I0818045

DREAMS OF DEBT AND DEITIES

CELIA RALK

Editor: Cat Jay PA & Authors Services
Proofreader: Messenger's Memos - Fiction Editing Service

First published in 2025 by Celia Ralk
ISBN 978-1-7635903-4-2 (paperback)
ISBN 978-1-7635903-3-5 (ebook)

CONTENT WARNING

Dreams of Debt and Deities is an adult fantasy novel, the first instalment in the ***Crooked Crowns*** series and some content may be triggering for some readers.
This book contains

- Blood
- Violence
- Death
- Funerals
- Unintentional cannibalism
- Explicit sexual content
- Consensual non-consent
- Breath play/choking
- Physical abuse
- Degradation/name calling
- Slapping
- Biting
- Voyeurism
- Sex work
- Exotic dance
- Drug addiction and recovery
- Homophobia
- And as always, coarse language

This book is intended for mature audiences.

If you are feeling distressed or need to talk, please reach out to your local services and supports.
Your mental health and wellbeing is important.

Dreams of Debt and Deities has been written using the Australian English dictionary, so readers familiar with American English may find inconsistencies within the grammatical language. I, as the author, am Australian, so take that as you will.

Crooked Crowns is an LGBTQI+ friendly and inclusive (on page) series.

DREAMS OF DEBT AND DEITIES

Sorry about Neven…
I hope this makes up for it xo

GLOSSARY AND PRONOUNCIATION GUIDE

Elanist - El-ah-nist - The centre-most continent, home to Vequil fae.

Tirenas - *Ti*-reh-nas - The largest eastern continent, surrounded by few islands. Tirenas is home to predominantly Darsmun fae.

Morrin - More-in - The largest western continent, home to Resmigian fae.

Vequil - Ve-kwil – Those with an affinity for elemental magic. These fae reside in courts inspired and powered by one of the following elements; fire, water, earth, air or spirit.

Vequil Inalis - Ve-kwil In-*ah*-lis - These fae come from a dwindling heritage able to channel and draw power from each element, effectively being able to manipulate *all* elements. They are unable, however, to draw from the additional power a Vequil fae might have, specific to their court.

Darsmun - Darz-mun/mon - Fae with an affinity for solar magic. They reside in one of the two solar courts (day or night) and their affinities usually correlate to their home court. Those belonging to the night court tend to channel a gentler version, though both the Obsidian and Cerulean courts magic wielders have the ability to manipulate the mind and sight.

Resmigian - Res-*mee*-jan - Fae with an affinity for seasonal magic. They reside in one of the four seasonal courts (summer, autumn, winter, spring) and their affinities correlate to their home court. The magic of the Resmigian fae is predominantly passive. Traits specific to the Resmigian fae include slanted, upturned eyes and what one dwelling outside Morrin might consider abnormal height. For those with mixed heritage, carry-over identifiers include elongated fingers, longer necks or torsos, etc.

Soliqe - *So*-leek – Shifter fae who once had the ability to transform into any number of animals, people, objects, etc. depending on their origin both familiarly and geographically. Some bloodlines have diluted over the centuries, with majority of the shifter fae in Tirenas bearing wings and remaining in a state of partial shift where their wings are always there, though they cannot shift further in either direction. Telltale signs of a Soliqe fae are the longer, more sharply pointed ears than other fae. They hail from northern isles that no longer exist, and now the majority take up residency in Tirenas to work for the king. A Soliqe fae will also have increased hearing and sense of smell.

Daemdrana - Daym-drana - A dragon like creature bearing feathers as well as scales and who's wide, feathered tail can also spark flame, albeit less powerfully than their mouth.

Phoenix - A creature with the ability to be reborn after death.

A BRIEF GUIDE TO THE VEQUIL FAE

All Vequil fae, the race of fae native to the continent of Elanist, belong to one of the five courts. Once, Elanist was governed by the Golden Kingdom. While that is no longer the case, the land is still divided geographically by the court borders and continues to follow the naming conventions begun aeons ago.

Any Vequil fae whose powers have manifested are identifiable by the markings found on specific parts of their bodies, in tribute to the magic they possess. The court of a Vequil fae who has not yet manifested can be identified by their skin colouring.

COURT OF WAVE

Court of the water fae. These fae possess the ability to manipulate water in any form, along with the ability to heal. Water fae generally have wide eyes, round features, and a fair complexion. Many water fae have varying shades of blue undertones to their skin, or simply patches of skin that shimmer blue. All Vequil fae are marked by the power of their house, though universally among the courts those markings are the colour of ash. The water fae hold their intricate swirls along their throats, over their collarbones and under their chins, surging up like rolling waves. Water fae are the most placid and docile of all the Vequil fae, and are normally the first to attempt to defuse any unpleasant situation or hostile conversation.

COURT OF FLAME

Court of the fire fae. These fae control and wield flames at whim, along with the elements of fire. This might include bringing water quickly to the boil, conjuring a flame, burning someone without touching them, or even warming the surrounding air. Those belonging to the Court of Flame generally have hair that ranges from auburn to copper and the most common eye colouring is shades of brown and hazel. Their skin tone appears in shades of copper, rose gold, and rust. Fire fae are marked by raging tongues of ash-coloured flame, dancing around the sternum and ribs, and sometimes extending downward. Fire fae are the most antagonistic and easily offended of all the Vequil fae.

COURT OF SOIL

Court of the earth fae. These fae are able to manipulate the earth, be it the dirt, the trees, a flower, or a single leaf. Some have the ability to speak to animals or to shapeshift. However, the process is taxing and the occurrence of these abilities has dwindled throughout the ages. They are typically the shortest of the Vequil fae, though this is beneficial for those who can shift into an animal form as it makes the shift an easier process. Their skin tends towards various shades of brown or green. Those belonging to the Court of Soil have marks that run up their spines, shaped like vines or branches, or like the roots in the earth. Earth fae are the most excitable of the Vequil fae and absolutely abhor footwear.

COURT OF BREATH

Court of the air fae. These fae have the ability to manipulate the air to their will, whether to provide or remove. These fae are lethal, perhaps more so than any other Vequil fae, though they are also the most light-hearted and easy-going. Telltale signs of an air fae are the sharp facial features such as a pointed nose or high, angular cheekbones, and the silver tinge to their skin, eyes, or hair. Air fae bear marks along their hips and below their navels, with some even extending to wrap around to their spine. Like gusts of wind drawn by an abstract artist, some form tight coils and others flow like a soft breeze, the tendrils billowing gently around the skin. The Court of Breath is where the artists and visionists dwell. Air fae are the fastest of the Vequil fae.

COURT OF CANDOR

Court of the spirit fae. Their magic is connected to the spirituality of the individual as well as their surroundings, the ether. The Court of Candor was once a repository of the knowledge and history of the Vequil fae. The Court of Candor disappeared not long after the Golden Kingdom fell. Maps no longer mark the locations of the temples, libraries, or any of the spirit court. Instead, they show empty land. Fae from the Court of Candor don't typically have any obvious outward signs aside from the lack of other courts' traits and characteristics, and a slight violet shimmer to their skin. They have the ability to speak mind to mind, and to see the future in varying degrees of clarity or accuracy through waking visions, dreams, or nightmares. The Court of Candor's history is shrouded in shadows, though it is rumoured their charcoal markings climb from the nape of their necks and circle their scalp, fashioned almost like a scrolling ancient language. Spirit fae are generally the quietest, and most reserved of the Vequil fae, though have always held themselves with a sense of surety.

THE VEQUIL INALIS

Directly translated means *the original vequil*, meaning the very first of its kind. Something new. These fae have the unique ability to harness all elemental power, rather than being limited to only one. However, a Vequil Inalis may not draw on the additional strengths and attributes of a single-element fae. Where an air fae possesses increased speed, or the water fae are able to heal, a Vequil Inalis does not possess such power. They may only pull from the water, fire, earth and air, with the exception of intuition and other Candor related power. An Inalis can be identified by their multiple markings, though they bear no other telltale signs of heritage. The Vequil Inalis fae originated in royal blood, and while they are not limited to such bloodlines now, a royal Inalis will be far more powerful than their non-royal counterparts. They are uniquely identified by markings made not of charcoal, but gold.

CHAPTER ONE
CLARA

The soldiers closed in on Clara, cornering her against a marble pillar almost twice her size, and the cold splintered down her back as she collided with the rock. Excitement shone in the males' eyes—excitement and greed.

Clara's jaw clenched. Her tongue pressed into the back of her teeth and against the roof of her mouth, the discomfort providing a welcome feeling. It was something to focus on, to distract herself from the heartbreak which tore and shredded its way through her body.

She felt silly, really. It had taken Beau dying for her to realise—or, rather, *accept*—her feelings towards him. But it was too little, too late.

He died for her, though he likely died for nothing, and the grief sat heavy in her chest. It filled the hole Beau had left when his heart stopped beating, when he ripped hers out and destroyed it.

When the king had killed him.

She was remarkably calm for someone who had just felt her heart, her very essence, shatter. Had felt it happen so thoroughly, she could have sworn her heart had torn in two. Though perhaps she was simply empty now, since a part of her she did not realise was so important was now gone. Even her magic receded, as if it, too, were lost. Maybe part of it died with Beau. She wanted to touch him, to lay a hand over his chest—to be certain he was dead—or against his cheek, or his forehead. She wanted to lie with him, drape his arm across her stomach, and close her eyes and forget he was gone. To pretend, for a moment, they were anywhere but here.

Only she couldn't.

Bitterness coated the air as thick as Beau's body was covered in his blood. His skin had already turned ashen and sickly, and if he wasn't already, soon he'd be cold to the touch. Clara spared another second to glance at him before she looked back at the soldiers in front of her. If she looked any longer, she'd break down and cry, or maybe the bile which threatened would spill over. Neither option was ideal, and both would have to wait.

The king's voice echoed in the room, but she couldn't hear him, not over the persistent ringing in her ears or the rumbling beneath her feet.

Maybe she imagined it, as no one else paid any mind to the shuddering tiles, or the tinkling of the ornamental chains pointlessly hung from the braziers.

"Clara," the king coaxed, his voice far sweeter than he should be able to manage. He clicked his fingers twice in front of her face before she realised how close he now stood, and it sparked a smirk from the Tirenas king. "For the last time, sweetheart, remove your shirt or someone will do it for you."

Sweetheart.

Beau had called her that once. A single butterfly danced in her chest, then died in her throat. She narrowed her eyes at the king, who rolled his own in response.

“Do not call me that,” she growled, her voice rough but somehow steady. Snickers came from every direction.

Someone mumbled, “Lover boy call you that, did he?”

“Back when he could call her anything, you mean?” another responded.

Clara closed her eyes and attempted a calming breath. When she inhaled, she imagined one of the soldiers stepping forward and impaling himself on her sword. On the exhale, she thought of incinerating his carcass.

Of course, she didn’t possess any weapons. Though she felt her hands tingle at the faintest sense of her magic—it hadn’t completely vanished. She said nothing and made no move to undress.

A thin soldier stepped forward, his sand-coloured wings tucked tight, so they didn’t brush against anything as he moved. It sent another painful stab of longing through her as they made her think of home.

He pulled a small knife from his belt and flipped it in his hand. It landed hilt down in his palm, blade pointed at Clara. A surge of fear raced down her spine, dancing in the soles of her feet. The ghost of a breeze teased her cheeks.

The soldier smirked as he raised his hand to her abdomen. He tugged at her hem with his free hand, then used the knife to slice the front of her shirt in half in one move.

Clara held her breath until he grabbed her wrist, tugging her towards him, then a small, choked gasp escaped as she abruptly stumbled forward. She looked past the soldier with sandy wings, to the others who grinned like sadists and the king who waited expectantly.

Then the winged male moved behind her and tore her shirt from her body without warning. Now she stood almost bare from the waist up, with only a bra to keep her somewhat covered. At the whistle from a male with wings a shade of brown so dark they could be mistaken as black, Clara bared her teeth. Though he appeared confident, two beads of sweat formed above his brow and slowly dripped down his face.

The prickling in her hands intensified until it felt as though she were playing with needles. Clara squared her shoulders and took another deep breath.

Then she looked at Beau again—she couldn't help it. He lay still, untouched since he'd fallen. The earth seemed to cry out under her, from under the castle, as if it, too, had lost him.

"Another set of markings, Your Majesty." The male with sand-coloured wings had a voice like a pepper grinder. Cracked and disjointed, and far too nasal for someone in good health.

His words hit Clara like a bag of rocks. Another mark. When did that even happen? Surely, she would've remembered it . . . How could she not have known?

"Colour?" the king asked.

"Gold," the soldier responded. "Same as the others."

The king nodded, waving a hand lazily over his shoulder as he walked back towards his throne.

Clara scoffed. "That's it?"

"Would you like me to say more?" he countered. "The only words worth saying now are those chanted in the Convergence Ceremony. You will be collected momentarily for bathing and preparation. That will be all." He sat, not bothering to look at her. Clara glared at him, her hands curled into fists, the pain from her nails digging into her palms like hot iron brands. "Oh," the king added, gesturing to Beau's body. "And someone clear up this mess. What a waste."

A spark erupted inside Clara; one she hadn't expected, but now embraced. Like a slack band she hadn't realised was slowly being pulled taut, she finally snapped.

Mess.

Waste.

The only mess, the only *waste* Clara could see, was the damned tyrant who sat in a chair he didn't deserve with a title he sullied.

King Urian was right.

That would be all.

She would not inflate his ego or his arrogance by submitting. She would not allow him to terrorise her further, to take even more from her. He *would not* acquire her powers.

Her mother would be okay. Jacob and Evian would make sure of it, just as they would take care of each other.

Her sister would also be fine. Clara had lived her whole life never even knowing her sister existed. She'd never wanted one; Seren had been the closest she'd had to a sister, and she was enough. Clara wouldn't miss a woman she had never met, nor would she grieve what she could've had. She wouldn't have the time.

With another deep breath, Clara closed her eyes.

As she inhaled slowly, she thought of Neven. On the exhale, she thought of Beau. Before she opened her eyes, she pictured seeing them again, together. Digging deep within herself, to every corner of her being, Clara reached for any trickle of magic she could find. She pulled on every thought, every emotion which had sparked power before and imagined amplifying it. Of making it as big and as loud and as devastating as she could manage.

She raised her hands in front of her, towards the soldiers and the king, and smiled softly to herself. If any of them noticed, they said nothing. A shimmering veil of amber coated her fingers, spreading up to her elbows, and the briefest vision flashed before her.

Beau's body bursts into flames and extinguishes just as quickly. A pile of gold-speckled ash is left in its wake. A pile large enough she can almost see his body hiding beneath it, like some cruel joke. The ash disappears, and a hazy image of Beau's wolfish smile replaces it. The cheeky grin she wished she could see once more. He winks, then that, too, disappears.

Then it was gone.

The swell of magic she'd drawn, and the hum of power that surrounded her, had simply vanished into the air that now felt too quiet and still.

The king tsked and shook his head, disappointment clear on his face.

"No, Clara, there will be no outbursts. If you insist on being unwilling to control yourself, I will see to it for you."

Clara looked down to find, not only had the shimmer disappeared from her skin, but a barbed iron binding hovered around her wrists in a figure eight design. It curved and writhed, as if it were alive, and glittered as though the stars had bled for its brutality. She did not doubt the entrapment would have her bleeding too.

A snarl she could not help, nor bothered to rein in, left her throat as she bared her teeth. The king only chuckled and waved his hand in dismissal.

The door Clara had burst through opened again, this time for June to scurry in. She bowed before the king, then grabbed Clara by the elbow with no semblance of gentility and dragged her from the room.

June did not look at Clara, but the disgust was clear on her face. She was glad the grouchy old woman kept her mouth shut.

There was no breeze on the way back to Clara's room and since she was no longer properly clothed, she was grateful.

Her room had changed little since she'd been here last. June had put away the clothes she'd left draped over the bed—that beautiful gown she'd likely never wear again—and replaced the comforter and pillows. Otherwise, the only difference was the time and day.

June let go of Clara's arm and she ached to rub where the old woman's spindly grip had dug in, but as she couldn't, she sighed and waited for June to come back. June walked into the bathroom, turned on the tap and had taken a few shuffling steps before she stopped. Clara's hearing was not as fine-tuned as a shifter, but she'd heard June stomp and scuttle about her room so many times the woman's gait was a familiar one. Familiar enough to notice its abrupt halt.

Clara's eyes flew towards the door, where she'd expected someone to enter, but no one did. A few seconds went by with no visitors and no more movement from June. Clara shuffled on her feet, a wave of nerves coursing through her, but with no idea of the source or what she should be doing.

Then the water turned off, and June walked back out of the bathing room. Her expression had softened, but not with kindness, more apathy and emptiness. If Clara squinted, she might even consider June's eyes to have glassed over.

"I will remove your cuff, Clara. Do not make any sudden movements, nor sounds. Then I will bathe you."

June's voice was more monotone than Clara remembered, but her world had been turned upside down more than once since she'd seen the woman last, so Clara ignored the change.

She nodded once and kept her mouth shut. No sudden movements, nor sounds.

Why she would remove the cuff, Clara didn't know, but she also didn't question it. One of the barbs uncoiled from the other and the shimmer dissolved into a dull glow. The second it unwound from her wrists, Clara felt a surge of power race through her.

It started at the base of her feet, tiny pinpricks of magic, then raced up her legs and warmed her spine, heat coating her abdomen and stretching to the tips of her fingers. Her head felt clearer, and her lungs felt open again. She hadn't realised she had struggled to breathe, and perhaps she hadn't been, but the second she was free Clara felt like she could finally take a deep inhale.

Free wasn't entirely accurate, but at least she was no longer bound.

A million thoughts whirled through her mind, escape plans forming so she might actually be free. She could run, but the likelihood of her getting far was slim. Running and hiding was an option now that she was alone, but she did not know the grounds well enough, nor the staff rotations, to feel confident with such a plan. While murder was definitely on the table, as rude as June could be, Clara couldn't bring herself to justify a possibly innocent woman's death.

The king. His death was justifiable, and his murder was something Clara would ensure, even if it killed her too. Maybe not today, but the tyrant would pay for his actions and Clara would be the one to claim the debt.

CHAPTER TWO
CLARA

Clara stayed silent while she undressed. June assisted, though her apathetic mask was not enough to cover her reluctance or disapproval.

She, too, stayed silent. Her instructions came without sound, and she inclined her chin towards the bathing room before giving Clara a forceful shove. Clara did her best not to snarl, but her face twitched with ire, regardless.

For a moment, Clara considered simply enjoying the bath. The king had said she would now be treated as a prisoner, and while Clara did not doubt him, it was yet to be the case. A warm bath would be wonderful, and given all the king had done, the least he could do was allow her a moment to breathe.

Though June had other plans, it seemed. She gathered soap bars and vials of all colours and sizes, causing an abundance of smells to hit her all at once. It was horrid. Clara took a deep breath in through her mouth to avoid the discordant odours.

As the bottles clinked against the stone countertop, a flash of colour flew through Clara's mind.

Red roses. Crimson gloves. The velvet sheath of a sword decorated with a ruby at its pommel.

The clang of swords rang through her mind as June turned to face her.

"Come now," she said, again in a monotonous tone.

However, Clara was distracted, too busy remembering her previous visions. How she should've learnt to heed them by now.

First her father, then Neven, now Beau.

This one may have been simple and vague, but it came for a reason.

The colour red—for a reason.

So, when June knelt beside the tub and dipped her hand in to test the water, submerged almost to her elbow, Clara made a decision. Without a second thought, she heated the water, and it bubbled around June's arm.

The woman screamed and pulled her limb from the boiling water, cradling it close to her chest.

Clara opened her mouth to apologise, but before any words could spill out, her bedroom door burst open. She spun and her eyes darted in a frantic search for something to defend herself with while June cursed her, calling her horrible names. Her apathy had sure worn off.

A soldier grabbed Clara by the biceps as she lunged for a lamp. It wasn't close enough she would've reached it anyway, but she'd had to try.

The male was tall and built so similarly to Neven—minus the wings—that a lump formed in her throat and burned while it grew. His skin was a dark and rich brown, as were his eyes and hair, which curled tightly. It was long enough to frame his face, and his Darsmun ears poked out, adorned with subtle piercings.

He looked Clara over once, quickly, before turning to June.

"Are you alright?" he asked, his tone gruff, and it suggested he'd take no nonsense.

"Not in the least!" she cried. "That careless, thoughtless—"

Her screams were cut off when the soldier interjected. "Perhaps you should seek medical attention. I will watch the girl in your absence."

"No." June shook her head. "I will send another maid to assist. She may be a prisoner, but it is improper for a male to bathe a female, and *she*," June hissed, turning her nose up at Clara as she pointed viciously, "is disgusting and not fit for the ceremony at all."

"Of course." The soldier dipped his head as he agreed. Clara rolled her eyes and tried to jostle herself from his grip.

June muttered more crude things as she walked out of the room. When the door thudded closed, the soldier lessened his grip and Clara seized her opportunity.

She kicked him in the shins.

He swore and bent to rub his leg. Clara reached for the lamp, successfully this time, and slammed it into his back.

The soldier shot up and grabbed Clara's wrist, hard enough she thought she might bruise, and she thrashed as she tried to get away from him.

Then he surprised her by tugging on her arm, in a gentler fashion than she'd expected. "Clara," he said sternly, but not aggressively.

She stopped moving and really looked at him. There was an air of familiarity about him, though she couldn't say she'd ever met the man.

He did not fight her, nor did he keep her detained. He let her go and the act alone was enough to stun Clara.

"I'm sorry for the disguise earlier," he continued, making no sense. "This is what I actually look like, minus the guard uniform. Stars, it sure is scratchy material. You'd think the king would splurge a little more, considering how he loves to flaunt his wealth." The male shook his head, while Clara cocked hers to the side. She couldn't tell where she'd seen him before, or how he knew her.

"Ryland," he said, gesturing to himself.

Clara shook her head. "No, Ryland is a boy. One a third of your size and with poor posture. You must be confused."

"I assure you, I'm aware of who I am. My name is Ryland, and we met not that long ago. You threatened my beating heart and working lungs, if I recall correctly, if I accompanied you to His Majesty."

A pulsing ache formed along Clara's hairline. She contemplated whether it would be rude to rub her forehead before conceding and deciding she did not care. She truthfully would've enjoyed a bath.

"I don't understand."

"I know and I'm sorry, but allow me to explain. I work for your sister. She sent me after you, to make sure you got home safely. I am to escort you back to Elanist, where she will meet you and fill you in on everything."

"That is not a good enough explanation! How did you appear as a boy at first, but are now a fully grown man? Why would you bother?" Clara asked with far less patience than she'd intended.

"Would you have been as likely to allow me to join you if I'd approached you as I am now?" Ryland countered. "I am a Darsmun fae, capable of sight manipulation."

Immediately, Clara's shoulders straightened, and her hands rose. Her feet screamed at her to move, to run, *anything*, but they'd frozen in place.

"You can mind play?"

She barely formed a coherent sentence. It was as if her tongue had swollen and turned to stone in her mouth. She eyed him sceptically, and he did nothing to ease her suspicions or to convince her he came to her in good will.

He shook his head.

"No," he replied softly. "Sight manipulation works a little differently. I am only able to bend what you see. For example, I could have you see an ocean before you, but you could not hear it. Nor would you feel the water if you stepped forward and walked through what you saw. A Darsmun capable of mind play has a much wider net to cast and incredible flexibility with the power they possess. They can make you feel—"

"I know what they can do." She cut him off dryly.

An expression of surprise covered his face, though he didn't say anything further. Instead, he urged her to leave with him.

"I am currently naked," she said, crossing her arms.

He shrugged. "It is of no matter to me."

Clara scoffed and placed her hands on her hips instead, leaving her breasts on full display.

"A rather impressive set you have, Clara, though it is not breasts I like to put in my mouth when taking a bed partner." He raised his eyebrows and encouraged her to figure it out on her own. She simply shook her head and continued.

"Regardless, I don't think I should leave the room undressed." She turned and moved to the wardrobe, assuming there would still be clothing in there for her. Then she called over her shoulder, "Have you heard anything of Beau?"

"I haven't seen him, if that's what you're asking," he called back.

"I'll kill the king for this," she muttered, angrily pulling drawers from their racks.

"You will not be killing any king today, I assure you. What for, anyway?"

Clara rolled her eyes at the male. He could *assure* her until he was blue in the face. He'd simply be blue and wrong.

"How long have you been together?" he asked, walking up to lean against the doorframe.

Her breath caught in her throat. This damned male, bringing lumps to her throat and causing her eyes to burn. She blinked them rapidly to will the tears away. Now was not the time.

"We're not," she said, clearing her throat. "Not like that. We only met a few months back."

"Oh."

It was quiet for a moment until Clara slammed one of the drawers shut. She couldn't find anything suitable to wear. Countless silk garments and frivolous gowns. Nightwear and useless slippers. She spun to leave, but an overcoat hanging precariously from the rack caught her eye.

A tear slipped free this time, and she let it. Clara pulled the coat from its hanger and wrapped it around herself.

Hoping it might still hold a trace of him, Clara breathed in deeply through her nose. She held her eyes closed tightly when she could only smell the perfume June spritzed her with all those days she'd worn it. Not a hint of him.

Is that how it would be from now on? Memories and longing? She supposed so.

"It's a lovely colour. Compliments your hair nicely." Ryland nodded towards the coat. He hadn't moved from the doorway.

Clara managed a small smile in appreciation before she set her face again. "I assure *you*, Ryland. I will kill the king for all he has done. He deserves nothing less."

"But why, Clara? He is a *king*."

"Because he deserves it, Ryland! He killed Neven, he killed Beau, he's killed Mother knows how many others who didn't deserve it. I was tortured because of him. Enough is enough."

"Clara, grieve and move on. You said yourself, you were not even with Beau—"

"No," Clara held up her hand as she cut him off. "Do not insult me by assuming you know anything about my relationship with him. If you have nothing helpful to add to the conversation, keep your mouth shut. I don't need to explain myself to you."

"I'd like to know what I'll be dying for, if you'd be so kind." He folded his arms across his chest and raised an eyebrow in challenge.

Clara sighed.

"He was an asshole. The very first night we met, I was taken aback by his damned good looks. The first words he spoke to me felt like a dream I couldn't remember, like they were tucked into the furthest part of my mind, and it drove me insane that I couldn't access it. That I couldn't remember.

"But he was rude and defensive, honestly—a prick. He held a blade to my throat, and I smacked him for it. I ignored that he was pretty, or how his voice filled me with familiarity. Oh, I enjoyed the days he kept his mouth *shut*." Clara looked at her feet and smiled fondly at the memory. "Then I spent more time with him and all of a sudden I realised my heart hurt when he wasn't around, and I looked for him everywhere, hoping to catch a glimpse of him. I couldn't ignore it anymore, much less him. He plagued my thoughts, and the only problem I had was that they were only thoughts."

"You didn't exactly seem friendly with him when I arrived."

"He hurt me. Made decisions that, in his defence, he thought were right. Though he was wrong and multiple lives were lost. I was forgiving him—or trying to—but I wanted to, and he didn't know." Clara looked at Ryland now, buttoning her coat and tying it around her waist. "For Beau's life, for Neven's and all the other undeserving souls who passed too soon under the king's hand. For the life I could've had, which he callously took away, I will take his and obliterate it.

"He took the lives of too many, and he does not deserve his own. So, if you insist on following your orders and keeping me safe, on returning me to Elanist, this is my one condition. The king dies before—"

Beau is sitting in the dust behind bars. His head first hangs, then tilts back to stare daggers at the ceiling. Finally, he looks blankly ahead with literal flames dancing in his eyes. Golden feathers float around him. Soldiers laugh and Beau shouts expletives.

Ryland gripped her elbow and stared at her intently.

"Well?" he asked. "What did you see?"

"I don't know what you're talking about," she said, looking away.

"Stop it. I know you have some level of foresight. You had a vision, and I would like you to tell me what you saw." He sighed, then added, "Please."

Begrudgingly, Clara told him. Though she didn't know whether to trust him yet, she didn't have many other options. If he was going to take her home and turn a blind eye to her assassination of a king, she supposed sharing one of her gifts wasn't so bad, especially considering he seemed to know already.

"Any identifiable soldiers? A sign of when this happened?"

Clara shook her head. "It was only flashes. I don't have full visions, only snippets."

It didn't matter, not really. June would've reached someone and sent them to her by now, so Clara didn't have the luxury of time. Luck did not usually grace Clara, and she feared today would be no exception.

"I am fairly certain that will change once your spirit magic manifests itself properly."

She shrugged, tightening the tie around her waist. "It doesn't matter—he's already dead. I watched him bleed out in front of me."

CHAPTER THREE
CLARA

Ryland adjusted the hood over Clara's hair, and ensured the clasp was fastened at her collar.

"Stop fussing," Clara hissed. "Someone will notice and grow suspicious."

"They ought to be, Clara!" he hissed back, running a hand down his face with a sigh. "Just please keep your mouth shut. Anyone who hears your voice will recognise it as yours."

"Only if they've had the pleasure of listening to me before." Clara winked, but Ryland only rolled his eyes. Footsteps approaching pulled them from their discussion.

It was go time.

Two guards walked towards them, both sets of narrowed eyes bouncing from Clara to Ryland and back.

“Excuse me!” Ryland called to them. One raised an eyebrow, but the other gestured for him to continue. “Where might we find the king at this hour?”

“What do you want with the king?” The guard who spoke squared his shoulders while the other reached for the sword sheathed on his hip.

“It is in regard to payment of a debt.” Ryland leant closer to the guards and lowered his voice as he continued. “The female, rather. I am simply dropping her off. King Urian shall want to know she is here.”

A look passed between the guards, and Clara held her breath. She said nothing, doing her best to look small and timid, like nothing more than a sex object.

“Remove her cloak.”

Clara looked towards Ryland. Oh, how she wanted to blow the guards up, to fill them with too much air or boil their blood until it decorated the walls.

Ryland grabbed Clara’s wrist and tugged her closer. His cold hands jarring against her skin. It was enough to knock her from the rage which filled her thoughts and to let her magic simmer back down.

She only had one thing on her mind and, frankly, did not care about anything else, let alone niceties and taming her power. Ryland, however, was much more level-headed and some small part of her appreciated him being here.

“I’m afraid she isn’t wearing anything underneath, sir.” Ryland spoke so casually that the guard who’d reached for his weapon snickered, but let his hand fall to his side.

The other sent him on his way before telling Clara and Ryland to follow. Clara had hoped they’d be pointed in the direction to find the king themselves. Though another small voice she'd rather ignore reminded her they needed the escort.

"Does the king know you're coming?" The soldier barely glanced over his shoulder, his steps sure and precise.

"No," Ryland answered. He shot a glare towards Clara, to which she returned one of her own. Looking back at the soldier before he turned around and questioned them further, Ryland continued, "It was more of an 'earliest convenience' sort of arrangement."

Clara held her breath and waited for the soldier to answer. If he suspected anything, she did not know how she would turn the tide back in their favour, as she wouldn't get another chance.

This was it.

The soldier only nodded. After another two turns, Clara recognised their path, and she remembered the room they were headed towards.

It was almost poetic, really, and smugness bloomed inside her. She did her best to stop an arrogant smile from spreading across her face. Another turn and her suspicions were confirmed; she could already see the gilt doorknobs ahead.

"Do not let him announce us," Clara whispered, her gaze pleading with Ryland.

He looked at Clara, searching her face, but nodded once and looked ahead. His face went slack, and though he continued walking, his footsteps slowed. The soldier's steps did as well before he turned to face Ryland, only paces away from the intricately carved double doors. The same vacant, almost apathetic expression masked his face, as had June's earlier. Had Ryland toyed with her mind like he played with the soldier's now?

Clara tried to rationalise that her lack of care was because he wasn't doing anything truly wrong. That his intention was to protect her and keep her safe. However, a gnawing feeling suggested perhaps she wasn't as opposed to manipulation as she'd originally thought. Maybe it was hypocritical, or maybe it was survival.

Regardless, she continued to stand in silence. Even when the soldier's face returned to normal, and he cleared his throat. When he nodded to them both and walked away, Clara took a deep, steadying breath, but still made no sound.

The wooden door creaked as she opened it. Clara groaned when she realised there were no more surprises up her sleeve. It was now or never. She threw the door open wide and stormed up to the king's desk.

King Urian jolted slightly but regained his composure easily. He was sly, if nothing else. A smirk crossed his face as he took Clara in, and she was unsure if she was still hidden under the blonde guise Ryland had set for everyone else; the hood only covered so much of her hair, after all.

"Miss Afron," he drawled, leaning back in his chair. "I had no idea you were so eager to meet your fate."

"I am eager for many things," she sneered. "Your fate, however, is at the top of my list."

The king laughed. The sound made Clara's blood boil and set her teeth on edge.

"*My* fate? Oh Clara, please." He stood, all humour wiped from his face. "You," he called to Ryland. "Go retrieve the—hang on." He cocked his head, seeming to notice Ryland was not his employee. That he was not wearing a soldier's uniform and had no solar crest in sight. "You're not one of mine."

"Apologies, majesty. I bow to another crown."

A look of realisation came across his face before the king stared daggers into Clara.

Immediately, Clara was thrust into a different time. A different setting.

Beau stood before her, and the king stood before him, less than an arm's reach away.

He looked at Clara with an ugly, evil smile before he drawled with far too little emotion, "You are already mine and I tire of these little games."

Beau opened his mouth, but no words came out. He spluttered, eyes widening, as a gurgling noise came from his throat, followed by blood spilling from the deep slice along his skin.

Clara vaguely registered the feel of hands as they pressed into her arms and clutched her jaw. Part of her wanted to look away, not wanting to witness Beau's death again. But she couldn't look away even if she tried. She wanted more time with Beau, even in this warped reality. Though she couldn't quite put her finger on why it was wrong, as it felt so real.

When the blood spilled from Beau's mouth, she screamed. The sound echoed off the marble walls, deafening all other sounds. Her knees went weak as Beau's gave out.

Even as he fell to the floor, red staining the pristine white beneath him, his eyes stayed locked on Clara's and hers did not move from his.

She tried to tell him everything, but her mouth wouldn't move and the screams wouldn't stop. Telepathy was not a power she possessed, yet she still tried.

He had to know she would forgive him. That she wanted time with him, for that and so much more. His eyes closed and did not reopen, and his chest lay flat and unmoving.

Clara blinked, and instead of Beau laying on the alabaster tiles, he once again stood in front of her.

And the scene reset and played out again.

And again.

And again.

Until Clara noticed how the minute details didn't match her recollection of the moment forever branded in her mind. That the soldier holding her now tried to pinch her, or whisper something incoherent in her ear. How a Darsmun fae with gold jewellery in his ears now stood behind the king and urged something of Clara she couldn't make out.

Until the floor was no longer marble and pristine, or the room sparkling white, but instead covered in a carpeted rug and cast in the low light of warm-toned lamps. Until the door was wood, with gilt doorknobs and etched in spiralling symbols instead of plain and ivory.

As reality returned, her throat burned and her limbs blazed. She tasted something bitter dripping in her open mouth, warm and metallic, while the soles of her feet tingled with such a ferocious level of power it was near painful to continue to stand.

The king loomed in front of her, with his hands pressed to each of her cheeks. His eyes bored into hers but did not truly see her.

She'd never known what his power was, but now she could make an educated guess. He dealt with memories and for Mother knew how long he'd held her there, replaying her worst moments over and over again.

Ryland now stood behind him, concern flooding his face as his eyes darted over her. Clara blinked as she realised she'd been screaming.

The lamps spread around the room flickered in a frenzy, the flames bending to her will. A rumble rose from the floor beneath her, strong enough to rattle the shelves and desk. A headache bloomed in her temples, extending down to her jaw, though that seemed like the least of her worries as the king continued to use her memories against her.

She still saw them replaying in her mind. Saw Beau fall again, never taking his eyes from hers.

Enough was enough.

"It's beautifully ironic," she whispered through a snarl. "Don't you think, *Majesty*?"

The king did not answer, only responded by baring his own teeth.

"You *punished* me in this very room and now you'll meet your own punishment here. Not that it will ever compare to the evil you've spread into this world, but I will certainly sleep a little better knowing I've rid the world of you."

Objectively, Clara held a lot of power. Even in her current state, with the control the king still held over part of her mind. Yet even as inexperienced as she was, she knew her well of power ran deep. It was a well she felt swelling and rising and filling as magic flowed more freely through her. She drew on it quickly and with intent.

Papers flew across the desk as a wind tore through the room. Pages flipped in the books which lay open on the desk or had fallen from the shelves in the aggressive eddies. Clara's hair whipped around her face, and her cloak flew out behind her. A water decanter rattled, the overly ornate glasses shook, and the contents spilled out. Amber liquid sloshed in a heavy glass bottle on the desk, as the matching glass tipped to its side.

Pain shot through her head, spreading down her neck and spine. It wrapped around her bones like barbed wire or thorny vines.

She'd thought anger was the only feeling she'd have towards the king. Anger, then victory once his head rolled from his body. Then maybe relief when she left his corpse to rot.

Instead, rage was fuelled by the deaths of those she'd loved as Beau and Neven filled her mind. Her love for them filled her heart. A love so strong it filled the entirety of her, and it was for them she broke the king's hold.

For them, she grabbed his wrists with her searing hands and felt perverse joy at the look of confusion on the king's face, at his pain as he realised she'd burned his skin, at his fear when he gazed at her face and realised she was not done.

Clara pulled up every ounce of power she had with her, and with a scream, she released it.

She hadn't really thought ahead enough to plan *how* she might kill the king of Tirenas, and like every other time, her power decided for her. As a frozen shard speared through the middle of his chest, and at least two dozen smaller shards cut his bare skin, she didn't bat an eye.

The king dropped to the carpet in a gurgling heap. Rage filled his eyes as he glared up at Clara, though beneath the fury was fear. Clara didn't stop to consider what her pleasure at the sight of him frightened at her feet might mean for her soul or her character. Or that she revelled in how powerful it made her feel.

King Urian spluttered a few times, though he did not try to stand as his breaths came short and fast. An empty glass lay on the floor next to him, the decanter on its side and bone dry.

Without a word Clara leant over the desk and grabbed the bottle of amber liquor, filling the near empty glass beside it. She took a swig from the bottle and threw the glass at the king. His pain-filled cries at the alcohol seeped into his open wounds were a sweet song.

She bared her teeth at the king, now cowering and whimpering, and crouched beside him. For a second, Clara allowed herself to truly look at the tyrannical leader this continent had served for centuries. Pride bloomed in her chest at having brought his reign to an end.

With the flick of her wrist and barely a thought, Clara lit the unfit, unfeeling ruler on fire. His cries turned to screams, and a cruel smile spread over Clara's face. The smell of his burning body assaulted her nose, any sound of disgust Ryland made drowned out by the dying king's pleas for mercy.

He deserved no such thing.

As his screams stopped, the pile before her now ash, Clara doused what was left of King Urian with the contents of the bottle in her hand. Then she dropped it into the pile of sludge. It was a fitting end. Once a stain on fae kind was now merely a stain on the carpet.

Clara clicked her tongue. "What a waste," she muttered, shaking her head.

As she stood and Ryland held her to inspect her for injury, the pain of new marks appearing hit her. Once from the base of her chin to just below the dip of her collarbones. Twice more, on either side of her face, from her temples to just above her jaw. She didn't know what these marks would look like, aside from being gold, but she knew they marked her as a spirit fae.

She cried then, as she was marked for the last time. When she returned home, which she was now more determined than ever to do, she would return as one of them, at least partly. A water fae

CHAPTER FOUR

CHAPTER FOUR
BEAU

Beau's body stirred before his mind woke. He'd only ever experienced a handful of rebirths, and he doubted he'd ever get used to it. There was no one for him to ask whether the process got easier.

Pins and needles tore through his naked body. They started at the tips of his fingers and toes and spread like wildfire through his body until every inch of him felt their touch. It started as a gentle niggle, a slight tightening of his skin, but grew rapidly to become the thousand cuts he now felt. Some of his muscles twitched, the one near his eyebrow particularly persistent.

All of him ached.

He hadn't been in any pain before he died and for that, he was thankful. Every other time had been a slow and agonising experience.

However, all of him was in pain right now. His eyelids as they tried and failed to open, his fingers as he stretched them out, even the insides of his nose as he inhaled. Smoke filled his nostrils, and his automatic grimace set his face ablaze in even more pain. His throat burned, and his lungs felt sodden—heavy and entirely uncooperative.

Beau hated resurrection every time. This time, though, a flicker of hope—almost excitement—sat in his chest at the thought of waking and reuniting with Clara. He prayed it would be different from the last reunion they shared.

Then he remembered she hadn't known.

That every breath, every heartbeat, was for her. That her hot little hands had branded his heart, and he now only felt alive with the warmth. He felt stupid for not telling her sooner, because he couldn't see or speak or think straight without *her*.

She didn't know of his true nature. Of his Phoenix heritage and ability to resurrect. She had watched him die, and he had watched it shatter something inside her.

He did that with his omissions and secrets.

She had to watch him die without knowing it would not be permanent.

A pit formed in his stomach—a dark hole of nerves and uncertainty over how she'd react when she found out.

When he finally peeled open his eyes and the ringing in his ears settled, Beau saw he had not been moved. He noticed the two soldiers in the room and was keenly aware of the lack of anyone else. The king had left, and Clara was nowhere to be seen. Fear spiked in his chest and his throat burned.

“Welcome back to the land of the living, Hawthorne.” Both soldiers snickered, but Beau ignored them.

On wobbly limbs, he rose to all fours, then attempted to stand. He attempted poorly and failed miserably. After rebirth, while a Phoenix resurrected in the same physical shape as they died, initially all their motor skills were weakened. It was almost as if his body and memories needed to wait for his muscles to reset. So Beau stumbled and swore, then let out a frustrated sigh.

“Put these on,” one of the soldiers ordered, as he threw clothing at Beau. A shirt and pair of pants landed in front of him, and he sighed, sitting back on his heels. The taller of the soldiers continued, “I don’t care whether you’re about as competent as a fawn, Hawthorne. Let’s get moving.”

Beau said nothing until his eyes landed on another piece of fabric in a heap on the floor, close to where Clara had been the last time he saw her.

“What’s that one?” he asked, his voice barely a rasp. Clearing his throat, he jerked his chin towards the fabric.

“If you’d prefer a female shirt, you need only have asked. You’d be denied, but still.” The soldiers snickered again, but Beau wasn’t listening anymore. They’d all but confirmed it was hers. Beau clenched his hands into such tight fists, the fabric of his own shirt groaned beneath his fingers.

He’d not yet pulled his pants beyond his knees before Beau was hoisted up and dragged from the throne room. The soldiers spoke between themselves, but Beau’s mind raced with worry.

Where was Clara? Had the ceremony already taken place? Was she even alive?

Maybe she'd got out. The thought of her fleeing and him never seeing her again had Beau's lungs threatening to seize, and his heart broke a little more the longer he considered it. However, he couldn't help the hope which sat heavy in his gut that Clara was far, far away. That she was safe.

Beau hadn't paid attention to the route they'd been taking, and suddenly they were walking downstairs. Well, the soldiers were walking, Beau was stumbling, though they'd essentially been carrying him the whole way. The only reason they'd be going downstairs was to the dungeons.

"Where are we going?" Beau asked, his voice slightly less hoarse.

"Where do you think?" The shorter one scoffed.

"Why are you taking me to the dungeons? King Urian—"

"Has given us explicit orders," the taller soldier cut him off. "You are to be detained until further notice."

"Why?"

"You question your king?" The shorter soldier was less compassionate than his colleague, if any soldier of the king's possessed that trait to begin with.

Beau's thoughts turned to Neven—the one soldier he knew who had been compassionate. He'd been a good male and friend to Clara. Guilt settled heavily in Beau's gut and he kept his mouth shut.

Only one soldier sat on guard in the dungeons, though considering Beau was the only prisoner, he wasn't surprised. The cell he'd been thrown into smelt of mould and piss, with a bucket in the far corner of the small space and a floating cot hanging from the wall adjacent. Beau sat in the opposite corner to the poor excuse for a toilet he'd been granted, turning his nose up every time he considered moving the bucket to lie on the bed.

The floor was covered in dirt and dust and heavens knew what else, but his body still ached, and his legs didn't feel strong enough to hold him yet. Feeling had returned, so for that, and the lack of stinging and pain throughout his entire body, he was grateful.

Voices carried down the stone staircase, but he couldn't make out what was being said, only the hurried tone. Was something wrong? His thoughts immediately turned to Clara, and he sat up straighter, straining to hear the commotion from the castle above.

A soldier ran down to his colleague, armed and ready—for what, Beau didn't want to know. They spoke in hushed tones before the soldier on guard spared Beau a quick glance, then nodded and they both raced up the steps.

Beau pushed to his knees and crawled to the cell bars. His grip was tight, partly to hold himself up but also in the futile hope he might see or hear something . . . anything.

Prisoners were not left alone. Much less those who knew their way around the castle and had what might be considered *valuable knowledge* of the place and proceedings.

However, before he had much time to stew on it, two sets of footsteps made their way down the staircase. Beau could've sworn red hair peeked out from underneath the dark, hooded cloak.

Surely not.

He pulled himself to stand, his knees doing a shocking job at holding him steady, while his whole body felt weak and shaky. Beau blinked rapidly. Perhaps he was hallucinating? He'd never hallucinated after rebirth before, but there was always a first time.

Clara couldn't be here . . . she shouldn't.

"You piece of shit!" She stormed towards him, pointing a porcelain finger at his chest.

When she was close enough to touch, Beau saw a golden glow emanating from her. It distracted him enough he barely saw the cell door fly open, or her hand fly to his face.

"How could you do that to me?" Clara shrieked as her hand connected with his cheek.

She'd slapped him.

Not hallucinating then.

"What the fuck was that for?" he asked, rubbing his face where her hand had struck. He wasn't even upset. Relief overwhelmed him and all he wanted was for her to touch him again, even if it was another slap. Okay, perhaps not an actual slap, but touch him nonetheless. She was here.

"You let me believe you *died,* you fucking asshole!"

The guilt was back.

He raised his hands defensively. "Okay look, technically I died." Even as the words came out, he knew it didn't help. While his tone was soft and gentle, the words were wrong. Not incorrect, just unnecessary.

"Oh, sure," Clara said, throwing her hands up before resting them firmly on her hips. "Distract me with the fucking semantics. You didn't stay dead, but I watched you bleed out in front of me." Her voice broke over the last few words, and Beau had never felt such remorse in his life.

Not when he couldn't save Brielle, when he couldn't help his mother. Not when he knew he'd been the reason Neven got killed. His heart cracked hearing her pain, knowing he was the reason behind it.

Clara stuttered. Clearly there was more she wished to say, but she couldn't find the words. Or didn't know where to start. He'd stay there and take it all, whatever she said, as long as she would speak to him.

It hadn't been all that long ago, but it felt like a lifetime since he'd heard her voice.

She shocked him entirely as she let out a frustrated breath and wrapped her arms around him. Clara clung to him so tightly. She shook softly against his chest, but she held onto him like nothing else mattered. He was shocked at first, but after a second his shoulders relaxed, and he draped his arms around her too. With one hand placed behind her head, and the other wrapped around her lower back, Beau held Clara, and for a second, his world was at peace.

"I'm sorry," he whispered.

She pulled back to look up at him, her brows drawn close in a frown.

"So you stars-damned should be, you prick. Do you have *any idea* what that was like for me?" Clara groaned and narrowed her eyes, curling her hands into fists. "I could just—" she said through gritted teeth, pulling her hand back, no doubt to slap him again, making Beau regret his earlier willingness for it.

Instead, he caught her wrist and lowered her hand, then threaded his fingers through hers. Her skin felt icy, and he noticed her shivering.

"No, no more of that, thank you."

She sighed but squeezed his hand.

"You lied to me," she said softly.

"I did no such thing," he responded, and shook his head. "Not about this. I have only ever lied to you once, and it is something I plan never to do again."

"What was the lie?"

When she looked at him, worry was etched into her soft face. Those beautiful green eyes stared up at him, seeming to look right into his soul.

"That I didn't care if you slept with Neven," Beau answered quietly.

Someone cleared their throat from outside the cell, and Beau wrapped his arm in front of Clara, shielding her. He had seen no one enter, though he'd been completely focused on her. He was always focused on her.

"This is touching, truly, but we need to get a move on. The king is dead. Your condition has been met. Now let's go."

The male stood with a hand outstretched towards the stairs, impatience clear in his manner, but there was a familiarity Beau couldn't quite place.

"Hang on," he said, turning back to Clara as the stranger's words sunk in. "What?"

Clara sheepishly looked away and pulled a face. "Long story short, I got angry and vengeful, and the king got what he deserved."

She nodded once, then made to leave. Clara tugged on his hand, but Beau didn't move.

"No," he said. "Not long story short. Tell me the truth and don't omit any details for a speedy retelling."

Clara sighed and closed her eyes. She didn't look at Beau when she opened them again, nor while she spoke.

"After you—" she swallowed.

Beau hated he was forcing her to relive the memory, so he squeezed her hand. The faintest ghost of a smile tugged at the corner of her mouth. Beau blinked and looked away. If he started staring at her lips, he'd finally kiss her like he should have months ago and now wasn't the time.

Clara continued, "—died, King Urian, may his soul eternally rot, examined my body and found new marks had appeared along my spine. He sent me off to bathe and prepare for the ceremony, of which I no longer wished to take part. I was cuffed, but for some reason, June removed them before undressing me."

She turned to the stranger, who now stood with his arms folded across his chest.

"Why did she take the cuffs off? Was that you?"

"It was a friend's doing." He shrugged and cocked his head slightly, the gold jewellery in his slightly pointed ear dangling.

"Why not you? You dealt with the soldier earlier," Clara pressed, and her eyes narrowed.

"I manipulated him into believing he'd already announced us. He saw it play out in front of him, but someone had to manipulate June on a much deeper level than I can do."

"Right," Clara said. Beau could see the cogs working overtime in her mind, though what exactly, he wasn't sure. "Well, I had no magic while I was cuffed, but when it was removed, power flooded back, and I took the opportunity I was presented with. I boiled the bath water with her hand in it and she left to seek medical attention. Ryland and I spoke briefly of you, which brought to the surface a lot of rage, and thinking of Neven only added fuel to the fire. I requested the king's corpse in exchange for Ryland escorting me back to Elanist to meet my sister.

"The king is now dead. I overdid it a touch with the power surge—hence the currently glowing skin. We were leaving when we overheard a few soldiers in the courtyard speaking of you, and that it was a shame you were locked up. I couldn't leave without seeing for myself."

"You have a sister?" Beau had so many questions. He wasn't sure why that was the first to escape, but he supposed it was as good as any.

"Apparently." She shrugged. The movement caused her cloak to sway, and Beau got the briefest glimpse of her bare legs.

"Clara," he said, unable to tear his gaze from her body. "Are you naked under that cloak?"

She winked, and he could almost forget they were standing in his prison cell. For the briefest moment, it felt normal and *right*.

He had more questions, but the stranger was right. If Clara had killed the king, they needed to leave.

Quickly.

CHAPTER FIVE

CLARA

Beau's hand didn't leave hers, and Clara felt calmer the longer he held on. The longer they touched, the more content she felt. Regardless, time was not on their side here.

When Beau finally looked up from her legs, his eyes dragged over her slowly. Clara couldn't deny it had her feeling warm in all sorts of places. A small grin spread over Beau's face before he shook his head.

"Alright," he said, after clearing his throat. "Where is Ryland? And Ronnel?"

His face was neutral and calm as he mentioned Ryland, but hostility and violence painted his face and filled his voice as he spoke Ronnel's name. He bared his teeth and looked at no one.

"We haven't seen Ronnel since we were together last," Clara told him gently. She sensed Beau was far angrier at the shifter than she was.

"And Ryland?" he pressed.

"Present," Ryland piped up from the walkway. He threw a hand up sheepishly and gave a lopsided smile.

"No." Beau shook his head. "Ryland is a child of no more than fifteen, surely! Skinny and awkward, not built like a godsdamned soldier."

"Ryland is a Darsmun fae capable of sight manipulation. He's older than fifteen years, though by how many, I couldn't say." Clara shrugged again and held her hands out, gesturing towards Ryland as she made her grand reveal.

Beau's eyes narrowed, and he closed the distance between himself and Clara. He might've even moved around her, so he now stood between her and Ryland. She couldn't be sure and didn't want to make assumptions.

Sure, he cared for her, but did he have *feelings* for her? Her gut told her yes, though her ears were yet to hear the words. After all they'd been through, she wanted to know for sure. Mother be damned, she murdered a royal—a king, no less—for Beau. Yes, also for Neven and for herself and countless others, but she could not lie and say Beau wasn't the leading factor.

Her heart burned for him.

His face plagued her thoughts every time she closed her eyes. Did she plague him?

A chaotic flurry of emotions rampaged through her. She wanted to speak with him properly, but now was not the time nor the place to broach such a conversation. They didn't have the luxury. So instead her hopes stayed firmly seated as she tried to focus on the conversation happening in front of her.

She'd missed what Beau said, though it wasn't hard to catch up.

"No," Ryland answered. "That's a little different. Sight manipulation is purely for what one can see. There is a little leeway for sound, though I can't explain why. It worked to our advantage today, so I'd call that a win. If I were to manipulate you, it would be like looking through a window in your mind, be it entirely fabricated or only partially, and you wouldn't be able to touch any part of it. A Darsmun capable of mind play can do a great number of manipulations. They have no qualms with making you see, hear, feel, smell—"

Beau cut him off, sending butterflies through her as he squeezed Clara's hand and took an assertive step forward.

"You say this all as if you're envious."

Clara couldn't see his face, as he'd turned away and stood in front of her, but she could imagine the raised eyebrow and set jaw.

"Perhaps I am," Ryland said nonchalantly. "Though perhaps that isn't any of your business." He turned to Clara pleadingly. "Clara, please, for the sake of my head not resting on a pike by the end of the week—which is precisely how long it would take for your sister to learn of my failings and come here herself—do not make me ask again. We need to leave."

He waved his hands, ushering them towards the staircase. Clara nodded, and Beau followed suit.

She took this moment to really look at Beau. He still watched Ryland suspiciously, and Clara understood his mistrust. But for the briefest moment, she could breathe a little easier seeing Beau really, truly, and completely alive. How it was possible, she had no idea, but it was something she'd find out, sooner rather than later. For a second longer, Clara allowed herself to appreciate being able to look at him in the flesh.

He was alive.

His sun-kissed skin, covered in freckles. Amber eyes, so warm and inviting. Full lips and beard, so contrasted between soft and rugged. Dark, curly hair that reminded her of the chocolate spirals and shavings she'd always give generously to cake orders at the bakery. All the things she realised she'd taken being able to stare at for granted.

She took a breath and gave Beau's hand a squeeze and a tug, then made to leave the dungeons. Though he wasn't lagging too far behind, Beau wasn't able to keep up with them easily. His steps were clunky and disjointed, even compared to her.

Clara ducked under his arm, silently praying this didn't end up with them both falling face first into the tiles or landing in a jumbled pile of limbs and bruises. She wrapped her other hand around his waist and slowed to match his pace.

Ryland didn't look back, but he didn't need to. As they ran towards the meeting point, Clara hoped she was actually helping Beau. Only a handful of seconds passed without him looking down at her, as if maybe he, too, worried she wasn't

truly there. That this was some sick joke, or mind trick they couldn't wake from.

Finding Ronnel wasn't all that hard. Ryland asked a soldier passing by where he might be and was answered immediately. It was almost laughable to learn he was lounging by the very tree they'd agreed to meet at prior to their audience with the king. The carriage sat just outside the property's edge, in a line of trees beyond the one Ronnel lay beneath, with only one horse in view. Iivan was tied up, though Nisaa was nowhere to be seen.

"Fae or not," Clara called, stopping mere paces from where Ronnel lay, clasping her hands behind her back. "You sure have a talent for deceit."

She'd never seen the male move so quickly or scramble so fast as he bounded to his feet.

"You're one to talk." He jerked his chin towards her. A sound almost like a scoff came from him, but it was a weak noise, like he couldn't fully commit to it. "I've heard all about your half-truths and deception."

"Which makes me even more qualified to discuss such matters, don't you think?" Clara raised her eyebrows calmly, increasing Ronnel's nervousness.

Perhaps it was the murderous rage emanating from Beau. Or the cold indifference from Ryland—who Clara suspected he did not recognise, seeing instead a tall, built, fully matured fae. Maybe Ronnel was right to fear the odd little trio before him. For his life, indeed, because he certainly wasn't leaving this encounter with it.

“Do you recall,” Beau growled, his voice pitched so low and calm compared to the tension in his face and his body, “when I offered you alliance in Flame?”

Ronnel’s eyes flickered between Clara, Beau, and Ryland. Beau took a step closer.

“I warned you. ‘*Disappear, or you will die’* were the words I said. I was very clear you were to stay away from the king.” Another two steps forward. Ronnel glanced almost pleadingly at Ryland, perhaps hoping he was a neutral party in this encounter. “Yet here you are, back on royal grounds, kissing the royal ass. Now your king is dead, you fool, and you are next.”

In a heartbeat, Beau flew past Ronnel and spun. One arm reached around Ronnel’s collarbone, and Beau’s hand firmly gripped the shifter’s biceps. The other held a blade to his throat.

“You wanted to come back here!” Ronnel hissed at Clara. “I helped you!”

Clara smiled at how quickly his tone turned pleading.

“Yes,” she said, and nodded slowly. “Though I did not ask to be double-crossed in the process. Nevertheless, what’s done is done. Time to move on, and quickly at that.”

She nodded once more to Beau specifically, who lowered his blade.

“You’re lucky her heart still beats, asshole,” Beau spat. “I would’ve enjoyed killing you slowly.”

Ronnel’s posture relaxed. He even breathed a sigh of relief before he spoke. “You’ve convinced him not to kill me, then? I’m most apprec—”

“No, you idiot.” Beau laughed, though it wasn’t the joy-filled, infectious sound she’d grown to crave. Instead, it fell flat, and she couldn't blame him. "She convinced me to kill you *quickly*. We don't have the time to dilly-dally."

Ronnel's eyes widened, as did his mouth, when Beau's blade lodged itself deep in his throat. Much like when Beau died, Ronnel's blood poured out quickly, then his parted lips stained crimson, and blood overflowed, spilling down his chin.

A spluttering noise came when Beau removed his blade, followed by a dull thump as Ronnel hit the grass. Beau grimaced, looking for something to wipe his weapon clean, and gave Clara an apologetic look as he reached for her cloak.

"You really should put some clothes on," he said, not looking at her face.

"I have your bags in the carriage," Ryland said, as he walked past them and towards their transportation.

"Bags?" she repeated, turning to follow him. "As in more than one?"

"Yes, both yours and your deceased friend." His soft smile was filled with empathy, an understanding of the sorrow she felt.

Part of her appreciated his attempt at delicate wording, but part of her wanted to scream.

"I have another condition," she said, pausing before climbing into the carriage. Ryland held the door open for her and gestured for her to continue. "I need to make a stop before we leave Tirenas."

Ryland sighed, but said, "Of course you do." He stepped aside as Beau followed her into the carriage.

"A stop?" Beau asked. He sat next to her, instead of on the seat opposite as she'd expected. Butterflies exploded in her gut when he draped his arm around her shoulders casually.

"Yes, do you know Neven's parents' address?"

"Are you sure this is the right house?" Clara asked for a second time. Her fingers ached from where she'd picked at them so much. The nerves of having to tell the family of her friend he was dead—and that it was her fault—threatened to overwhelm her.

However, she couldn't in good conscience go back to Elanist without making sure they knew. Neven was a good male with a kind soul, and Clara could only assume he learnt it from his parents. There certainly had been no one who possessed those qualities at the castle.

"Take a breath," Beau whispered, then knocked on the door three times. Clara had barely inhaled before she heard footsteps headed towards them.

The wind caressed the back of her neck, but bit against her cheeks.

A short, plump woman with the warmest of smiles opened the door. Her grey hair spilled from a loosely tied bun at her nape, but she bore no other outward mark of her age. The tawny wings were smaller than Clara had expected, though they sat well on the woman's shoulders. But it was her striking cobalt eyes which stared at Clara that robbed her of her words.

"Hello," she said, as she gave Clara and Beau a thorough look over. "How can I help you?"

"May we come in, Mrs Dalys?" Beau asked softly. It was such a friendly tone, one Clara hadn't expected, but one she appreciated all the same.

She ran her nails around her cuticles, waiting for Caryn to answer. It felt like an eternity of silence before she stood back and welcomed them into her home. Her smile didn't falter, and it caused nerves and guilt to grow in Clara's gut.

Neven's mother led them into a quaint kitchen and dining space, offering them a seat at her wooden table. Two hallways jutted off opposite to where Clara was seated, and behind her Caryn flittered around in the kitchen.

"Tea?" she called out.

"Please," Beau responded. He then turned to look at Clara, concern etched on his face. "Do you want me to handle this? You don't have to—"

She cut him off with a gesture of her hand. "Yes, I do." Clara nodded, more to herself than Beau. She took a deep breath, trying to centre herself before Caryn returned. A small breeze swirled through the room and Beau cut her a warning look.

Caryn returned to the table, handing one ivory teacup to Beau and the other to Clara as she asked, "What brings you both here?"

"My name is Clara, Mrs Dalys. Neven and I—"

"Oh, Clara!" she interjected, her face lighting up and her smile widening. "I'm so pleased to meet you! Neven's told me so many wonderful things about you."

Before she joined them, Caryn walked back to the kitchen, no doubt to collect her own cup of tea. She patted

Clara's shoulder as she passed, and Clara's nerves built until they lodged in her throat, burning and immovable.

"I'm so honoured," Clara started, clearing her throat. "But I'm afraid I'm not here socially." She wanted to be tactful, but she feared if she took any longer, the words simply would not come. So as Caryn sat in front of her, lifting the cup to her lips, Clara spoke.

"I'm so sorry, Mrs Dalys. Neven is dead."

Shards of porcelain flew in every direction as the cup hit the table. Gone was the warm, welcoming expression Mrs Dalys had greeted them with. Instead, disbelief and fury stared back at Clara. A sneer replaced her smile as Caryn shook her head slowly and narrowed her eyes.

"No, I'm sorry. You're going to have to repeat that last part, dear. I don't believe I heard you correctly."

From one of the hallways burst a male, whose appearance almost reduced Clara to tears.

He looked so similar to Neven. From his height and build to the same sandy-coloured wings and dirty-blonde hair. Even his eyes were that familiar shade reminiscent of a winter's morning.

Clara's nostrils flared and her lips pursed tight as she blinked rapidly. Anything to avoid crying. This was not her place to grieve.

She dug her fingernails into the palms of her hands to distract herself from the heaviness of a cement block on her chest. Or maybe several, as all of a sudden her lungs wouldn't work.

Unable to pull her eyes from the male, Clara now noticed the scar that ran from his earlobe to his jawline. Then that his hair was long enough to brush against his eyebrows.

Those points of difference calmed her, reminded her this wasn't Neven. They did not, however, ease the pain in her chest.

Beau's hand landed on her thigh under the table, and he gave her the gentlest squeeze. A wayward thought of another time, when his hand might find its way up her thigh, passed quickly through her mind. It most certainly wasn't appropriate, but she smiled internally. Neven would've encouraged it, at least.

"Clara?" the male asked, looking at her. Stars, he even sounded like Neven. Before she could respond, Caryn stood and spoke for her.

"Yes. Clara. The one your brother spoke so highly of has now come to inform me he is dead. Please go on and explain how, exactly, my son lost his place among the living."

Caryn slammed her hands down on the table, paying no attention to the shattered teacup and remaining shards. She glared at Clara. Unblinking, unforgiving, and unwavering.

Neven's brother hurried towards his mother and wrapped her in his arms. He attempted to pull her closer to him, but she did not budge.

So Clara told her what had happened, from start to finish. She explained how she met Caryn's son, of his kindness and loyalty. And finally, that he died to ensure she survived.

"Get out." Caryn's voice was low and murderously calm. Beau's hand had remained touching Clara the whole time, which had helped. However, the way Caryn looked at her now felt as if she'd flung those delicate shards of porcelain at Clara's chest.

Clara stood without question. She was officially no longer welcome, though she couldn't blame the woman.

Lifting the bag full of Neven's belongings, she tried to hand it to his mother.

"Keyne," she said, still eerily calm as she turned to her son. "Your brother, my *son,* is dead because of her. I want them both out of my house before I return the favour."

Mrs Dalys did not look at Clara, nor at Beau, as she snatched the bag from Clara's fingers. It was time to go.

Keyne spoke as Clara turned to leave and Beau stood.

"I'm sorry about her," he said as he gestured to the corridor where his mother had disappeared. "And I'm sorry for what you've had to go through."

Reaching over to take Clara's hand, Keyne twisted the ring on Clara's thumb. Neven's ring. She'd grown so used to wearing it, the thought hadn't crossed her mind to take it off, and selfishly she didn't want to.

Regardless, she let go of Keyne's hand and twisted the ring off. She held it out to him, but he shook his head with a kind smile.

"It suits you," he said, taking it from her only to place it back in its original position. "And Neven would want you to have it. He did indeed speak fondly of you and held you in such high regard. If you need anything, reach out, yes?"

Clara nodded hesitantly, only giving in when Keyne raised his eyebrows expectantly.

He pulled her in for a hug, and for a brief moment, she pretended it was Neven. Almost immediately, Keyne burst her delusional bubble, but for a split second she got to pretend it was nice.

"My mother never wanted him to join the king's ranks, but Neven always knew what he wanted." Keyne held her tight while he murmured, resting the side of his chin on her head. "He said he knew he could do some good one day, but he had to be in a position to do so first. I laughed at him when he suggested it. Despite this court's silent following of the king, we are not ignorant to his ways.

"Regardless, Neven insisted, and he had his wits, so I didn't question him. He knew the risks and took them, anyway. When you feel guilty, remember that, will you?" He pulled back to look at Clara earnestly.

She smiled and softly replied, "He knew you'd understand."

"I'm sorry?" Keyne asked.

Clara stepped away, moving closer to Beau, who welcomed her without question. "Before he died, Neven said to tell you he was sorry. That I should tell *you* because you'd understand."

Keyne laughed, and an odd feeling spread through Clara at the sound. Part of her noticed how similar it was to Neven's, while another part was strangely glad their laughs were different. Something of theirs must be their own, she supposed, considering how much they shared.

"No, Clara," he said as he led them towards the front door. "Oh dear, no. He was telling you." Keyne chuckled again. "Gods, even from beyond the grave, he's fucking apologising."

Clara couldn't help but laugh with him and found herself genuinely pleased when Beau joined in. "He did that a lot, huh?"

They bid farewell with a wave, a genuine smile on their faces as Clara and Beau returned to the carriage. Beau held the door open for her and offered his hand to help her step inside.

"Time to go home?" he asked.

"Time to go home," she replied.

CHAPTER SIX
BEAU

Four days later, the trio stepped foot onto Elanist soil, and Clara immediately relaxed. Her shoulders dropped as she flung her head back and sighed at the sky.

She'd stolen many glances at him during the ferry ride from Coultin but hadn't really spoken to him again until last night, when out of nowhere, she'd asked him about his heritage.

He'd told her he was not a fae, nor a shifter, to be specific. He'd spoken about his father and how his heritage was indeed as wasted as the king had said, at least regarding the wings. That he was sorry he hadn't told her sooner and she'd had to watch him die without knowing it wouldn't be permanent. He simply hadn't known when the right time to mention it was until it was too late.

Throughout the entire conversation, Clara traced patterns on her knees as she held them to her chest. She barely looked at him, a fact which left him nauseous. She only spoke a little more, saying she was still angry—something he had expected—and then thanking him for being honest.

"Any other life-altering secrets you wish to share, Beau?" she'd asked.

Stars, when she'd said his name, his whole body lit with warmth. Words would not form, so instead he'd shaken his head. She'd simply nodded and left, then all of a sudden he'd gone cold again.

Seeing her now, he couldn't help himself as he walked towards her and draped his arm around her shoulders. Physical recoil was not the reaction he had expected, but Clara jolted at his touch and moved out from under his hold. Shocked, he let his arms fall limp at his sides as his face contorted with hurt and confusion.

"Am I so repulsive?" Beau tried to keep his tone light, but the humour was missing.

Clara looked at her feet before answering.

"No," she whispered, then her beautiful green eyes looked up at him with sadness and confliction. "I need to process, and I cannot do that with you touching me." She shook her head and looked away.

"Process what, exactly?" he asked, not quite as gently as her. "You lay on me the whole carriage ride, with no qualms about me touching your leg, or holding your hand." He threw his hands up in frustration, and Clara mirrored the sentiment, then dragged both hands down her face.

"You died, Beau! That is what I need to process!"

Beau wondered if she'd meant to shout at him. He hoped if she kept shouting, maybe she would get whatever she'd bottled up out of her system and then they could move forward. Maybe then she might let him help her move on.

"You didn't say anything and now a part of me does not trust you. A bigger part of me doesn't want to risk getting involved and losing you all over again. For good next time!"

Her eyes welled with tears, but she blinked them back and pinched her lips. Only neutrality stared back at him now, and even though he knew he shouldn't, his anger at seeing every emotion wiped from her face got the better of him. So Beau said one of the stupidest things ever to spill from his mouth.

"You're such a hypocrite," he huffed out as he stormed past her.

Clara scoffed before stomping after him. "Excuse you?" she demanded.

Beau vaguely heard Ryland make a comment in the background, but he wasn't listening to the Darsmun. From the corner of his eye, he watched Clara wave Ryland off, and the male threw his hands up in surrender and walked a few paces away. At least he pretended to give them some privacy.

"You heard me," he said.

Clara grabbed his elbow and shoved him. Though Beau spun to face her, he wouldn't meet her eyes. Instead, he looked anywhere else—past her, above her head, towards the mountain range they'd have to pass over the next few days. Fucking stars, this *woman*. She managed to find every one of his hot buttons and tap dance on them. Clara riled him and ruined him, but he could *not* look at her or his resolve would crumble, and his stubborn streak was far too strong for that to happen.

"Asshole," she spat. "Yes, I had secrets, but the difference is I did not know what my secrets truly meant. Whereas you were well aware of yours. I kept my secrets out of fear, and not only for myself, might

I remind you." She crossed her arms over her chest and glared at him with distaste, causing his heart to crack a little. "You kept your secrets out of cowardice. We are not the same."

"I suppose not," Beau ground out. His eyes betrayed him as they glanced down at her. A second was all he allowed himself before he turned his entire body away.

"Come on, Ryland. Let's go," she called, before storming past him to entwine her arm with the fae's.

Beau couldn't help his empty laugh, though it sounded more like a scoff than anything.

"What?" Clara paused, whipping around to face him.

He couldn't stop the next words from coming either, though he regretted them the second they were out.

"Replacing Dalys so soon?"

Hurt flashed across her face, fleeting before it was replaced by the iciest stare she'd ever given him. Slowly, she stalked towards him, her finger pointed violently at his face.

The surrounding air turned hot. Oh, he'd really fucked up now.

"First of all," she said, venom coating every word, "how dare you!"

"Uh, might I suggest—" Ryland interrupted.

"No," Beau and Clara shouted simultaneously, cutting him off.

"More importantly, and most impolitely, *fuck you*." Clara bared her teeth, but she needn't have worried—the bite to her words was enough.

"Clara," Beau said, no longer looking at her but behind her. Any anger he'd had, any other emotion, was instantly replaced by fear. He tried to reach for her hand, but she pulled back.

"No, I have had just about enough of you. Your attitude, your brutishness, and insistence that you're right, your—"

Beau shook his head to cut her off. Her eyes widened in rage and her lips pressed firmly together.

"No, Clara. Listen." The beast behind her huffed, and she stiffened. "Turn around slowly."

For once, the stars-damned woman listened to him without hesitation, and he breathed a sigh of relief.

Clara spun and gasped. Her body went rigid as her head tilted upward slightly. Beau stifled a groan—now was not the time for a fucking vision.

The beast stood before them, watching them closely. Its head was cocked slightly as Clara remained unnaturally still, unmoving for seconds which felt like an eternity.

Sunlight bounced off the creature's scales, some shaped like standard reptilian scales but others like short, pointed feathers. Vibrant colour cascaded down from its spine, where the scales were bright orange. Then they transitioned into a flurry of burnt orange, copper, and crimson. Its feet ended in talons shaded so close to blood, he couldn't be sure they weren't dipped in the substance.

Clara released another soft breath, and the creature turned alert.

"Daemdrana," she whispered.

In response, the beast blew a puff of stiflingly hot air from its nostrils, which were easily the size of Beau's fist.

He reached for her arm, so he might pull her out of the way if the creature changed its mind about simply watching. Clara didn't flinch this time, nor did she resist when he tugged at her gently.

The beast took a step and Beau froze.

"Stay still." Clara spoke softly, her voice no longer laced with a single ounce of the fury it held moments ago. "Do not provoke her."

Clara didn't take her eyes from the beast—*daemdrana*. Beau had never believed they even existed. Though in their defence, his kind wasn't often spoken of either.

It took another step towards Clara and sniffed.

Beau's body stiffened, and after another two steps its face was close enough that if it chose to take a bite, Clara would lose her head, and likely so would he. On instinct, Beau pulled Clara back, but immediately, he knew that was the wrong thing to do.

His actions had, in fact, provoked the beast.

Pain lanced his abdomen and spread like wildfire through his body. He hadn't seen the creature's tail flick, or the feathers, which were as hard and sharp as steel. Beau's attention had been entirely on keeping Clara safe and making sure the beast kept its maw shut. It was only as he fell to the ground that he saw the orange blur before it settled on the dirt.

"That wasn't very nice," Clara scolded. Beau didn't know whether she spoke to him or the daemdrana, but it didn't matter anyway.

The daemdrana huffed, pressed its nose to Clara's stomach, and took flight before anyone could react.

Ryland and Clara were both at his side in an instant. The former searched through his rucksack, for heavens knew what, while the latter scolded Beau.

"I told you not to provoke her, you stars-damned fool." She shook her head as she lifted his shirt to inspect the wound. He tried to laugh, but it hurt and quickly turned into a cough, then a wince, and next he was struggling to breathe, so Beau stayed quiet.

"I don't know how to do the healing thing," she whispered.

"I have antiseptic but no bandages," Ryland said, finally looking up from the bag.

"It's alright," Beau said. "I'm fine."

"You fucking liar," Clara scoffed, but it was laced with fear. If there had still been leaves on the nearby trees, he had no doubt they'd be rustling by now.

"Truly, I'm fine. Here," he held out his hand. "Help me up?"

Clara looked at him for a long moment before she rocked back onto her heels. She bounced once—and *fuck*, if he wasn't immediately thinking of every other way he could watch her bounce—then aimed to stand. Unfortunately for Beau, Clara's inability to do anything simply or easily came crashing into him. As did she.

Her hands flew out to brace her fall, but she landed straight on him. Blood coated her hands, as it did his abdomen.

Beau couldn't help the gasp and subsequent groan as Clara landed on his wound.

"I'm sorry!" she blurted.

"On second thought, don't move." He winced, but then turned to face her. White spots marred the corners of his vision and closed in rapidly. "I enjoy watching you fall for me."

Clara rolled her eyes, and Beau's smirk was genuine.

"Fuck you," Clara whispered, though there was no bite. He might've even seen her lips quirk.

"I'm sure you'd like to."

The moment was ruined when Beau coughed and blood flew from his mouth. He groaned and closed his eyes. This, too, was another fatal wound.

"You know what?" Clara said. "This is the universe teaching you a lesson." She patted his face once, a little harder than was necessary. "Come and find me when you're reborn."

Then she stood and walked away.

"What? You're not going to wait with me?"

Clara didn't answer. Then the white spots took over completely, and Beau lost consciousness.

Once again, Beau's eyelids felt sewn shut. Pins and needles spread from the tips of his toes to the top of his head, painful and without mercy. One of the worst parts of the rebirth was when he could feel his body, with all the pain running through him, but couldn't move.

The first time had been frightening indeed. However, Beau was rarely frightened these days, except when it came to Clara. That woman had him fearing all sorts of things.

Clara, she'd left.

If he could, he would've rolled over and wallowed in self-pity, but he could only wriggle his fingers at this point. After minutes, though it felt like hours, his eyes finally obeyed his demand to open, and he pushed onto his elbows.

"Rise and shine, sleepy head."

Beau's heart squeezed she hadn't left him. Perhaps there was a benefit to dying. If he could keep her safe, there was no question, but if it also meant he woke to her gentle smile and caring eyes staring down at him . . . Hell, he'd face death willingly.

Clara tossed a shirt and pants at him.

With every death, a Phoenix burst into flames. They were then reduced to a pile of ash until the body reformed and the heart regained its beat. As any natural fire would, the flames incinerated anything not associated with the body.

He looked down at himself, then back to Clara, unsure whether now was the right time to comment on how she'd seen him naked, so fair was fair. Then he noticed she was also lacking clothing.

"You should take your shirt off more often," he croaked.

One side of her mouth twitched in what Beau would choose to assume was a smirk. "And you should be less of a jerk, but I suppose we can always dream."

Beau sat up and couldn't help the grimace as every bone and muscle in his body protested the movement.

"I'm sorry for what I said. I was rude and insensitive."

"Yes." She nodded, then cocked her head to one side. "You sure do apologise a lot. Projecting, were we?"

Clara raised an eyebrow. Or at least, she tried. It was an adorable attempt, truly. Still, he knew what she attempted, so he kept his face neutral.

"I can admit when I'm wrong," he said. "I'm not perfect, Clara. Quite possibly the furthest thing from it, in fact, so I can promise there will be more slip ups and apologies to come." Beau took a deep breath before he continued. "Yes, I was projecting. I am scared to within an inch of my life that when you get home, you won't have any need of me anymore . . . I am easily replaced."

Another deep breath.

"Beau," Clara said, but he shook his head.

"Please, let me finish."

She nodded, so he kept going. He was entirely out of his depth, but he wanted to tell her. After everything, he *needed* to.

"From the second I laid eyes on you, I knew you were meant to be something to me. I didn't know what, but suddenly there was a gaping hole in my body I knew would never be filled by anyone else. All the walls I'd worked so hard to build started to fall. I have no rational thoughts when it comes to you, so I make no promises to be perfect. I told you I wouldn't lie to you again.

"I believe my death tally now comes to two. Twice I've died for you, and for you I would die a thousand times more. I'd live a thousand painful, miserable lives and level every world to know you are here and to be by your side. I choose you today, I will choose you tomorrow, and the next. I will choose you forever and yet pray that forever never ends, because forever will simply never be enough. I choose you in every capacity, and whether you choose me or not, I will be here. In whatever way you'll have me, I'll be here because I am entirely, irrevocably, unequivocally yours."

Clara's eyes glistened with tears. Her mouth opened and closed twice before Beau stopped her.

"Please don't say anything now," he said, moving a hand to place on hers. He quickly thought better of it and instead collected the shirt she'd passed him. "I don't want to push you for a response or put you on the spot." He pulled his shirt over his head. "All I ask is that when you're ready, take my hand or touch my shoulder, or *something*." A soft chuckle escaped, and relief flooded him when she smiled back. "Unless you've fallen into dangerous waters again, in which case, I will drag you back to land and scold you like the last time."

Beau winked and Clara's smile grew ever so slightly as she moved to sit on her knees, leaning closer, though Beau noticed she didn't venture close enough to touch him.

But that was okay, he'd said his piece. He'd told her in the only way he knew how, without frightening her, that he loved her. And when she was ready, he'd shout those very words for the entirety of Elanist to hear.

But for now, he would wait.

"Are you hoping I might so that you can see me naked again?"

Though waiting was already proving to be difficult.

"Fair is fair." He shrugged, then added, "Are you hoping for a different outcome if that happens?"

Clara smiled and stood.

"Come on," she said, before she turned and started walking away. "Ryland will be hours ahead by now, and he has all the food!"

She didn't look back and neither would Beau. He'd pledged himself to her, but actions spoke louder than words. Clara made him want to be better, so he would be.

For her.

CHAPTER SEVEN
CLARA

Catching up with Ryland hadn't taken as long as Clara had expected, or perhaps it'd only seemed that way because she was distracted by Beau's confession.

He'd all but professed his love for her. Not in so many words, but she wasn't so daft she couldn't put two and two together.

She hadn't been able to look at him since and had intentionally maintained her pace a step or two ahead of him. Though the heat of his stare suggested perhaps he'd intentionally stayed behind her.

Weeks ago, a confession like that would've had her melting. However, now it left her more conflicted than before. Part of her questioned whether it was a trauma response. How many times had he died and been reborn before they met? At only thirty-four years, Clara couldn't imagine it had been all that many. Yet now he'd died twice—with her and because of her—so maybe it was a symptom of something entirely separate from love.

Another part of her weighed the likelihood of him dying again, considering their track record. Was she capable of watching him die over and over again while not knowing if his lives were infinite? If not, which would be his last? What would happen to her if she gave herself to him and then he was ripped from her? She knew losing him would break her heart—that is, if she gave it to him in the first place.

Then she remembered all the times her heart ached when he simply walked away from her, be it down a hallway or around the corner. How she longed to be near him, even if he riled her.

She thought about Nyrene and Helmos, and their epic and world-ending love story. Clara wanted a love like that, one so strong it could level worlds. And that was what Beau had said to her. He'd level worlds for her, even only to be by her side.

Clara had to admit, his words had melted her heart and anger—at least a fraction. She also couldn't deny how only days ago she would've done anything to have him back. She couldn't forget that fact, nor did she want to.

Emotions and thoughts warred within her, and she hadn't noticed when Ryland fell into step beside her.

"I'm afraid we have limited clothing left," he said, surprising her so much she jumped and barely managed to stay upright. Clara stumbled over a large stick, tripping a few steps before righting herself and shooting Ryland a glare.

He laughed at her, which was much less surprising, then he handed her a shirt. Without hesitation, she took it and threw it over her naked body, but it was only once it cleared her face that she realised who it had belonged to. This was not one of her shirts. It had been Neven's. A new wave of grief washed over her, and once her arms were through the sleeves, Clara hugged them tightly around herself.

"What did you see earlier?" Ryland asked. "In front of the daemdrana."

Clara turned to her right and spared Beau a quick glance as he followed them. She looked away again before answering.

"Exactly what you did . . . immediately following the vision," she said. "You were right. Now that all the elements have manifested, the vision had more details." She sighed, then let her arms hang loosely by her sides and stretched out her previously clenched fingers. "I watched Beau move quickly around me, then she got defensive and swiped at him. He fell, and it ended."

Beau let out a long breath, and from the corner of her eye, Clara saw him rub the back of his neck.

Ryland only nodded, then asked, "Do you know the history of daemdrana?"

Clara looked at him briefly, eyebrows furrowed, then shook her head.

"They were born of another world," he said. "One with a different magic. Power less interested in being confined within specific boxes. Daemdrana was a family name, a clan particularly fond of shifting.

"The stories never corroborate why, but the family was cursed. On each member's eighteenth birthday, they would shift involuntarily into the beast you saw earlier and be unable to turn back. It is said they do not trust males, that they have been taught not to for whatever reason. And that the one who will free them from their curse is an out-of-place young female."

Clara did not like where this speech seemed to be headed. The last thing she needed was to be at the centre of more history that could come to kill her. The creature was magnificent, her deadliness only adding to her appeal, but she was lethal nonetheless.

“Some say it will be a member of the Golden Kingdom who can reverse the curse, yet others are of the opinion that the Golden royal will simply help, perhaps point them in the right direction. Most believe it will be a woman who does not belong to the Court of Flame but is instead passing through. Hence, the stories speak of the daemdrana’s search for the lost kingdom, scouring Flame and approaching only females.”

Her shoulders sagged. Though she hadn’t been holding her breath, her exhale was full of relief. In this case, she was simply a female passing through.

“They have an impeccable sense of smell.”

“Of course they do,” Beau muttered. “Did you see the size of its nostrils?” He physically shook off the memory.

“You’re just bitter she didn’t like you,” Clara snarked back, though she felt much more comfortable being playful than she’d expected. Confusion aside, she enjoyed the Phoenix’s company, and her stomach fluttered when he smiled.

“Is that why she sniffed me?” Clara asked, and Ryland nodded in response.

“Most likely,” he said. “Though she mustn’t have been interested. From what I’ve read, if they take a particular liking to you, they’ll sit at your feet or become overly protective.”

“What would you call killing me for grabbing her hand, if not *protective*?” Beau asked, his last word dripping with sarcasm, and Clara rolled her eyes.

"I'd say it suggests she felt threatened by a male. Regardless"—he shrugged, his tone nonchalant—"I thought it was an interesting piece of history."

The remainder of their journey was slow, but uneventful, although travelling the entire distance by foot was not Clara's preference.

Beau kept his word and didn't touch her, and she wasn't sure whether to be pleased or disappointed. Her gut twisted every time he moved a little further away, and with each passing day, the urge to be closer to him grew. However, she would not hurry this decision, as rushing into things had not benefited Clara in the past.

By the time they were through the mountain passes, the winter frost had bitten away at her fingers and toes. She could hardly feel the tips, and they were a permanent rosy colour, matching her nose and cheeks. Oh, how she wished for the maroon coat she left in Tirenas. Leaving it had not been her choice, but it had been the smart one. It wouldn't have fit into either bag, and her disguise would've been compromised had she worn it under her cloak.

Winter had stripped the trees bare, leaving no cover at nighttime. It was another—perhaps selfish—reason for wanting to stay close to Beau; he always ran warm. Ryland made no complaints. He only commented every so often about the history of the mountain pass, or a fact about the flora and fauna they passed.

He was an incredibly intelligent man, and while Beau likely would've been capable of getting her home, Clara was glad to have someone with a level head and the knowledge to guide them.

At least she had enough control of her flames that she could light a small campfire every night once they stopped. Though, since no one wished to attract unwanted attention, they never let it burn for long.

Could she have used her power to warm herself from the inside? In theory, absolutely. In practice, she was too nervous to try. Now wasn't the time for unnecessary experiments, especially with more travel ahead and their limited medical supplies.

The night before they were to cross the Kiyan Rapids, Beau sat with her after Ryland had fallen asleep. The fae male seemed to nod off so easily, and Clara found herself irrationally jealous.

"How are you?" Beau asked, after gazing at her in silence for a moment. He lounged back, his straightened arms holding him up and his legs crossed at the ankles.

In contrast, Clara's body was curled in on itself for warmth. She was cross-legged and hunched over, with her head drawn down all but in her lap.

Beau's hair was tousled and messy, barely held back in a bun at his nape. He wore an ill-fitting shirt, loose around the neckline, but tight where he'd rolled the sleeves around his elbows. It tucked into his very well-fitting trousers, and truthfully, Clara couldn't help her wandering mind. He looked tired and worn, but so handsome Clara found herself staring, at least for a second.

"Shitting myself," she said, and offered a weak smile. He returned the expression before turning his gaze to the sky.

Very few stars graced them tonight—too many were covered by the fog and clouds.

“Sleep, Clara.” Beau stood, though where he intended to go, she had no idea. They had no tents, and once she slept, the fire would extinguish, eliminating any light.

He made to turn, but paused, then added quietly, “If you would like any assistance crossing, I’m here. You need only ask.” With a single nod, he walked around the fire to where Ryland was sleeping and lay down too.

He was giving her space to process, not touching her because she’d told him she couldn’t think if he did. He’d listened and done exactly as she’d asked.

Even though her intent had been to reduce the possibility of regrets, Clara worried perhaps she’d done the opposite. Yet again, her chest squeezed uncomfortably as she watched Beau walk away.

Sleep had not come easy last night, though truthfully, she hadn’t expected it would. When she woke, the fog was thick and her side touching the ground was damp.

What a fabulous way to start the day.

In addition to the discomfort of sleeping outdoors in the sodden dirt during winter, Clara’s dreams had been filled with scraps of visions.

She wasn’t sure whether her power still manifesting was the reason her visions were not consistent or complete. Perhaps those she had while asleep were contending with her subconscious mind and unable to form. Or maybe all she’d ever get was a random assortment.

Regardless, all she had last night were exhausting snippets, ones which made no sense at all.

First there had been a vision of a handful of flowers, known to only bloom in spring, frozen in a solid block of ice. Then came windstorms full of autumnal tones and fallen leaves, coursing across a beach shoreline. Next, Clara sat alone in an empty room, devoid of all colour or personality. The only break in the alabaster walls was a window which showed both hail and sunshine striking the same field beyond the glass.

She woke to the scent of blood.

However, Clara was not bleeding, and neither was either male. Nor could she find any animal nearby who had died of an open wound.

As she waited for her companions to rise, the only sound Clara heard played on a loop. In the otherwise tranquil early morning, all she could hear was a woman screeching.

"We will take what we are owed," was shrieked over and over, the voice high-pitched and scratchy.

Beau woke only a moment before Ryland. As he sat up, he met her gaze, as if she was the first thing on his mind.

The thought warmed her, though not enough to shake her nerves. Thankfully, the air was frigid enough that the wind Clara unintentionally drew upon went unmentioned.

He nodded once, then busied himself with something else.

Clara kept staring at him, though.

CHAPTER EIGHT
CLARA

Her gut had churned all day, in symphony with the wind which danced around them. The soles of her feet prickled more ferociously the closer they drew to the water.

Beau glanced at her frequently. Wary looks, with a glint of hope, which Clara could only assume stemmed from the possibility of her asking for his help.

And though she wanted to ask, pride gave her pause.

Strength and courage were traits Beau possessed and demonstrated frequently, and Clara wanted to show she could be strong and brave as well. To prove that her mother was right in calling her strong; to remind herself she was brave without a man. She was capable of controlling herself. Her fears and urges and magic alike. Clara wanted to ask Beau for help, yet her tongue would not form the words.

Then logic trampled over her prideful thoughts, as she remembered how few steps she'd made across the rapids the last time. When she looked down, she found her hands shaking, and it was not entirely from the cold. However, would Beau assume it meant she was ready to welcome him back into her heart entirely? Was she willing to risk hurting him further by informing him it didn't?

No longer able to rely on the Mother for help, and frankly questioning whether the goddess ever cared to begin with, Clara stopped at the river's edge and turned her eyes to the Phoenix. She trusted him to get her across the water swiftly and safely. Mere seconds after she looked at him, Beau locked his eyes with Clara's, almost like he felt her gaze had shifted to him.

She hoped he saw the silent request in her eyes for the help she could not voice.

He nodded and closed the gap between them in a heartbeat. Her own fluttered when he reached her.

"May I?" he asked cautiously.

All she could do was nod, curling and flexing her fingers, as she tried desperately not to touch her sensitive cuticles, already picked to shreds. To not think about the tightness in her chest, which had nothing to do with how close they now stood to one another. Before she could blink, Clara was flung over Beau's shoulder, and his warm hand rested on the back of her thighs. Again, she admired his wings—the colour and shape. The magical fluidity of each feather, so delicate but forceful.

"In the name of honesty and transparency, I would like to inform you your ass is incredible from this angle."

Clara smiled, then responded without thought. “My ass is incredible from every angle.”

For the first time in what felt like so long, Beau laughed. Freely and loudly. Clara couldn’t regret what she’d said, even if the signals she sent were murky.

All too soon, he planted her safely on the other side of the rapids and clasped his hands behind his back. The hope in his eyes was a touch stronger now, but so was the confidence in Clara’s chest that all was not lost between them.

Beau cleared his throat, and Clara nodded once before he stepped around her and continued into the Water Court. Ryland followed but made sure she noticed his single raised eyebrow and smirk as he passed. Clara did the only thing she could think of and stuck her tongue out at the back of his head before following as well.

Being back on Wave soil was something Clara hadn’t been confident would happen again. It felt surreal, but Clara was apprehensive. She was plagued by a foreboding feeling, which became thicker and more intense the closer she got to her home. Clara couldn’t help her fidgeting.

First it had been a loose thread on the cuff of her sleeve, then she’d fidgeted with her fingers. Clara pulled at the sides of her nails, bit the ends of them, and pushed her thumbnails into the pads of other fingers until the crescent shapes were stamped into her skin. Next she fiddled with her hair, which had been twisted into a bun at her nape, then undone and retied at her crown. Still unhappy with it, Clara unwound it once more and braided it slowly.

"Your fingers will fall off if you keep that up," Ryland said quietly from her side. She ignored him and continued the braid. Then he asked, "Have you spent much time in the Court of Breath?"

"A little," she responded with a shrug. She'd worked in Breath many times, but aside from the last New Moon festival the court had hosted, it'd been years since she'd spent any time there. Except, of course, in her recent travels.

"Did you know there is a central field there which exhibits every season every day?" Clara's lips quirked up on one side. Ryland's love of history and geography was sweet. "It's called Florence Hills, in part for its naturally occurring miniature hills throughout the field, but also after the Resmigian fae who enchanted it as a gift for the Air Court. I admit, I don't recall the particulars of why it was created, but it's truly a sight to behold. All four seasons in one day, could you imagine?"

His brown eyes lit up and Clara wondered why he hadn't said anything previously—they'd just been in Breath, after all. Surely a small detour wouldn't have been an issue.

"Some call the field cursed because seasons come and go for a reason. They say you should not alter the workings of the universe. You should simply appreciate what there is to appreciate and be mindful and cautious of everything else. But one day, I'd love to visit. Perhaps you'll join me? I have a feeling you would find the respite and solace rather enlightening."

"Ryland," Clara said, narrowing her eyes at the man who maintained his innocuous and too innocent expression. "Why are you being cryptic?"

"I was being honest." He shrugged, and though Clara knew there was more than mere honesty behind his words, she didn't push further. He seemed as though he wanted to say something else but didn't, and Clara didn't pry.

Her hands grew clammy, which made for an uncomfortable attempt at weaving her unruly locks. The outskirts of Iloura came into view and a burning lump formed in the back of Clara's throat. She willed her breaths to come evenly, and for the winds around them to slow.

Warmth radiated at her back, and she knew without turning it was Beau. He walked close behind her, though still far enough away his fingers did not brush hers nor his toes clip her heels. Still angry with herself for asking him to stay away, Clara grumbled internally at the slim space between them that felt mountainous.

After what felt like a lifetime of being away, and yet all too soon, Clara found herself at the property line of her mother's house. Her home.

She took a deep breath, begging for the stinging in her throat and eyes to subside. Shaking out her hands, Clara raised her chin and closed the distance to the front door.

As soon as she opened it, the smell of fresh flowers hit her. A tear overflowed then, as even though she'd hoped to return, her fear at never coming home had been stronger. She'd never truly thought she would get back here.

Everything was exactly as she'd left it. The smell of potatoes wafted through the hallway, and Clara's stomach grumbled in response. It had been months since she'd had a proper home-cooked meal, much less in the company of her family.

Ryland and Beau followed behind her silently, their footsteps barely making a sound along the floor.

Rounding the corner into the dining room, she saw her mother stood with her back to Clara, hunched over the sink with the tap running, peeling more vegetables. Evian stood beside her, pulling cutlery from a drawer.

"Something smells good," she said, as loud as she could manage. Both her mother and Evian spun immediately, and the former clapped her hand over her open mouth as tears welled. The latter stood still, his mouth also open.

Felicity ran to her and wrapped her thin arms around Clara so tight the bones dug in and breathing became a struggle. She didn't care, and wrapped her own arms around her mother, squeezing her back just as tight.

Clara laid her face in the crook of her mother's neck, and Felicity's hands roamed her daughter's back. As if she needed to be sure Clara was real, whole, and safely in front of her.

Words did not come to her mother, only free-flowing tears and a hesitancy to let go. Even when her brother finally strode over, and the siblings shared a similar embrace, Felicity kept hold of Clara's hand.

It was only when she pulled away from Evian that Clara's mother spoke.

"Clara," she said, her voice wavering. She opened her mouth and her lips moved as if she were physically contemplating what to say. She settled on, "I love you so much."

"I love you, too, mother—so stars-damned much. You have no idea what it took to get back here to you, but I don't wish to leave for a long while."

"Perhaps you should stay here forever." Her mother chuckled softly, then did a double take. "Oh, Clara!"

Felicity gasped, her eyes wide as her hands flew to the sides of Clara's face, then down to her collarbones, then she lifted the hem of Clara's shirt and inspected more of her gold marks. She'd only been marked as a fire fae when she left her mother.

"I think you best fill me in on what exactly it took to get you home."

Clara nodded. They walked to the table and sat, Beau on one side and Ryland on the other. Evian and her mother sat across the table and eyed the males warily, but listened while Clara told them everything.

She spoke, missing nothing from the moment she left them, to each new mark she gained. Including her treatment at the castle and her escape, Neven's and Beau's deaths, and King Urian's, who she still could not mention without disdain. Finally, her second escape, and that she was currently, *technically*, on the run from the Solar Kingdom. And the daemdrana incident, which caused Evian to scoff.

"Orange daemdrana wasn't so far off then, was it?" He waggled his brows, and Clara rolled her eyes.

"Hush, you. The townsfolk couldn't possibly have known, and you're clutching at straws because you want to be right." She couldn't help but smile at her brother, though.

"I hope the dagger came in handy," Evian said, brows drawn more seriously.

Clara winced. “Unfortunately, I lost it more than I used it. Then I incinerated it. I’m sorry.”

Evian flung his head back and laughed. Clara intended to replace it, but he cut her off mid offer.

“Of course you did, little sister. Don’t fret, I have others.”

At that she simply nodded and smiled appreciatively.

It wasn’t long until dinner was ready, and Clara was famished, so she helped set the table. Beau and Ryland tried to help her but had no idea what they were doing. Any attempt to hide her chuckles failed, and they both gave her unimpressed looks. Her mother and brother continued to watch the males sceptically, though neither said anything.

She learnt Jacob had organised to stay the night at a friend’s house, and Felicity repeated the little boys’ intentions to study with next to no confidence. She offered to go and collect him, but Clara shook her head. Though her heart ached to see her little brother, there was no need to pull him away so soon.

“There will be plenty of time to come, Mother,” Clara assured the fretting woman. She’d nodded and wrapped Clara in another hug before she laid out food.

Between bites, Beau spoke. “This is incredible.” His voice was low and quiet, and Clara wondered whether he’d meant to speak aloud.

“Oh, you’re sweet.” Felicity’s voice was light, as was her smile, but it took a more serious edge as she continued, “Though flattery will get you nowhere. My daughter may swoon, but my head is level. You will do well to remember that, as I recall who arrived at my door all those months ago.”

She raised her eyebrows in challenge, a dare that only a mother could.

Beau swallowed nervously and nodded before he responded.

"Noted," he said, dipping his head in acknowledgement. "However, I assure you that your daughter does not swoon. I don't even think she likes me all that much." Ryland made a snorting sound, which he failed to cover with a cough. Clara glared at him, but he wouldn't meet her eyes.

Beau shook his head and glanced down at his plate before he speared a potato with his fork. "Regardless, my compliments are sincere. I haven't had a home-cooked meal in years, and never anything quite like this. I appreciate you accommodating me, and these potatoes specifically"—he paused as he lifted the fork in front of him—"are incredible."

Felicity nodded, apparently satisfied.

"The trick is to sear pig rind in the dish first. Then throw the potatoes in the fat. I'll teach you," she offered tentatively. "If you'd like?"

"I would like that very much."

Clara's heart squeezed, and in response the water in everyone's glasses pulsed, rippling for a second, and then stilled as if nothing had disturbed it.

Beau turned to her before she could think too long on her accidental magic outburst. "Aren't you a vegetarian?" he asked in no more than a whisper.

Clara smiled, and the water rippled again. He'd remembered. It was such a minor detail she wouldn't have expected him to even register during their argument, let alone remember so many weeks later. Though he did, and the flutters in her stomach and chest doubled at the realisation.

“Yes,” she said softly.

“Her food is cooked separately,” Felicity interrupted. “Roasted in butter and rosemary instead.”

“Not too shabby a chef, our mother.” Evian spoke with *most* of his mouthful swallowed. Clara pulled a face of disgust and shook her head, looking away from her brother. “Sweets, on the other hand . . . well, you’ll have to fend for yourself.”

Clara and Evian both chuckled, and Felicity smacked her son on the back of the head, though he only laughed harder, then planted a kiss on their mother’s cheek. The woman softened instantly.

At the end of the meal, Clara stood to take her plate to the sink. She noted how silent Ryland had been throughout dinner. Perhaps he was being polite or was simply nervous. Either way, Clara didn’t mind.

A knock on the door made her heart skip a beat.

“All of a sudden I’m having flashbacks,” she muttered with a glare at Beau. Though the expression held no real fire, and certainly no bite.

He seemed to know, because he scrunched up his face and it relaxed into a smile.

“I’ll get it, shall I?” Clara asked, staring pointedly at her brother.

“Since you’re up.” Evian shrugged, not even looking at her as he shovelled more food into his mouth.

Clara rolled her eyes and walked to the door. She raised an eyebrow at Ryland when he stood and followed her.

At least the bird inside the wooden clock on their hallway wall was silent tonight—otherwise, it might've felt a little too similar for comfort. Unintentionally, Clara held her breath as she pulled open the front door.

A woman stood beyond the threshold. Her expectant, almost annoyed features softened as her pale-green eyes raked over Clara. Thin, pursed lips pulled into a sweet, almost excited smile. Light-blonde hair with the subtlest rose tinge was pulled into an updo, and though Clara couldn't see it entirely, it gave the woman a regal aura and a sense of importance. She had the slightest button nose, but otherwise her features and bone structure were sharp and aligned well with her oval-shaped face.

Golden Candor marks glittered along the sides of her face, from her ears upwards to where they were hidden beneath her hair.

The woman would've fit with the courtiers and nobility in Tirenas, an observation which left a sour taste on Clara's tongue and immediate distrust in the pit of her stomach.

"Oh, my sweet girl!" The woman beamed, clearly elated to see Clara. Though Clara did not recognise her, a vague sense of familiarity bloomed at her choice of words. "Do invite your big sister in, won't you?"

Her tone was gentle and warm, her smile friendly and inviting enough. Though Clara couldn't get past her unease, nor the deviousness hidden behind the stranger's too perfect teeth and overly made-up face.

Sister?

CHAPTER NINE
CLARA

"Sister," Clara repeated as her brows drew together. It wasn't a question, but the woman answered anyway.

"Yes," she said, nodding slowly and eagerly.

Clara didn't move, nor offer for the woman to enter.

"My name is Elisabeth. I'm sorry I didn't sign the letter I sent, but it was best kept anonymous." Elisabeth raised a shoulder, then opened her mouth, but Clara interrupted.

"Letter . . . That was you?" Her tone was accusatory, though she couldn't find it in her to feel apologetic. Her hands warmed instantly, and the chill around them lessened. The breeze, however, did not; instead, it now bit at her nape and pricked along her arms.

Elisabeth gave her a flat stare.

"Oh, stop it," she snapped, planting one hand firmly on her hip. "You'll burn the house down and I am in no mood to be turned into a mound of soot. Hasheem." Elisabeth moved her gaze to beyond Clara and dipped her chin in acknowledgement on her last word.

"Ma'am," Ryland said evenly. Clara spun around in time to see him mirror her nod.

"Hasheem?" Clara asked him, her eyes narrowed so fiercely they ached. Of their own accord, her nostrils flared.

He looked down at her, and his features softened even while hers did not.

"My family name," he explained. "Ryland Hasheem is my *full* name. You are already aware I work for your sister."

Clara turned back to her *sister*.

The concept was absurd. While this woman obviously knew Clara existed and had kept tabs on her to some extent, she'd never bothered to introduce herself until now. Why was that?

"What do you want?" Clara asked, crossing her arms.

Elisabeth inclined her head, looking down on Clara for a second before regaining her neutral expression. Ire filled her pale eyes, a fact Clara did not fail to notice.

"I thought it high time we became reacquainted."

Before she could ask what the hell Elisabeth meant by *re*acquainted, Clara's mother hurried down the hall.

"Hello," she said, friendly as usual. "Who are you?"

"Elisabeth Hayes, Mrs Afron. Clarenna's biological sister."

Clara's mind raced as her foot tapped against the wooden floor.

Felicity had invited Elisabeth inside, apparently ignoring her daughter's silent pleas not to do so. Now Elisabeth, along with Felicity, sat at the round table in the dining room. Evian had made himself scarce after clearing the table with Beau. He made some excuse about meeting someone important and him not wanting to be late.

Clara couldn't sit; she was barely able to stand still, so sitting would've driven her totally mad. Ryland stood a few paces behind Elisabeth at the table and Beau stood between Felicity and Clara. Some of the heat from her hands shifted to a warmth in her chest at seeing him stand as protectively of her mother as Ryland seemed to do for Elisabeth. Though his gaze intermittently flicked to both Clara and their unwanted guest.

Elisabeth explained she'd heard Clara was headed home and wanted to stop by, check in, or whatever else was deemed appropriate of a sister who cared. However, Clara was not convinced that her motives were entirely genuine.

"How, exactly, did you hear I was leaving Tirenas?" Clara asked, scowling pointedly at Ryland. He shot his hands up in defence and gave an expression as if to say, *Not me*.

"Through a mutual friend," she said, before she pulled a small pocket watch from the waistline of her dress. "Who should be here any moment." Elisabeth looked back towards her with a too-sweet smile.

"No friend of yours is a friend of mine," Clara countered, her nose twitching slightly.

"Ouch," Ryland muttered, and placed his hand over his heart in a feigned display of hurt. Clara gave him a flat look in return.

"Your letter," Clara continued on, finally able to ask the question she'd been most eager to have answered. "You mentioned sending me to the king. Why?"

"To keep you safe," Elisabeth answered immediately. Her tone and facial expression suggested Clara should've already known this. That she was irritated at being questioned. Yes, she would've fit in well in Tirenas indeed.

"So you said, but *why*? What did I need to be kept safe from? And why, of all the fucking places, did you believe me being held in the tyrant king's clutches was the safest? How many times did you have to fall on your head to think that might be a good idea? Were you dropped as an infant?"

"Clara," her mother chastised with a low voice.

Elisabeth's expression didn't change, nor did her tone give away what the woman might've thought of Clara's words.

"I possess a variant of foresight. It showed me a version of the future in which you were harmed. He likes to collect things, and I knew under his watch no one would murder you. Excuse me for trying to keep you alive, you ungrateful child." She'd started out matter-of-factly, but by the end, her resolve had slipped and Elisabeth sneered.

Surprising herself and a couple of the others, Clara laughed, though it was empty. "*He* almost murdered me, you foolish woman. He would have, too, if his plan had worked."

Clara curled her hands into tight fists. She'd narrowed her glare at her *sister* so much she hadn't noticed Beau closing the gap between them, not until she felt the ghost of his touch on her hand as he ever so slightly brushed his finger along hers. As quickly as it happened, he moved away again.

It was a reminder that he was there if she needed him. That regardless of what had transpired, they were alive, and he was there. His presence calmed her. Clara sucked in a deep breath and took a step closer to him before she continued speaking.

"Do you know why he liked to collect things?" she asked. "Powerful things, to be exact."

"Please, do enlighten me, Clarenna." Elisabeth waved a lazy hand and sighed.

There was that name again. She thought she'd misheard when Elisabeth first said it instead of Clara. The name itched her spine.

"My name is Clara," she corrected. "He wanted my magic. He wanted to perform the Convergence Ceremony on me—at any cost, I might add. Could you not *see* this future?"

Clara folded her arms over her chest, unable to shake the distaste from her face. Elisabeth's expression faltered.

"I'm sorry," she said, which somehow Clara knew was not in character, even if she knew nothing of the woman. The apology sounded foreign on her tongue. "I did not know. Unfortunately, that isn't how my magic works. I saw—which is a very loose term—a female enemy and you dying. A war is coming, and I expect that has not changed. I only wanted to keep you safe. I have waited for years to see you again, and I will not apologise for doing whatever I could think of to allow this meeting to come to pass."

Her admission was vulnerable and likely as close to an apology as Clara would get. Unless, of course, she was a skilled con-woman and had deceived them all.

Though in the name of maturity and growth, Clara had told herself if she made it out of Tirenas alive, she would slow down. With her judgements and reactions, with plans, and whatever else she might rush into in the future.

The self-reflection had her glancing at Beau, who already gazed at her patiently. Subtly dipping his head, he signalled his confidence and support for whatever she decided. She nodded back, then turned to Elisabeth.

"Yes, well," she said, attempting a light-hearted tone. "Seems your plan didn't fail entirely. Though the execution could've done with more thought."

Beau didn't hide his chuckle. Elisabeth's face held what she believed was an honest look of hope.

Perhaps having a sister wouldn't be entirely disappointing. It remained to be seen, but maybe it wasn't such a bad thing after all.

Ryland answered the door when Elisabeth's guest knocked four times. It was an unusual number of raps, and so gentle Clara barely registered the noise. However, she refused to answer the door a second time, especially considering the last two times she'd done so, things hadn't panned out well.

All things considered, having Elisabeth arrive wasn't so terrible so far. The unpleasant part—which was generous in Clara's opinion—was finding out her sister was the reason King Urian had come looking for her in the first place. So Clara found it difficult not to rest the blame for everything that had happened since then on her sister's shoulders.

Sister.

Such a foreign term for Clara. She'd grown up with Evian, the furthest thing from a sister. Then Jacob had been born, and she was no longer on an even playing field. He had been the household tiebreaker, and she was the only girl.

Not that she minded. She'd never craved a sister. Seren had been her best friend for so long she could barely remember meeting the woman, so Clara had never lacked female companionship.

Now a female sat before her, telling her how much she was like their mother. How while Clara was the near spitting image of her father, she had her mother's personality and disposition.

Elisabeth told Clara of her parents' names—Fintan and Lenore—and random stories of them both. From before Elisabeth was born, to her childhood, adulthood, all the way to her mother's death. Specifics were not shared, and in truth, Clara did not want them. She felt no connection to this family, and no desire to know more.

Clara had a family. She had a mother who she loved dearly, and who loved her even more in return. A father who was a good and kind man, who was taken too soon. And two brothers who would just as quickly laugh at her falling face first into the pavement as they would take a knife to the heart for her. Perhaps not Jacob yet, but Clara had no doubt when the boy was old enough to understand what it meant, and the stakes, he wouldn't hesitate. Just like she wouldn't hesitate for them.

Ryland re-entered the living space, a short woman with a bounce in her step following immediately behind him. Her shoulder-length green hair gave her away immediately.

The woman smiled warmly at Clara before dipping her head in acknowledgement to Elisabeth, who returned the gesture in kind. She greeted everyone in the room, complimented Clara's mother on her home, and then looked to Elisabeth as if they were having their own private, telepathic conversation. She then took a seat beside Clara, patting Clara's knee as if she remembered Clara as well.

"You were in the art gallery," Clara said. "Diandra's."

"Indeed, I was." She nodded, flashing near-perfect teeth as she smiled. Another look passed between her and Elisabeth, and Clara was certain Elisabeth nodded ever so slightly before the woman continued. "My name is Poppy," she said, with a contemplative expression and a bobble of her head. "In truth, it's Philipa, however I'm far too young to have such an elderly name, so I go by Poppy. How have you been?"

Poppy scooted a little closer, as if they'd been the best of friends for years and were catching up. Clara noticed Beau looking cautiously at the strange woman they'd met months prior, but he said nothing. She gave him a small smile when his gaze turned to her. His shoulders relaxed and his lips softened into a smile of their own before he turned away.

Clara scoffed in answer to Poppy's question.

"I honestly don't even know how to answer," she said as she shook her head and lowered it.

"Well, never mind that then," Poppy replied cheerily. "How are you feeling now that you're home?"

"Do you always ask questions about how someone feels, or do I spark a particular interest?" Clara asked, then winked at the small female. Though she was average height for a fae female, Poppy's features and overall appearance were reminiscent of a pixie.

Poppy laughed. "Perhaps it is both."

The room continued with idle chitchat until Ryland spoke quietly into Elisabeth's ear and her face hardened.

"Clarenna," she said, and Clara rolled her eyes. "Apologies, *Clara*," she amended. "There is a matter I wish to discuss with you before we part ways for the evening."

Clara only nodded and gestured for Elisabeth to continue. Her gut told her this would no longer be idle conversation, nor would it be pleasant.

"What transpired over the last three days you were in Tirenas?"

Beau stiffened. Ryland shot him an almost apologetic glance, then turned to Clara to offer her the same expression. She wasn't looking at him, though, instead narrowing her eyes at Elisabeth.

"It feels like you already know the answer to that question," Clara said evenly, despite her heartbeat turning erratic.

Elisabeth nodded.

"Unfortunately, I do," she said, disapproval clear and present on her face. "Since your assassination of the king, Crown Princess Eveline has stepped into her role as impending queen. Her coronation is due any day now, and I have it on good authority that things will not go well for you once she has been crowned."

"Not go well for me *how*, exactly?" Clara asked.

"A war is coming, girl. How exactly did you think killing the king of a continent, her *father*, was going to sit with her?" Elisabeth spoke ice-coated words as her face morphed into one of outrage and disgust.

"Do not take that tone with me," Clara spat back. She stood, firmly planting one hand on her hip as she violently pointed the other at Elisabeth. "Need I remind you that you sent me to that castle in the first place?"

Elisabeth only scoffed.

"We will not go round in circles on this, Clarenna. The fact is, you killed a king, and his daughter is going to request your life in retaliation. Blood for blood, an eye for an eye." Elisabeth waved her arm, as if mentioning this was beneath her.

"I sure hope you're mentioning this because you have a plan, *sister*," Clara snarled, her top lip pulled back. "Otherwise, you're wasting your breath and taking up space in my house."

"No, I do not have a plan yet. I mentioned this as a warning, so be on your guard. I have not received a death warrant, but I do not doubt it is coming. War is coming. Your enemy is female. I get the sense it is sisters you should fear, so perhaps do not throw the word around so freely."

Clara resisted the urge to swear at this woman. She'd been in Clara's house for hours, yet only just thought to mention the impending war? She felt that the moment before she left was the best time to inform Clara that she was, yet again, in some form of trouble. That her life was on the line thanks to Tirenas royals.

This time deep breaths did not calm her. Warmth spread rapidly through her fingers and up her arms. Some of the heat which crept up her arms subsided when Beau stepped in to stem her rising emotions. Clara's shoulders relaxed a fraction as he thanked Elisabeth for sharing and promptly guided her and Ryland to the door.

Screw Elisabeth and screw the twins.

Maybe Elisabeth had been right to choose now to speak up. She was not welcome in Clara's home, nor did she wish to look at the woman a moment longer.

Poppy's cherubic voice flitted over Clara's stiff shoulders. "You would, by the way." Clara did not know what she was talking about, but before she could ask, Poppy continued. "Sleep peacefully and without nightmares or visions if I spoke to you as you fell asleep. I'd likely have to hypnotise you a tad, but it would be harmless, and you'd wake feeling so well rested."

Clara only vaguely recalled thinking such a thing the first time they'd met, though she knew she'd never voiced her musings aloud. But again, Clara could not ask before Poppy bounced down the hall and out the door.

CHAPTER TEN
CLARA

"Is this really necessary?" Clara's mother asked for a second time in as many minutes. "You're willing to sail across seas, then attempt to convince the most emotionally detached of all the royal families to ally with you in a war?"

Felicity had as little respect for the Morrin rulers as Clara, though she always did her best to not speak ill of others. Clara had no such reservations.

"I do not trust Elisabeth at all, but I will not bring war to your home—"

"Our home," she interrupted.

Clara continued without pause, though she acknowledged the love and relief which filled her heart at hearing her mother dismiss any doubt Clara could've had about returning home. "The vile man had it coming, and if I can arrange for allies, Mother, I will. Regardless of how lazy and fragile they may be."

"Clara," her mother scolded.

Clara shook her head in response, as she would not speak kindly of those who stood by and let Urian overrun the continent. His distaste for her kind, but Clara specifically, frequently darkened her mood. However, for her mother's sake, she would try not to let that happen today.

She took a deep breath and continued, her voice now much calmer. "If war is coming, they have a right to know, do they not? They may do nothing, but they should at least be informed. And if I can arrange for allies, I consider it a positive."

Beau sat at the kitchen table, a silent observer to the women's conversation. Resting against the counter, her mother fidgeted with a tea towel. Clara had started the conversation seated in the chair next to him, but quickly moved to pacing. Remaining still had never been easy for Clara, let alone at a time like this.

Realising Beau had said nothing since Elisabeth left with Poppy and Ryland in tow, Clara halted and turned to face him. Hands planted on her hips, she tapped her foot before calling him out.

"You're uncharacteristically quiet," she said, while she folded her arms across her chest. She pressed them firmly into her, in an attempt to be still for the moment at least.

Beau made a noncommittal noise, to which Clara rose both eyebrows. She levelled an unwavering stare until he conceded.

"I am here to support you in your decisions," he said. It was possibly the first time he had weighed his words carefully, instead of saying whatever first came to mind.

Clara didn't know what to do with this development, and her arms slackened slightly in surprise.

"But I have to agree with your mother." Felicity huffed triumphantly, though said nothing, and Beau continued, "If you want to go to Morrin, I'll follow, but I strongly advise you to make proper plans rather than the 'act first, think later' approach." He tilted his head towards her with a knowing look.

Clara didn't wish to voice it out loud, but she knew he was right. It didn't matter how cowardly she perceived the king and queen to be—they were still king and queen.

"Do you . . ." Clara started, then took a deep breath and turned away from Beau's gaze as his stare pierced into her soul. He knew her better than she wanted to admit, and they both knew how little she liked to ask for help. Though perhaps he might take it as a peace offering, a step closer to letting him back in. "Have any suggestions?"

The bastard didn't even attempt to hide his smirk, which leaked over the rest of his face. Clara narrowed her eyes, and she saw the corners of her mother's lips perk up.

"I do, actually." Beau leant back in his chair, and his smirk turned into a grin that threatened to melt Clara.

"Go on then." She waved her hands in front of her, gesturing for him to elaborate.

"Your sister seems to have connections. She has a Darsmun fae and whatever kind of fae Poppy is working for her, and both have mind-based magic, though that isn't entirely important. But it goes to show she has powerful employees. She may be able to organise an audience with the king and queen, and we can meet with them and discuss our case."

"*Our* case," Clara scoffed. She thought it was under her breath, but evidently not.

Beau gave her a flat look before he continued. "I will support you with whatever you choose," he repeated. "But I will not let you lead the audiences with royalty. I love you, but you'd have us in a cell within minutes."

Beau chuckled under his breath, but Clara's lungs emptied. Those words played over in her mind and her heart simply stopped so she could hear them clearly.

I love you.

She'd guessed as much after the daemdrana incident, when he'd professed all manner of beautiful things to her. But hearing them outright? Her heartbeat thundered in her ears when it started again, and for a second she had no thoughts at all, just an empty mind save for those three words on loop.

Clara cleared her throat.

"What do you propose we tell them?" she asked.

"The truth." Beau shrugged. "That the tyrannical reign of Tirenas is done. The fallout, however, is that war is now on your doorstep. Likely on theirs, too, if they choose to remain impartial. Eveline is a woman who gets what she wants and will not settle for less, regardless of its attainability. We will tell them that forging an alliance is what will help turn the tides and keep many of their kind safe."

“And ignoring this warning will end in millions of deaths?” Clara didn’t consciously speak, though her tongue still formed the words.

“No,” Beau said slowly. “I don’t think that’s what it will come to.”

Felicity eyed her warily, but said nothing.

Clara shrugged and played off the odd statement as pessimistic, though it wasn’t necessarily a far-fetched outcome. The endless loop of Beau telling Clara he loved her had since ended, replaced by the repetitive screams and flashes of blood and weapons.

Clara couldn’t shake the unease that washed over her, nor the ominous feeling that what was coming would be bigger than what anyone had conceived.

The next morning, her mother informed Clara that Jacob was due home by lunchtime. There was no school today, and she warned Clara he would likely cling to her like a barnacle. Clara couldn’t wait. She set off towards the bakery with Beau by her side, so she might have something sweet to offer her brother on his return. She knew she spoilt the boy, but she couldn’t help it, nor did she plan on stopping anytime soon.

Their walk into town was mostly silent, with Clara sharing pieces of her home and its history with Beau along the way. She pointed out the road that led to her various schools, where Seren’s house was, and the tree they’d carved their initials into as children. Clara shared the pact the two girls had made to marry each other if they were still single at a few hundred years—though she couldn't remember if they agreed on three or five hundred years—laughing as she recalled the promise that two small children had made to one another, and the endless back and forth on the terms of their agreement. Beau smiled softly the whole time, taking in her words, or at least he attempted to, which Clara appreciated.

She pointed out her mother's workplace, and Evian's, though he hated nothing more than to be reminded of his terribly mundane job.

"Sometimes a quiet life is the preferable option," Beau said distantly.

Clara responded without thinking, scoffing as she said, "You certainly won't find that with me."

"No." He laughed back. "I most certainly wouldn't. Though I believe I said *sometimes*."

Clara smiled but said nothing else.

When they arrived at the bakery, a swell of air flew around her, sweeping stray locks from her face and cooling her neck. Beau waited patiently, his soft smile waking the butterflies in her stomach. He stood silently until she was ready, and at the single dip of her chin, Beau stepped forward and pulled open the door.

The smell of jam hit her first. Strawberry and plum—Nerrida's two favourite flavours. Then apricot, and her nose turned up instinctively. She would never understand why anyone would like apricot jam; the texture was gross, and the flavour was awful.

Then she laughed and inhaled again. She smelt the bread next, which wasn't a surprise. Nerrida baked fresh bread daily, but it was done so early that by the time the shopfront opened, the smell had dissipated or been overwhelmed by whatever sweet treat she'd whipped up afterwards.

Clara was so preoccupied, caught in her reminiscing, she hadn't noticed the large winged male waiting with a pleasant enough smile on his face to take her order.

"Who the fuck are you?" she spat out loud, without thought or consideration. The possibility of Nerrida hiring someone in her absence was not slim, and Clara had expected as much. But to come in and see it first-hand felt like a slap to the face.

"Clara," Beau scolded, albeit lightly, perhaps as more of a reminder. Though if he were reminding her to be polite, she would impolitely remind him not to be a hypocrite.

A clang sounded from the kitchen, followed by a series of smaller crashes, then the sound of hurried footsteps.

Nerrida filled the doorway, which separated the kitchen from the storefront, halting abruptly as her hand flew to her mouth.

"Clara," she breathed, and ran so fast she was a blur of cream and ivory, from her pale-blonde hair and fair skin to her uniform of a cream apron dusted with flour, off-white shirt, and matching pants.

Nerrida hugged Clara so tightly, a fresh wave of emotion threatened to spill out. And she hugged the woman back, breathing in the familiar smells and feeling just a little more at home.

She blinked a few times, while over Nerrida's shoulder, Clara saw Beau introduce himself to the winged fae, and the males conversed quietly.

They spoke briefly, Clara highlighting the positives of her time away and her pleasure at being home. Even after mentioning her impending trip to Morrin—while omitting any frightening information—Nerrida offered Clara her old job back, and she immediately accepted. It was another step towards normalcy and would be good for her. She hadn't considered what it meant for the other employee, but truthfully Clara couldn't find it in her to care.

After purchasing a variety of pastries for Jacob, they left the bakery and headed home. The wind picked up the closer they got to the house, but it was gentle this time, not aggressive like it normally would be. She barely felt the tingles in the soles of her feet.

This breeze—her *magic*—felt a little more in control, and stars, if that wasn't one of the best realisations she'd had lately.

CHAPTER ELEVEN
CLARA

Clara and Seren lived only a few streets apart, so Clara's shock at seeing her friend wasn't due to the water fae being out of place. Instead, it was the overwhelming sense of relief that washed over her. The normalcy and familiarity were unexpected.

Beau stopped less abruptly than Clara, though he was also more graceful. A few of his feathers brushed along her arm and sent tingles down her body, but she didn't look at him. Instead, she remained staring wide eyed and slack jawed at her best friend, who seemed almost as shocked to see Clara standing at the opposite end of the footpath.

Both females took a step forward at the same time, and Clara breathed, "Seren."

Seren's hand flew to her chest, to her collar, before she wrapped both arms around her middle and lowered her chin.

Clara vaguely heard Beau's murmured questions beside her as she handed him the bags and rushed forward.

Clara stayed silent as she collided with her oldest friend, wrapping her arms around her so tightly she feared the tiny woman might have trouble breathing.

Seren seemed to hold her breath for a moment, her whole body still, until she relaxed and held her back.

Clara didn't know how long they stayed in their silent embrace in the middle of the walkway until Seren pulled away.

"You're home." It wasn't a question, but Clara nodded anyway. Seren's voice was soft and small, like always, though there was now a note of something Clara couldn't identify. Unease? Discontent? She wasn't sure.

"I got back yesterday," Clara offered, then stepped back and allowed the apparent separation between them to grow. Awkwardness had never been something the two of them experienced and, frankly, it made Clara nervous.

"You're safe?" Seren asked. "You're . . . okay?" She seemed concerned.

Though Clara wouldn't have doubted it yesterday, today the relief in Seren's eyes was clouded with hesitation. Clara nodded, unable to form words without mixing them with an accusation. She'd been gone a long time, and anything could've happened since she saw Seren last to account for her strange behaviour.

Seren sighed and her body relaxed more, then she let her hands fall to her sides. She closed her eyes as she inhaled a second time and smiled at Clara when she released the breath. Some of the hesitation dissipated from her bright-blue eyes, and a little of the distance between them disappeared.

The water fae linked her arm through Clara's and they started walking. She stared at her feet for at least a dozen steps until, without warning, she blurted out, "I'm romantically involved with your brother."

And it caught Clara completely off-guard. No wonder she'd been acting odd! Seren was fucking Clara's brother.

Clara chuckled and patted Seren's hand, which had stiffened around Clara's biceps. She'd always been timid and had a tendency to be nervous.

"Is he good to you?" Clara asked.

"Yes," Seren answered immediately. "He's kind and gentle and compassionate," she gushed, listing all the traits Clara already knew her brother possessed.

"And you are happy?"

"Very," Seren said again, nodding fervently.

"Then I am happy for you, silly girl. You need not have worried about my approval, if that's what has you all jittery and strange. I love you both, you know that."

Seren nodded, and Clara saw a single tear roll down her cheek before she sniffed, shaking off whatever still sat heavily on her shoulders.

Beau continued walking behind them, and Clara appreciated the semblance of space and privacy he gave by holding back a few paces. Though he could likely hear everything, even without a Soliqe's advanced hearing, he made no sound or any attempt to catch up.

As if knowing where Clara's mind had wandered to, Seren poked her in the ribs and asked, "And who might your friend be?"

Friend.

Was that what he was, or was he more?

Stars, how many months had she dreamt of being more than friends? Was her stubbornness really the only thing that stood in the way now?

How could she possibly summarise their journey? That he'd been her captor, teacher, mentor, then friend, and finally someone she flirted with and fell for? But also someone who ripped her heart out when he died in front of her, only to be resurrected, yet he'd lost all her trust in the process. Now he was intent on being there for her and proving his commitment to her.

"It's complicated," she said with a sigh, and remembered his ability to overhear their conversation.

"Then uncomplicate it," Seren pushed.

"I think I fell in love with him." The words came easier than Clara had expected, though they were anything but simple.

"You *think*?"

"It's complicated . . ."

"Clara." Seren stopped, pulled Clara around to face her, and blue eyes bore into Clara's own. "His eyes have not left you, and I can almost guarantee neither has his mind." Clara scoffed and rolled her eyes instinctively, but Seren clicked her tongue and continued. "Uncomplicate things, because you deserve to be in love and happy about it."

She *wanted* to be in love and happy about it. Clara wanted so badly to move on, to move forward with the regenerative prick. She understood why he didn't say anything before, and she understood everything he'd said afterwards. Though she certainly didn't agree with it all, but what *exactly* was her problem?

Did she not trust him? Or was she unsure if she wanted a life with him, in case his infinite number of lives were cut short? Would she rather take the risk of love and loss or lose out altogether?

In reality, she was a stubborn girl who was hurt and shied away from experiencing it again. Deep in her heart, Clara already knew what path she should choose.

Now for her tongue to catch up and say the words which would leave her vulnerable.

That might take some time . . . and alcohol.

Clara barely noticed that they'd continued their stroll, but when she glanced back at Beau, she could've sworn he'd put more space between them than before. She didn't know what to make of that, but guessed he'd been eavesdropping, noticed Clara's lack of a response, and gave her more space. Though whether the male had the emotional intelligence to come up with such a gesture, she wasn't sure.

"The New Moon festival is in a few days," Seren piped up cheerily. "Please tell me you'll be there!" Her voice was a squeal, and all she needed now was to jump excitedly, then Clara could pretend this conversation was happening a year ago and the past few months hadn't happened.

"Days?" Clara scoffed, with a shake of her head. "We have at least a week. I wouldn't miss it," she added softly as a genuine smile lit her face.

"Irijna and David are coming, apparently with exciting news! I wonder if she's with child!" Seren was practically bouncing.

Clara snorted. "You know her preferred positions do not lead to babies."

They both laughed, but all too soon, they were at Clara's door. Beau still hung beyond at the property line, giving the two women their privacy. Laughter fizzled out, and Seren dropped her arm to hold Clara's hand, squeezing before letting go completely.

"I am so glad you're home," Seren said solemnly. "And safe."

Clara nodded, then hugged her friend once more before she flitted away. Clara waited for Beau to walk up the walkway before she opened the door.

"How much did you hear?" she asked.

"It's complicated," Beau answered with a devilish smirk. Clara couldn't help her pursed lips from spreading wider until she was smiling too.

The fear that blossomed on Jacob's face as he walked in only an hour after Clara was enough to crack her heart. The tears that ran down his pudgy little face and the fracture in his voice as he spoke into Clara's chest had her resolve breaking as well.

She'd done well not to cry until this point, but seeing Jacob let all her emotions escape. She held him as he cried and soaked both his collar and her shirt with his tears. It was too much.

"I hardly even got to say goodbye," Jacob said between hiccups. "I didn't think I was ever going to see you again." His words trailed off into a whisper.

Clara grabbed his shoulders, which still shook in her hands. "You cannot get rid of me that easily, little brother." She knelt in front of him, pressing her forehead to his. It was a gesture she'd done since he was born.

As a newborn, she'd hold him to her chest and bring her head down to him or lean over while he lay on the floor or in his bassinet. When he grew enough to sit and then stand, she would lean in a little, and he learnt to lean in with her. It'd been something they shared and something she adored. Something Clara had not truly realised how much she'd missed.

"Please accept my sincerest form of apology," Clara whispered, pulling away slightly with her hands still cupping Jacob's cheeks. His usually clear, pale skin was now covered in red splotches, especially around his eyes. "There are four almond pastries in the kitchen for you, plus an assortment of others to share," she added, and he bounced over to the kitchen bench. "But the almond ones are yours."

Clara sniffed and sat back on her heels with a chuckle, watching her little brother. Oh, how she'd missed him. Missed them all.

Three days later, Clara had already started back at work. A small feat, really, but one she hadn't realised would feel so empowering.

In the castle, if she wasn't with Beau, Neven, or a staff member—usually June or Agnes, the cranky old wretch—she was asleep. She had no time to do what *she* wanted.

Now that she was home, Clara woke when she pleased and spent her days much the same way. She'd been to work twice, in fact. One shift had been spent with the newest member of Nerrida's staff, Mikhail, who Clara hated to admit wasn't entirely a waste of space. Nor was he someone she could continue to dislike for reasons beyond his control.

So she was polite—civil and amicable—though not going so far as to behave as a friend. They had a nasty habit of leaving her, one way or another.

She'd seen Seren a handful of times, but Elisabeth hadn't come back, which was entirely for the best.

No death marks had arrived. Though as angry as Clara was with her sister, she couldn't deny the marks were coming and she should heed Elisabeth's warning.

Beau quietly questioned her decision to go to Morrin; however, Felicity was far more open about her distaste for the idea. She'd only just got her daughter back and did not want her gallivanting off again so soon. Every time they discussed Clara's plans, she sighed and muttered, "My strong, stubborn daughter. Halfway to fearless, indeed," and conceded.

Despite everything going on, Clara's mind never strayed far from the Phoenix in the next room. He walked her to bed every night, hovering by the door for a fraction of a second—

long enough Clara thought he might say something. Then, every night, he nodded and left.

Clara's home did not have a spare bedroom. There was a bedroom for each sibling, a suite for their mother, and a study which could be converted in the case of an emergency but was entirely too small for someone with wings to occupy.

So, Beau slept on the settee.

Her room was on the opposite side of the wall to where he slept, and Clara contemplated every night before she fell asleep whether to invite him to share her bed.

She chickened out every time.

Pathetic, really.

Clara rolled her eyes and kicked off her blankets with a huff. Another night of disturbed sleep.

In the mornings, just for a second before she was lucid and conscious, Clara forgot. About Neven being dead, the fact that she'd killed the king, and that he'd killed Beau first. She forgot about all the death she'd dealt, and how she didn't feel even slightly guilty—it was like she'd never been taken at all.

Then she'd remember, and a wave of heartbreak and pain and anger would crash over her all at once.

Yesterday she'd woken from a truly awful sleep and the pain had been so bad the windows shook.

Yesterday, when her memories flooded her mind, a fresh feeling bloomed in her chest. Warm and excited and nervous, almost. Like butterflies.

So when it happened again this morning, she decided. Today she would tell Beau.

Grab his hand, or fuck, maybe she'd simply jump him. Either way, today she would tell him. She would finally follow her heart instead of her head—it belonged to him, after all. If she thought about it, Clara's heart had been his for quite some time.

She threw on some loose trousers and an old tunic, and stalked from her room.

"Well, isn't this a sight for sore eyes." Evian chuckled as he watched from the bench. He sat holding a cup of tea in one hand and a newspaper in the other. If Clara squinted, she could see their father staring back at her.

She turned, hoping to see Beau, but found the couch empty.

"Oh, ha-ha," Clara mocked, then stuck out her tongue. "Might want to watch your tongue, Evian. I'd hate for you to burn it on your tea."

Clara poured her own cup, not sparing a glance for Evian, but she didn't need to. She could call on her fire powers fairly easily these days, and for something so trivial as boiling water, she barely even had to spare a thought.

Evian chuckled again, then set down his cup.

"Seren told me you saw her the other day," he said, glancing at Clara. She nodded and raised both brows. "And she told you?"

"That you've been banging my best friend?"

Evian sighed and pulled a face.

"Yes, Evian. She told me."

"And?"

"And nothing, you fool. I'm happy for you, as I am her. Excluding your inability to keep your mouth closed while eating, you're a decent male. She could do far worse."

"Was that a compliment?" Evian raised a brow, the grin on his face lopsided and cocky.

"More like not an insult," Clara said with a shrug.

"Did she mention anything else?" Evian asked. His tone was serious now.

"No," Clara said. "What else should she have told me?" She put her teacup on the counter and spun to face her brother. He so rarely had nerves etched on his features, and he never took so much time to consider his words. "Evian," she prompted.

"It isn't entirely my place to say," he started. Though before she could remark how he shouldn't have brought anything up if he didn't wish to continue, Evian kept going. "But I feel it is something you should know. Something you'd want to know, at least."

The butterflies Clara had felt flittering earlier now felt leaden and hot. The heels of her palms tingled as her mind concocted a string of wild theories for what Evian might say next.

"A few weeks back," Evian said, unable to look Clara directly in the eyes. "A group of Tirenas soldiers stormed through every house, business, and building with any connection to you. They said there would be consequences for those unwilling to help them. Seren was here when they broke the front window, thundered in, and started throwing chairs and pulling doors from hinges as they looked for you."

Clara bit the inside of her cheek, her thoughts now completely overtaken by guilt.

"One of the soldiers grabbed Seren by her shirt, pulling her off the ground, and snarled at her how she should do well to remember what happens to the unhelpful, and the rewards given to those who help. I felt a furious pounding in my chest, and I could barely hear over the ringing in my ears.

"Seren told them you weren't here, and despite me shouting that at them the entire time, they finally listened and dropped her." Evian's face grew murderous. "Before they took their leave, they picked up the side table from the sitting room and smashed it and glass flew everywhere."

"Were you alright?" Clara gasped and couldn't help but interject. Evian nodded.

"A few minor scratches, but it was Seren who got hurt. A dozen glass shards embedded in her chest and neck, plus one in her face, and another in her shoulder. Honestly, she looked like a beautiful, horrific painting." He smiled softly, and Clara joined him. She enjoyed seeing him express such content and loving feelings for her friend, though it was only the fact that she'd seen Seren alive and well the other day which kept her from worrying too much for her friend's safety.

"I don't really remember what happened next. Just being so angry, so furious, it felt like steam radiated off me and every surface in the house." He shook his head and looked down at his hands. "I pulled each shard of glass from her skin as gently as my shaking hands could manage. By the sixth or seventh shard, I noticed the wounds weren't bleeding anymore—they weren't even open. Once the last shard was out and she was entirely healed, a bolt of pain shot through my chest. When it stopped, I did what any sane individual would do."

"You took your shirt off?" Clara snickered in jest.

"Yes." Evian chuckled with her. "I took my shirt off and inspected my skin to find I'd been marked. My magic manifested, and I healed her. Then she broke down, sobbing and shaking in my arms. Mother, she felt so small and frail. I held her until she calmed.

"She told me what happened with her father. Do you remember when the soldiers stormed the town before Bird Boy One and Two came to collect you?"

"Arrest me, you mean?" Clara folded her arms as a sinking feeling enveloped her. A chill settled on her shoulders, but thankfully, no wind brushed through the house.

Evian nodded. "Two soldiers beat her father to within an inch of his life, looking for information on you."

"I knew that's why they were here," Clara whispered. "But what does that have to do with anything? Darin is okay, yes?"

"Darin is fine," Evian confirmed, still weighing his words. "But only because Seren told them where to find you."

Clara's back straightened, and she looked away, her jaw set. She kept her face neutral, but frankly didn't care whether she succeeded.

"Clara, wait," Evian said, his hands held up. "If she hadn't, he would have died."

All she could do was nod, though she did not meet his eyes. She didn't wish to ruin the happiness he'd found with Seren.

But all Clara could feel was betrayal.

Had Seren's intentions been justified? Of course, and Clara would've encouraged her to do exactly as she had done. The problem was, Seren had been a coward and a liar by omission. They'd seen each other since, not once or twice, but multiple times. She could have mentioned her actions, warned the woman who was supposed to be her best friend that she'd had a hand in her being taken hostage. Held prisoner.

No wonder she'd acted so strange the other day. She felt responsible. And she should.

The window behind the sink rattled, as did the vases on tables and shelves. Clara's fingers warmed and a bead of sweat formed on Evian's forehead.

"Were they fatal or superficial?" Clara asked, her tone flatter and steadier than she'd expected. "Her wounds."

"Superficial, why?"

Clara stared at her brother. No doubt the only thing that showed in her eyes was fury, as it was the only thing she felt.

She spoke calmly as she pushed off the bench and stalked out of the house, pausing only to call back over her shoulder, "You should've let her bleed."

CHAPTER TWELVE
CLARA

Clara stormed from the house. She'd left intending to find Seren, so she could tell her exactly what she thought of this secret she had been keeping. When she arrived at Seren's house, though, Clara saw Darin in the front yard. He had a limp, and scars dotted his body, clearly seen from the other side of the path. Darin straightened, carrying a handful of weeds and sticks to a compost pile, then he turned and spotted her.

His face was full of love, happiness, and pleasure at seeing her. His smile spread from ear to ear, and he beamed with joy at his *unbiological* daughter. That was how he referred to her. Clara had always been Darin's unbiological daughter to anyone who asked, or anyone who would listen. He waved, and Clara returned the gesture—albeit half-heartedly—as all the anger slipped from her body.

Now she just felt hollow.

Her shoulders sagged, and she gave Darin a weak smile as she continued walking. She wouldn't rip into Seren today, maybe not even tomorrow.

She wouldn't speak to Seren, nor seek her out. Clara wanted nothing to do with the woman. At least not for now.

Her feet moved automatically, and she stared vacantly, taking in nothing. Clara wandered aimlessly around town until she found herself sitting outside her house.

Sometime later, the door behind her opened, then closed with a soft thud. Footsteps approached her, but she wasn't paying attention. She didn't look up, though she didn't need to, knowing who it was by the warm citrus notes which filled her nose. Somehow she found comfort in that familiarity, much like with the heat radiating off his body, fighting off the chill of the changing season.

Beau sat next to her silently. He didn't prod. He sat and provided her with a sense of calm Clara hadn't expected, but definitely welcomed. So she rested her head on his shoulder and sighed.

Beau's body was so still, for a moment Clara feared he'd stopped breathing. Then he let out a long, slow exhale and his shoulders relaxed. He didn't move closer, nor did he speak, and Clara enjoyed the serenity and closeness of his presence.

That night, Clara hardly slept. Nightmares and visions plagued her from the moment she closed her eyes.

A three-headed snake writhes and hisses in a cloud of smoke. Slime and scales shimmer, morphing into a woman somehow simultaneously hideous and enticing.

The otherworldly female calls Clara forward, captivating her with an intoxicating beauty which brings goosebumps to Clara's flesh, even here in this dreamlike plane.

Goosebumps not created entirely from awe.

Fear coats her tongue, filling her throat and sitting heavily in her gut.

Hair reminiscent of spilt oil sticks to her skin, leaving only the female's full, pale lips bare and the tattoo on her chin on full display. It seems to writhe like the snake, more swirl than serpent. It morphs, moving down until it wraps around her gangly wrists.

A sword shimmers in her hands, shifting in and out of reality.

Next, the swirl moves between her brows and along her forehead, looking more like a crown of thorns before repeating the cycle.

A snake on her chin.

A sword in her hand.

A barbed crown set above unnerving eyes.

Slick hair parted around her face, framing a small, pointed nose, and round, milky-white eyes shimmering without irises.

Her lips pull back slowly, and Clara realises the woman is smiling.

Teeth like a monster who dwells in the deepest ocean cave fill her mouth, sharp and thin and far too many to count. She opens her mouth wider than should be possible for a female so small.

The unfamiliar being shrieks.

Water splashed her face. It filled her open mouth, causing Clara to cough and splutter in a poor attempt to not choke. She heard a woman hiss in the background and immediately Clara's spine tingled, as did the soles of her feet, and air swirled violently around her.

"I apologise for soaking the sheets," Beau said, though to who, Clara was unsure.

The water fell from her face, and she wiped her eyes, but fear still coated her vision, and her breathing was quick.

"It worked the last time," Beau added as his hand found the side of her face. Breathing came a little easier, and the whooshing sound she hadn't realised had filled her ears subsided.

Clara blinked rapidly, then noted it was her mother who had been hissing and pacing, while flinging her arms around and scolding Beau.

He had yet again doused her with a bucket of water, though this time, it was a mixing bowl.

He handed her a handkerchief and turned back to her mother.

"Where do you keep the linen?" he asked calmly.

"Third shelf in the cupboard down the hall, in front of the bathing room," Felicity answered, gesturing towards the hallway.

When Beau nodded and left, Clara's mother immediately sat on her sopping-wet bed and took Clara's hands in hers.

"What happened?" she asked, fear dripping from every word.

"I didn't even realise I'd fallen asleep." Clara shrugged and shook her head.

"You've not had such a nightmare in years, Clara. Not since your father . . ." Felicity trailed off, and neither woman looked at the other.

"And much like then, this one made no sense. Already it's turning to a hazy memory, like something I should remember but is slipping away. It's like trying to catch smoke."

Clara let go of her mother's hands and stood from the bed.

"I'm going to get a towel," she said, making for the door. Turning back, she asked, "Where are Evian and Jacob?"

"In Jacob's room," her mother said, a hint of sympathy lacing her tone. Clara's nightmares frightened Jacob at the best of times, let alone when she woke in a screaming fit.

Clara left her room without another word, popping her head into Jacob's room to find him playing cards with Evian on the bed. With a quick apology, she promptly left, closing the door before either of them could ask if she was alright.

Fae could not lie, but she couldn't tell them the truth. She was the furthest thing from alright, and her entire body felt like it was still shaking. Pins and needles tracked all the way from her heels to her head, painful and tight, and a biting chill sat at her nape, while goosebumps covered her skin.

The feeling of impending doom, the end of the world as she knew it, sat heavy in her gut. Life-shattering dread she couldn't shake left her wanting to scream and cry and throw something in the hopes it would dispel this feeling of despair. The absolute fear that filled her body and seeped out her pores.

If the world crumbled, Clara would not be surprised. Nor if it opened and simply swallowed her, then stitched itself together with her stuck inside.

Beau stood waiting, leant against the linen cupboard with a set of fresh sheets and pillowcases in hand, and a comforter draped over his shoulder. Somehow, the sense of dread got a little better and a little worse at the sight of him.

"What did you see?" he asked.

"I don't remember," Clara sighed out with a shake of her head, then threw her arms up with a grunt. "What's the point of having visions if they don't make sense? Nor remain in my mind long enough for me to recall?" She was a second away from stomping her foot, or perhaps actually throwing something.

Beau chuckled softly and offered her a genuine smile. Some of her frustration melted away at seeing him like this. A small amount, at least.

Beau opened his mouth to speak, but Clara beat him to it. If she didn't say it now, she'd chicken out. She was determined and stubborn and would never allow herself to be seen as weak and cowardly. Prey to her own feelings.

"Will you stay with me?" Clara blurted out. Perhaps a little thought into her words wouldn't have gone astray, but it was too late now, she supposed. "Tonight . . . I mean. I've no doubt the settee is entirely too small and not as comfortable as a bed would be." Clara stepped forward and took the sheets from him. "Plus," she added. "I could use the company."

Beau's eyes lit up, but he maintained a neutral expression.

"And will this be for mounting? Or sleeping?" he asked. "I know you prefer to keep it to one or the other." A grin spread over his face.

A flash of a memory crossed Clara's mind of the last time Beau had woken her as he had done tonight.

"*I prefer to be awake, you know. The next time you mount me.*"

Laughter bubbled from her chest, and Beau's smile widened.

"Perhaps tonight we could simply lie together," Clara said, before she turned on her heel. Beau didn't move at first, until Clara added, "But you never know where the lying might lead."

Fear and dread still rippled in her body, but as Beau followed her into her room, Clara felt a little lighter.

Safe in the knowledge he wouldn't leave again, at least for the night, Clara was content. Stars, she might've even been happy. Not that she'd admit it to her fool of a Phoenix. He'd only get cocky, and Clara was too tired to put up with any chest puffing.

By the week's end, Beau had made himself right at home in Clara's room. He started picking up her discarded clothes, separating the clean from dirty laundry, and he even organised her books, cosmetics, and jewellery.

She had to admit the male wasn't useless, and for whatever reason, he felt the need to nest in her bedroom.

Clara appreciated his efforts, as he had a good eye for it, so she wasn't complaining.

The past two mornings, she'd woken up so warm it was as if the sun had serenaded her personally. Instead, it was Beau. Either with his leg entwined in hers, his arm wrapped around her, or simply his hand lying next to hers. Clara wasn't complaining about that either.

For the past two mornings, she'd woken from an undisturbed sleep and in a content mood. Had the sleep been restful or any good? No, but she'd learnt not to pray for a miracle a while ago. Clara took what she could get.

"So," Beau said, breaking their long but comfortable silence. "Are we going to discuss our sleeping arrangements of late? Can I to expect it to continue when we get home?"

He said *home* so casually, like he felt comfortable with her in her house, and warmth fluttered in her chest.

"You have grown rather comfortable in my bed." Clara nodded, folding her arms and leaning back in her seat. She looked him up and down slowly, as if considering. "And who am I to interrupt your beauty sleep? You've been practically glowing for days."

"Oh, I don't think you can give all the credit to your bed, sweetheart." Beau leant forward, resting his elbows on his knees, his hands dropped so casually between his legs.

“You flatter me,” Clara said, as she fought hard not to stare.

“You deserve to be flattered.”

Clara’s breath caught for a moment, and she couldn’t look away from his piercing amber eyes. Regaining her composure, Clara straightened and inclined her chin. “Yes,” she said. “Yes, I do.”

Beau chuckled and shook his head, though light danced in his eyes while something else crept over his face. Clara couldn’t be sure, but it looked a hell of a lot like pride.

“Anyhow,” she continued, “there is nothing to discuss. One bed is plenty big enough for the two of us.”

“And that’s all?” Beau asked, his smirk cocky.

“That’s all.” Clara nodded, looking away.

She wanted nothing more than for him to share her bed. She desired to share a great number of things with the male—her life, days, nights, herself.

But something had felt off the past few days. Something to do with the vivid dream she’d had the other night. It was a vision she could barely remember, yet knew it was important. Her focus was divided, and now was not the time.

“Okay,” Beau drawled. “And what about that sweet little friend of yours? The blue fae . . . what was her name?” He paused for a moment, feigning deliberation.

Clara whipped her head around, turning to him, her lip pulled back in a snarl. His confidence was attractive a moment ago, but now all Clara saw was arrogance.

“Seren,” she said flatly. “And she is spoken for.”

Beau’s brows knitted together, his head cocked to one side. For a moment, he looked almost comical, but Clara wasn’t laughing.

He referred to a woman she'd considered her best friend until recently, who was now involved with Clara's brother, and Beau was suggesting taking *her* to bed?

Jealousy built rapidly until it bled from her tightly clenched fists. Anger, too, and a lot of envy.

Clara was jealous.

And, quite frankly, disgusted at the thought of Beau sleeping with another.

If they hadn't been locked together in a rather comfortable carriage, and she had any other means to travel to the Court of Breath for the upcoming festival, Clara would've stormed off by now. Maybe she should order him to leave and find his own way there.

As Clara turned away, Beau's eyebrows rose and his eyes widened. His hands shot up defensively.

"Oh, that came out wrong," he said quickly. "What I meant was she's sweet . . . because . . . she said . . . I mean, the other day . . ." Beau spluttered over his words, and Clara fought to suppress her laughter.

Poor man, fumbling and unable to string a sentence together. Was it guilt causing his nerves?

Beau sighed and ran a hand over his face.

"I overheard you two," he said quietly. "I wasn't eavesdropping before you hurl accusations at me."

He knew her well, though Clara hated to admit it.

"You told her you fell in love with me," he said. His hands were back in his lap and his eyes stared intently at them. Away from Clara.

A chill settled in her chest.

"I told her I *thought* I fell in love with you," she corrected.

“And what do you think now?” he asked earnestly, and a fraction of the ice in her chest melted.

“I think it’s complicated,” Clara repeated. “And I’m not in the mood to discuss it further.”

Beau nodded, looking almost defeated. The cold seeped away entirely, replaced by a dull and steady ache around her heart.

She knew she needed to give him something. Inviting him into her bed had been the first small step, but the first of many towards their forever, hopefully.

Had he known? Or was he a male who couldn’t read subtle hints, or any hints at all?

While her jealousy had dissipated, Clara’s body was still stiff, and the insides of her cheeks stung from how hard she’d bitten them in an attempt not to lash out at Beau.

Clara’s default emotion was anger—she knew that—but she wasn’t angry with Beau. Seren hurt her, had betrayed her and their friendship, and that’s the reason Clara was angry.

Regardless, Clara was in no mood to talk. Though that didn’t stop her from stretching out her leg and running one foot up Beau’s calf. A peace offering maybe, or perhaps a reminder that fire did more than burn. Fire could heal and warm, if one would let it.

He looked at her with something she couldn’t decipher. His eyes stared further into her soul than anyone’s ever had, just shy of being uncomfortable. She let him stare but didn’t say anything.

Neither did he.

Beau simply looked at Clara, then shifted to recline in his seat.

CHAPTER THIRTEEN
ISOBEL

Isobel had always gravitated towards art. Expression of self through painting, chalk, charcoal, and sculpture, even stitching for a time.

With her body covered in not only the markings of a Vequil Inalis, but also her own designs, Isobel's skin bore many tattoos, though some held a deeper meaning, like her sisters' names, which were scribed on her wrists. "*Even when the lights are off*" was scrolled in the Old Language between her fire and air marks—a phrase her mother spoke when Isobel needed to be reminded that she was strong, or brave, or beautiful. Even when the lights were off, and the sun was asleep, and no one else could see, her mother told her she still *was*. Whatever she wanted or needed to be, she *was*, and whether anyone else noticed was irrelevant.

Some designs meant nothing or very little, like the butterflies and peonies which encircled her arms, or the insects and roses along her legs. The dagger in front of one ear, and spear behind the other.

The crown over her heart meant everything, but when she first got it she hadn't known what it would mean to her now. She'd traipsed through the Court of Breath a few years prior, and it left her wanting the piece on her chest. Forty-eight hours later, the ink was forever etched on her skin.

Art was important to her, it was therapeutic.

She sat before her slightly opened window, wearing coveralls stained with every colour, her bright-pink hair pulled back from her face, with a paintbrush in hand. Slowly, intentionally, Isobel stroked peach and lemon and lavender paint over her canvas. Eventually, it would turn into the background of a freshly risen sun—like most of her paintings.

A knock on the door pulled her mind from wandering to intense shades of red, or gentle gold-flecked jade.

Isobel turned as Poppy peeked her head around the door and asked, "Got a minute?"

Isobel nodded, putting her paintbrush down.

"She's off to the New Moon festival. No marks have been sent, no word from Tirenas at all. Elisabeth is growing more agitated by the day."

"I went to a New Moon festival once," Isobel said. "I don't even remember why I was in Elanist, but I felt so alive and at home in the court. Breath, if memory serves." Isobel smiled softly.

"That's where this year's festival is being held," Poppy said. "You would've been at the last one in Breath. You wouldn't have been old enough prior to that."

Isobel nodded again, swirling her dirtied brushes in a jar of water.

"Four years ago," she confirmed. "I wasn't there the whole time, though. The sunset was so blinding, with flashes of gold, and I had the strangest feeling." Isobel shivered, as if she could physically shake off the memory. "Like I was frozen and on fire at the same time. I honestly thought I'd been drugged, so I left." Isobel shrugged. "I'd only been sober a few weeks at that point, so it was better to be safe than sorry."

Poppy listened intently—she always did.

"Elisabeth wants to go back," she said. "When Clara is home and Maja is ready. Getting any more information from her is like pulling teeth, though I suppose she needn't share more with her grunt workers." Poppy rolled her eyes, and Isobel fought to restrain herself and not smile at the blatant disrespect her friend only ever divulged in private.

"Think she'll allow me to accompany you back?" Isobel tried to mask the desperation in her voice.

"Not a chance," Poppy said softly, then patted Isobel's hand as she rose to leave. She turned, and just before she reached the door, she added over her shoulder, "Her Majesty is looking for you, by the way." Her words dripped with sarcasm at the mention of Elisabeth, who truly held herself as a queen. It was unlucky for her that neither fate nor the Elanist government worked like that—not even the monarchy, when their thrones were full.

Fabulous. Just the meeting she needed.

Clinking rang through the grandiose hallway as Isobel walked towards Elisabeth's study. Family paintings hung on every wall, including pieces commissioned of Clara. An unwelcome wave of professional jealousy swept over Isobel as she considered the fact that she'd never once been asked.

She pushed the unhelpful thoughts aside and tucked the few unbound locks of hair behind her ears before she knocked.

Four short, precise knocks.

The door opened with a warm breeze and Isobel entered to find Elisabeth with her hands clasped in front of her unimpressed face. Her elbows were pressed onto the desk she sat behind.

"You asked to see me," Isobel said, dipping her head in acknowledgement and submission. "Do you have any updates on the archaic wolves?"

"The search in Tirenas was unsuccessful, as mentioned." Elisabeth scoffed as she stood and rounded the desk, sitting on the closest edge.

Isobel kept her spine straight and her shoulders back. Her eyes focused on the ever-growing, disorganised stack of paperwork as she continued, "Poppy found two last known locations of the wolves in Morrin. One was searched and appears abandoned, likely in the last week or so. I was waiting for your approval for the second search. I can leave by sunset tomorrow."

Elisabeth nodded, though her face remained impassive. She always looked that way at Isobel, if not with a varying degree of distaste and disapproval. Half the time Isobel wondered why the woman took her in at all. Elisabeth clearly disliked her, though she never outright spoke of it.

It never stopped Isobel from doing her job, though, and from finding the silver lining and remembering to smile.

"Maja and I, along with the twins, will head back to Wave in the coming days. Be sure to have an update when I return." Then Elisabeth dismissed her with a lazy gesture towards the door.

Isobel told herself it was futile to ask, but she just couldn't help it. "Might I join you, ma'am?"

Instead of answering politely, or even curtly, Elisabeth laughed. "Do your job, Jeffreys, and do not concern yourself in business not your own."

Isobel pursed her lips and nodded once, leaving without another word.

Regardless of how murderous she felt, she smiled genuinely at the few witches she passed. By the time she reached Maja's room, her fury had ebbed away.

Isobel knocked on the door, and this time it was opened by the plump old woman herself with an equally genuine and welcoming grin on her face.

"Isobel, sweetheart," she cried, welcoming Isobel into her suite.

It was far simpler than Isobel's, but Maja rarely stayed long at the palace, so her accommodations never seemed to matter to her.

"Maja," Isobel crooned. The woman who'd been like a grandmother to Isobel for almost half a decade embraced her warmly. Isobel hugged her back as vigorously as always. "May I ask a question and be assured it will not find its way to unwelcome ears?"

Maja's face pulled into a knowing grin, as if she could sense where the conversation was headed. She sighed and nodded, gesturing for Isobel to continue.

"When is Clara's birthday?"

Isobel held her breath. It was a multilayered question, as its answer held so much. Isobel wasn't sure she even wanted to know.

Maja's face softened, and she planted a kiss on Isobel's temple. "Why?"

"Do you need to ask?" Isobel replied, and her attempt at a laugh came out flat and full of nerves.

Maja chuckled, then stepped towards Isobel. She cupped Isobel's cheek with one hand, wrapping her wrinkled fingers around Isobel's wrist with the other. Her gaze fell to the lined tattoo on Isobel's forearm.

"No," she said, meeting Isobel's eyes again as a soft, almost sad smile pulled at the woman's lips. "I suppose not."

"I got that six years ago." Isobel traced the letters that somehow held a numerical value. "They are called *Roman numerals*, though I don't even know who Roman is, let alone why he has his own numbers." Isobel huffed. "I was high and didn't care to ask."

Maja ushered Isobel towards the table. Isobel sat with a sigh and continued speaking.

Maja propped her hands under her chin. She never rushed or interrupted, rather nodded along and allowed

Isobel the space she needed. Much like Poppy, Maja was someone Isobel considered a friend.

"I knew the date was important, so wanted it etched somewhere I could see it." Isobel sighed and rubbed both hands over her face.

"It's hers," Maja said, then eyed Isobel sceptically. "But why do you worry now?"

"Because Elisabeth will never allow anything more than a professional relationship. I have to keep my mouth shut and stay away."

"Why?" she pushed, though it was more of an encouraging nudge than a forceful pry.

"Why what?" Isobel asked, as she threw her hands up in frustration. "Why won't she allow it? Why must I lose something I never had in the first place? Or why is that somehow more painful than the alternative?"

"Darling girl," Maja said, clicking her tongue. "Elisabeth does not speak for her sister. I think you'll find the firecracker has a mind and heart of her own. You do not need to do anything you do not want to do, regardless of Elisabeth's opinion on the matter." Maja leant across the table and patted Isobel's hand. "You need not lose anything—love her instead."

Isobel nodded, unconvinced but hopeful.

Maja put on the kettle and brought out biscuits shortly after as they spoke of their families. Maja's children, now grown, and their current adventures. How the eldest who was travelling but now had taken over running the tea shop while his mother was otherwise engaged. Or rather, while she was taking orders from Elisabeth.

She had a decent heart and usually meant well, but truthfully, Isobel found the ruler to be entitled and more than a little arrogant at times. Though she'd been a welcome refuge when Isobel needed it and helped her to detox, recover, and stay sober. It was almost four years now—and counting—thanks to Elisabeth.

Isobel guessed she wasn't entirely bad.

Maja asked about Isobel's family. When she'd seen them last, when they'd spoken. Though the conversation didn't last long.

Isobel had stacks of letters addressed to each of her family members tucked into the back of a drawer in her room, but had never been able to work up the courage to send them.

So Isobel tried not to think of them at all.

Thankfully, Poppy burst into the room in time to save her from Maja's scrutiny. Leather pants hung from her thin frame, tightened by a belt with daggers affixed on either hip.

Poppy was vehemently against pants in any scenario except in an emergency. This wasn't good.

The second clue something was wrong was when Samara stepped in silently behind her sister.

The Mute and The Master.

She who never made a sound, never spoke out loud. Only ever communicated through the mind.

Samara was one of the strongest telepaths born in centuries.

Whereas her sister had a way of forcing others to do her bidding. Whatever it was she instructed them to do. Isobel didn't know what to call Poppy's ability, but she sure knew to stay on her friend's good side.

Half Darsmun, half Vequil fae.

An iconic and dangerous duo.

Almost identical, save for body hair and skin colour.

While Poppy preferred to remove her hair almost entirely, so only the thinnest line remained of her brows, Samara left all her hair alone. Her hair was so long she now braided it and wrapped it into a circlet twice around her head before she secured it. That, and the shade of green Samara coloured her hair. Poppy's was bright, almost luminous, where in contrast Samara's was dark enough to rival an oil spill. However, both were stunning against their respective creamy-fair and rich-umber skin.

Samara nodded to both Maja and Isobel in greeting, though her lips stayed pursed. A second later, her lilting voice filled their heads.

Bad news, I'm afraid.

Isobel had learnt of Samara's gifts the hard way, as the woman apparently preferred. She said she liked to gauge people's honest reactions, and Isobel's hysterical jump quickly enamoured her.

"What's happened?" Isobel asked, her voice betraying her nerves. Her gaze flitted between Samara and Poppy.

"The death marks," Poppy said slowly, her eyes glued to her sister's in a way that usually meant they were conversing in private. "They've been issued."

Maja sucked in a breath, stepping forward to place a comforting hand between Isobel's shoulder blades.

Follow up warrants are outstanding for any co-conspirators, those who offer assistance, and those who obstruct the investigation.

"Elisabeth is furious," Poppy said. "She wants to warn Felicity before the marks are physically delivered."

"How long?" Isobel asked, as she looked between the twins.

I'd expect they'll be formally notified and the marks will be delivered within the next seventy-two hours.

"What about Clara?"

Poppy didn't say anything.

Once Elisabeth speaks with Felicity, she intends to collect Clara from the Air Court and return her to her adoptive mother.

"Where is Clara right now?" Isobel asked, encouraged by the approving tap Maja landed on her back.

"Elisabeth will punish you," Poppy said, with a shake of her head. Samara pulled a face in agreement.

"Where is she, Philipa?" Isobel repeated.

Poppy rolled her eyes. "You know I hate it when you call me that," she retorted with a sigh. "She's at The Wetler's Estate, an inn close to the town centre."

"Thank you," Isobel whispered, then gave her friend a kiss on the forehead. She clasped both Maja and Samara's hands in a fast goodbye, then planted her thumb over her pendant and braced herself for the travel.

CHAPTER FOURTEEN
CLARA

The sun, blinding and shimmering over buildings and streets, circles the horizon from right to left in seconds.

Close on its tail is the moon. Bright and awe-inspiring.

Stunningly captivating, yet its only purpose seems to be to follow the sun.

A thousand stars twinkle alongside the sun and her moon. Dazzling. Subtle. The softest of connection in between.

The sun.

Her moon.

And her stars.

Clara stirred gently, though her neck ached furiously. Unsure of how long she'd slept, or even when she'd fallen asleep in the first place, she peeked out the window.

Their carriage stood still, and all too slowly, Clara realised she was alone.

Wind stirred the curtain which covered the small window set in the carriage door, even though it was firmly closed. A prickling, almost pinching sensation, ran up her arms and down her spine.

Her mind told her to breathe. They'd likely stopped for Beau to stretch his legs or to relieve himself. Though Clara's heart sped up at the need to find him. To find him whole—before it was too late.

This was a dreadfully familiar experience.

Clara's mouth dried, and her tongue felt heavy. Then, as clumsy as ever, Clara bounded from the carriage. Stones and dirt caught her as she fell to her knees. Blood beaded on her palms, which had taken the impact, though the sting hardly even registered.

Instead, Clara felt the weight of a thousand bricks piled atop her chest when Beau was nowhere to be seen.

And no driver either.

Clara couldn't see much farther with her vision now blurring.

Where the fuck was he?

A strange noise came from Clara's throat. Somewhere between a choked sob and a muffled, grunted scream.

He promised. Beau swore he would stay with her.

Well, where the fuck *was* he?

She hadn't realised she'd stood, or that she'd started pacing, when a warm hand grabbed her shoulder. Clara spun instantly and wobbled on her toes, latching onto whoever touched her for stability.

It would've been incredibly foolish, had it not been Beau who stared down at her. Concern crinkled his forehead and parted his plump lips, filling his golden eyes as he looked her over. His arms ran up and down her body—in the most boring sense, checking for an injury—and his warmth spread through her.

It chased away her chilling fear.

"And just where the fuck were you?" she demanded.

"Settle, sweetheart," Beau said. He cupped her cheek with one of his large, normally comforting hands. "We needed to stop for directions, and I didn't want to wake you."

"You couldn't have left a note?" Clara hissed with a scowl.

"Oh, of course," he said as he rolled his eyes. "With the abundance of paper I always keep on me. And ink." Beau folded his own arms, then held her stare.

He made a solid point, though she refused to admit it. All Clara could think of was how she'd fallen asleep with Neven, and when she'd woken from the vision-filled slumber, she'd found him dead.

The wind had settled now that Clara's fear had subsided, but the chill in the air remained, as did a subtle breeze. It was slight enough to only rustle the outermost leaves on whatever scarce trees surrounded them.

The immediate danger might've been non-existent, but Clara was still scared, as there was always the chance Beau would take his final breaths before her. How immortal was a Phoenix, anyway? How many lives were they granted before the fates decided they were no longer deserving?

Would Clara's heart cope if she found Beau the same way as Neven? Still. Unseeing. His heart no longer beating.

Perhaps some space would do her good. The bubble she and Beau had been living in the past few days was her favourite escape, but it was growing complicated.

Thankfully, the rest of their ride was swift, and by the time they arrived in the Court of Breath, the sun was down and the celebrations were in full swing.

The carriage stopped outside a dingy-looking inn, with at least seven people waiting by the counter. It was hardly unexpected, though, considering the New Moon festival had begun, which meant so had the alcohol.

Water Court wine was mostly terribly flavoured water, but the wine here was something else entirely. Something Clara wanted an entire bottle of, and soon.

Beau carried their overnight bags into the inn and nodded to the scrawny male at the desk before bypassing check-in altogether. Clara followed with her mouth slightly agape, unsure exactly why the Phoenix knew his way around so well. If she were honest with herself, Clara might've admitted to herself the attraction which swirled around in her belly. It made her heart flutter just a little faster, watching him rugged and dishevelled from their journey, sleeves rolled up and hair tousled, brimming with confidence.

For once, Clara intentionally kept her mouth shut. If she opened it, she knew nothing appropriate would come out. Fear and lust warred in her heart and head, enough to give Clara the start of what she knew would be a blinding headache. Though another feeling niggled and Clara knew that, too, was the start of something.

Painful, but so stars-damned worth it.

After what felt like a million dodgy, creaking stairs, and three corridors with distinct odours coming from between their walls, they arrived at their room.

"This place is disgusting," Clara muttered.

"Listen to you." Beau chuckled. "Miss Hoity Toity Princess. Heaven forbid you stay anywhere less than fit for royals."

"Shut up, asshole." Clara glared at him, then folded her arms. Inclining her chin, she continued, "You cannot tell me this is a quality establishment."

"Just wait until you see the inside," Beau said with a wink. Clara physically shuddered.

"We should've stayed with Finn, like I suggested."

Beau ignored her, and when he swung the old door inwards, Clara immediately knew why.

The room was dark and mostly barren. A standard double bed on one wall, a frosted window with a balcony to the right, and the kitchenette and bathing room were along the far wall. The room was dressed in shades of charcoal and amber, with golden stitching on the comforter and pillowcases, brushed gold lamps, and a yellow-toned lightbulb hanging from the ceiling. Surprisingly well-maintained carpet lined the floor, and everything appeared dust free.

It was simple, clean, and masculine. Everything a single male would need while travelling, likely for a decent price.

"Is it yours?" Clara asked as she lowered her arms and stepped inside.

Beau nodded. "Mostly, anyway. The owner is a distant relative, so he keeps the room free for me in case I need it."

“That must get awfully expensive for you,” Clara said, blowing out a long breath.

He shrugged. “It’s not so bad. I pay him annually, so once a year, most of my month’s pay goes straight out the window. It’s worth it, though.”

“So you can flex the dingy inn to passersby?” Clara laughed, but Beau levelled a flat, uninterested stare at her.

“No, smartass.” Beau put his hands on either side of her hips, then spun her towards the bed. “So I can lure pretty redheads with foul mouths to the *one bed* we’ll have to share.”

Clara laughed a little harder as the butterflies in her stomach fluttered.

“Likely naked, considering I didn’t pack any nightwear,” Beau said, as he brought his mouth so close to her ear she could feel his breath. “*And* huddled in for warmth—it gets cold here in the winter.”

“That’s awfully presumptuous of you, sir,” Clara said, stepping out of his reach and turning to face him again. She placed her own hands on her hips and raised an eyebrow.

Humour and barely veiled desire filled Beau’s eyes. An odd combination, but one that had Clara’s breaths coming a fraction faster.

“The next time you call me *sir*,” Beau said, his tone now deep and gravelly and entirely too seductive, “I’m going to remove your clothing.” He stepped forwards as he spoke. “Bend you over.” Another step towards her, and his voice dropped to barely a whisper. “And take you then and there.”

Clara’s heart beat rapidly. She licked her lips unconsciously, and the second Beau’s eyes dropped to her mouth, his hands stiffened by his sides. When those beautifully enticing amber irises rose again, carnal hunger was the only thing staring back.

As she contemplated saying it again, Beau cleared his throat and stepped back.

“Consider that your official and only warning, sweetheart.”

She all but melted. Clara needed no warning.

However, the male, for whatever reason, decided on restraint.

Clara huffed, but nodded.

Aside from Clara telling Beau he would stick out like a sore thumb if he kept his boots on, and him grumbling in response, they dressed in silence. The butterflies hadn’t left Clara, though they were now joined by an unexplainable sense of dread. It sat heavy, and paired with the butterflies, was making Clara nauseous.

It was nothing a little alcohol couldn’t solve, or at least ease, but for that they needed to leave the room, and Clara didn’t entirely want to.

Beau wore tight linen pants that left nothing to her imagination, and a loose black shirt. Half the buttons had been ignored and Clara struggled to focus. His smirk told her he was well aware of the effect of his bare chest, and the cocky bastard was enjoying it.

So Clara did the mature thing, undressing slowly in front of him. Two could play that game, *sir*.

Exactly what game they were playing, she didn't know nor care. But what she wanted to be playing was something horizontal between sheets.

Alcohol would fix that too.

Beau cleared his throat and stood from where he'd sat at the end of the bed, waiting for Clara. He took a step forwards as Clara bent over. She could've sworn he cursed under his breath, but before he could do anything else, Clara stood and slipped into the second option she'd brought.

It was simple, casual, and relaxed. Everything she was hoping to portray this evening. Soft, somewhat sheer and shapeless, but comfortable, the cream-coloured linen dress with a halter neckline would have her breasts on display before the sun made its appearance.

It was a little boring and nothing like what she would've normally worn, but perhaps blending in would be a good thing. After the spotlight had been on her so blindingly as of late, perhaps the change would be welcome.

From the corner of her eye, Clara watched Beau grin and shake his head. He walked to the door, then held his elbow out for her to take. Eagerly, she linked her arm in his and together they walked into town.

Music blasted from every direction, so loud it rumbled beneath her feet. In the middle of town was a massive bonfire and surrounding it was easily a few hundred folk, drawn from all across Elanist.

A female with deep-brown eyes smiled at Clara as she walked past, her entire arm glittering green amidst the light of the flames.

Clara grabbed the woman's empty hand and nodded towards the glass of sparkling wine in her other.

“Where might I find some of that?” Clara asked.

The woman’s smile grew, but instead of speaking, with her free hand she cupped the back of Clara’s neck, and with the other, brought her glass to Clara’s lips.

“I insist,” she purred.

Beau interjected, muttering about not taking drinks from strangers, but Clara opened her mouth instead.

Of all the courts to be worried about spiked drinks, Breath was the least dangerous. Hell, she’d be more concerned about accepting drinks from strangers in her home court than here. Trouble did not dwell in the Court of Breath.

“And where might I find some more?” Clara asked again with a small chuckle as she wiped a drop from her chin. The woman took Clara’s hand again, so Clara took Beau’s, and the three of them walked towards a bar.

Two shots and a glass of wine later, Clara was much more relaxed. A niggle prickled at her nape, but only slightly, so she ignored it.

Beau cradled his ale as though he wanted to savour it and honestly Clara couldn’t blame him. The alcohol of the Air Court was the finest of Elanist, excluding a few choice liquors from Flame. The term “firewater” was aptly given, considering their liquor went down hot and stayed that way. It was strong and potent, but here, everything was fresh and inviting.

“Miss Afron!” a familiar voice called from behind her, and Clara spun around. Obviously too quickly, and she stumbled, Beau catching her by the waist before any damage was done to her ego. She patted his thigh in thanks.

Auburn hair flew at her faster than Clara could register, but she knew who barrelled towards her. And who followed the mischievous woman wherever she went.

"Why are your hands empty?" Irijna squealed, wrapping Clara in such a tight hug she could barely embrace her back. "And what in Mother's name are you wearing?"

"Hello, little one." David wrapped an arm around Clara as soon as Irijna let her go and stepped back. He pecked her cheek and added, "It's strong—I'd recommend you sip this one," as he pulled away and offered her his glass. The liquid inside looked so close to the shade of Beau's eyes, Clara couldn't help but smile.

"Little one?"

"Because you're short." David shrugged.

Clara scoffed. "You weren't complaining about my height the last time I was here."

"I'm not complaining now, darlin'." He winked, and Irijna playfully smacked his biceps. David reached to grab her hand, his tattoos turning hazy, like smoke from the raging fire.

Beau's hand twitched on Clara's waist, but he remained silent, only pulling her a little more into his side.

Completely ignoring David's earlier suggestion, she downed the contents of his glass in one foul-tasting swig. She stuck her tongue out and handed the empty glass back to him.

"That was disgusting," she said, as she pulled a face and coughed. David laughed and Irijna shook her head, while Beau's hand stayed firmly planted on her waist.

She could barely make out his expression, but Clara would've put money on it being concern. Apprehension, at the very least.

"So is your dress!" Irijna turned to face Beau. "Not your doing, I hope."

The hand not warming Clara's side shot up in defence as Beau shook his head.

"I had no say," he said, before he added, "I'm Beau, by the way."

"Irijna," she said with a genuine smile. She leant into David's side and laid her head on his chest. "And David." She patted his chest affectionately.

Beau nodded but didn't say anything else.

"Come," Irijna said, her tone gentle but without room for arguments as she grabbed Clara's arm, tugging her away from Beau. His hand pressed a little heavier on her hip, before she took one step too many and his hand fell away. Then her entire left side went cold.

Clara took the short glass of shimmering rose-coloured liquid from Irijna and downed a third.

"I have news," Irijna said as they walked away from the bonfire, from the party, and Beau.

"So I heard . . ." Clara said and waggled her eyebrows.

"What's that look for?"

"Seren believes you are with child." Clara gave a flat laugh, though it sounded light enough that Irijna didn't question her.

"A baby cannot come from the places David sticks his cock in me, I assure you."

Clara laughed more genuinely at that, as did Irijna.

"So what is this news then?" Clara asked.

Irijna hesitated and bit her lip before she stopped altogether. She took Clara's hands and faced her.

The wind picked up, rustling Irijna's free-flowing hair and Clara's dress. Irijna raised an eyebrow, but thankfully didn't question it. Instead, she replied, "David and I are going travelling."

A brief flash of a red suit and old cell bars flashed in Clara's mind. She ignored it and hoped Irijna didn't notice. That was part of a conversation Clara was not yet ready to have.

"You act like this is something I ought to grieve."

"No, not grieve, per se. I just—" Irijna sighed. "I'm going to miss you, Clara. And I have no time to visit before we leave!"

"Well, when do you leave?"

"Tomorrow night." Irijna bit the inside of her cheek and Clara's jaw dropped.

"How long have you known? Where are you going?"

"Since Scilla's wedding. I was going to tell you then, but you were otherwise engaged."

"How long will you be gone?" Clara's voice was soft and small now. These were more friends she was going to lose.

How many more would there be?

"We aren't sure." Irijna looked away. The normally brazen and carefree fire fae now stood nervously before her. A lump burned in Clara's throat.

She attempted to put on a happy face, but was unsure if she succeeded. Clara took Irijna's elbow and continued walking.

"I love you, Irijna, you and David both. I want you to be happy, so if travel is what you want, run wild and free across the continents. But promise to stay safe and to write."

Clara couldn't look at her friend, but her words were honest.

Irijna patted Clara's hand. "Your mailman will be tired of me in record time, I assure you."

It only took a few more moments of relatively comfortable silence before Clara knew where Irijna was taking her.

Finn sat on a wooden swing on his front porch, and at their appearance, the widest grin spread across his face. He abandoned his ale swiftly and ran to greet them by his gate.

"I would've expected you to be at the festival by now," Clara said as she hugged her friend.

His ash-blonde hair had grown since she'd last seen him, and it was now tied in a knot on the crown of his head. He wore grey leather pants and an emerald shirt he hadn't bothered to button at all. Clara grinned.

"I'll be heading down shortly," he said. "We have a guest currently getting ready. I didn't want to leave her alone, as who knows who might slip in?" Finn winked, and both Irijna and Clara rolled their eyes.

"We need your wardrobe, kind sir," Irijna requested with a lazy flick of her wrist and dip of her chin.

"By all means, ladies," Finn said as he chuckled and waved them inside.

Clara had been here many times before. At the last New Moon festival, she'd raided Finn's closet as well.

Before they made it to the hallway, Finn steered them towards his kitchen.

"Drink first," he said. "Undress second."

So they did. They drank until Clara was spinning and tumbling, but by whatever miracle managed to stay upright. Mostly. She laughed with her friends and cast the thought of losing another two from her mind, at least for now.

By the time Irijna hiccupped and fell off her seat, Clara announced it was officially time to get a move on.

Finn's lady friend left, not before she gave everyone a smack on the ass and blew them a kiss, and Clara giggled like a child.

Irijna and Finn helped her get dressed and fix her hair. For a while, she spoke without a care—without the burden of the last however many months—and Clara felt lighter. At ease with her friends.

With a final tug and tightening of her straps, Clara was dressed and admired herself in the mirror.

It was the perfect colour for her hair to pop. Her markings were on display, though now they filled her with pride rather than caution, so she admired them too. Fabric was draped loosely across her body, so soft and shimmering, she was sure she'd sparkle by the fire.

Clara let loose a breath.

"Fucking stars." Finn whistled, then stepped back to look her over properly. "He won't be able to keep his hands off you."

Clara smirked. "Now, where have I heard that before?"

Irijna chuckled, but waggled her eyebrows and said, "When has he ever been wrong?"

CHAPTER FIFTEEN
BEAU

Beau saw the small female making a beeline for Clara, and the mountain of a male—bulky as many of the soldiers Beau had worked with—who followed her with a subtle look of adoration and pride. It was an expression Beau knew well.

"Miss Afron!" she called, and Clara spun with excitement.

After barely a handful of drinks, the woman was already falling over herself, though admittedly, even sober, that wasn't uncommon. Beau caught her mid fall and set her straight.

Her hand slapped against his thigh, then there it stayed, resting on his leg. Their usual banter had returned, though Beau knew Clara was still holding back.

It didn't matter. He'd made a vow and had every intention of keeping it, regardless of what Clara chose. But when she did things like rest her hand on his leg, his heart skipped a beat in his chest. No one had ever warned him that love was so painful.

Absent were the warnings for what he might feel watching another male kiss her cheek, hearing others call her sweet pet names, or to so clearly display their history.

"Come," Irijna said as she took Clara's empty hand. Beau hadn't meant to hold on to Clara, but his body craved any touch she would give. Beau held on until she was out of reach, and then his hand was brutally empty.

As the females walked away, arm in arm, David spoke.

"How did you two meet?"

Beau swallowed. "I was a bounty hunter for King Urian. She was the bounty."

He watched Clara move through a sea of people, then she was swallowed whole. Only when he couldn't see her anymore did Beau turn to face her friend.

"And you?" he asked.

"Four years ago, Irijna and I met her at the New Moon festival. Here, actually, in Breath." David seemed to watch where Clara and Irijna had disappeared as well. "Irijna and I grew up together."

Beau nodded, then registered what the male said.

"Wait, four years?" he asked.

David nodded. "Why?"

"It's not important," Beau muttered and shook his head.

Thankfully, David did not push. Instead, he ordered a jug of ale and two shots of whatever he'd given Clara. He explained he and Irijna were from the Court of Flame and the amber liquid was the drink of choice within their borders.

They clinked the shot glasses, Beau tapping his glass to the bar twice before he drank. It was one of the few traditions he cared to continue from his own homelands.

"Clara was right," Beau said, pulling his lip up a fraction. "That's foul."

David laughed heartily and clapped Beau on the back. "It takes some getting used to," he replied with a mischievous grin.

The conversation flowed easily between them, which Beau appreciated. He was apprehensive at first, especially with how David looked at Clara and the fact that he'd kissed her. They were important to Clara, though, so Beau kept his territorial mouth shut.

As they spoke, Beau learnt of the greeting traditions in Elanist. Pecks on the cheek were standard among friends and family, and David found a great deal of humour in confronting Beau on his jealous expression—even more so after having explained the customs. He also learnt of David and Irijna's travel plans, something he had a feeling Clara wouldn't be entirely pleased with.

As if he'd summoned the woman herself, Irijna bounced over and latched on to David's side. He kissed the top of her head and a strange pulling sensation sparked in Beau's chest.

"How did you know we were speaking of you, love?" David asked, adoration blooming in every word.

"Because you rarely ever speak of anything else," she answered, and grinned up at him. "What's he been blabbering on about?" she asked as she turned to Beau.

"Your upcoming travels," Beau answered. "Does Clara know?"

He looked in the direction she'd come, but he couldn't see Clara anywhere. Irijna glanced at her feet briefly before she raised her milky-blue eyes again.

"I told her earlier," she said. "How is she?"

Beau didn't know how to answer.

Okay? Alive? Lost? Trying?

Clara was so many things and yet trying to be a million others. She was doing her best.

Again, Beau looked out into the crowd of people but couldn't see her. "I'll admit, I didn't know her long before her world was spun on its head. She's—" He paused, trying to find the right words. "Different to when I first met her. So much has changed, and she's lost a lot." Beau sighed. "But she isn't dead, even though the odds weren't in favour of her survival. I don't think she's living again yet, but she's breathing."

Beau looked down at his hands, unable to meet their eyes any longer. Not since he felt partly responsible.

"Take care of her," Irijna said, gently placing her hand on Beau's cheek.

"Where is she?" he asked, unsettled by her absence and unsure why she hadn't stayed with Irijna.

The fire fae female shrugged. "She'll be around here somewhere. She finds a little more of herself at these festivals. Let her learn to live again."

Beau fought the urge to scoff, as if he couldn't help her with that. As if she couldn't find herself, or learn to live again, with him around.

Frankly, he was offended.

However, he was sure Irijna meant well. At least, Beau told himself she did.

Four rounds later, and Clara still had not been seen. Beau excused himself from her friends, who looked like they'd rather spend some time alone anyway.

The music was so loud the ground shuddered beneath his feet with each note. Drums pounded and something rattled like rice in a shaker.

Fae swarmed around the fire, or around each other. Many had lost their clothing and instead donned the body of another, or multiple others. For a second, Beau thought he saw Seren weaving in amongst the crowd, but he'd only met her once, so couldn't be sure.

Either way, she was not who he was searching for.

Finally, down a side street somehow also filled with fae, he found a brilliant head of fiery hair and the smell of apples, albeit somewhat doused in alcohol. Unfortunately, a grey-haired male danced far too closely to Clara for Beau's liking. Though she certainly was enjoying herself.

Beau told himself she'd made no promises to him, regardless of what he'd said to her, so she was free to dance with whomever she chose. But when the male ran his undeserving hands up her body and pressed his lips to hers, any rational thought left Beau's mind. He saw red and clenched his fists so tightly they ached in an effort to stop himself from throwing one into the male's jaw.

Instead, he stalked over to them and grabbed the male by his silver ponytail. Yanking it a little less gently than he should have, Beau growled, "Leave."

When their lips parted, Clara's face was contorted with ire, but the clearly intoxicated male took one look at Beau's face, which was filled with rage, and obeyed.

Clara took a step back and glared at Beau.

"What is your problem?" Her speech was slow, as were her movements as she straightened and folded her arms.

She'd changed. When she'd left him, she'd been wearing a simple linen dress that barely covered her thighs and had her breasts tempting him. Now she wore a silk dress that hugged every part of her in a soft shade of green, a touch lighter than her eyes. She sparkled like a spring goddess.

Stunning.

She was so captivating that for a second, Beau was speechless.

Then Clara pushed, "Well?"

Beau's face hardened.

"My problem"—he tried to keep his tone in check—"is that you're face fucking and grinding up against some tosspot whose name you don't even know."

"Oh, I know his name," Clara scoffed. "So, go away and find somebody else's fun to spoil." Clara flailed her arms in exasperation and made to turn, but Beau caught her wrist.

"I told you I would be here in whatever capacity you allowed, and that remains true. But I cannot stand here and watch you throw yourself onto the mouths and laps of others. I'd rather you tell me now to fuck off entirely."

He dropped her wrist. His voice somehow remained steady, even while his heart pounded loudly in his ears.

"Why?" Clara asked, quieter than he'd expected. Her shoulders relaxed.

"Because it should be *my* tongue in your mouth, *my* hands on your body." He stepped a fraction closer. Dared not release his relieved breath when she didn't step back. "My cock inside you."

Clara cast her gaze away and muttered, "Well, thanks to you, his cock never made it inside me."

"Good," Beau growled as relief flooded his chest.

"What do you want, Beau?"

There it was again, the irritation. But his name on her lips was like a melody he never wanted to stop hearing.

"You! I am incapable of wanting anything as much as I want you!" Beau came to the realisation that his feelings were not reciprocated. He sighed and stepped back.

Shock covered Clara's face. "Come and fucking take me then!" she shouted back.

His heart stopped entirely. For a moment, Beau was speechless.

"Coward," Clara snarled.

Something in Beau snapped, and in a heartbeat, he was standing only a breath away from Clara. So close her breasts pressed against his abdomen.

He should've taken her, ripped the tempting excuse for a dress from her body. But as badly as he wanted her, part of him didn't truly believe she wanted him in return. Not intoxicated as she was. So no, he wouldn't take her now, as badly as he wanted to.

"Do not tempt me, Clara," he spoke low, and Clara's mouth parted in response. Everything in him wanted to bite that bottom lip until she bled and desire filled her eyes. Stars, this *fucking woman*. Beau's cock twitched, begging to be touched by her.

"Or what?" she asked, her voice a whisper as she raised her chin, meeting his eyes with the defiance he loved. "You'll spank me?"

The corner of her mouth twitched up, and her smirk taunted him even more than her words.

Beau lifted his hand and cupped her throat, pressing his thumb in firmly, so close to her wild pulse. Clara gasped, only a quick intake of breath, but Beau's cock ached at the sound as he imagined how many other noises he could draw from her pretty little mouth. "Only if you ask me nicely."

Pulling back from Clara, taking his hands from her body, and turning away was far more difficult than he thought it would be. She smelt intoxicating, and the way her eyes had flickered between his, sparkling with desire—*fuck* if it wasn't the most incredible thing.

He didn't expect her to follow him when he left, intending to cool off, but suddenly she was there, slowing her unusually fast pace to walk beside him.

Beau cast her a sideways glance and saw her bite her lip. He also saw her wring her hands a few times, then heard her huff and sigh and grumble. His lips twitched into a smirk, but Beau quickly looked away so she couldn't see.

Stars, if she saw his smirk he'd never hear the end of it.

Her skin was cool as she slipped her hand into his. She was silent, but her action spoke loud enough. His jaw might've dropped a little, though he quickly interlaced their fingers and squeezed.

Clara spent the rest of the night drinking as if her life depended on it and dancing as if she were on stage in some underground whorehouse. However, at least now she drank arm in arm with Beau, and danced close enough he could run his hands over her body the whole time. Sometimes close enough for her breath to run along his collar, or so there was no breath left between them.

Temptation danced so close in front of him, Beau could barely control himself. But he did—to prove to her he could be better. He could be a good male for her.

Drink after drink, Clara grew sloppier, and her smile widened. She giggled more freely than she had in some time. Beau couldn't bring himself to cut her off; instead, he stayed, enjoying the touch he was allowed, and remained watchful.

She didn't notice any of the males staring at her, nor the ones who dared to step too close. A brief glance by Beau had them retreating before they ever sought her out. As they should—none of them deserved her.

Irijna and David twirled around them a few times. Or rather, Irijna twirled and David followed her contentedly. He clapped Beau on the shoulder before they moved on.

When Seren spotted Clara, she waved. It was a nervous gesture, her face contorted and hands skittish.

Clara simply turned the other way and stormed towards the drink table, downing another two shots and a tall flute filled with shimmering pink liquid in speedy succession. She then spun away from Beau, and as usual, oversold the gesture. He fought to keep himself from laughing, instead flinging an arm out around her waist before she landed in the dirt at their feet. Rather than him steadying her, Clara doubled over and barely missed the ground.

It was time to go.

Once again, Beau threw Clara over his shoulder. This time, however, Clara was unable to control herself. She ran her butter-soft fingers along several of his feathers, sighing and moaning as she connected.

Fucking *hell.*

This woman was going to be the death of him in so many ways.

"Bedtime for you, miss," Beau grumbled.

Clara giggled. "Yes, sir," she slurred.

He could've sworn she saluted him as well, and Beau's cock jerked in his far too restrictive pants. His mouth was so close, he could've taken a bite of her ass then and there. A growl came from deep in his throat, nostrils flaring, and his grip tightened on her legs.

Beau's earlier sentiments looped in his mind.

The next time you call me sir, I'm going to remove your clothing, bend you over, and take you then and there.

Her elbow dug sharply into the back of his shoulder and her hair whipped around his throat as she likely propped her head up.

A light drizzle started as they walked. Not enough to soak them, but enough that the cold droplets sobered him a little.

Clara crossed her ankles and flung her feet up, her ass bouncing in the process.

Fuck.

"And are you going to sleep—" Clara hiccupped. "On the floor—" Then yawned. "Like a gentleman?" She sighed and her head flopped forwards.

"I am no gentleman," he ground out. "And I plan on taking full advantage of you being so close in such a small bed and cosy up for warmth."

"Liar."

Beau grinned, but said nothing.

By the time they arrived at the inn, Clara's dress clung to her in the damp air and Beau's shirt hung a little closer to his chest as well. As they crossed the threshold into his cousin's establishment, Beau lowered Clara to her very unsteady feet. Her eyelids drooped, her lashes grazing against her cheeks with slow blinks.

As difficult as it seemed for Clara to keep her eyes open, she had no issues staring at his open collar.

He enjoyed having her rake her gorgeous jade eyes over him, and her lips parted ever so slightly, almost as though she were too wrapped up in him to notice. Part of him hoped she noticed him staring at her the same way.

Getting her up the stairs proved far more difficult than he'd anticipated.

Clara took every step as though it were a metre high and covered in spikes; she moved incredibly slowly, and half bent over with her hands out in front. Not that it did her any good.

The first flight of stairs, Beau thought it was humorous, maybe even a little cute, but by the end of the second flight, he had her back over his shoulder.

Again, she played with his feathers, and the sensation had him biting the inside of his cheek. He pressed his tongue to the roof of his mouth and set his jaw, so he didn't moan at her touch.

This *fucking* woman.

If she hadn't been so intoxicated she could barely stand, he'd have her on the stairs.

After what felt simultaneously like an eternity, yet only seconds, Beau swung open to door to their room. He then simply walked over to the bed and, less than gracefully, dropped her onto the mattress.

The woman was already asleep, snoring quietly, with one of her arms bent under her in a way that looked almost painful and one of her legs hanging off the bed. Beau sighed and might've chuckled a little before he pushed her further onto the mattress and moved her arm. She would wake feeling rather poorly, so the least he could do was help her sleep more comfortably in the meantime.

She burrowed her head into the pillow, drool already spilling from her lips. Clara was the most beautiful, enticing creature he'd laid eyes on. Simply stunning. And yet again, he found himself so incredibly grateful to know her.

Strange dreams of debts and deities filled Beau's sleep. He wasn't normally one to dream, so he passed it off as a combination of the foreign alcohol and the strange bed, then tossed the already blurred memories aside.

Warmth flooded from the window; a hazy orange-and-white light soaked the room. A subtle snore sounded close to his ear.

Beau turned his head, causing his nose to brush along Clara's cheek. Fuck, what a sight to wake to. He hadn't noticed her cosmetics the night before, but after sleep, kohl was smudged beneath her shuttered eyes.

As Clara stirred, Beau realised how close she'd crept to him overnight. As her leg moved, Beau noticed how it was contorted between his own.

As he woke, so did the rest of him.

Though he hadn't packed nightwear, Beau hadn't thought it was appropriate to sleep naked while Clara lay unconscious beside him. He'd kept his clothes from yesterday on, including his pants, which were now becoming restrictive.

Beau ran his hand along the side of Clara's body. With his finger, he traced her curves, the rise of her hips and the dip of her waist. Oh, how he craved more, to touch all of her.

Most of him believed that waking with his fingers, tongue, or cock pressed into her body would excite Clara, but part of him wasn't sure, so for now his painfully restrictive pants stayed on.

"Did you mean it?" Clara asked, her voice husky and laced with sleep. Her eyes were still closed, and she was likely not completely awake yet.

"Mean what?" Beau answered in barely more than a whisper.

"What you said last night." Her eyes fluttered open slowly, then locked on his. "About wanting me."

Beau brought his hand up to cup her cheek. To his surprise, she leant into his touch, and all of him melted. "Every word, Clara. Every fucking word."

Her eyes took on a feral glint, full of passion.

"So, if I say *please*, sir." Then he felt her trace his leg with her hand, moving up towards his desperate cock.

"You'll spank me. But what will you do if I beg?" Sultriness coated her voice, warmer than the sun.

"Struggle," he said through gritted teeth. Struggle, indeed.

"Why?" she asked, as her hand climbed his body further, coming to rest over his bulging crotch. Fuck. Her fingers splayed and her palm pressed down. It was all he could do not to flip her over. He wanted this. Wanted her, so stars-damned badly.

"Because these walls are paper thin. And if you beg, all I'm going to want to hear next are your screams," he growled.

Clara smirked. It was such a devilish expression.

"I certainly couldn't scream with my mouth full, now could I?"

"Fuck," Beau drawled. He closed his eyes, barely able to look at her while she tempted him this way.

Would it really be such a problem to have the neighbouring rooms hear her scream? For the floor to know his name by the hour's end?

"Oh," Clara said, propped up on her hands and knees. She still palmed him through his pants, even as she leant forward and whispered, "I'd like to."

The knock on the door felt like a bucket of ice water. Now was not the time for a visitor, and Beau was not a fan of sharing. Another curse flew from his tongue, although of an entirely different nature.

Clara laughed seductively, removing her hand from his crotch. Beau grumbled, but it didn't decrease her mirth.

The knock turned into an aggressive rap. Whoever was on the other side was in a rush and damn near beating the door down.

"One day," Clara whispered, "you're going to wake with your cock in my mouth."

Fuck.

"You're going to be the fucking death of me, woman."

CHAPTER SIXTEEN
CLARA

Clara didn't acknowledge her frustration at the interruption. Instead, she maintained her smirk until she was completely off the bed before turning to the door. Energy pulsed along her skin and in her bones the closer she stepped to whoever was on the other side.

Slowly, Clara reached towards the knob while holding her breath, half expecting it to burn her upon contact. Then a gentle feeling spread through her chest, yet no less overwhelming.

Behind the door stood a woman with bright-pink hair and fear plastered on her face. Jewellery hung from her ears, nose, and mouth, but even then, she was a picture of beauty. In Tirenas, or at least in the king's presence, she would've been shunned.

It was no wonder she'd been blonde then and had removed her piercings. The tattoos now lacing her skin weren't visible before either. Though Clara didn't know her name, she captivated her all the same.

"You," Clara whispered, and felt like she could finally breathe properly for the first time in forever.

The woman opened her plush lips, but before she could say anything, Beau's hand wrapped around Clara's waist.

"Who is it?" he asked, his eyes darting between them both. The woman's mouth closed to a thin line, and one of her eyes twitched slightly.

Then she looked back at Clara and any animosity from her face vanished, replaced by one of contentment. Clara might've hoped a little affection filled her crystalline-blue eyes as well.

"We have to go," she said to Clara, taking her hand. Her voice was as dreamy as the last time they'd spoken. "I'll help you pack."

Beau tightened his grip on Clara's waist, and for a second, the strangest spark of anger flared, but it was gone as quickly as it came.

"She won't be going anywhere until you introduce yourself, at the very least." Beau's tone held no room for arguments.

Her eye twitched again, and the woman sighed. "My name is Isobel. I work for—or rather with—I'm not quite an employee . . . I know your sister," she finally settled on, seeming almost nervous.

Clara didn't mind, she enjoyed hearing Isobel speak, and now she had a name for the face she never wanted to forget.

Isobel. If the heavens were real, that's where she came from. She was stunning and angelic.

Clara was captivated.

"Has she sent for us?" Beau asked quickly. Clara noted his furrowed brows and the tightness of his lips—not in anger, but in concentration.

"Not *us*," Isobel said with a sneer. "Technically, she hasn't sent at all yet, and I'll be reprimanded for speaking to you, let alone being here and warning you." She lowered her head and shook it slowly.

"Why will you be reprimanded?" Clara asked, ignoring what felt like the more important part of the statement. She would speak to Elisabeth, as there was to be no reprimanding, punishment, or scolding.

"That's not important." Isobel shook her head again, this time as she urged Clara and Beau into their room. "Eveline has been crowned queen and has issued the death marks on both of your heads." She gazed past Clara and Beau before she looked back at Clara earnestly. "I know you don't know me, and Bird Boy certainly doesn't trust me, but I swear to you, I am here for your safety, nothing more."

Clara's heart skipped a beat at the chivalry, but her stomach turned leaden at those last words.

Nothing more.

Was it right to feel disappointed? Likely not, though it didn't stop the unpleasant feeling from lingering.

"Elisabeth has left to inform your mother," Isobel continued. "Then she intended to collect you herself. She'll have a conniption if she learns I've come to you first.

"There will be further warrants issued for anyone who aided you in your escape from Tirenas, as well as anyone who obstructs the investigation and execution."

"Why did you feel the need to tell us yourself?" Beau asked, narrowing his eyes.

"Because I have a softer heart than Elisabeth, and I care what happens next, more than of a political nature."

Clara nodded. "I suppose we should go then," she said, turning from her companions. A trio she imagined was going to grow uncomfortable before it became pleasant.

Transportation was never something Clara considered could be conducted in a moment, up until Isobel and Beau disappeared in front of her eyes. Isobel reappeared less than a minute later without him, and Clara marvelled at how she'd just vanished and popped back up again.

Clara shouldn't have been surprised, considering all she could do which defied the laws of accepted truth. Nevertheless, when Isobel told her they'd be *transporting* back home, she'd laughed. Her jaw had dropped upon actually seeing the reality.

Isobel smiled sheepishly as she reappeared, no doubt at Clara's incredulous expression. She walked over to Clara and asked if she was ready.

But as she held out her hand, Clara blurted, "You knew who I was at the feast day, didn't you?"

Isobel faltered and dropped her hand and her gaze. "Not entirely," Isobel admitted, "but partly. Yes, I knew."

"I prefer the tattoos," Clara said. Though she immediately felt stupid, she didn't correct herself. Isobel smiled, and the golden flecks in her eyes sparkled. At the mesmerising sight, Clara couldn't help but smile herself.

"Brace yourself. It can be a rough first ride." Then Isobel took Clara's hand.

Before she could consider what that meant, Clara's entire body felt as though it had turned to putty. Stretched in every direction and pounded back together into an indescribable mess. Pain danced over every extremity and nerve, as somehow she felt light and heavy all at once. Then, faster than she could blink, she stood by the kitchen table in her mother's house. She was back home.

She felt nauseous. Dizzy and ill.

A cold sweat formed at her nape. Ringing pierced her ears. It only took a few seconds before she opened her eyes, but Clara kept her hand braced on the back of a chair, just in case.

Beau sat on the settee, his head between his knees and his fingers interlaced behind his neck. It caused a grin to spread across her face. At the same moment, he looked up and scowled at her, muttering something about his ailment not being funny.

Elisabeth stood in the middle of the room and spoke to Clara's mother, who paced and wrung her hands in front of her. She didn't look at Elisabeth, but the woman seemed unphased. She simply continued speaking, as if she were reciting a grocery list.

Evian stood near the hall, speaking in hushed tones with Ryland, who appeared as enthralled in their conversation as her older brother.

Poppy and another woman sat on the couch with Beau. The former ran her hand up and down his back, likely to ease the nausea Clara had no doubt was roiling through him.

Despite knowing this, she couldn't help the set in her jaw or the flare of her nostrils. Isobel placed a cool hand on her forearm to halt her steps towards them. Clara hadn't noticed her automatic response, nor how hot her body had become.

Then all Clara felt was an overwhelming and violent urge to rid her stomach of its contents. She quickly made a beeline for the sink and threw up. Beau's chuckle was a touch weaker than normal but was still loud enough to reach Clara's ears. She flipped him off as she threw up twice more, then cleaned the sink and rinsed her mouth.

"I thought it wasn't funny, asshole." She glared at Beau but walked over, sitting down on the floor in front of him anyway.

"So considerate of you to join us so early," Elisabeth said, distaste in her tone, though perhaps not entirely directed at Clara this time. "And of you, Isobel, to collect them so promptly." Elisabeth spun, crossing her arms as she faced Isobel. A slight intake of breath and the bite of her lower lip were the only signs that Isobel was affected.

"Yes, considerate indeed," Clara said loudly, narrowing her eyes at her sister. The stare Clara received in return was volatile, like Elisabeth was unfamiliar with someone calling her out, but Clara hadn't even begun yet.

"Oh, your confidence is admirable, girl, but it's misplaced." She took a step towards Clara, menace clouding her pale eyes. “Do you realise the political nightmare you’ve created, Clarenna?” Elisabeth snarled. As she pinched the bridge of her nose, she hissed, “Did you *have* to kill him?”

“What would you have rather I’d done, Elisabeth?” Clara shot back as she stood, baring her teeth and throwing her hands up in frustration.

Political nightmare. Clara could only imagine what the woman would do when faced with a real nightmare. She fought a scoff.

“Invite the barbarian to tea so we might discuss our grievances?” she continued. “He deserved to die, and I’m glad I was the one to deliver him his fate.”

Elisabeth rolled her eyes, pulling her own lip back, and Isobel took the smallest step towards Clara.

It was reminiscent of the first day she’d encountered foreign soldiers in her town. Seren had shied and stepped away, but now Isobel stepped towards her.

Her heart warmed.

“Clara,” her mother whispered into her hair as they stood by the front door. They had already said their goodbyes and argued the merits of this trip. “My strong daughter. Halfway to fearless.”

Felicity sniffed, and Clara knew the woman was holding back tears, though for her own benefit or Clara’s, she was unsure.

"I love you," Clara replied. Anything else and her mother would use it to convince Clara to stay.

Evian had insisted he come along, and Elisabeth offered Ryland and Samara. Clara was incredibly unnerved by Poppy's sister, and also rather intrigued and impressed if she was honest.

They'd only met the day before, but Clara had a feeling their relationship would bloom into a friendship—at least, she hoped so, as every instinct told Clara she ought to stay on Samara's good side. Isobel hadn't said goodbye when she left with Elisabeth and Poppy, and Clara debated whether she should have attempted to convince her to stay.

Now Clara stood with Beau, Evian, Ryland, and Samara, their travel bags packed, an abundance of food prepared, and a letter from Elisabeth stowed safely within Ryland's pocket.

When her mother finally released her, Clara turned to Jacob and held him just as close. Evian kissed their mother's forehead, assured Jacob they'd return with nary a hair out of place, and then nodded to Clara.

It was time to leave.

To travel to Morrin.

CHAPTER SEVENTEEN
CLARA

The little over a day's trip at sea was spent quietly. Each of them was nervous. Evian and Ryland mostly kept to themselves, though Clara overheard snippets of conversation between them. They discussed employment, politics, and passions, but truthfully, Clara found their conversation to be dull.

Samara was polite enough. Friendly and open when approached, but happy to sit in solitude. Clara found her staring off into the distance—unblinking and unseeing. She assumed Samara was communicating with Poppy, but she never asked. They simply smiled in passing and left it at that.

Beau had asked Clara what she'd intended to say to the royals when they arrived. The question was raised less than an hour into their trip, but it ended their conversation as quickly and abruptly as it began.

In short, Clara did not know.

Elisabeth had organised an audience with King Taron and Queen Sylvina. She'd seemed less than pleased by the entire arrangement, making pointed sniffs and huffs and grumbles. Though Clara ignored her attitude entirely.

Their night at sea had been decent enough. The sound of crashing waves and midnight sea birds lulled Clara to sleep.

Beau slept as close to her as he could manage, which was bittersweet. On the one hand, Clara loved the feel of his body pressed against hers, craved it more than she'd anticipated, but on the other, it was a constant tease—and not the fun, anticipatory kind. One neither she nor Beau enjoyed. They fell asleep cradling each other, and woke even more frustrated than when they closed their eyes.

At least once they were home, she could put an end to this extended suffering.

The sun shone brightly in the clear sky, yet as soon as the boat docked in the Winter Court, snow fell around them. Tiny flakes clung to their hair, clothes, eyelashes. Her shoulders were damp by the time the royal escort arrived to collect them, and rosy splotches covered everyone's noses and cheeks.

Clara pulled at her magic. Focused it on her fingers and toes, then slipped her warmed hand into Beau's. She placed her other hand on Evian's back and chuckled when her brother let out a soft moan. Vequil fae were not fans of the cold.

Despite the constant snowfall, the streets were filled with smiling faces, chatter, and laughter. Clara relaxed just a fraction at the thought this might not be the disastrous experience Elisabeth expected. If their subjects were happy and healthy, surely the king and queen couldn't be all bad.

Clara spun in the mirror, double checking that the laces of her dress were fastened and none of her undergarments were peeking out.

Upon arriving at the castle, their group was shown to their different rooms. Samara and Clara were led by a tall female with a far-too-tight chignon at the top of her head, and the males were led away by similarly rigidly dressed servants.

The large, pointed-nosed woman then left them with what Clara could only assume was her first attempt at a smile in decades. Samara fitted Clara into a four-layer ensemble, comprising a frilled undershirt and compression stockings, two different corsets, then finally a dress that Clara swore weighed more than her. Although she had to admit, the structure of the bodice did wonders for her already full breasts, and the cinching at her waist accentuated her hips.

However, the shade of purple was truly awful and clashed with just about everything, but Clara reined in her grimace—or at least tried to.

Even Samara stifled a laugh, although she never made a noise. Rather, Clara heard it as a quiet tinkle in her mind.

A knock on the door stopped her from wagging a finger, as she needed both hands to carry the heavy fabric.

Ryland stood waiting on the other side, one hand behind his back, the other held out as he offered Clara his arm. She took it willingly.

No one spoke on the walk towards the throne room. Surprisingly, Clara didn't feel any wind bite her neck or her cheeks. Perhaps she'd got ahold of her powers.

Doubtful, yet so was the notion that, instead, she was calm.

Beau and Evian stood by the throne-room doors, waiting for them, and as the Phoenix saw her approach, his mouth pulled into a grin. It was then she realised the reason no fear-induced wind circled her.

For as much as she disliked the Morrin rulers, she did not fear leaving their grounds without him, nor without her other companions. Clara was confident they would depart as they'd arrived, so while she was nervous, she was not afraid.

Clara climbed the few steps to her brother and Beau. Evian stood on one side of her, while Beau moved to the other. She reached out to clasp Beau's hand as she smiled back appreciatively at Ryland, who moved to accompany Samara.

Though before she could place her hand in Beau's, a vision flooded her mind.

Dark, wet hair covers the male's eyes. Blood spills from his wide, open mouth at an alarming rate.

"A debt will be paid . . ."

The vision is the wrong way up, with blood flying upwards, and his body upside down. His feet are high above his head, hands resting by his side.

Clara blinked rapidly, disoriented and lightheaded.

Beau's concerned face filled her vision, and Evian opened his mouth to speak, his brows furrowed. However, no question left his lips, as thumping sounded from the other side of the mahogany doors and then they were pulled open.

King Taron and Queen Sylvina sat atop matching wooden thrones and waited for her mismatched group to enter.

Clara walked slowly towards the royals, Evian and Beau on either side and one half-step behind, then Samara and Ryland a full step behind the trio. She kept her face relaxed, and as reverent as she could manage.

Three paces before the dais, Clara stopped, lowering herself to her knees as gracefully as she could manage in so much fabric and such a restrictive dress.

Someone called their names, and the king and queen nodded after each introduction. Beau and Evian bowed as well, bent horizontally at the waist. Clara kept her head and gaze lowered until King Taron's voice boomed through the wooden room.

"Rise," was all he said, yet his tone was commanding. It was a voice that bade others to listen.

Though Clara fought the niggling voice that reminded her he had remained silent when her continent had been overrun by a tyrant.

Clara stood but remained focused on a grain in the floorboards until she was upright. Only then did she raise her gaze to the king and his queen.

"Clarenna Hayes," Queen Sylvina said. Her voice was soft, but her words were barbed and poised.

Clara strained to keep her face neutral as she dipped her chin in respectful acknowledgement. "Your sister gave quite the endorsement, dear. What is so important you required an immediate audience?"

Light poured in from the windows on the left side of the room. It highlighted Queen Sylvina's long, delicate fingers as she waved her hand, and her blonde hair, which glowed in the sun.

"I appreciate your accommodations, Majesty," Clara said, lowering her chin again. "I have come in the hope of aid. A barbaric leader once sat atop the Tirenas throne, and he raised his successor in kind. While King Urian's reign is now over, the tyranny will continue.

"Violence, war, death. It will not stop on its own. So I humbly ask for your assistance in establishing peace. I cannot do it alone, nor am I so ignorant or naïve to think I might. I am seeking an alliance, a pooling of resources and manpower. To make peace no longer a far-off ideation, but a reality. So we do not cower, but bring forth a better, united future for our folk. Please, Majesties, will you consider it?" Clara curtseyed again, her head bowed until her chin nearly rested on her breasts.

"Did you not murder their king?" King Taron asked. There was no accusation in his tone, only incredulity and perhaps a hint of humour and disbelief. "Yet you seek our power and resources to stop violence and war. Peace. Does it not sound hypocritical, child?" He scoffed.

Clara raised her chin, clenching her fists in her skirts so they might stay unnoticed. "I am no child," she said evenly. "But I am the change, whether you will accept it or not. If you ignore me, war and dissidence will fall at your doorstep. You cannot run from what is to come."

"Are you threatening our kingdom, Clarenna Hayes?" Queen Sylvina stood, her eyes narrowed, and she stared daggers down at Clara.

Shit.

The cell door slammed shut and the sound echoed through the dungeon. It smelt like mould and urine. And Clara swore something had died in a far corner, though she was grateful she couldn't see exactly what.

Her cell contained a dirty bucket and a straw pallet, almost entirely deconstructed and spread about the small space.

Another female sat in the corner, with her knees drawn up and elbows resting on them, and her back pushed against the stone wall opposite the bars. All her fingers were swollen and coloured various shades of green and yellow. Bruises decorated every knuckle but were not entirely recent. Every finger was broken and left that way.

Her dark hair was wild and unruly, more so than Clara's. A white line ran from below her right eye to her jaw. It might have been chalk, standing stark against her skin, though it appeared half brushed away. Dirt smudged her forearms, face, and clothes.

"How long have you been here?" Clara asked, before she could stop herself.

The woman cracked open a deep-brown eye, then closed it again with a sigh. "Unsure."

"Unhelpful," Clara muttered.

"Sorry to disappoint you, princess." The woman shook her head, and somehow Clara knew if her eyes were open she'd have rolled them as well. "The entire dungeon is warded, so time moves differently to above the ground. It feels different—to entirely mess with your mind and senses. I might've been here a day, a week, maybe even a month. I couldn't tell you."

Clara let out a long breath. That, too, while unhelpful, was good to know. "What are you in for?"

"Are you supposed to ask felons their crimes?" The woman raised her eyebrows but smiled. "I was caught stealing. The queen sentenced me, and her captain dished out additional punishment for sticky fingers. They're less sticky now."

"What did you steal?"

"A loaf of bread, a pumpkin, and two ears of corn."

The woman shrugged, but Clara could see her nerves. The smile that did not meet her eyes, the subtle break of her voice. Her gaze which flitted about the room, and the broken skin on her lips as she bit them.

"I don't suppose you know a way out of here?" Clara asked, far more light-heartedly than she felt. To her surprise, the stranger laughed, though she didn't answer the question.

"Stop communicating with the convict, Clara, and enlighten me on what the fuck just happened?" Beau demanded, gripping the bars of his own cell.

"Don't you take that tone with me, sir." Clara planted her hands on her hips and raised an eyebrow. "It will get you absolutely nowhere. Try again."

Beau sighed.

"What's your boyfriend's problem?" the stranger asked, now standing much closer.

Clara looked to Samara, who shrugged and put on a noncommittal expression.

"He's sexually frustrated," Clara whispered, though loud enough for everyone to hear.

Evian groaned and scolded her.

"I thought you had a plan," Beau said, shaking his head as he scrubbed his hand across his face.

Clara shrugged.

"Sister, please, do not wave this off as anything but serious. While you may be well versed in being held prisoner, that does not extend to the rest of us." Evian paced his cell.

The males had been separated, though Samara and Clara had been kept together. Clara rolled her eyes at the notion women were less powerful or less likely to escape. It was an unfortunate and misogynistic oversight.

"Calm down, Evian. We won't be here long," Clara tried to convince him.

"You threatened a king and queen. Not to mention their son, their subjects, and lands. Clara, you threatened their damn dog." Evian threw his hands up and continued pacing.

She hadn't . . . not really. Though Evian was in no mood to listen to her outline *his* mistake.

CHAPTER EIGHTEEN
CLARA

Hours passed with no sound—it was maddening. Though her heartbeat continued to pound in her ears.

She sat at the barred door, her hands clamped around the giant padlock. Clara tried to pull the damp humidity in the cells into the metal device, then quickly freeze it. She hoped her actions would weaken its structure, and she slammed it against the bars. Unfortunately, her attempts so far had been futile.

A rich voice echoed through the room, confident and ostentatious.

"Not trying to escape, are we, pet?"

"I am nobody's *pet*," Clara snarled.

Beau growled in response, and both Ryland and Evian took a step closer to their bars. Not that they could do much, but the gesture was appreciated.

A male dressed in shades of blood sauntered towards the females' cell, wearing a mischievous smile and a small ruby-encrusted crown atop his head.

On his hip hung a dagger, sheathed and decorated in the same rich shade of red as his suit.

His nose and jaw were angular, every bone in his face pronounced. In a pretty way, sure, but his inflated ego suggested he knew as much and milked this genetic blessing. For anyone not from Morrin, his limbs would be far too long for his body, but here the arrogant male fit right in.

Lanky, tall, and smug.

This must be the prince.

Jude Lorson, only heir to the seasonal courts' throne. Playfulness and excitement danced in his hazel eyes.

"Need any help?" he asked, as he leant against her cell's bars. He had crossed one foot over the other and folded his arms in the falsest display of innocence he could muster.

"No," Clara grumbled, dropping the lock. A clang rattled the bars and echoed under the high ceiling. She sat back on her heels as she looked up at the prince.

"I'll leave you to it then," he said, not hiding the humour from his face. Clara glared at the prince, who raised his hands in defence. "You seem to have it under control."

Before he could bid her farewell, Clara called out, "You know I could get out!"

"Clara!" Evian hissed.

Beau pinched the bridge of his nose, and Ryland stood by, stoic but silent.

"Go on then," the prince scoffed, hand on his hip, gesturing with the other for her to show him.

Honestly, Clara hadn't thought that far. Impulsivity was her worst trait, and one of these stars-damned days she was going to have to learn to rein it in.

Today, however, she just had to improvise and hope this royal did not take after his mother.

Clara sighed and wrapped her hands around the bars on either side of the padlock. She focused all her pent-up anger and channelled it into something useful, such as heating her hands and melting the iron in her grasp until it was malleable enough for Samara to squeeze through.

The woman was essentially an oversized pixie, petite, and often severely underestimated. Clara had no doubt the fae possessed incredible talents. She would have the keys in seconds.

Then they could leave.

Aid would not be found here.

Clara sat on her knees, pulling at her magic and tugging on the solid bars for what felt like a lifetime without reprieve. They didn't budge. Letting out a frustrated shriek, she glared at the prince.

"Well done." His words dripped with sarcasm. "But would a key help?" On the end of his now outstretched forefinger, the prince held a wire ring, six keys hanging off it.

"What's the catch?" Clara asked as she stood and wiped her hands on her dress, her eyes narrowed.

"I didn't say there was one," he shot back without blinking.

Clara recognised that answer for exactly what it was: an evasion. Unlucky for him, Clara used the technique herself one too many times not to notice.

"I think I'll pass," she said, kneeling back down, and she could've sworn at least two of her male companions sighed in relief.

“I don’t think you have that option,” Prince Jude whispered as he unlocked the cell, swinging the door open. He held out his elbow for her and smiled. “Shall we?”

Jude patted Clara’s hand as they walked along, arm in arm. Clara expected him to remain in the castle; instead, he took her on a silent tour of the gardens. Stepping stones made up mosaic walkways through rows and rows of flowers. Every colour and variety. Her mother would love it here.

For a moment, Clara closed her eyes and pretended their walk was not a reprieve from barred captivity. That it was a friendly stroll.

Then the prince opened his mouth and burst Clara’s delusional bubble.

“So, how are you enjoying your stay?” he asked, smirking down at her. “Please do be honest, as our prisoner accommodations are due for an update and first-hand knowledge would be helpful.”

“Are you enjoying yourself, prince?” Clara spat. Having to tilt her head back to meet his gaze did nothing to help her temper.

“Aren’t you?”

“Quite frankly,” Clara said as she stopped and pulled her hand from his elbow, “no, I do not consider the inside of a cell to be enjoyable accommodation. Nor do I consider being a prisoner to be an enjoyable pastime.”

Jude leant down with a genuine but apprehensive smile. “I may have a solution for that.”

“Do enlighten me.” Clara raised her eyebrows.

Jude took a deep breath. “Marry me.”

Her jaw dropped and eyes widened before her face set in a scowl. Then she took a step back and turned so he wouldn’t see every emotion which ran across her face. “I beg your finest pardon, sir?”

What the fuck.

“Finest indeed,” Jude crooned behind her, though he did not attempt to coerce her back.

Clara, now furious, spun only to see that he stood relaxed, wearing a smug grin.

“Mother, you’re full of yourself.” Clara sighed and shook her head. This was not the conversation she was expecting to have with the prince and sole heir to a kingdom. “A proposal,” Clara continued, “—and a most unromantic one, I might add—is the most absurd thing to come from your mouth.”

Jude feigned outrage, but his smile and the playfulness in his soft hazel eyes gave away his mirth.

“Come now, pet, we’ve only just made acquaintance.” He looped his arm through hers and started walking, and Clara had no choice but to join him. “How would you even know?”

“Because it is an utmost idiotic idea,” Clara said without forethought. She’d effectively called a prince stupid twice now. She sighed and shook her head again, but he patted her hand, almost in reassurance.

“Clara,” he said, in a far more genuine tone than he’d used yet. “I can ask you romantically if you would like. I can wine and dine and court you until you’re permanently blushing. Whatever you want, I can do that, but I don’t think you truly care for theatrics.

“The truth is, my throne cannot seat two males, and I refuse to give up the love of my life to serve my kingdom. So I am asking if you will marry me, and I am counting on what I know of you that you will allow my love his place beside me every step of the way. As I will allow yours. It will be a relationship built for business, that I hope will progress into friendship, but nothing more. I need a queen to satisfy my parents. They’ve already given me a deadline.”

"Jude," Clara said. "If I may call you as such." He nodded. "After today's events, I strongly believe I am the last option that will satisfy the king and queen." She couldn't help but wince at the thought of their reaction to Jude announcing her his betrothed.

"Ah, but they've run out of options, my dear. If they are to insist I marry at my rank, they've lowered their standards so much you just might live to see the wedding."

"Rude," Clara scoffed. However, to her surprise, the prince was not so arrogant after all, and her smile was genuine.

"Honest," he replied, and Clara chuckled quietly.

"And what's in it for me?" she asked.

Jude nodded. "For one," he said, and held up fingers as he spoke. "You'll no longer be my mother's prisoner. Two, you'll have aid for this upcoming war that you are adamant is coming. Three, as much gold as your pretty little heart desires. Fortune is no object, I assure you."

"You must think me vain, prince," Clara said dryly.

"I think you are intelligent, princess. Smart enough to know the value of this deal and what gold is good for. If not for yourself, then surely for others."

He wasn't wrong, and Clara nodded.

"Is that all? Are you done blowing smoke up my ass?" She raised a single eyebrow, and he chuckled.

"For now." He nodded and pulled away, holding his hand out for her to shake. "Do we have a deal?"

Clara reached out, but before she placed her hand in his, she had a thought. "Mend the prisoner's fingers and let her go with no strings attached or hidden loopholes. Then yes, we have a deal."

Jude raised his eyebrows and gave her a look that suggested he was surprised, then his smirk was back. He put his hands in his pockets before she could take one.

Then he leant down and whispered, “Shall we shake on it, or share a kiss?”

Clara rolled her eyes. As they turned towards the dungeon, something Jude said registered. “Hang on.” She pulled to a stop and firmly placed her fists on her hips. “I don’t have a rank.”

Jude only winked again and continued towards the cells.

CHAPTER NINETEEN
BEAU

Clara returned with the prince in a much better mood than Beau had been expecting. Hell, a smile even tugged at the corners of her lips. He caught her eye as soon as she crossed the wide steps into the dungeon, and she winked at him. Beau couldn't help but grin back.

The prince paid him no attention. Simply walked from cell to cell, releasing the locks and swinging open the doors. Quizzical, apprehensive expressions covered his companions' faces, as well as the prisoner who had already been here.

She looked at Clara, clearly unsure of what was happening, but expecting her to provide insight. Knowing Clara, she likely would.

"Your charges have been dropped," Clara said with a smug, satisfied expression. "The prince will take you to a healer and if the healing is anything less than immaculate, you'll return to Elanist with us and have a professional tend to you."

Beau opened his mouth to protest, but Clara held her hand up without so much as a glance his way.

The woman stuttered a few times, stunned, before she nodded and thanked Clara and the prince. Then Clara rounded up their band of misfits and took Beau's hand.

"You want to tell me what happened?" he whispered as they left the dungeons.

"Not entirely," she admitted, while refusing to look at him.

"Clara," Beau pressed, as an uneasy feeling spread in his chest.

She sighed, then said, "I am unofficially betrothed to Prince Jude."

"You're *what*?" Evian hissed. He beat Beau to the punch—it was exactly what he was about to say.

Clara groaned and threw her head back, closing her eyes, and the light from the dusk sky illuminated every freckle on her face, turning them golden in the setting sun. She looked so serene, so captivating, it was difficult for Beau to hold on to any frustrations or accusations.

But he managed.

"You were gone for all of five minutes, and you come back *engaged*?"

"First of all," Clara said. Her eyes narrowed at Beau, then she turned to level the same stare at her brother. Ryland and Samara wisely kept quiet. "I was gone longer than that. Second, I considered the outcomes, and the benefits outweighed the drawbacks." The woman had the nerve to shrug.

Beau looked to Ryland and Samara, who shared a look between them but said nothing. He wondered what Elisabeth would think of this arrangement. Likely nothing good, at least for Clara.

Things were moving too quickly, and Beau did not trust that the prince would follow through on any offers or benefits. He didn't trust the prince at all.

Beau would have to call on someone he could trust, at least more than a cocky prince. For the time being, maybe it would distract him from all the questions which warred in his mind. The emotions which riled his gut into a nauseas frenzy.

He'd not considered marriage, not really. Not yet, anyway. But his heart cracked at the thought of another male proposing and Clara saying yes.

Jealousy hurt like a bitch.

When they returned to Elanist soil, Ryland and Samara went their separate ways, leaving Clara, Evian, and Beau to wander home in uncomfortable silence.

Evian looked as though he wanted to say something but refused to spit the words out. He reminded Beau of Neven in the early days, when the soldier got on every single one of Beau's nerves. He reminded Beau of Neven in general, but the annoying attributes were near identical. Maybe that was why Clara had befriended Neven so easily, as she subconsciously felt comfortable around the male.

Clara said little during their journey home, though Beau was unsurprised. Truthfully, he didn't want her to. Didn't want to have that discussion with her brother so close. So they travelled in silence.

After a little more than an hour's walk, they were back in Felicity's kitchen, preparing for dinner. No one said much during the meal and the only thing which kept Beau sane was Clara's knee pressed against his while he ate. A reminder, he hoped, that there was more to her engagement than she'd let on.

She would tell him when she was ready, and likely, without her mother and brothers being present for the conversation.

Beau stirred before Clara the next morning. He'd slept terribly, as constant images he couldn't make any sense of flashed through his mind. Phrases about spare lives played on a loop in various languages, some he recognised and some he didn't, though subconsciously he knew they all followed the same theme.

He didn't know what to make of this recent development—these dreams—but he knew what he felt every time he woke. A heavy gut, jittery bones, hot-and-cold sweat simultaneously along his spine. Every time, Beau spent the following day nervously watching every corner, trying to identify the threat he could feel but couldn't see. Danger sat heavy in the air.

He wondered if Clara was projecting. Neither of them knew the extent of her power, so it was entirely possible.

He'd ask her later.

A soft thud came from outside. Clara stirred a little and snuggled further into her pillow. Beau stifled a chuckle and slowly got out of bed. He pulled on some pants and a sweater, then stepped into the hall, closing the door as gently as he could. If he woke Clara, she'd grouse at him all day.

Today, they had work to do, and she'd be much more productive if she was in a good mood.

The sky was still purple, so it was likely everyone else was still asleep. Beau walked towards the front door and opened it quietly, stepping outside to greet his guests.

Keyne stood with a genuine smile, loaded down with bags and training equipment, as did his companions. A female and male with raven-coloured hair, who looked so similar, Beau was sure they were related.

"Thank you," he said, offering his hand to Keyne.

"Of course," Keyne replied as he shook Beau's outstretched hand, then gestured to the pair beside him. "This is Oren." He pointed to the male, who gave Beau a lazy salute. "And Aleska." The female gave a half-assed curtsy and a smirk. "Your letter sounded urgent. What do you need from us?"

Beau rubbed the back of his neck and winced.

"Clara is engaged to the Prince of Morrin," Beau blurted. "A war is coming, so she's formed an alliance, but it will only get her so far. We returned yesterday, and considering

I have an unknown amount of time before violence knocks down her door, I need help to train her."

"Not going to make her sit safely on the sidelines?" Oren asked, eyebrows raised.

Beau snorted. "You'll do well not to suggest such a thing in front of her. No, I want her to be able to protect herself as well as anyone she insists on stepping in front of."

"Do you have a plan?" Aleska asked, her voice much lighter than her hard facial expression suggested.

Beau shook his head again. "Not really. I began training her magic in Tirenas but never worked on physical combat or self-defence. I was hoping you'd be able to help me with that." Beau turned his gaze back to Keyne.

When he'd first been paired with Neven, Beau investigated the Dalys family and learnt of Keyne's martial arts and self-defence school. After Clara's rushed betrothal, Beau realised he and Clara needed help, and Keyne seemed like the best person to ask.

He nodded, and Beau sighed with relief.

"There's a wide shoreline along Ira Bay, only twenty-five minutes north of here by foot. Clara should know how to get there. Wake her, let her know we're here. We'll meet you there in an hour." With a nod, the three winged fae stepped back, then shot into the sky.

So much for letting Clara sleep.

Beau grimaced and mentally prepared himself for the attitude she was going to sling at him for waking her before the sun.

Or tried to, anyway.

One thing Beau could always count on was Clara's hatred of waking early. How she ever worked in a bakery, he couldn't fathom. He'd tried gently caressing her face, moving the wild hair from over her eyes, but all she'd done was smile and cosy further into the mattress.

He'd pulled opened the curtains, but she turned away from the light and dragged the comforter over her head. Beau bit back the frustrated growl in his throat, instead taking a deep breath and ripping her covers away, then he bolted for the far wall.

It was not far enough.

Clara was up in an instant, fury written all over her sleep-muddled face. As soon as he reached the wall, Clara was in front of him, jabbing her finger into his chest.

"What the fuck do you think you're doing, Hawthorne?" she demanded.

"I don't know how I feel about you calling me Hawthorne, sweetheart," he answered.

"Perhaps I will call you nothing instead," she grumbled, turning back towards the bed.

"Or," Beau countered, moving around Clara to stand between her and the comfort of sleep, "perhaps you could spend your morning compiling a list of your best insults?"

Clara narrowed her eyes, and her brows drew together. "Am I going to need them?"

“I fear so,” Beau said with a sigh.

Clara groaned as she made her way to her wardrobe. She dressed in silence, forbade him from following her into the bathing room, then snapped her fingers at Beau when she was ready to leave.

After Beau explained where they were going, most of their walk was made in silence. That was until he realised he might not get a better opportunity than this to discuss her dreams.

Beau considered his next words, not something he would normally do—outside of working with the former king, Beau had never found a reason to be careful when he spoke.

Clara was the total opposite. She chose certain words for certain folk and situations, and she read further into every word to grace her ears. So Beau had to be careful.

“How has your magic been lately?” he asked, settling on speaking generally to start. Beau cast a sideways glance at her in time to see her shrug.

“Present,” she said, her tone was still clipped and annoyed.

“I’ve noticed you have an effect on water,” Beau said casually. “Though it seems a little more unpredictable than fire and air.”

“That’s hardly surprising,” Clara scoffed.

“Agreed” Beau said, and tried to hide his chuckle. “What about your earth magic or Candor?”

Clara shrugged again. “I do not know how to tap into either of those, so we’re shit out of luck. I’m sure you’ll wake me the second you figure it out.”

Beau grinned. “If the need arises.”

"And what was the *need* this morning?" Clara stopped to face him, her hands on her hips.

"Training." Beau continued to walk. "Hurry up, I have more questions."

He chuckled when Clara muttered something about him being an asshole under her breath. She fell back into step with Beau.

"Had any visions or nightmares lately?" He feigned a nonchalant tone.

Clara raised an eyebrow but didn't question him.

"Sure," she said. "A few in Morrin centred around the colour red. A male bleeding from his mouth, but the entire scene was upside down. That was disconcerting, and I felt nauseas when I woke. I don't know," she said, shaking her head as she shrugged. "There have been a few that make no sense but leave me with a feeling of concern and dread. They're cryptic and I rarely understand them until it's too late, except for the daemdrana's. I understood *that* one perfectly, but you ignored me."

Beau rolled his eyes.

"Why do you care about my visions?" Clara asked.

Beau didn't know how to answer. His heart wanted to tell her everything. He'd dreamt for the first time in decades, and he believed those dreams belonged to her. Similar to when he alone heard her scream in Flame. He believed she was projecting—a manifestation of her Spirit Court magic. However, projection was a gift she would never be able to control, and it would drive her insane.

So his traitorous mouth opened and spilled the second lie he'd told her. Hopefully, it would be the last.

"No reason."

"Liar," Clara hissed, but it was playful.

She knew he was hiding something, but at least she didn't sound angry. Or at least not more than she already was this morning.

Thankfully, they arrived at Ira Bay before Clara could question him further.

CHAPTER TWENTY
CLARA

Three bodies danced along the waterline of the bay. Though as she drew closer to them, she realised they were not dancing; they were sparring. It was an easy thing to confuse, considering the flow, rhythm, and intricacy of their movements.

A raven-haired couple and a blonde moved seamlessly around one another, striking and dodging.

The stones crunched and gave way beneath Clara and Beau's feet as they walked towards the shore. They were certainly not locals.

It was confirmed when the blonde male turned to face the noise and Keyne was now looking at them, a wide smile lighting up his face. He ran a hand through his hair and jogged to meet Beau with a handshake and Clara with a hug, while the dark-haired couple continued to spar.

“Are you the reason I was dragged from my bed at such an ungodly hour, Mr Dalys?” Clara asked, a touch more accusatory than she’d intended. She pressed her folded arms more firmly to her chest as she inclined her chin and narrowed her eyes.

Keyne chuckled and rubbed the back of his neck briefly. When he turned around, she could almost pretend it was Neven. Clara twisted the ring on her thumb subconsciously.

“Clara,” he said, and stopped in front of his companions. Keyne gestured towards the woman first, whose hair shone almost blue in the morning light and fluttered around her shoulders in the breeze. “This is Aleska.” The female dipped her forehead in acknowledgement and smiled. “And Oren.” His hand waved towards the male, who beamed at her and waggled his eyebrows.

Clara chuckled but swiftly attempted to cover it with a cough. Beau glared at her, though he was all bark and no bite. The daggers he stared at Oren, however, were much less empty. Clara patted his biceps before she walked to the water’s edge.

She’d surmised they’d be training her magic, though she’d incorrectly assumed it would only be Beau and herself. Unsure what court, or even which continent Oren and Aleska hailed from, and only knowing Keyne was a Soliqe shifter, Clara couldn’t fathom what help they’d be for training her power.

“We’ve been made aware of the coming threat,” Keyne said. “So we’re here to help better prepare you physically.”

“You’re going to train me in combat?” Clara asked. She felt stupid for not having considered it already, though she’d blame the early start and still-lingering sleep.

"They'll teach you about form and balance, and I will teach you all the invaluable tips and tricks for when a male underestimates you based solely on the fact you have breasts." Aleska nodded with a grin. Though she didn't know Aleska from a bar of soap, Clara liked the woman.

The more instruction Clara received, the more she found she enjoyed it. Regardless of the time, moving felt productive, even if it was nothing more than practice. It wasn't enough to stop her frequent glances at Keyne, as if looking at him enough would turn him into his brother. Maybe this was her sign to say goodbye to her friend. Until now, Clara hadn't even considered a funeral past the wish to hold one. Though perhaps seeing Keyne was the shove she needed to carry out her plan.

Thankfully, Keyne didn't seem to notice her staring at him constantly, as it wasn't a conversation Clara wished to have with him today.

Instead, she focused on the siblings who were teaching her how to fight. Or more accurately, guiding her in the most basic foundations of self-defence and teaching her to how to stay alive.

Oren was large, bulky, and made of muscle. His midnight hair whipped around his face so many times it was comical, though frustrating to watch.

As he meticulously explained the proper foot position, weight distribution, and balance, his long hair flicked Clara more than a few times despite it being tied back. He stood close by while Aleska—who Clara learnt was his sister—gave her a lesson in defence.

When the next gust of wind hit, but before Oren's hair connected with her face, Clara threw her hand up and caught his ponytail. She tugged it with enough force that Oren jolted and then pulled him in front of her until their noses were a finger's width apart.

"Move back, or I'll cut it off."

Oren chuckled, but raised his hands in surrender. Clara let go of his hair, and Oren walked off. She couldn't help but watch the first few rounds between him and Beau.

Clara knew her mistake when Aleska elbowed her playfully in the ribs and informed her it was probably for the best she watch closely because she'd be sparring Beau next.

Keyne and Oren pulled thick mats apparently out of their asses, as Clara had seen none all morning. It was now near midday. She had yet to eat, and the only thing that kept her from wandering off was the reminder that had she been better prepared, Neven might still be here.

He might've even been the one to teach her.

Dwelling on the past did her no good now. Though she couldn't help it, especially when she saw her friend every time Keyne walked past.

Clara exhaled slowly and rolled her shoulders. Beau handed her a bottle of water, which she accepted greedily. He said nothing, but his face expressed his question and concern. His eyes raked over every inch of her face and flicked lower once or twice. She nodded and shooed him away before turning to Aleska.

"What exactly am I to do?" she asked, closing the bottle. Aleska took it, replacing it with a wooden pole.

"Fend him off," she said with a quirk of her lips, as if it should've been easy enough for Clara to guess. "He's far more skilled than you are, which is likely what you'll face even if you were to train for months. Defend yourself, keep him and his weapons from any vulnerable spots, and stay upright."

Clara made a noise somewhere between a scoff and an empty laugh.

"I'm in for a real treat, then. I struggle to stay upright on the best of days, let alone when the goal is to knock me over."

"Use your strengths. If you're standing, you have a better chance at escape than if you're prone or sitting." Aleska jerked her chin towards where Oren had Keyne pinned to the ground in a demonstration for Beau. "But if your opponent is bigger than you, using their altered centre of gravity and their ego against them can benefit you."

Keyne rolled his head to the side as Oren threw his elbow downward. A second too slow and Keyne's nose would've been broken, likely along with the rest of his face.

"Oren is significantly larger than Keyne," Aleska continued. "But that is not a benefit—he's slower because of it, and cocky."

Keyne used Oren's momentum to lodge his elbow into the ground, then slammed his own elbow into the side of Oren's face.

"Most times, that move would surprise your assailant, giving you a second or two to manoeuvre your way out from under them as they regain their balance and position. It isn't foolproof, but survival isn't about that."

Clara nodded. Before she could plan, Keyne was up and calling her over.

"We will use mats for now, but only for the first few training sessions. Do not rely on them to best your opponent, as they will not exist in war."

How pleasant. Clara fought to keep her expression neutral.

Beau stepped onto the mat, bouncing on his toes a few times, then had the audacity to wink at Clara. Her eye twitched and nostrils flared. He spun his wooden pole a few times, like the cocky bastard he was, then waved her onto the mat.

"Remind me why we're doing this again?" she said as she circled the mat with Beau. He grinned, a wickedly beautiful expression no doubt meant to distract.

It was working a little.

"Because you have a tendency to be rash, wild tempered, and—"

"Thank you," Clara snapped, cutting him off. "Got it."

His charm was now working a little less.

Beau chuckled, then pounced, his wooden pole aimed for her face.

Instinctively, she swung her own, and when they slammed together, the impact ricocheted up her arm. Clara growled unintentionally and Beau's eyebrows rose—in surprise or because he was impressed, she wasn't sure.

They continued in much the same way. Beau struck, and Clara made a haphazard attempt at defence. Shrill and guttural noises spilled from them both for what felt like hours. Clara was sweaty and Beau had removed his shirt, his chest now glistening.

Use your strengths.

Assets and strengths were two very different things, though for today, Clara didn't mind blurring the line. She removed her own shirt, and she heard Aleska laugh behind her. Oren hooted and clapped. Clara smirked as Beau stared daggers at their mountain of an instructor. From the corner of her eye, she saw Keyne pinch the bridge of his nose and shake his head, but the slightest hint of a smile also grazed his lips.

Clara used her few seconds wisely. She drew on the wind above the water, where it was always at its strongest in Wave. She pulled it to her, then past her, towards where Beau stood with his disrupted focus. His wooden pole flew from his hand.

He spun, watching on with shock as it sailed through the air and landed a decent stretch inland. With his back now turned, she quickly kicked the back of his knee, and Beau stumbled forward. Clara used her own wooden pole to prod him in the side until he rolled and ended up on his back. Clara pressed one bare foot to his abdomen and the end of her wooden pole to his throat.

"I win," she purred, her expression full of self-satisfaction.

Before another gloating word could leave her lips, Beau threw a leg up and hooked it around her own. In a heartbeat she was falling, then warm hands wrapped around her sides, and she stilled. Lying flat on top of Beau, her breasts were dangerously close to his face, though his eyes only fluttered down once before his hips bucked and they spun. Then Beau straddled her, one hand pressed to the mat beside her face, while the other held a blade to her throat.

"I'm having flashbacks," she breathed.

"You're presumptuous and impatient and severely underestimating the seriousness of what is coming." His cocky grin disappeared. They hadn't spoken about Jude yet, but Clara had a suspicion the conversation was not far in the future.

"Oh?" she asked. "And you're the expert here. Tell me, Beau, what else am I lacking?"

"Do not put words in my mouth," he hissed. "You need to expect the worst of your opponents, or you'll end up dead. Always assume there's another threat, another weapon or attack. Do not claim the win until their lungs are void of air and their heart no longer beats. Do you understand?"

Beau pressed the blade more firmly into her skin, and a prickle of pain and pleasure danced from her jaw to her collar. While it was not the time to consider taking the male to bed, there were worse times for inappropriate thoughts. Clara sighed and glanced at their companions, who were all somehow suddenly more interested in themselves than Beau or Clara.

"Yes, sir." Her smirk was half-assed, and the flirtatiousness was absent from her tongue.

"You're distracted." Beau's amber eyes flared briefly. "Distracted, indeed."

CHAPTER TWENTY-ONE
BEAU

Beau ran, the breeze cool on his face. Not that he was in a rush, but he was grateful for the air brushing his skin and the silent moment to breathe.

He should've expected Clara would use her body to distract him. Hell, her goal was to throw off his focus, and she succeeded. That trick wouldn't work with Eveline. She would likely admire Clara's boldness—it might evoke a chuckle, but she'd remain focused. She would take the debt she came to collect, clothing or no.

Once he got back to the house, it didn't take long to locate the half-emptied bag in Clara's room. It was under the side table in the far corner, exactly as she'd said. Beau reached in and pulled out the crumpled white shirt, still marred with smudges of dirt and smelling of stale rain. It was not overpowering enough to wrinkle his nose, yet strong enough the scent wafted up as he held the shirt in front of him, and for Beau to realise Clara hadn't washed it.

He couldn't blame her.

None of Brielle's belongings had been touched until almost a year after she died. His mother couldn't bring herself to step foot in Brielle's bedroom for months, and when she finally did, Beau couldn't pry her out.

Beau sighed, unsure whether to say anything. The gods were not among his beliefs, and neither were lingering spirits who eavesdropped on the living. Yet guilt shrouded him anyway, for a death he could've prevented and for which he held a piece of the blame.

Words wouldn't help Neven now.

Beau held the soldier's shirt and ran back towards the bay, to where Keyne and Clara waited.

They sat waiting at the tide line. No one spoke, but Clara's eyes were red rimmed, and her lips were pursed. She offered him a tight smile in acknowledgement as he crouched beside her, handing her the shirt. At that Clara stood, and Keyne followed suit.

"In Elanist," she said, as she walked out into the water, "we have traditions for honouring and mourning the dead. They vary based on where you live, and to which court you belong." She sighed, stopping once the water reached her hips and turning to face the males. "In Wave, we wrap the body and send it off to sea so the soul of the water fae can return to their kin and find peace among the waves. In Soil, the bodies are buried with something to keep them safe on their journey to the afterlife, and something to connect them with those still living. Sometimes it's as little as a charm on a string, wrapped around their finger."

She rolled Neven's ring on her thumb.

Clara fidgeted with it constantly, often subconsciously. Her voice caught, and Beau fought not to wrap his arms around her in comfort. Though that wasn't what she needed now.

She looked down at Neven's shirt and took a deep breath before she continued.

"In Breath, the bodies are burned and the ashes thrown over a cliff, or somewhere high, so they can fly free from this world to the next. A family member will recite the Ad'a Everlife, which is a poem for safe passage through their lives. From living, to death, to whatever comes next." Clara shrugged. She folded the shirt awkwardly as she held it above the water, careful not to get it wet.

"In Flame, the body is also burned, but the ashes are not scattered. A fire fae is the only Vequil fae to be able to withstand the heat of a burning body, burned anything, really. So while the body is burning, an officiant will hold their hand to the deceased's chest and the ashes will collect on their skin. They mark the family of the deceased, so their spirit lives on in those still breathing. It is tragically beautiful to watch."

"What are we doing in the water, Clara?" Keyne asked gently.

She looked up at him, eyes already misty. "I don't know which court I fit into." Her voice broke and Beau's heart cracked at the sound. "All of them, I suppose, so I figured I'd combine them together."

"What about Candor?" Beau asked.

"Honestly, I'm not sure of their tradition." Clara shook her head. "The entire court disappeared before I was born. All I know is they have a similar verse to the Ad'a Everlife."

"What would you like to do? What would you like *us* to do?" Keyne gestured to himself and Beau.

“I’ve only ever been present at a few services. You”—Clara pointed at Beau—“I want to be quiet and supportive. I want you to be present.”

Beau smiled softly at her. He raised his hands and walked over to Clara without a word, taking a place behind her, and he laid a hand on Clara’s waist in an offer of silent support.

“And you,” she said to Keyne. “He was your brother. What do you want to do?”

“Help you heal,” Keyne said earnestly. He took a step closer to Clara and rested his hand over hers, above Neven’s shirt. “We have our own traditions, and I’ve grieved my brother. I will continue to do so for the rest of my life. Now you should honour him and let yourself move on. He would not be pleased that you continue to blame yourself for what happened. Take your time, honour and mourn, but don’t let his death consume your life or distract you from your future.” He levelled a pointed stare at Clara, and she avoided his gaze.

“Is that why you’ve been so distracted today?” Beau asked, then clamped his mouth shut.

“Quiet,” she hissed, and Beau fought a grin.

Clara took a deep breath.

“Soul to sand,
dawn to dust.
Blood to bone,
raw and rust.”

Keyne removed his hand, and Clara followed suit.

She lowered her hand into the water until she found Beau’s, leaving Neven’s shirt supported above the water in her other palm. While this was not a moment for him, Beau couldn’t help the warmth which bloomed in his chest as she interlaced their fingers and squeezed. She took a deep breath before she continued.

"I hold you dear,
I set you free.
Wherever you land,
forever you'll be."

The shirt burst into flames. Heat crackled and as Beau peered over Clara's shoulder, he saw fire engulf her entire hand. His instinct was to put the fire out, then he internally smacked himself for being so stupid. She was part fire fae, or depending on who was asked, she was a fire fae.

"Among us here,
near and far.
Kinfolk alike,
sun, moon, and star."

Her voice lilted, and as she stood in the lapping water, Beau had no doubt of her likeness to a siren.

"I'll hold you close,
no matter you'll stray.
Be safe—"

Her voice broke, and Beau rubbed her hip with his thumb, reminding her he was there.

"Be sound . . ."

Clara's shoulders dropped and shook, and Keyne shot Beau an expression he couldn't quite decipher, so he glanced at Clara instead.

Her eyes were pressed closed, and tears streaked down her cheeks. Her lips twitched, and her nostrils flared as she inhaled slowly.

"Until, I pray,
we meet again.
At noon, or night,
you won't be far."

For someone as strong as she was, it was unusual to see her so fragile. Beau was unable to do anything but let her fall into him, and catch all the pieces, then help her sort them later.

While he appreciated her ease and willingness to be vulnerable with him, Beau vowed he would not allow this feeling to befall her again, not if he could help it.

"In hearts alone,
if not in sight."

A swell of air surrounded the trio, circling them. The fire went out, leaving a pile of ash in Clara's hand. She opened her eyes and removed her hand from Beau's, then dipped her thumb into the ashes.

She dragged her thumb over Keyne's nose twice, marked two horizontal lines, then kissed his forehead.

"I'm sorry," she whispered.

"How many lines for you?" Keyne asked.

Clara shook her head.

"It's two across the nose horizontally for siblings. Twice vertically on the forehead and once vertically on the chin for mothers. Vertically from the hairline to the lowest part of the nose once for fathers. Once vertically over a cheek for male kin, and once horizontal in the same spot for female kin." Clara sniffed, then attempted a reassuring smile. The expression fell short. "Friends do not receive marks."

"Today," Keyne replied, as he dipped his thumb into the pile and winced at the touch, "you do."

He marked her left cheek horizontally, the width of her eye, though she washed it away with her silent tears. Keyne held his forehead to hers as she cried.

Beau scooped the remaining ashes from her palm and waded to shore. Keyne and Clara followed shortly after.

She wrapped her arms around his neck the second she reached him, and again, warmth exploded inside of Beau.

"Thank you," she whispered into the crook of his neck.

Beau simply stroked back her hair and kissed her temple, holding her until she was ready to leave.

CHAPTER TWENTY-TWO
CLARA

Clara woke to the feel of Beau's fingers tracing slow, tantalising patterns along her skin. Up and down her side, circling over her hips and thighs, then following the golden lines which already marked her. She smiled before she opened her eyes, knowing he'd be propped on his elbow, his gaze fixed on her.

In the past four days, he'd hardly left her side. Aside from while she worked, Beau followed her around, providing her comfort like a blanket on a winter's day.

Though the cold was dissipating, mornings were still brisk, making scarves and beanies necessary. However, the sun warmed her more than the air chilled. Spring was moving in.

Each day that followed Neven's funeral, Clara felt a touch lighter. A fraction less distraught at her friend's fate. Now when she looked at his brother, all she saw was Keyne—her trainer and new friend—not the ghost of someone she loved and lost. While it would never be something Clara was okay with, the weight and bitterness of his death lessened a little more each day.

Her eyelashes fluttered, and she opened her eyes to find Beau exactly where she'd expected. Though his face was shrouded by apprehension.

"What?" she asked.

He blinked a few times, then offered her an unconvincing smile. Clara simply raised her brows and waited for him to answer.

Beau sighed. "I have to leave for a few days."

Clara's face fell. "When?"

As she sat up, the comforter fell and exposed her naked torso. She smirked at Beau's blatant ogling, then cleared her throat loudly.

"Today," he answered. Before Clara could protest, he added, "Shall I walk you to work first?"

"I'd like that." She patted his hand before she stood.

"How's the new employee?" Beau asked, as he, too, stood and exposed himself in all his naked glory.

Clara couldn't help but stare back.

"He's not so bad," she murmured before she shook her head, clearing her throat again. "I found out he's part Vequil, part Soliqe. Apparently, his sister has claws and they can both communicate with birds."

"That'll surely come in handy," Beau scoffed. "Will he be in today?"

Clara eyed him suspiciously, then shrugged.

"I'd assume so."

Beau nodded, and they dressed in silence.

The bell rang above her head as Clara opened the door to Nerrida's bakery. Mikhail smiled, offering a slight wave, before he continued loading pastries into the display cabinet. Seeing him behind the counter no longer filled Clara with the rage or guilt it once had.

Beau cleared his throat behind her, where he waited in the doorway. Clara wished him good luck on his trip, though he hadn't told her where he was going or why. Before, she would've been angry at his secrecy, but now she trusted him enough to be sure he would come home and tell her when he felt it was necessary.

So she simply squeezed his hand and flitted towards the kitchen. Clara turned to wave at Beau from the hallway, but he was no longer in the small shop. Instead, he and Mikhail stood just outside, having what seemed to be a civil enough conversation. Beau's eyebrows drew together and his top lip lifted enough to show the point of a canine. Clara couldn't see Mikhail's face, but when Beau's face relaxed, she let out a light huff and continued down the hall.

"Clara!" Nerrida screeched as she exited the cool room. She hurriedly dropped sticks of butter and milk cartons on the bench and rushed to Clara. Halting abruptly, she placed one of her delicate hands on Clara's chin and turned her head to the side, while the other hovered just above her bruised skin. "What in Mother's name happened?" she demanded, her eyes clouded with worry.

"I've been learning self-defence." Clara shrugged, downplaying the injuries. Truthfully, they looked worse than they were. "You should see the other guy."

"Oh?" Nerrida asked.

"Indeed." Clara nodded her head, likely too eagerly to be convincing. "He doesn't heal nearly as fast as I do."

"Oh, dear." Nerrida brought a hand to her mouth but failed to hide her chuckle. She turned to collect her ingredients, calling over her shoulder, "You've got bread to bake this morning. Off you go!"

"Yes, ma'am."

Clara smiled, eager to begin her day, but winced as she brought her hands to the sink. "Do we have any gloves?"

"No, why? Just wash your hands."

"I have—" Clara contemplated her words. Open wounds felt like the wrong choice. "Scrapes."

"Clara." Nerrida's tone was much more sympathetic this time. Less scolding, more friend than parent.

"I may have fallen a few times," Clara added. She felt she should explain herself, though she didn't need to. She'd visited Nerrida's bakery thousands of times as a youth, and by the time she was old enough for a job, Clara knew the bakery inside out. Nerrida knew Clara almost as well.

Walking over to Clara with understanding and concern in her gaze, Nerrida placed a gentle kiss on Clara's forehead and whispered, "Be careful. Please?"

Clara nodded. Her injuries were from the absence of training mats, which Keyne felt should be removed. Now every time she stumbled or fell, it was onto coarse sand or the various rocks that lined the shore.

"You do the cookies then, and I'll do the bread."

Clara nodded as she heard the bell chime in the front. A second later, Mikhail's voice rang through the bakery.

"Only me!"

Which meant Beau had officially left. A strange pang spread through her chest. She didn't miss the Phoenix already, but she had a strong suspicion she would soon.

By the end of her shift, Clara was unsurprised to find herself displeased to be going home. The bakery was a place she could relax, switch off, and run on instinct and muscle memory. A kitchen was a place of solace for Clara. Sparring on uneven ground, while a mass of rocks and sea spray prickled her bare skin, less so.

Her arms ached simply thinking about it.

Unintentionally, she groaned. Though she knew physical training was necessary—at the very least, self-defence was essential—she couldn't help but dawdle as she crossed the threshold out into the street.

Mikhail loitered on the footpath, and when she looked at him, he smiled and stepped towards her. At Clara's questioning look, the unnaturally chipper male only chuckled.

"Heading down to the bay?" he asked.

Clara's eyes narrowed, and her spine straightened.

"I might be . . ."

"You're training there, yes?" Mikhail pushed further, rocking forwards on his feet slightly.

"And how might you have come by that information?" Though she was suspicious, she walked slowly so he might follow.

"A little birdie told me," he said with a wink as he fell into step with Clara. Despite the absurd cliché, and the lack of an actual answer, she couldn't stifle her grin.

"Of course it did," she muttered.

"May I walk you there?" Mikhail asked, his tone low and serious.

"You may." Clara dipped her chin.

"Excellent." Mikhail beamed and clapped his hands together. "We need to make a detour."

She turned fully towards him then, incredulity plastered over her face.

"Mikhail," she chided.

His expression didn't falter, a charming smile still firmly planted on his sun-kissed face.

"Clara," he all but sung in response.

"What detour?"

"You'll see. So, how is your training?"

Clara sighed, but relented. "Well enough. I've had my ass handed to me more than I care to admit, but I'm learning."

"And Keyne is teaching you?"

"What does it matter who teaches me?"

"I meant no ill will," he said, hands held up in submission. "I was only going to say that you won't find a better instructor. Aleska and Oren are superb, but Keyne is far superior. You'll learn a great deal from him, ass handings and all."

"How do you know them?" Clara asked.

They'd left the town centre, now walking down a much wider dirt path. It wasn't her normal route to the bay. Homes and fruit trees dotted either side of the path, though they weren't as closely packed as in the middle of the village.

"Keyne is a distant friend of the family," Mikhail said, as he directed Clara towards a line of log-cabin-style homes. "A few times removed, a cousin's friend's someone or other. Truthfully, I don't know the exact connection, but when I was a child, my family would go to Tirenas for the summer and visit my mother's relatives." He stopped in front of a small cabin with large grey stepping stones placed almost haphazardly from the property line to the viridian door. Mikhail turned to face her with his hands behind his back. "As soon as I was old enough to take a class, I did. I then spent every subsequent trip taking as many classes as possible. That training has saved my life twice now." His smile softened for a second, before he told her to wait as he bounded towards the front door and disappeared inside the house.

When he returned, he held a small cylindrical flask.

"What is that?" Clara asked, her brows furrowed.

"It'll help you focus," Mikhail answered and held out the flask. "It calms the body but enhances the mind. Most find it incredibly helpful for strategising and observation in battle." He cleared his throat, then amended, "Or in your case, self-defence training." Mikhail's smile turned sheepish as he rubbed the back of his neck and extended the flask towards her for a second time.

"Are there drugs in this?" she asked with a pointed look.

"Helmos, no."

Clara recognised the deity he named from the statue at King Urian's palace. From the lovers, destined to chase each other forever and to never have more than a glance at their other half. Helmos, the god of the sun, and his counterpart, Nyrene, the goddess of the moon. Part of her envied a love so powerful it could level worlds and shatter existences. Though deep down, Clara knew it was not something to crave, for it could bring nothing good. Only longing and heartache.

"It's tea."

Evidently, her scepticism covered her face.

Mikhail sighed. "Would you like me to drink it first? To prove it to you? You know, despite me being a fae incapable of lying and all."

"Even if you drink it, that proves nothing." Clara tightened her arms across her chest. "The effects could be slow to develop, or you could play a mind trick. You are a fae incapable of lies indeed, but you're still a Darsmun fae, and they're trickier than any of us."

Did Clara truly think Mikhail was trying to poison her? No. Though she hadn't ruled out the possibility entirely, she didn't truly believe his intentions were nefarious. Unfortunately, her stubborn streak could not allow her to back down now.

"I did not inherit any Darsmun abilities."

"You could be manipulating my mind as we speak."

"Oh please," he scoffed. "Like that would fool you. Give yourself some credit! Especially as an Inalis, you'd see right through any mind games." Mikhail smiled, his tone light and jovial.

But Clara wasn't laughing, and the smile which had tugged at her lips vanished. "What the fuck did you just say?"

"You're a Vequil Inalis, are you not?" Mikhail asked, his face now filled with nerves, his eyes unsure where to land. His smile fell and his gaze lowered to his hands. "I apologise if it was not public knowledge, or my place to speak. But your markings gave it away, and you did not seem to hide them."

Clara was uninterested in correcting him and was unwilling to remember the time she had fallen prey to the mind play of a Darsmun fae. Instead, she took the flask from Mikhail and opened the lid. She swirled the liquid, inhaling the subtle scent of bergamot, lemon, and something else she couldn't identify.

"If there is poison in this, I'm going to kill you."

"Thank you so much, Mikhail," he mocked, his voice three notes higher than normal. "You're so welcome, Clara," he added in his regular voice.

As if his playfulness were contagious, the tension in Clara's body evaporated, and her own smile bloomed. Once it spread wide across her face, she stepped closer and tugged on his collar until he lowered his face to hers.

"Please believe me when I tell you that if I find out you are anything but an upstanding citizen, I am going to take this flask and shove it so far up your ass you can taste it," Clara told him sweetly.

She released his collar and started walking towards Ira Bay.

"Truly, anytime."

"With my foot."

"How pleasant."

“Widen your stance.” Keyne spoke with a deep, sure tone. He was here for instruction, critique, and correction, and Clara appreciated his lack of bullshit—something that could not be said for her brother.

Evian had been standing with Keyne when Clara arrived and insisted on joining their training session.

Mikhail had stayed only long enough to let her know Oren had two of his toes severed on his left foot, and his balance suffered for it. He’d then spoken to the three instructors for a moment before he ran off, leaving Clara stuck with Evian.

Her brother had pushed even harder to stay once he heard Beau had left. His argument had centred on: “Well how am I supposed to know what I can help with if I don’t know what you already know?” Eventually, she’d relented, knowing he needed the training as much as she did. Perhaps something valuable would come from this, taking him away from this court where he didn’t wholly belong.

“Hands up,” Keyne repeated.

Clara grumbled and let out a frustrated breath. Not only was it an unnatural position for her to stand in, Evian moved so slowly she had ample time to block his attacks.

She dropped her fists to her sides, and instead of focusing on the hand-based attacks they had been practicing today, she swung her leg out and hooked her ankle behind Evian’s.

He toppled, landing with a thud and a groan.

"What was that for?" he asked as he stood, dusting sand from his backside.

"You've been going easy on me all day," she said, her voice high and too fast. "I won't ever learn if I don't fail, Evian! If I do not learn, I will never best anyone."

"You cannot blame me, little sister, for trying to keep you safe instead of throwing punches."

"You cannot keep me safe by coddling me."

Something like hurt flashed briefly over Evian's face, but thankfully, Oren jogged over to them before her brother could respond. "I'll take over," he said and clapped Evian on the shoulder. "I believe your missus is here, anyway." He pointed inland, towards the town, where a short female with a bright-blue shimmer to her skin on her arms now stood. A crack spread through Clara's heart when Seren waved to Evian and her smile faltered as her gaze turned to Clara.

Seren had been Clara's longest and truest friend. Her sister in all the ways that mattered. The reason behind a million laughs and less than half as many tears. Her heart hurt at the rift between them. How Clara longed to run to her friend and wrap her arms around the petite woman, pretending like nothing had happened. To gush about her feelings, to rant and rave about all the warring emotions she'd cycled through of late.

To not be without another friend, especially one so important as Seren.

Perhaps it was stubbornness, or her heart's inability to place itself in a position where it could be hurt again, but Clara held her tongue and averted her eyes.

Evian kissed the side of Clara's head, then whispered something about Seren being there when she was ready to mend their relationship. Mechanically, Clara said goodbye to her brother and stalked towards the water bottles at Aleska's feet.

The raven-haired female raised a brow as Clara approached but said nothing.

Oren walked up behind her and collected a pair of training poles in place of his matching daggers.

"On second thought," Clara said, after swallowing a mouthful of water, "I'm done for today."

Before Oren could say anything, Clara resealed her bottle and stalked away. As she walked, she ignored the violent thumping in her chest that threatened to overwhelm her entirely.

CHAPTER TWENTY-THREE
BEAU

Dirt and gravel crunched under Beau's feet as he walked through Tirendell, searching for the town centre. It was located close to the Wave-Flame border, just over the mountain passes.

For the umpteenth time since he crossed the mountains and moved through the clearing, Beau patted the breast pocket of his coat to ensure the pouch sat safe. Then he let loose a relieved breath and let his arm fall.

Birds trilled above, and the few trees decorated with early or evergreen foliage swayed in the wind. The whooshing sound had Beau on high alert, with his hands held stiff and his wings pulled up slightly—not that they'd be any help if he needed them. Beau was glad they had some movement at least, and maybe one day he'd learn to use them.

Though today would not be that day.

He set that thought aside and turned his face upwards to scan the sky. He surveyed all directions, but there weren't many places a being could hide. Open grassland stretched far and wide, though it was splattered with rocks and stones, gravel, and dead shrubs. Trees were scattered and filled the considerable space, but there was no forest.

A slow flap sounded from the sky, and the back of Beau's neck grew damp. Not from sweat or nerves, though he couldn't deny he was on edge with what circled above him.

The surrounding air heated, reminding him of Clara, though her heat was almost always more inviting.

Another flap, closer this time, which Beau realised came from a different set of wings.

Scaled in colours from orange to red, with vicious claws to match, the beast huffed a scorching exhale through its far-too-large nostrils. Its black eyes narrowed on Beau.

He fought the urge to reach for his sword or simply run. But the last time he'd been in the presence of a daemdrana, he'd paid the price for acting without thought. So this time he remained frozen in place, still as any statue, enduring the creature's glare.

It huffed, and Beau could've sworn light-grey smoke plumed from its snout. The ground crunched as its claws dug into the gravel. Its tail then swung around, and one of the spikes struck its leg, dislodging a single crimson scale, which clattered to a stop at Beau's feet.

For the one who does not need you to save her but will require help to survive.

Beau's jaw fell slack as his eyes bulged.

The daemdrana's voice echoed in his mind, simultaneously low and masculine, and light and feminine. Somehow, it was a single sound and a chorus of voices. He hadn't known they could speak, let alone to another's mind.

"And what is she to do with it?" he asked carefully, not wanting to offend the creature.

It huffed again.

It matters not, only that she keeps it close and passes it on when the time comes. She has a brain, Phoenix. Allow her the chance to use it.

Without warning, the daemdrana flared its wings and shot into the air, leaving the echo of wingbeats and a chill in its wake.

A bell chimed as Beau opened the door to the jewellers. It was dainty and small, but rung loudly. A female with hair more vibrant than Clara's jumped up from behind the counter.

He entered the shop and closed the space between them in two strides. A quaint store indeed. Yet perhaps the workspace out the back was larger.

"Are you the goldsmith?" he asked, realising he should've led with something else as he watched her face harden. "I need your help, please."

She nodded and gestured for him to continue.

Beau pulled a hessian coin pouch from his belt and put it onto the counter, then drew the smaller, lighter pouch from his chest pocket and placed it side by side. He described his time-sensitive request and explained the extra coins he offered to accommodate the rush.

Her face softened, and her mouth quirked as she inspected the bag of coins.

"I can have it done by this time tomorrow," she said, as she emptied the money into the register. Then she took the small pouch and made to turn around.

"Oh, almost forgot!" Beau added, and she paused. He plucked a single feather from his wing with a wince and handed it to her. "I'll be needing that back," he added. "It's for design purposes only."

She chuckled and walked towards the back of her shop, hopefully to get started.

Beau left to find a decent enough inn to spend the night and counted down until he could leave this court to return to Clara.

CHAPTER TWENTY-FOUR
CLARA

Clara knew something was off as soon as she reached her property. Tingles danced along her spine, nape, and between her temples. The start of a headache formed at her brow, and she audibly groaned as she reached for the door handle.

The smell of spiced fruits and ripe berries wafted through the hallway, and soft, lyrical voices carried down the corridor.

As Clara entered the living room, she found Samara, Poppy, Elisabeth, and Isobel spread about the dining table and settee. Poppy sat with her feet curled beneath her, a cushion held to her stomach. Samara stood, leaning against a chair, her own arms folded loosely. Isobel stood at one end of the table, Clara's mother bustling about behind her, while Elisabeth sat at the table looking more appalled than ever.

“Nice of you to join us.” Elisabeth spoke with the kindness of a sword aimed at an undeserving man. Distaste and superiority dripped from her tongue.

“Hello, Elisabeth,” Clara said with a sigh, before she spared a brief glance at Isobel. Their eyes met for what felt like eternity, then she greeted her mother and the twins.

Elisabeth scoffed, then spoke down her nose at Clara. It felt like a reprimand, as though Elisabeth was telling off a child. Clara tried to tune her out until Elisabeth’s volume increased.

“You were brash and thoughtless, and so incredibly juvenile! Queen Sylvina wrote to me, you know? How could you be so foolish as to *threaten a queen*?”

“Threats mean nothing.” Clara shrugged. “I killed a king, remember? If she was worried, I succeeded. She should be concerned.”

“Clarenna!” Elisabeth’s jaw dropped and her eyes widened slightly.

“My name is Clara,” she corrected. “And I am not apologising. I did not threaten her—well, not intentionally—but she’s right to feel threatened. War is coming and everyone will be affected. It is a cause for concern, wouldn’t you agree?”

“Mother, help me.” Elisabeth whispered. “Perhaps it’s my fault, leaving you here to be raised by some woman I didn’t know—”

“You will not speak poorly of my mother in her own home, Elisabeth.” Clara pointed to Elisabeth with a calm fury she’d rarely displayed. It was truthfully a little frightening how liberated she felt, doused in tranquil wrath. “I do not care who you are, where you come from, or what you intend. In this house, your opinion is non-existent when it comes to her. The only exception is when you grant her the praise she so rightfully deserves for having to raise a child she did not ask for."

Elisabeth raised her hands submissively. "Of course. Felicity, I apologise. That was rude of me to insinuate. Clara, my sweet girl, I only meant—"

Clara cut Elisabeth off again. "I do not care what you meant, Elisabeth. Watch your tongue. If you think I have any issues cutting it from your mouth, think again. I am not your sweet girl; I am *her* strong daughter."

Ire flashed in Elisabeth's eyes, though her face remained neutral.

"Do also remember, Elisabeth, I am now betrothed to their son, which makes me the queen's heir by matrimonial bond. Take that as the threat it is."

From the corner of her eye, Clara noticed Isobel's face fall. Her eyes dropped to her feet as her middle finger traced circles around her thumb. A strange feeling, a lot like guilt, flared in her chest, but she couldn't place why.

"Perhaps we should take a break and reconvene tomorrow?" Felicity spoke up as she flittered around Elisabeth and stared intently at Clara. "Morning tea might be nice. Clara, would you see Nerrida about organising some pastries, please?"

"Of course, mother." She walked over to hug Felicity, pressed their foreheads together, and whispered, "I love you."

"I love you, my darling."

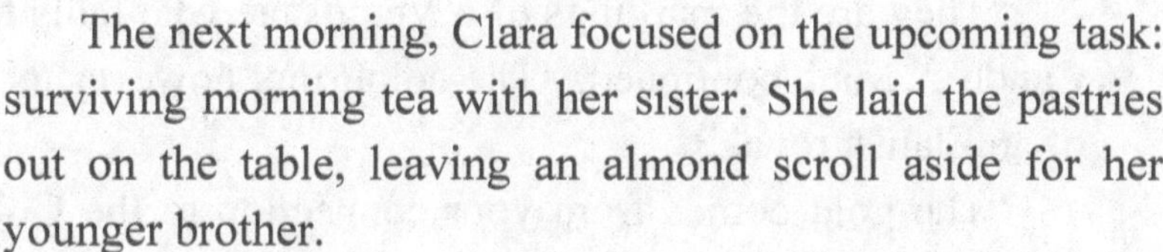

The next morning, Clara focused on the upcoming task: surviving morning tea with her sister. She laid the pastries out on the table, leaving an almond scroll aside for her younger brother.

Elisabeth entered with Maja walking behind her, an almost proud smile on her face. Clara resisted the urge to hug the woman or berate and demand answers to the questions which still plagued her. Samara followed Maja, but Poppy was nowhere to be seen. Isobel was also absent, causing an ache to caress Clara's heart.

Maja leant in to hug Felicity, thanking her for her hospitality, though Clara didn't miss the subtle movement of Maja's lips as her mouth brushed past her mother's ear.

Her mother politely, but quickly, excused herself from the kitchen as Maja took a seat at the table.

"Still drinking fruit-flavoured sugar water, girl?" Maja grinned playfully at Clara, who couldn't help but smile back.

"Is there any other kind worth my time?" she countered. They both laughed until Elisabeth cleared her throat.

"We need to discuss your lineage," Elisabeth said, her tone grim.

"If this is about my being a Vequil Inalis, you can skip it. I am aware."

Maja and Elisabeth shared a look, then Maja spoke.

“Not quite, dear. You see how Elisabeth is marked along the sides of her neck, and behind her ears?” Maja gestured to Elisabeth, who turned her head to show her marks of Candor.

For a second, Clara didn’t question, then realised how few marks her sister possessed.

“They are the markings of a Vequil fae who hails from Candor,” Maja continued. “The colouring, however, is that of an Elanist royal.”

“The gold comes from your connection to the Golden Kingdom. Our father is the son of Prince Vaughn. He died not long after father was born and as the only living, legitimate blood relative of the crown, it was passed down to him.” Elisabeth spoke in a soft tone.

“Except he does not possess golden markings, and it was decreed centuries ago that the throne was only fit for an Inalis to sit upon. The throne has sat cold and empty, and the crown on a pillow in a glass cage, for centuries. That was, until my power manifested, and I was marked golden. The kingdom was maintained but not governed. Now I am the closest our continent has to a queen until you are coronated or my son bears Inalis markings.

“Our mother was a spirit fae, and her magic passed to me. When you were born, you projected your first vision to her. We assumed you would hold only Candor magic also, but new intel shed doubts upon that theory, and, well, you know how that ended. Felicity has gone to fetch something I think might help, or perhaps only bring more confusion. Truthfully, I am unsure.

“It’s a lot of information and I don’t think now is the time to discuss it. Though since you are betrothed to a Crown

Prince, you ought to at least know you have a throne of your own. Provided I die before my son is old enough to sit upon it, that is."

There were far more important elements to what Elisabeth had said, but her eyes bulged as she asked, "You have a child?"

"Yes," she said, with no change or falter in her expression. "His name is Christopher, and he is three. In Elanist culture, tradition states the firstborn of the current king and queen is the heir. The position of next in line falls to their firstborn before any subsequent children of the king and queen, unless the child is under the age of maturity. If I die before Christopher reaches twenty-seven years, the crown will fall to you."

Clara didn't know what to do with that information. It was bad enough she'd be inheriting a kingdom by marriage, but to know there was a possibility of a second? And that she came from royalty? Yesterday's headache made a sudden return.

"Why are your marks different to mine?" she asked, ignoring the pounding at her temples and the realisation that Jude already knew of her heritage.

"Genetics are a fickle thing, Clara. Your true power comes from our mother, from the spirit fae. Much like my own.

"I can sense oncoming events and can occasionally speak to into another's mind. I cannot see the future, nor have visions or premonitions, but I can feel shifts in emotions or when the future has changed. It's an internal feeling rather than sight. You have the sight, however clear or unclear it may be at present.

"Our mother was telepathic and had entire visions of the future. So clear and intense she said it was as if she were standing right there. Our father was born from a Flame-Inalis coupling and I wouldn't be surprised if that was the second element to manifest in you. Prince Vaughn was a Vequil Inalis, and his bride was a fire fae. I inherited our mother's Candor magic, while the Mother gifted you with that of the Inalis. The ability to harness all."

Clara refrained from rolling her eyes at the mention of the Mother. The goddess who had conveniently disappeared when Clara needed hope and hadn't reappeared since. Clara wondered whether she had ever been there at all.

"I don't know why," Elisabeth said with a subtle shrug. "But either your groom doesn't know, which I doubt, or he's keeping your future in-laws in the dark."

What could he possibly have to gain by keeping her royal heritage a secret? Surely King Taron and certainly Queen Sylvina would be more amenable to their engagement if they knew she held rank.

What else was her husband-to-be hiding?

"Thank you," Clara said as she bid Elisabeth good day and walked her to the door. Maja and Samara wandered ahead, their elbows linked.

"Whatever for?" Elisabeth asked.

She paused in the doorway, looking at Clara with confusion. It was not a familiar expression for Elisabeth to wear and Clara fought to rein in her smirk.

"For giving me some answers," Clara replied. She had more questions than she started the day with, but at least now she had some answers.

In a way, the water court was still her home, even though she bore marks that labelled her as something else.

Elisabeth had explained how their father had searched for other Vequil Inalis fae as soon as their mother had died. She'd omitted *how* exactly Lenore had died, though Clara supposed it didn't matter. Elisabeth told her about her home, the Golden Kingdom, and that one day soon Clara would be expected to visit the palace. How it hadn't disappeared, but rather been preserved and protected.

Maja told her of a letter her biological mother enlisted her help to write and insisted Clara should read it after her birthday. She'd muttered something about it all making more sense once she'd reached maturity, but the sentiment only confused Clara. All intent to ask more questions vanished with the reappearance of the throbbing ache behind her eyes.

Call for me once you've read it.

Samara's voice rang softly in Clara's mind. She didn't ask for clarification—which she likely should have—as another question stood at the forefront of her mind and burned Clara's tongue.

"Isobel has the same markings as me, though hers are grey. Why?" she asked, uncharacteristically nervous.

Ire danced over Elisabeth's face. She didn't even try to hide it. "Isobel Jeffreys is of none of your concern."

Clara didn't bother to hide her annoyance.

"That's my business, don't you think?"

She raised a brow expectantly and waited for Elisabeth to answer her question. An answer didn't come.

"Well?" Clara prompted.

"Clarenna." Elisabeth sighed again, more resigned this time. "Clara," she corrected, with a dip of her chin. "Isobel Jeffreys is an employee of the Golden Kingdom. She has the markings of a Vequil Inalis because she has the power of one. But what she lacks is a connection to the throne, hence the lack of colour."

Clara nodded. Despite the attitude, her sister had given her a straightforward enough answer, but then Elisabeth ruined the moment.

"Listen to me very carefully, *Clara*. You are not to cavort with the staff. You will remember their place. The only individual on my payroll who comes anywhere close to being considered for a relationship past professional boundaries is Ryland Hasheem. Even then, I would not approve of such a thing without careful deliberation.

"Isobel Jeffreys is not your friend. You will not spend time with her. Your paths will not cross, and I expect you to remember to keep your personal life separate. Quite frankly, you need not even speak to her."

"Elisabeth—" Clara protested, the pang in her chest thrumming.

"No." She cut Clara off, her face twisted in disgust. "That is final. Goodbye."

Then she closed the door behind her.

Clara stood frozen in the now too silent and empty hallway, wondering why it felt as though she were grieving.

CHAPTER TWENTY-FIVE
CLARA

Clara woke to a trumpet blaring outside her door. Thankfully, her sleep had been restful, void of any visions or nightmares. Without Beau, her mattress had felt empty and cold. He'd already been gone two days, but who knew how long *a few days* truly meant, and Clara missed him already. His steady breaths by her side as she fell asleep and whenever she woke throughout the night, or the gentle sparks along her skin as he traced circles with his finger whenever he woke before she did.

Jacob chuckled from the hall, then knocked, pulling her lingering thoughts away from the Phoenix. She kept her eyes closed but didn't stifle her smile, as the ruse of her still being asleep was a pointless one.

Her mother and both brothers bound into her room with laughter and shouted birthday wishes. Clara shot upwards as Jacob pounced onto the bed, dragging him backwards to the mattress. His giggles were contagious, and she laughed alongside him.

Felicity shuffled around the bed to plant a kiss on her head, handing her a small wooden box. Two cards sat atop the gift, one tied to the box with cream-coloured ribbon and the other had Clara's name written across the top in an unfamiliar scrawl.

Jacob pulled a blue velvet pouch from his pocket and dangled it in front of Clara, a wicked grin on his face.

"That's from the both of us," Evian said, inclining his chin towards the bag.

"Thank you," Clara responded as she tucked Jacob under her arm.

"Happy birthday!" he squealed again.

Putting the cards aside, she untied the small bag and tipped out its contents. Three differently shaped dice fell to her lap, each varnished a rich mahogany and outlined in fine lines of paint. The first, with nine faces, was decorated in silver numbers. One, with a different letter on each of its twelve sides, was painted in gold. The final die painted in a bone colour bore symbols she did not recognise, though she could immediately appreciate its beauty.

"I made them," Jacob said proudly. "For board games."

"And I have an instruction manual for bedroom games," Evian added with a wink.

Felicity's hand quickly collided with the backside of his head, but he only chuckled harder. Clara followed suit before she covered the sound with a cough. Her mother was unimpressed with them both.

Finally, she opened the box from her mother. Inside was a blue apron with two front pockets, trimmed with lace and embellishments and some sort of embroidery along the ties. Upon closer inspection, she noticed the water fae marks in thick stitching along the waist ties, and *Afron* stitched along the neck.

"It's so no matter which family you end up a part of, or which ground you land on, you'll know you always have a place here."

As a single tear ran down her mother's face, Clara shimmied from the bed and closed the gap between them. She wrapped her arms around the emotional woman and embraced her.

"I could never forget, Mother," she whispered into Felicity's hair, then kissed her cheek. "Never."

Her mother nodded and squeezed Clara back, sniffling. "Happy birthday, my strong daughter."

"Halfway to fearless," Clara whispered with a smile.

"Oh, I think we're long past that point, darling. Don't you?" Felicity gave her a pointed look, laced with humour. Clara cackled as her mother shook her head. "Your father stitched it. He decided you needed one after the first orange-and-poppyseed cake you baked."

The room erupted in laughter, except for Jacob, who hadn't even been conceived yet. Clara had been only four years, though she'd been successful in all her baking endeavours to that point. To her credit, the orange-and-poppyseed cake had also been a success in the end, even if it was a horrifically messy experience in the making.

That, and she'd lost her two front teeth, squashed butter up her nose, and somehow managed to squirt orange juice into her eye.

"That card is from us," Felicity said as she smiled. Then she gestured to the other envelope. "That one arrived this morning."

Jacob's messy handwriting filled the card with a heartfelt note about how glad he was to have Clara home, causing a lump to form in the back of her throat. Condensation on the windowsill spilled over, dripping heavily to the floor. The second card smelt of sunflowers and summer rain, and it seemed to almost sparkle in the morning light.

It's not much, but I couldn't let the day pass without reminding you how special you are. May the sun take note of your shine and endeavour to replicate it for everyone else to stand in awe.

Happiest of turns, Clara. I hope to spend the next one with you, and many more to follow.

All my love,

Isobel

Clara closed the card quickly, then gently pressed it to her chest. Closing her eyes for a moment, she inhaled the scent and smiled. Warmth spread through her body, tingling from her toes to her fingertips.

When she opened her eyes, Evian waggled his brows with a smirk. Clara ignored him, giving her little brother another squeeze before she ushered them all from the room.

Felicity approached Clara where she sat, curled on the settee with a glass of water in hand. She'd been attempting to recreate the magic which she had used to manipulate water in the past, but so far had not prevailed.

She knew fire could be manipulated by anger, and air was triggered by fear. Any neurological magic Clara possessed happened at random, so she had decided not to bother attempting to control it. Water and earth evaded her. So she set the glass on the floor with a huff before turning to her mother.

"You've been called to the bakery," Felicity said.

Clara's brows drew together. "But it'll be closed by now," she muttered, standing to check the clock in the hall. It was nearly dinner time, and there'd be no reason for Nerrida to call her in now. Besides, she wasn't even rostered for today.

Felicity shrugged as she walked back towards the kitchen, calling out for Clara to be safe and not dawdle. Clara sighed, moving her disappointing glass of water to the table before she left.

When she arrived, Mikhail stood outside, beaming eagerly, his hands clasped in front of him and his teeth on display.

Clara raised her eyebrows.

"Happy birthday," he said in a tone that sounded as if he were trying much too hard to be casual.

"Thank you," she replied hesitantly. Then, as he handed her a blindfold, somehow his smile grew. "What the fuck is that for?"

"Generally, surprises work best when you don't know every single detail."

"Ha-ha," Clara muttered dryly as she rolled her eyes. "Really, though, what's it for?"

"To ensure you are surprised, Clara. Put it on." He thrust his hand out towards her, the velvet hanging loosely over his palm.

Clara sighed and gave in, wrapping the blindfold and securing it. Suddenly, she was lifted off her feet, Mikhail snickering as she screeched. Then the only sounds were his wings flapping and his incessant talking.

Mikhail spent the entire flight telling her about the surprise party he threw for his sister when they were still in grade school. He'd decorated their house with scales and ribbon, and everyone who arrived wore reptilian themed costumes and cosmetics.

"We come from a feather and claw line of shifters," he said, as his feet dropped to the ground. "Her face was priceless when she saw everyone looking a little more like her. I won that year."

Gently, Mikhail untied her blindfold, and his grin was still plastered on his face. He leant in closer and whispered, "I like to think I've had a hand in the win this year too."

Then he kissed her cheek quickly, called out more birthday wishes, and shot back into the sky.

"Did he really kiss you in front of me?"

Clara whirled at the sound of the voice she knew so well. His unkempt hair was in a sad excuse for a bun, pulled back from those bright-amber eyes she saw even when hers were closed. She was overwhelmed by a level of excitement and relief she didn't expect.

Beau stood in the open doorway of a small wooden home. A dish towel hung from his shoulder and food was smeared across his hands and forearms. She ran to him and wrapped her arms around his neck, pressing her face to his chest, and inhaling his familiar spiced-orange scent. He squeezed her back without hesitation, then chuckled.

"If I knew this was how you'd greet me, I'd leave more often."

"If you leave me again," she snarled, narrowing her eyes at him, "your next return won't be so pleasant."

Beau laughed and kissed her forehead. It was such a simple gesture and yet she melted. Her face relaxed and the tension in her arms evaporated as quickly as it formed. Her gaze fell to his lips, and her thoughts followed suit.

Ruining the moment, Beau added, "I will have to leave again soon." Though noting her expression, he rushed to continue before she could accost him further. "But not yet. So for now, happy birthday."

An appreciative smile bloomed on Clara's face, as did the warmth and butterflies in her chest.

"Why are we in the middle of nowhere?" she asked, finally taking note of the lack of anything but the trees and otherwise empty land surrounding them. Mountains lined the horizon, shrouded in the orange glow from the setting sun.

"Privacy." Beau shrugged, then ushered her inside.

Clara didn't *need* privacy. Stars, she'd fuck him in the middle of the street if the opportunity presented itself.

Her thoughts turned to the New Moon festival and flutters filled the deepest part of her stomach.

Their footsteps echoed along the entryway and throughout the empty house. Mostly Beau's booted footsteps, as Clara hadn't bothered to put shoes on before she left home, knowing she wasn't needed at the bakery for work. Thick brown drapes hung over the windows, leaving only the few candles Beau had lit to cast light about the rooms. A small round table sat in front of the oven and cooktop, covered in potatoes, herbs, and cutlery. A pot boiled on the stove. There was a white box on one of the two chairs, with a smaller box balanced atop it.

"How did you find this fine establishment, Beau?"

He chuckled. "Never mind that. It's ours for tonight."

"And how did you know it was my birthday?"

"I asked," Beau said with a soft smile. "Now, I didn't make the cake, but—"

"There's cake?" Clara squealed. Beau feigned offence, but his expression broke as he collected the white box.

"Of course, it's your birthday." He handed her the smaller box, wrapped in pearl-covered lace, and opened the cake box.

It was *covered* in frosting. Clara couldn't hide her grin, even if she wanted to.

"Mikhail made it, so I have no idea the quality, but baking is far from my specialty. Frankly, I can't cook much of anything." He closed the lid and placed the box back on the chair.

"Are you going to poison me, Beau?"

"Not tonight, my love." He winked, and Clara fought to keep her expression neutral despite the butterflies which spread to every inch of her body. "This is a recipe passed down from my mother's grandmother and hers before that. It's one of the two recipes I ever bothered to remember."

"I'll report back, in that case, whenever I meet your mother. So don't ruin it." Clara rested her arms across her chest.

"You'd like to meet her?" The hope in Beau's eyes was almost too much.

"Very much," she said softly.

"I'm glad."

"What's the dish?" she asked.

"It's called poschappi," he said, and looked up to list ingredients off on his fingers. "Rice, potato, onion, a bunch of herbs, and far too much oil. Ingredients one might easily find in times of financial strain."

"Are you having money troubles, dear?"

Her eyes roamed his forearms, bared from the shirt he'd rolled to his elbows. Veins and muscle bulged as he worked. She couldn't help but stare, taking all of him in.

Beau answered as she pulled her gaze slowly back up his chest, where oil stains scattered his loosely buttoned shirt. "Not today, but if you keep looking at me like that, I'm going to find myself deep in debt."

"Looking at you like what?"

"Like you might like to remove my clothing and admire what's beneath it." A coy smile danced over his face. "Like you might've missed me a lot more than you're willing to admit out loud. Like you might even grow to love me."

Two could play a game of teasing.

“And why would that put you in debt?” she asked, refusing to acknowledge his last statement. She pressed her arms closer, pushed her breasts up.

Beau stared for only a moment before he cleared his throat. “Because among my kind, it’s instinctual for us to want to shower our”—he paused, uncertainty clear in his eyes—“loved ones with gifts. And also with acts of service, which I hope you keep in mind.” He looked as though he wanted to say something else, but didn’t.

“I will be sure to,” Clara drawled slowly. Stepping around the table, she stood behind him and wrapped her arms around his waist. “I’d hate for you to fall into poverty, after all. I think we can find other ways for you to keep me happy, sir.”

Beau’s body tensed under her, and she smirked. He rolled his neck before clearing his throat.

“Excellent.” His voice was like melted gold. “But before that, I have something for you.”

Clara couldn’t help the laughter that spilled from her throat. Of all the times for him to change the topic, she hadn’t expected it to be then, especially knowing what the term *sir* did to the poor male. Truthfully, his struggle was intoxicating, and a little humorous.

As he placed the lace-wrapped package in her hands, Beau averted his gaze. He continued preparing the food and placing the now rounded balls onto a tray. He looked nervous.

Clara eyed him curiously before removing the wrapping and opening the box.

Gold reflected the candle flame and for a moment Clara didn’t realise what it was besides jewellery. As she lifted it, the charm dropped and dangled from her fingers. A tiny feather, no larger than her thumbnail, hung from a delicate gold chain.

"Now," Beau whispered, placing the tray in the oven, "even when I'm not around, you'll have a piece of me."

"It's one of yours?" Clara gasped, realising how similar the feather was to the ones at his back.

Beau nodded. "And the rest of me is yours, too, if you'll have me." His eyes gleamed, nervously flicking between hers as if he couldn't bear to look away.

"I will have you, Beau." Clara whispered, closing the space between them. She dropped the empty jewellery box and cupped the back of Beau's neck.

"Thank the fucking stars," he breathed.

"Oh, they have nothing to do with it."

"I like to think," Beau murmured as he moved around her and took the necklace gently from her grip, "when we die, part of our soul lives on in the stars."

"Fuck, that's one way to bring the mood down." Clara rolled her eyes, but they both laughed quietly. The slightest brush of his skin along hers brought goosebumps to her flesh as he draped it around her neck and clasped it. It was oddly reminiscent of another moment–a lifetime ago it seemed–when he lingered close and spoke softly behind her.

"Look closer at the feather, Clara."

She searched his eyes as he moved to stand in front of her now. Then she studied his face, lingering a moment on those plump lips she desperately wanted to kiss before she obliged. The small golden plume was scattered with flecks of silver and grey. Her brows pulled together as she cocked her head and looked back at Beau, waiting for him to answer her unspoken question.

"So you can have your friend with you too."

It took a second for Clara to understand, but then her eyes bulged, and her jaw dropped, as did the charm from her fingers.

"You stole Neven's *ashes*?"

"Technically, I stole a handful of the shirt you cremated. It was supposed to be a nice gesture and you're ruining it."

"*I'm* ruining it?" Clara asked, a bark of laughter escaping her. "You're lucky you're pretty."

"No, Clara." Beau shook his head, placing his warm hands on either side of her face. "I am lucky for so many stars-damned things, but being pretty hardly makes the list."

"How long until dinner?" Her voice was low and breathy.

"Long enough."

CHAPTER TWENTY-SIX
CLARA

Beau slammed his lips into hers, and they were as warm and soft as she'd expected. His hands pressed to her cheeks for all of five seconds before they were moving, roaming down her neck and body. Clara's hands dug into his hair, clenched and pulled it as she ran her tongue along his bottom lip. Heat pooled at her core and fireworks and lights burst behind her eyes, just as the romantics promised.

Kissing him felt like she had taken a breath for the first time while simultaneously struggling for air.

He opened his mouth and teased her tongue with his, eliciting a short gasp from her.

"Fuck," he groaned. "I've wanted to do that for the longest *fucking* time."

Beau guided her through the house, one hand gripping the back of her neck while the other fumbled along the wall. Clara barely registered when they'd entered the bedroom, startling when her knees buckled against the edge of a bed.

Gasping, she fell onto it. Or rather, Beau pushed her down until she was sitting. He swore again, the sound sending flutters to her core. Clara bit her lip as she looked up at him, leaning forward so her breasts threatened to spill from her shirt.

In a heartbeat, it was pulled from her body and tossed aside. Followed by her pants, until she sat naked on the edge of the bed, Beau's eyes raking over her.

He nudged her legs apart as he leant in to kiss her again. Stopping short, his nose barely touching hers, he whispered, "You have the most beautiful eyes."

"You think they're nice now?" Her words were slow and sultry as she traced a finger along his jaw . . . followed by her tongue. "Just wait until they're filled with tears while I'm on my knees in front of you with my hands tied behind my back."

His growl had goosebumps erupting over her body.

"On your knees," Beau demanded.

For once, Clara followed his orders without complaint.

"So obedient, for a change." Beau wrapped one hand around her jaw and pressed his fingers in firmly, while the other hand adjusted his bulging crotch.

The sight of him had her insides coiling, and the smug bastard fucking knew it.

"Open." His voice was rough.

Without hesitation, Clara opened her mouth. She desperately needed him to fuck her, to ruin her. She needed him to violate her body, while looking down at her with ecstasy and passion and lust. Beau didn't seem like the kind to shy from roughness, and stars if that didn't turn her on even more.

Clara ran her tongue along her teeth, then settled it on her bottom lip.

Beau threw his head back and swore. "Are you ready?"

Clara only nodded and kept her mouth open, her tongue held where it was.

Beau spat into her mouth.

Her core tightened, and her thighs subconsciously pressed together, her body needing friction.

"Swallow."

She did. And the heat rose.

Beau leant forwards and spoke so close his lips and facial hair brushed her cheek.

"You took that so well," he drawled. "Now let's try something bigger."

This stars-damned prick. He knew all too well what he was doing to her. How he was slowly unravelling her and leaving her aching. If he wasn't inside her soon, she'd take matters into her own hands.

Before she could ponder further, Beau's pants were gone, and his rock-hard cock was thrust into her mouth. Clara gagged at both the lack of notice and the sheer size of him.

His hand tensed around her jaw and Beau grunted as his breath came faster and his hips bucked forwards.

Clara closed her mouth around him, his sweet slick leaking from the tip and coating her tongue. With her hands held tight against the backs of his thighs, Clara encouraged his movements, urging him to continue. She sucked hard and slow, revelling in the rasped curses and grunts of pleasure which erupted from him.

Removing his fingers from her chin, Beau fisted both hands in Clara's hair. With every ragged breath, he pulled her closer to the base of his shaft. Tears welled in her eyes from the force, though she had no complaints. She kept as much suction as she could manage while Beau fucked her mouth, and drool spilled from the corners of her lips.

"Fuck," he moaned. "*Fuck*, Clara."

His voice set off a frenzy in her, a near painful throb. And the thought of him easing himself inside her left her eager to feel it build higher. Anticipation was half the fun, after all.

Beau pulled her head down so far her nose touched his pelvis, and he held her there. His hips bucked a few times, and he grunted as she worked her tongue along the sensitive underside of his cock.

His eyes flared with desire as he tore himself from her. "On the bed and on your knees," he growled. "I'm going to fuck you from behind until you're screaming."

Fuck.

Clara obeyed without hesitation and crawled onto the bed, spreading her knees and pressing her chest and forearms to the mattress.

Beau's cock twitched as he ran it along her slick pussy. She arched up and back, desperate for as much of him as she could get.

"So fucking wet," Beau drawled, and Clara purred in response. "So fucking perfect."

Wholesome butterflies were not the kind she'd expected, but they warmed her chest. A few flew lower, beating rapidly and much deeper.

Heat swelled within her as Beau slowly entered her, his cock covered in her juices. He eased in and out far more gently than she wanted.

All he was doing was teasing her.

And likely himself, if his strained groans and vice-like grip were anything to go by.

But Clara didn't want to wait. She wanted all of him, and all of him *now.* Rolling her hips slightly, she slammed back towards him, crying out as she buried him inside her entirely.

Beau cursed and dug his fingers deeper into her skin.

She grabbed at the sheets above her head and moaned into the mattress as Beau's tempo increased. Ecstasy, the perfect mixture of pleasure and pain, burst within her. It danced along every nerve ending, sparking up her spine as Beau dragged a hand up her back, then wrapped around her neck.

He pulled her up by the jaw, his fingers back where they belonged, squeezing just enough for her head to spin. When he tugged her up further, his grip firm and his pace not slowing, Clara gasped. Her breath came out in short pants, accompanied by incomprehensible sounds as Beau pounded into her frantically.

Hungrily.

Aggressively.

He raised her until his damp chest met her back.

More pain and pleasure shot through her core and exploded out into her chest. Her breath hitched and choked sounds gurgled from her.

“I can’t,” she whimpered. “Fuck, I can’t.” Clara shook her head, as she tried to pry herself from his grip and move back to where it felt like divinity and magic existed.

Beau’s hand snaked upwards until his thumb caressed her bottom lip. “You can, sweetheart.” He slowed slightly as he bit back a groan. “And you will.”

Clara whimpered and moaned as he lowered her until her hands found the mattress again. Until all she could hear were the sobs and screams he pulled from her.

With every noise she made, Beau’s breathing grew more rapid, his curses more aggressive, his thrusts wilder and somehow deeper.

Clara bit into the mattress to stifle her screams.

Beau’s hand reached around her body. His fingers traced her sensitive outer lips as his palm pressed hard against her aching clit.

She screamed and her tears dampened the sheets as Clara begged him for more.

His deep chuckle sounded like gold and leather, smooth and rich.

Beau dragged his fingers slowly upwards until he settled his middle one on her clit, then he circled it with firm pressure. He growled and bucked faster as she cried out.

Her knees and thighs burned as her climax drew closer and closer.

“Fuck, you feel so good,” Beau grunted. Clara was so close, the pressure near to bursting and the heat coiled low. “Clara,” he ground out, half pleading and half in warning. “I’m going to come— Fuck!”

Her body erupted in pleasure, and Clara screamed.

Beau swore as release barrelled through them both. His cock pulsed and jerked inside her. Clara clenched her fists as she rode the waves, and Beau continued to slam into her as he experienced his own release.

They came undone together in a swirl of torturous bliss. Heavy breathing and the pounding of her heart filled Clara's ears, her arms now limp above her head.

Beau wrapped his hand in her tangled mess of hair and yanked her upright, turning her face to plant a kiss on her lips.

Arousal heavy in his eyes, Beau murmured, "And I've wanted to do *that* even fucking longer."

CHAPTER TWENTY-SEVEN
BEAU

Beau lay with his head resting on his hands, enthralled by the lines and figures Clara traced along his abdomen. The weight of her on his wing was a welcome warmth, one he wished he could replicate for her by curling it around her and holding her closer.

They hadn't cleaned up, simply flopped down with a smile. Content was an understatement for how he felt, but truthfully, nothing could come close to describing the peace and tranquillity this fiery woman brought him. It was like bathing in the fiercest but gentlest sun.

"Are you on any contraception?" he asked quietly. He did not want to dull the moment, though the question and potential ramifications plagued him.

"No," she said and shook her head. "Why would I be?"

"You are aware how children are made, yes?" He chuckled.

"Smartass," she muttered. "We fae don't bother with contraception, as we're notorious for being unable to easily conceive. While contraceptives exist, accidental pregnancy isn't really a concern."

"Is it a female difficulty, or male?"

Children were something Beau dreamt of sharing with Clara, and the idea brought a smile to his lips—but not yet.

"I don't know. What does it matter?" she huffed, clearly uninterested in the discussion.

"I'm not fae, Clara. If it's fae males who are lacking, we might find ourselves inconvenienced by a growing womb and a child inside it."

Her hand stopped, hovering above his heart. "What a disturbing way to phrase a pregnancy."

"Would you like to be pregnant?" he asked.

"Fuck, no." Clara scrunched her face again and shook her head vehemently.

"Then take the contraceptive. Better safe than sorry."

Clara hummed in response and returned to dragging her finger along his chest and arm. Her touch brought tingles to his skin, the most casual of fireworks bursting under her fingertip.

Abruptly, she stopped, sat up, and inhaled. An amused grin graced her lips as she whispered, "I think you're needed in the kitchen."

Realisation flooded his mind as Beau recalled what he'd been doing prior to Clara's arrival. Bolting upright, he tumbled out of bed, not bothering with any clothing. He ran down the dimly lit hallway and skidded to a stop in front of the smoking pan on the stove. The smell of burned potato and rice assaulting his nostrils.

With a wince, he removed the pan from the flame and turned off the stove, waving at the hazy cloud which shrouded the room. Beau cursed violently under his breath, though Clara—who had followed him from the bedroom—chuckled from the doorway.

Beau turned towards her, levelling a flat stare her way before he sighed and closed the space between them. With one hand, he tugged Clara towards him.

She made a startled noise similar to those he'd pulled from her recently, gasps he was already dying to hear again. With his other hand he grabbed the cake box.

"At least there's still cake," he said with a shrug of his shoulder.

Clara opened the lid as she looked directly into Beau's eyes, her lips dangerously close to his. "That's far more than a consolation prize, if you ask me."

Beau grinned and reached into the box, grabbing a small fistful of cake. He brought the offering to her lips and fed it into her open and waiting mouth.

"I'm so glad you think so," he crooned.

Not all the cake made it onto her tongue. Some frosting plastered to her cheeks and cream dropped to her chin. He had half a mind to lick her clean.

"Don't waste it," she jokingly mocked, as her eyebrows drew together in the most adorable attempt at a reprimand.

Clara swiped up the excess from her skin and licked her fingers clean, her stunning green eyes never once leaving Beau's.

He couldn't look away—even covered in food, she was the most captivating creature he'd ever be fortunate enough to look upon. So why would he ever want to stop?

Her hand snaked around his wrist and Clara pulled his hand towards her lips, then her tongue ran up his palm, from his wrist to the tip of his middle finger.

Beau's cock twitched, and a growl escaped his throat.

Desire swirled in Clara's eyes as he was sure it did in his own. When she took his thumb in her mouth, pressed her tongue to his skin and sucked, he couldn't hold back his moan.

"I'm decidedly not hungry."

"Oh, no?" Clara taunted, as she sat on the table and spread her legs.

"Fuck."

Her smirk was pure torture, devilish and beautiful. He wanted to fuck it from her mouth and paint her face with what it did to him. Clara swiped a finger through the icing, then trailed her hand down her stomach, the frosting smearing across her skin.

"I thought we weren't supposed to waste it?" Beau sassed as he put the box down. He had a feeling he'd be needing both hands.

"I don't think it'll go to waste, do you?"

His erection grew, begged for her hand or mouth or body, but this time it was her turn to be worshipped.

He bent forward and pressed his tongue to her skin, licking from the lowest point of her golden flames below her naval, all the way to the highest point of the twin markings from her air court heritage.

Lowering himself to his knees, Beau placed his hands around her thighs and pulled her plush body towards the edge of the table. Clara arched and widened her knees. Pressing his lips to her inner thighs, Beau left trails of kisses along her skin until he reached her aroused pussy.

The smell of her enticed a low growl from him as he inhaled, and she purred in response. His cock hardened at the sound, at how wet she was for him, and the sight of her spread before him, ready for him to bury his face in her cunt.

He pressed his tongue to her entrance, then slowly dragged it upwards to her clit. As he circled the most sensitive part of her, Clara arched her back where it touched against the table. She moaned and grabbed at his hair, the sensation drawing tingles along his skin.

He stroked between her lips, coating two fingers in her arousal, then inserting them inside her. Her pussy walls clenched around the intrusion and her gasp felt like the most pleasurable nails dragging down his spine. Beau groaned into her cunt and dragged his teeth gently across her sensitive flesh.

She moaned again and rolled her hips, riding his face.

His throbbing erection was bordering on painful, desperate for her touch. Beau curled his fingers inside Clara, slowly at first and then faster until the rolling of her hips became a frenzied buck. Her moans grew louder, paired with soft whimpers and sharp breaths, which had him dizzy with need and desire.

He growled again, and she pushed his head down.

"Beau," she whimpered, her voice hoarse and deep. "Are you achingly hard below the table as I ride your face and fingers?"

"As a fucking rock," he murmured, his lips still pressed to her.

"Touch yourself," she purred, "while I come on your face."

Beau groaned, grazed his teeth over her clit, and bit her subtly. As she arched again, Beau wrapped his other hand around his cock. Slowly but firmly, wanting to savour the taste and sight of her before him, he jerked himself towards completion.

Clara swore, her toes pointed, and her thighs clenched around the sides of his face. Beau hummed, his tongue flicking her clit while he pressed his mouth to her pussy and sucked gently. She clenched around his fingers, which still stroked her inner walls, and Clara came undone in a symphony of screams and shallow breaths.

She clasped his hair in a tight grip with one hand while the other cupped her breast and squeezed. Beau had to slow himself, else he would explode from watching.

Clara closed her fist more firmly around his hair and pulled, so Beau raised his head and an eyebrow.

"Your turn now," was all she said, in a voice like molten gold. Silently, he stood. As he stepped back, Clara slid off the table, her body pure seduction. He bit his lip to stifle what he was sure would sound like a whimper.

Perfection, wrapped up in skin like porcelain, hair like fire, eyes like the first hint of spring.

Her hands, soft as silk, wrapped around his cock, bringing such excruciating pleasure.

One hand gripped his length, stroked him, while the other cupped the back of his neck and pulled his face towards her. Clara's lips crashed into his in a wave of lust and desperation. One he mirrored as he licked and nipped at her bottom lip. She hummed into his mouth, but the noise turned to a breathy exhale as his hands clasped either side of her jaw, his thumbs pressed against her cheeks.

Then she pulled away and lessened her grip on his aching cock. "Lie down."

And he did.

In the middle of the kitchen floor.

The tiles were cold against his bare skin, and his wings twitched on contact. Then Clara was on all fours, hovering over him as Beau shuddered beneath her.

"Fuck," he drawled, as Clara sheathed him within her to the hilt. He dragged his hands along her legs, up her sides until they cupped her full breasts. Covering his hands with her own, Clara squeezed and rolled his palms over her peaked nipples. Another breathy sound escaped her, and Beau fondled her harder, pinching and slapping her skin. She revelled in it, slowly rocking her hips.

"Clara," he whispered. "Touch yourself."

She silently obeyed his command. Leaning back and propping one hand on his thigh for balance, she slid the other towards her still soaking pussy. What a glorious sight to behold. Beau could barely contain his growl of approval. Her wrist flicked as she traced circles over her swollen clit.

Beau grabbed the backs of her knees and squeezed tightly as he thrust upwards into her.

The motion caused her eyes to close, and a husky moan left her lips.

"Look at me," he said, and her eyes fluttered back open, clouded with desire and arousal.

As Beau sped up, Clara's moans and grunts of pleasure grew louder. Her head dropped back, and her movements became jerky and uncoordinated. Fuck, if she came on his cock again, he was going to explode.

Despite him so desperately wanting to fill her, to satisfy her until she couldn't breathe, he'd made his instructions clear. So Beau stilled.

Clara whipped her head up, the lust on her face now tainted with fury.

"I want to see the stars dancing in your eyes when you come on my cock," Beau said. "So, look. At. Me." He enunciated every word as his fingertips dug deeper into her damp flesh.

She growled at him, and Beau couldn't help his smirk. Though she kept those stunning green eyes locked on his.

Beau swore when Clara muttered she was close, bucking into her harder and faster. Her fingers moved in a frenzy at her clit, his name a plea on her tongue.

"Fuck, Clara," he grunted, as her climax tore through her.

Her cunt clenched around his throbbing cock, and she screamed his name as she came. Then she leant forward, pressed her hands to his shoulders and bounced on his dick.

"Yes, fuck, *yes*." Beau slapped her ass, and the sound echoed in the otherwise quiet room—well, save for their heaving breaths and moans. Beau strained to savour this divine torment. He was close, yet he never wanted this to end.

Soon he couldn't take it any longer.

"That's it, sweetheart. Just like that," he groaned out, barely able to form the words.

Clara let out a throaty moan and whispered, "Come inside me, please."

The sound of her begging unravelled him. Beau cursed and let go, his hands digging into her body as release barrelled through him. As he exploded inside the love of his life.

"Fuck," he bit out as the waves subsided, and Clara playfully nibbled at his neck.

She chuckled, and all he could do was return the gesture.

Fucking perfection.

CHAPTER TWENTY-EIGHT
CLARA

Two days after they arrived home, Beau left again. This time Clara woke to a note on her pillow scrawled in his messy handwriting, telling her he'd be back as soon as he could and that he loved her. Her hand flew to the feather-shaped charm dangling around her neck, and she smiled.

A few days later, Clara met the largest male she'd ever stumbled across. His face was a mixture of hard, sharp bone structure and round eyes that looked almost too big for his face.

She first laid eyes on him when he was standing by a table laden with refreshments and fruit slices, nodding at something Oren was saying. Oren looked average size next to the stranger, and his cheerful demeanour made the newcomer appear imposing and tough. Though when Clara introduced herself, his face beamed in the most welcoming smile and his handshake was far gentler than she expected. Clara learnt his name was Finch, and he hailed from the soil court, and once the words had spilled from his mouth, she noticed the slight muddy-green tinge to his hair and eyelashes.

As he sparred with her, Finch made a point of mirroring her and then correcting her, which Clara found incredibly helpful. Instead of simply telling her what she ought to be doing, he showed her and then positioned her properly, and by the end of their session, she was making fewer repeat mistakes.

Even though her body ached, it was a good pain. The kind that left her feeling satisfied and powerful. Pride bloomed in her, and she felt more confident in her physical ability than she had in a long while. However, all Clara now wanted was to collapse on her bed and ignore the world for several hours. When she arrived home, she made a beeline for her room to do exactly that.

Except the rush of air as she dropped onto the comforter rustled the envelopes and paper which sat on her nightstand, including the one letter she'd been avoiding, for reasons she couldn't name. The letter from her birth mother. Maja told her to read it after her birthday, so she'd waited. There was no time like the present, she supposed.

With a groan, Clara propped up onto her elbows and pulled the letter from the pile. The paper had turned a dirty yellow with age, and the creases were fragile as she unfolded it. She then proceeded to read it over and over—at least a dozen times—each time with more emotion flaring in her chest.

First, she felt something like sympathy for the woman who wrote of her daughter being born not breathing. Clara had no desire to have children soon, perhaps not for a hundred years, so she possessed no maternal feelings. However, she knew of a mother's love and how her emotions, her priority, and her world changed once she held a babe in her womb. Clara could only imagine the fear it would cause; finally, to hold the child she'd waited months to meet, only to find its lungs not working.

Then came dread at the confession of her power, which presented so early. Moments after her birth. Clara's mother wrote of how she had projected a vision into her mother's mind. Frustration swirled as she read that part in particular over and over–as she learnt of a new magic she possessed. One she would never master.

At the heartfelt words of remorse and guilt and sorrow, Clara couldn't help but feel empathy for her birth mother. She could practically feel the emotion seeping off the page. Even with no memory of the woman, a string tugged in her heart at reading how much her mother loved her.

More fear and dread bloomed at the reminder of the sacrifices made, and those still to come. Plus a strange sense of longing she hadn't expected as she read the words at the end of the letter.

Eternally waiting, beyond the moon and stars, and further than tomorrow's sun.

Felicity had been everything she'd ever needed in a mother or could ever want. Clara's heart was whole, and her life had been good. Though she couldn't deny that aside from the confusion the letter sparked, Clara might've liked to have met her biological mother. Perhaps the smallest fragment of grief glittered in her chest at the reminder she'd never get that chance.

Guilt filled her at wanting to meet her birth mother alongside sadness at having lost her before getting the chance. But had she really *lost* anything? She had a mother. A beautiful, kind, and loving mother who had opened her heart to a child she did not create, and Clara had always felt honoured. Was her odd sense of grief a betrayal of that?

Samara had told her to call when she was done, but gave no explanation of how to do so. Clara knew she should've asked, as she sat with her legs folded beneath her and cleared her throat, then spoke into the empty room.

"Samara? I feel foolish speaking to nobody. If you can hear me, please put me out of my misery quickly, I beg of you."

Clara shook her head and let out a frustrated, and somewhat embarrassed, sigh.

"I read the letter," she added. "If you'd be so kind, I would like to speak with Maja."

Clara waited a few painfully long seconds before she grumbled and stood. She placed the letter on her side table and spun, only to be met with one of the most beautiful smiles.

Isobel waved awkwardly, her soft smile widening as Clara beamed at her.

"Hello again," she said, tucking a stray lock of bright-pink hair behind her ear.

"Hi," Clara blurted. This woman somehow filled her chest with everything she needed to breathe, while simultaneously seizing all the air from her lungs. It was the most blissful pain.

“I see you got my card,” Isobel said, as she jerked her chin towards the bedside table where the birthday card she’d sent stood upright.

“I did,” Clara responded. It wasn’t a question, though Clara nodded eagerly. “It smells divine.”

“I’m glad you like it.” Isobel chuckled as she took a step closer. “It was a little bewitching that almost cost me a kidney.”

Before Clara could respond, Isobel held out her hand and Clara took it instinctively. She subconsciously rubbed the back of Isobel’s hand with her thumb a few times before she realised what she was doing and stopped.

Clara could’ve sworn Isobel stared at their clasped hands far longer than necessary, though she wasn’t complaining, as Clara was looking at Isobel in much the same way.

Isobel finally met her eyes and asked if Clara was ready. When Clara nodded, Isobel squeezed her hand, then placed her free thumb over her golden pendant.

In a blink, they were standing in a small, open-plan suite. A kitchenette was to her left, the dining table and two-seater settee to her right. Two doors were evenly spaced over the far wall, and Maja stood directly in front of her with a welcoming smile and open arms.

The nausea wasn’t so bad this time, though she still wasn’t entirely sure the bile burning her throat wouldn’t spill over. She sat when Maja gestured towards the table, taking slow sips of water once Isobel handed her a glass. The water rippled in her hand, though she couldn’t be sure whether it was her magic, or if her hands were subtly shaking.

“You read the letter,” Maja announced, and Clara nodded.

“Who were you to my birth mother?” Clara asked as she placed the tall glass on a coaster, sitting straighter in her chair.

Maja nodded. “We were childhood friends. We grew old together, had children at the same time. Your mother was my best friend.” She sighed and looked away for a moment, lost in her thoughts. “When she married your father, I was her only guest in attendance, as none of her family was pleased about her inter-court relationship, regardless of his standing. She asked me to watch over you, where I was able. To take care of you.”

“How did she die?” Clara asked as quietly and respectfully as she could.

“She killed herself,” Maja said. While her tone portrayed a neutrality, her eyes darted away, and her hands jittered in her lap. “After a fortnight of such powerful and violent visions, she’d had enough. She bled from her ears and nose with each one and screamed so loudly she couldn’t speak the next day.”

Isobel sat in the chair beside Clara, her leg bouncing under the table. She didn’t mind though, as the jangling of whatever jewellery she wore grounded Clara. Like a steady beat of soft background music, it was the perfect soundtrack to a conversation Clara didn’t wish to have but needed to hear, nonetheless.

“And what were the visions of?”

“You, mostly.” Maja sighed, looking back to Clara, sympathy filling her dark-brown eyes. “In varying degrees of danger. Of the end of the world, both for you, and because of you. The night before she died, she saw the prophecy. It merged into a vision of you as an infant—dead and limp in her arms. She knew it couldn't occur if she wasn't alive, so she came to me and told me everything."

"Were you there?" Clara asked gently. "When she . . ."

Maja nodded.

"Yes, and so was your father. He held one of her hands, while I held the other as she fell asleep for the last time. She'd taken a powerful paralytic tea and paired it with a sleep draught. The draught worked quickly, and she simply dozed off, then the paralytic stopped her heart and lungs. It was peaceful." Maja sighed, though it was a lighter sound this time, and a sad smile tilted her lips. "It was the most serene I'd seen her in a long time."

Clara offered her a small smile of her own, though it felt disingenuous. "What was the prophecy?"

"From what we could translate, it was not good. She received it in a very primal version of the Old Language.

"*When she takes on all, and many fall to one, ashes rise before the sun.*

Fear not when he breathes, instead as he lies, for when feathers fall, carnage shall rise.

Sisters will strike under darkened skies and lives will end alongside the night.

Presumed unable to fall, the daughters will break. Seized and unfeeling, blood rains in her wake.

Between the clouds, truth is concealed, her wrath a reflection and fear revealed.

In soaring leap, their world will end, as their severed descent shapes doom she sends."

"You memorised it?" Clara asked, more than a little impressed.

Maja gave a knowing look.

"Your mother repeated it to me once, and immediately I was overwhelmed by dread and despair. The feeling only got worse as we worked to translate it. *Memorise* suggests I held onto it by choice."

CHAPTER TWENTY-NINE

ISOBEL

As soon as the words of the prophecy left Maja's lips, Isobel felt doom and danger thicken the air in the room. Even though the conversation had shifted to more idle topics, the dread and heavy feeling from earlier had not lifted.

It was clear in the way that Clara picked at the skin along her nails discreetly under the table, or in how Maja's smile didn't reach her eyes.

Isobel had never been one to stay quiet for long, so as the conversation hit a lull, she stood and offered her hand to Clara. Warmth spread from their entwined fingers and soothed all the tension Isobel hadn't realised had built in her body. "Want a tour of your kingdom?"

"I don't think Elisabeth would agree." Clara shook her head, and a few wayward curls bounced over her face. "But show me anyway." Her rose-coloured lips curled into a playful smile, and Isobel's grew in response.

Maja waved goodbye and reminded them both she was only ever a call away. They left Maja's suite, hands still clasped, and Isobel swore her heartbeat sped and stopped all at once, like it couldn't decide whether to freeze the moment and savour it or take Clara and run so they might have a million more moments uninterrupted.

Isobel guided Clara out through one of the back doors, into the well-manicured gardens. In Isobel's opinion, they were boring, and Elisabeth didn't seem to have a creative bone in her body. The architecture of the palace was of the old style, with intricate cornices and architraves. High ceilings covered in now-faded murals and delicate, decorative mouldings, though to her credit, Elisabeth maintained the building well. Everything else was standardised, and every feature was far too similar to the one beside it to be labelled anything other than dull. Clara's gaze raked over the outdoor space and she made a quiet comment on how similar it was to King Urian's grounds.

They hastened through the insect enclosure, though Clara lingered in the farlannen aviary. They were truly magical creatures—part bird, part butterfly. A hundred wings, all various greens in hue, glimmered as they flittered around the room. Yet none quite as magical as Clara's eyes.

"They're near extinct," Isobel whispered as Clara stretched out her hand and watched, captivated, as the creatures circled her. "Folk often mistake them for pixies."

"I thought pixies were gold," Clara muttered. A farlannen landed on her palm and she became as still as Isobel had ever seen her.

Isobel shook her head. "Pixies are green, most commonly the shade of new grass just past the season's turn into spring. Farlannen wings have nearly as much magic as a pixie, so even though they aren't hunted intentionally, no one is ever disappointed when they're caught instead."

Once they left the aviary, Isobel gave Clara a basic tour of the palace, including the library, the ballroom, and throne room, despite the space not having been touched in years. By Elanist laws, Elisabeth couldn't rule, so the throne was now covered in dust and the heavy drapes were closed. As Isobel gestured down the short corridor that led to the kitchens, Clara grabbed her wrist, and they halted.

"Can I see them?" she asked, as hope danced in her eyes.

"Of course," Isobel replied, sliding her fingers through Clara's again as she maintained a neutral expression. Their hands had parted for Isobel to unlock the farlannen enclosure, but reunited, her chest held a flurry of emotion.

The kitchens took up much of this side of the palace and one wall was lined entirely with stovetops and ovens, cooling racks and heating lamps. To the left were three trough-sized porcelain sinks, all slightly marred in places, though Clara didn't seem to mind. She floated through the space, tugging Isobel with her as she ran her finger along the marks in the sinks, and over the marble veining in the benchtop. Every time she moved, her body bounced with excitement. A niggling feeling told Isobel if Clara ever wandered, this is where she would find her. Much like the roof was her sanctuary, the kitchens would be for Clara.

"There are no staff," Clara said. No accusation in her tone, but also no question.

“Your sister employs many,” Isobel responded. “Though she is also somewhat frugal with money. The chefs are only employed to work every other morning and prep the meals ahead of time. Ryland or someone else will then reheat the meals, and occasionally she’ll even do it herself.”

“Of course,” she muttered, rolling her eyes, and Isobel realised she didn’t want to discuss it further. Instead, she tugged Clara towards the back of the kitchens, to the expansive pantry Isobel had always admired.

Sure enough, Clara’s smile returned, and warmth bloomed in Isobel’s chest.

“What do you like to cook?” Isobel asked, as they wandered back through the kitchens and out into the hallway.

“I’m a baker at heart.” Clara spared a quick glance at Isobel as they walked. “But I’ll cook just about anything. My mother is a wonderful cook, excluding anything sweet.”

“Well, what is your favourite thing to bake?”

“I don’t think I have a favourite,” Clara said with a soft chuckle and another shrug.

“Mother, you make it awfully difficult to get to know you,” Isobel teased, a playful smirk spreading across her face, mirrored by Clara.

“What’s *your* favourite baked goods?” Clara raised her eyebrows.

“Anything lemon flavoured.”

Clara turned her nose up a fraction, and Isobel couldn’t help but burst into a laugh. When Clara joined her, it was like time stood still around them; all she could see or hear or feel was Clara. A cloud of divine bliss settled over them, and for a single moment, it felt like perfection.

“Not a fan?” Isobel raised a brow and gave Clara a pointed look.

“All I’ll say”—she grinned as her gaze dropped to Isobel’s lips and lingered for the longest second before returning to her eyes—“is you will never miss out on my account.”

“I’ll hold you to that,” Isobel whispered, close to Clara’s ear as they continued down the hall towards Isobel’s rooms.

A low, sultry laugh left Clara’s lips and brought goosebumps to Isobel’s skin.

“You can hold me to just about anything,” she whispered back. Isobel’s heart skipped a beat and sunk to the deepest part of her belly, burning with the most welcome heat.

After a few turns and a flight of stairs, they arrived outside Isobel’s door.

“I have a question,” Clara blurted out as Isobel reached for the door handle. “Poppy once told me that the stained-glass windows in Tirenas were inspired by the ones here, but I’m yet to see any. Where are they?”

Isobel sighed as she sensed her answer would disappoint Clara. “The stained glass in Tirenas was inspired by the ones in the Golden Kingdom. However, before the royals dispersed, there were a series of attacks. So when the decision was made to keep the palace and eventually the court hidden, many of them were destroyed. Over the years, others have degraded, and Elisabeth decided not to repair them. Instead, she opted for plain glass.

“There are a few remaining,” Isobel added. “One in Elisabeth’s quarters, and one in yours. There are also two in the grand hall at the entrance to the palace.”

"I have quarters here?" Clara's eyes widened as she spoke. It was such an innocent expression, so pure.

Isobel nodded. "Would you like to see them?"

"I'd rather see yours." The words flew from her mouth, and without missing a beat, Clara waggled her brows. Isobel chuckled softly and opened the door.

The space was quaint, but it was home. Her washroom and wardrobe were set to one side of the room, the double bed placed squarely in the middle, and her art station set up beneath the window on the far wall.

Clara's hand left Isobel's as she walked straight to the small table scattered with paint pots, brushes askew over newspapers and protruding from the small jar of water. A half-finished painting sat on the easel, so far only covered by strokes of emerald, forest green, murky brown, and powder blue. She'd intended to paint the sunrise and her view from the window showcased it so beautifully over the trees inland. The wooded area was now blooming, thanks to spring taking hold. The trees were lush with foliage and cast a rich green-and-gold hue with every new day. Even with only the barest skeleton of the painting complete, Clara stood with awe and reverence, lightly tracing her fingertip along the edge of the canvas.

Pride flourished and spread from Isobel's fingertips to her toes.

Clara turned and spotted the other paintings along the shelves, drawers, and on her nightstand, flitting through the room to observe each of them. She took her time, looking over each painting with care and an intense eye. Isobel had never felt so bared, so on show before. And she'd never welcomed vulnerability with such open arms. Somehow showing Clara the deepest part of her soul, a part of her she held so close to her heart, wasn't as daunting as she'd expected.

"They're beautiful," Clara breathed.

"Thank you."

Isobel moved lazily to the bed, resting atop it with her elbows propping her up. She watched as Clara took in her room and the few knick-knacks she'd collected over the years. She seemed so interested in everything on display, all the while Isobel was entirely entranced by her. Everything in this room made up who she was, yet nothing compared to Clara.

Clara made her way around the room, then returned to the paint table, turning to face Isobel, who hadn't taken her eyes off the beautiful woman before her. Light poured in through the window, outlining her in a celestial haze, a halo gifted by the sun for its brightest creature.

"So many colours," Clara mused, gesturing to the array of splatters and globs on the palette. "Which is your favourite?"

Without hesitation, her eyes locked on Clara's. "Green."

Clara's lips pressed together, in what Isobel could only assume was an attempt to hide her smile.

"And yours?"

She looked towards the table again before she answered, "Lilac, I think."

Isobel stored her answer away, like everything she learnt about Clara. Locked it securely in her mind, so she might never forget.

They spoke for what felt like hours, lying across Isobel's bed. Clara lay on her back, while Isobel rested on her side and never took her eyes from Clara. Their knees brushed, as did their calves or feet whenever one of them moved. Their hands were a hair's breadth away, so close Isobel could feel the warmth which emanated from Clara's fingertips. However, every time Isobel moved to place her hand in Clara's or get closer, Clara gave her the same interested but nervous glance, and so Isobel backed away.

Instead, she asked questions and got to know the woman beside her better. She learnt of her favourite things, family, work, and the life she had away from Isobel. Even sporadic comments of the winged male who currently held her attention. The one she'd been with in Breath, who'd felt the need to step between them to protect her.

Her chest flared red hot at the thought of some unimportant male stepping between them again. Isobel knew the searing pull was the tetherbond itself. It was a living, breathing force designed to bring her and Clara together. Its sole purpose was to unite the females destined by the stars to live out their days beside the other.

How could he ever understand such a thread? What made him so special? To be deemed necessary and to be held in such regard by the one who was *hers*?

Thinking of him only riled Isobel, and the prickling in her hands was the first sign. She clenched her fists and tried to distract herself, but a single look at Clara only reminded her those lips had been shared by another. Likely many, for she was a beauty like no other, and all unworthy.

Isobel didn't care about her past loves. This love, however, was currently in Clara's life. Jealousy was a fierce emotion, and one Isobel was entirely susceptible to experiencing.

The curtains rustled on a phantom breeze, and those stray curls danced over Clara's face. Before Clara could question her, Isobel stood and offered her hand to Clara once more.

"Can I show you something?"

A devilish smile crept over Clara's face. "Of course," she said, taking Isobel's hand and gesturing for her to lead the way.

CHAPTER THIRTY
CLARA

Clara followed Isobel down a small corridor and up an even narrower, winding staircase. Above her, the ceiling was peaked, and beside her, only candles lit the way.

Soon enough, they reached a landing and an arched wooden door, which Isobel opened. It swung out on to a small landing, which showed off the most stunning view of the Spirit Court. Clara swore that if she squinted, she might even see the border between Candor and Soil.

Beyond the landing, she saw that a narrow ledge connected the tower they currently stood within to another nearly twelve feet away. Instinctively, Clara's hand flew to the door frame, and her fingers dug into the stone. The soles of her feet tingled nervously.

Isobel smiled and squeezed the hand she was still holding. "I come out here rather frequently."

Clara's gaze flicked between Isobel's striking blue eyes and her petite feet moving in the wrong direction along a route towards certain death.

"Just don't look down." Her voice was soft and calm. "Look at me and give me your other hand."

Clara placed both hands, albeit hesitantly, in Isobel's, and all of a sudden she felt steadier. Confident enough to take small steps, Clara placed one foot in front of the other and followed Isobel out to the middle of the ledge.

"Sunrise, sunset, dawn, and dusk. Even in the middle of the day. There isn't ever a bad time to be up here."

"Except, perhaps, in a rainstorm," Clara muttered.

"Even then." Isobel chuckled, and the sound left Clara feeling as though she were floating. "The rain is beautiful. Sometimes, when it's thundering and pouring down, I like to come out here and watch from the clouds' perspective. It's loud but oh, is it worth it. To watch them light up and spread so forcefully across the sky. It's incredible."

Clara smiled as Isobel spoke. Warmth bloomed in her chest and spread to her fingertips. It did not help her already clammy palms or her fear of slipping from Isobel's grip, but it calmed her rapid heart.

"Would you like to sit?"

"If I sit, I will never stand again." Clara shook her head vehemently.

Isobel rubbed the back of Clara's hand with her thumb, in slow strokes that had Clara's heartbeat skipping and skittish. An unfamiliar, although not unpleasant, fire burned in her chest. Almost like an internal tug-of-war, but she had no idea who pulled at each end of the rope. It flared, sending heat throughout her whole body until she felt dizzy, in the fun, giddy kind of way.

Isobel stared at her with such adoration and intensity it was as if she could see the rope itself, or perhaps Isobel was on one end of it. But then who was on the other?

Was it Beau? Or Clara herself? Maybe someone else entirely. Considering it turned the welcome heat to a chaffing burn, slicing at her heart.

If Isobel truly was tugging at this imaginary rope and drawing her in, what were her reasons? There was no malevolence or fear surrounding the pull, only a need to be closer, to be wrapped up together.

Isobel stepped forward.

Is this what a tetherbond felt like? The bond itself, which pulled two beings together, declared by the stars and the universe to be one. Was this hers? If so, did Isobel know?

And where did that leave Beau?

Clara's eyes dropped to Isobel's soft pink lips, which had parted slightly. She dragged her teeth along her own, confused by so many things, but absolutely certain that with Isobel's lips on hers she'd be content.

Just like every time before, Clara hesitated. Sucking in a sharp breath, she froze.

Though she wanted to kiss Isobel, for their souls to join as the stars intended, she couldn't.

Clara was a woman of her word; she was honourable and would not partake in infidelity. Clara was spoken for and was happy with Beau.

There was no doubt in her mind that Clara would be happy with Isobel, but not if their relationship began with secrecy and lies and hurt.

Thankfully, an alarm sounded as Clara pulled away. She would explain herself later.

Confusion and concern flooded Isobel's face. "We need to go."

Clara nodded, holding onto Isobel's hands as she guided her towards the door. Once they were inside, they both flew down the stairs.

Samara burst from a nearby room and the three of them raced through hallways and down a second flight of stairs. The alarm continued to blare, and a prickle along the back of Clara's neck suggested this was not normal.

They ended up in what Clara assumed to be the entrance hall, noting the two stained-glass windows on a far wall that Isobel had mentioned earlier.

Elisabeth rounded a corner, along with two females Clara didn't recognise. "I was not aware you were here."

"Now you are," Clara spat back at her sister's rude tone. "What's the alarm for?"

"Intruders." One of the small females spoke up, fear coating her tone and filling her dark-brown eyes. Her hair was a deep red, rich as soil or wine, and fell to the waistband of her pants in many braids. Her ochre skin was decorated in vibrant-coloured jewels, as were her braids.

The other stood slightly taller, though neither of them reached past Clara's collarbone. Her hair was a full crown of tight coils, the shade of honey. Their clothes were simple and plain, but exuded comfort.

"We set the alarms decades ago," the first female continued. "But haven't needed them since."

“Have we located the intruder?” Elisabeth asked, her tone far snappier than Clara appreciated. Though she understood the severity of the situation, so held her tongue.

The women shook their heads in unison.

“They haven’t arrived yet. The alarm sounds when someone unwanted intends to land on the grounds. I’d expect them to land any—”

Before she could finish speaking, a tall woman materialised in front of them. Clad in thick black leather, and tight black pants, the fabric somehow looked stiff but moulded to her legs. Her eyes darted around the room, jet black with no distinguishable irises or pupils.

A shiver raked down Clara’s spine.

“Who are you?” Elisabeth demanded.

“I think the better question,” the stranger rasped, “is *what* am I?” She winked and tossed her shoulder-length hair to the side, setting her eyes on Clara.

Isobel stepped closer to Clara, while Samara moved forward.

“Fear not,” the woman said with a sickly sweet smile, which something told Clara was sincere. “I’m not here for any of you today.”

Her eyes lingered on Isobel for far too long, and now Clara stepped towards her.

“Then what are you here for?” Clara asked.

“And how did you find us?” Elisabeth demanded. “We’ve been hidden for decades. No one should’ve been able to locate us.”

The stranger sighed, already seemingly uninterested in Elisabeth or their conversation.

"My name is Ryn." She folded her arms as she looked down at Elisabeth. "I go by many names in many worlds. My kin traverse the worlds, landing in many places for many reasons. You do not have the clearance to know more." She turned to Clara, and wickedness gleamed in her depthless eyes. "You, however, I will speak with."

Isobel and Samara reached out again, each grabbing one of Clara's arms. Elisabeth immediately fired off a disapproving sound.

Ryn only shrugged. "You do not need to speak with me, Clara. I am not here to harm any of you. I'll simply be on my way, and you can all go back to your day."

"Why do you wish to speak to me?" Clara asked, not moving from her place between Isobel and Samara, yet eager to know more.

"Because I think we can help one another," Ryn replied. "It is up to you."

"She will speak with you." Elisabeth gestured for Clara to follow the woman, who now walked towards the doors. Clara gave her sister an incredulous stare.

"It is not up to you, Elisabeth."

Ryn turned to narrow her eyes and bare her teeth at Elisabeth, who balked but stayed quiet.

Clara patted Isobel's hand and shimmied from the females' grips. She followed Ryn outside and closed the heavy door behind her.

Ryn handed Clara a picture drawn in such vivid colours it couldn't have been from her world. The edges were torn along one side and one of the corners was folded. It depicted a man with an arrogant smirk and jewels hanging from every surface. His robes were lined with fur and he had long blonde hair.

"He goes by many names, so I will not bore you with the list, but have you seen him during your travels?"

Clara shook her head.

"If you come across him, contact your seer friend—Ora. Let her know and she will pass the information on." Ryn took the image back and shoved it into her back pocket.

"Why was I the only one allowed to know of this?" Clara asked.

"Because I find it amusing to watch those who think they're entitled to everything be told there's something they cannot have."

"You simply wished to watch Elisabeth squirm?"

"Do you not?" Ryn raised an eyebrow and chuckled.

As she turned to leave, Clara grabbed her wrist.

"Bold," Ryn murmured, with a smirk and sparkle in her eyes.

"You said we could help each other." Clara let go of Ryn's arm and folded hers over her chest. "So far, you've only spoken of your own needs."

"Indeed," she said. "It may not help you much, in truth, but only you can alter your fate. You hold it in your hands, and you decide when to let go." She leant in close before she whispered in Clara's ear, "As it currently stands, they're all going to die."

CHAPTER THIRTY-ONE
BEAU

Beau knocked three times on the old wooden door. After a few seconds of silence, shuffling sounded from inside, followed by a thud and a string of curses. Beau chuckled and shook his head, then cleared his face of his amusement before the door swung open.

"Oh," his mother cried. "I'm so glad you're here!"

"Hello, Mum."

She welcomed Beau inside and embraced him before ushering him through the hall towards the living space. The house was as empty as it had been the last time he'd visited. It'd been empty for a while. The plain white walls adorned with nothing, old floorboards with no rugs. There was a small table accompanied by only two chairs in the middle of the dining room, and a single armchair was positioned across from the fireplace.

He sat at the table as his mother put the kettle on and pulled biscuits from the pantry.

"What brings you here?" she asked, as she sat across from him.

Beau sighed, knowing the topic would be unpleasant to broach.

"Spit it out, son." His mother's tone was playful, as was her facial expression, though Beau didn't miss the glint of apprehension in her hazel eyes.

Brielle had the same eyes, round and so full of hope. Perhaps it should've been the first clue she wouldn't survive the trial.

"How many lives does a Phoenix have?"

Her eyebrows shot up, and her hands twitched. Almost as if she wanted to slap the thought from his mind or cover her mouth from the shock of him bringing the conversation up at all.

But he had to know.

"Mostly," she mumbled, her words almost skittish, "they are infinite."

"Can I share the lives with another? Is there a way to offer them to someone else?"

"Why would you ask such a thing, Beau? Why would you want to give yours up?" Nina's lips quivered slightly before she pressed them together. As the kettle whistled, she stood abruptly, all but stomping to the counter.

"I'm sorry, Mum. I don't mean to upset you."

"What did you think was going to happen when you started asking about giving away your lives?" she demanded.

Beau took a deep breath.

"Not all of them," he assured her. "I merely wanted to know if it was possible. And where the immortality and rebirth come from."

Nina sighed, then shook her head and placed it in her hand.

"The magic is in your wings. Theoretically, you could pluck up to half of your feathers to give away and they would regrow with your rebirth. But if they are severed, you will not return." She paused, her voice breaking. "Without your wings intact and attached to your body, your death will be permanent."

Beau nodded and stayed silent as his mother filled two cups with tea and hot water. He'd never had the heart to tell her herbal tea made his stomach turn, instead thanking her and slowly sipping.

"Why?" she asked, her voice barely a whisper. "Why bring up such a topic . . . after everything?"

After everything.

She referred to Beau's father, Rillian, and how he had died. He'd been a bounty hunter for King Urian, a role which extended to Beau after Rillian's death, where the likelihood of death was unsurprisingly high. Though, as a Phoenix, it should've been temporary and was one of the reasons King Urian had employed Beau's family for generations.

Two letters had simply arrived at their house one day, one for his mother, and another for Beau. The former advised Nina of her husband's death, and the latter offered Beau the newly available position of bounty hunter on the king's payroll.

Knowing he would be gone some months, Rillian had Nina promise to carry out Brielle's Phoenix trial when she became of age. Once he might've loved Beau's mother, but all Beau ever knew of his father was a careless, manipulative male.

Less than four weeks after his departure, the letter arrived, and a fortnight after that, Brielle's trial had been scheduled.

Beau knew, deep in his gut, that Brielle did not possess the Phoenix gene. Her eyes were the rich hazel of their mother's, with not a trace of the glowing amber of a Phoenix. Her ears held the slightest peak, and while not enough for the fae to consider her one of them, it was enough that Beau—who had rounded ears—could see the difference. His mother knew it, too, but she'd made her husband a promise.

Brielle hadn't survived.

"I wouldn't bring it up if it wasn't important." Beau tried to calm his mother.

She huffed, but otherwise didn't respond.

"If I pluck a feather and gift it, how does it turn into an extra life?" Beau felt stupid as he asked the question. He hardly even knew how to phrase it, and it sounded as foolish as he felt.

His mother's eyes softened. "The magic is within your wings. The extra life cannot be granted if the magic does not also run through their veins. You'd somehow have to push it into their bloodstream, but without destroying the feather. If it burns, it will simply cease to exist." She shrugged, the movement forced. "You could melt it, but it would have to be done incredibly carefully."

Beau thanked her, and they returned to sipping grass-flavoured tea in silence. He contemplated telling her of King Urian's death but was uncertain how she'd react. So he opted to stay quiet—he'd upset her enough today.

Once she was finished, Beau's mother collected the teacups and walked through the kitchen, placing them in the sink. She gave him a knowing look as he feigned disappointment. A mother always knew, even something as trivial as him not liking her tea—at least not enough to finish it. As she emptied what was left in Beau's cup, she gestured towards an opened gift box, which sat atop the bench.

"Thank you," she said. "What happened this time?"

Beau hadn't originally told his mother that the constellations had been painted for the worst night of his year. Not until she finally asked him what he drew inspiration from. He'd laughed at first, that she thought he'd painted them himself.

By that point, Nina had somewhat recovered, and was no longer a shell of an individual, showing signs of life. She laughed again, albeit rarely, and started cooking and cleaning. Though she wasn't as vibrant as she once was, Beau figured losing a husband and child would change her. All he wished was that he could take some of the burden from her. As useless as her husband was, Rillian was well loved. Undeserving, but incredibly well loved.

So when his mother had asked, with the faintest glimmer of light in her eyes, Beau told her. She'd cried and hugged him, then truly held him for the first time in years. A tear or two might've slipped free of his own eyes that night.

"I met someone." He answered his mother's question succinctly. "Stars, she's ruined my life." Beau shook his head, but his mother smirked and waited for him to continue.

"She left and ran off with another male. But I didn't know then what I do now. Poor choices were made, and that male is now dead."

"Beau!" his mother scolded. "Did you murder him for entertaining some girl?" Her hands found her hips as her brows drew together.

"No," Beau grumbled, then sighed. "That isn't the point, anyway. That night, she left with him, and through my actions, he died. I do not have fond memories of that time."

Instead of delving further into a night filled with regret, his mother asked, "What's her name?"

"Clara." Beau let her name roll off his tongue, and the sound soothed his unsettled heart.

His mother gave him a knowing look as she rounded the bench and walked to him, patting his face gently. "Did she come back?"

Beau nodded, a smile easing across his face. "She's the reason I'm here. I've come to ask for your mother's engagement ring."

A few days later, Beau knocked on another woman's door, but this time it felt like he'd come home. It wasn't the house; rather, it was the woman who occupied his every dream and waking thought, and every heartbeat in between.

Unfortunately, it was Evian who pulled open the door and informed him Clara wasn't home. He chuckled at Beau's disappointment and clapped him on the shoulder, retreating into the house. Beau followed silently, acknowledging Felicity with a smile.

He continued to Clara's room and dumped his bag on the floor, pulling out the daemdrana scale from an inside pocket of his jacket. Gently, he placed it on her nightstand and wandered back towards the kitchen.

"How long do you expect you'll stay with us, Beau?" Felicity asked, handing him a glass of water. She was an observant and eager hostess, though Beau wondered if he'd outstayed his welcome.

"Truthfully," he said, "I'm not sure."

"It's no bother, dear." Felicity smiled politely when Beau looked back up at her. "I'm yet to teach you how to cook anything, for starters, and Clara mentioned the meal didn't go quite as planned for her birthday. Also, I wanted to let you know the front door is usually unlocked, so you're welcome to let yourself in."

An unfamiliar emotion unfurled in his chest, and Beau smiled at the sweet woman.

"If you spend all your time waiting for Evian to open the door, you'll spend near an eternity outside."

"I appreciate your hospitality, Mrs Afron."

"My daughter indeed swoons for you, Mr Hawthorne. My only request is you keep her safe and happy."

"That is my only goal."

Felicity squeezed Beau's upper arms. Her approval and welcome left a warmth in Beau, which spread from where her hands pressed his biceps throughout his body.

More like home, indeed.

For the better part of an hour, Beau sprawled over the couch reading a newspaper. Though *reading* was a bit of a stretch, as he had been unable to focus and had attempted the same paragraph more times than he cared to admit. As he finally groaned and tossed the paper to the side, he heard the front door open and sprung to his feet.

In only a few strides, he met her in the hallway, beaming at seeing her again.

However, the Clara who stood before him was covered in a dozen bruises, her hair a mess, and all her weight balanced on one foot. Though her blood-smeared face lit up when she saw him, her mischievous grin spreading from ear to ear. Blood stained her teeth and leaked from a split in her lip. She was beautiful, but gruesome.

"What the fuck happened to you?" he growled, furious at seeing her in such a condition. He'd ensure whoever brought pain upon her was met with a fate far worse. For this to happen after he'd promised her mother he'd keep her safe? Guilt niggled at him and formed a heavy lump in his throat. Did this happen because he wasn't here?

"You should see the other guy," she said, far too cheerily. "I got him pretty good by the end." Something like pride glistened in her eyes.

"A male did this?" Beau's voice dropped even lower.

"Yes, Beau." Clara rolled her eyes. "I was training. Now move. I need a hot bath and a cold drink." She shooed him, and her fingertips brushed along his chest.

A furious calm washed over him, though he relaxed his voice enough that it sounded half pleasant as he asked, "Who were you training with today?" Then he planted a kiss on her temple as she bounced past him towards the kitchen.

"The new guy," she called over her shoulder. "His name is Finch. He's good."

Beau muttered a barely coherent response, then stalked from the house. Behind him, he heard Clara shout, but the sound was dulled by the growing space between them. His brain shut off as Beau canvassed the town, not knowing where he was going or who he was looking for. Then he heard Keyne's familiar voice call to Finch, and Beau's vision turned a much more vivid shade of red.

In a violent haze, he wrapped a hand around the male's biceps and dragged him towards Clara's house. The male questioned and complained the entire walk, but Beau ignored him.

"Clara!" Beau shouted from the front yard, finally letting go of the brute's arm.

She burst from the house, securing the tie of a bathrobe. Her hair was wet and dark, stuck to her porcelain face. The contrast only accentuated the beautiful green of her eyes as they widened at the sight.

For a second, the haze lifted, and all he wanted was to rid her of the robe. Then he noted the still raw scrapes on her knees and a large bruise on her thigh.

"Is this him?" Beau ground out. "Is this Finch?"

Clara scoffed and flailed her arm towards the male.

"Yes. Could you not tell from the bloodied lip and the half-missing ear?"

Not hearing anything after her first word, Beau swung at the brute. He punched him so hard the taller male stumbled backwards and pain flared in Beau's wrist. Finch fell to the ground, and in the next instant, Beau was straddled atop him with a knife poised at his throat.

"Beau, what the fuck?"

His name on her tongue brought the vaguest sense of rationality back, and he lowered the blade. Slightly.

"You think it acceptable to beat a female to the extent you did to her?" he growled out. "To touch her *at all?!*"

The male said nothing. He stayed perfectly still, only barely narrowing his eyes. So he wasn't a complete idiot, then.

Clara placed her small hands on Beau's shoulders and attempted to pull him off. After she had finally given up on yanking at him, she did not remove her hands. Beau was glad, as she grounded him. It gave him space to actually listen to her and finally register what she'd said before.

Half-missing ear.

A smirk spread over Beau's face.

"First of all, he was *helping* me. Evian goes too easy and I learn nothing. And you refuse to tangle with me if we aren't between the sheets, so all I ever learn is new ways to get you undressed. Not to mention you've hardly been here of late. Now get off the poor sod—he's had enough for today."

"You touch her again," Beau said, his voice less lethal than before, though not by much, and his blade still pressed to the male's throat, "and I'll cut off the rest of your ear, then I'll start cutting off other body parts."

Finch scoffed and finally spoke. "I will not take orders from you. If she asks me for help, I will gladly give it how I see fit. You do not frighten me with your blades. She bit my fucking ear off. *That* frightens me."

Pride warmed Beau's chest, and his smirk grew. He stood, then offered a hand to Finch. The male took it and once he was standing, he dusted himself off.

"You bit him?" Beau asked, honestly a little in awe.

Clara grinned wickedly at him, the sun catching the glint in her eye and magnifying it. Now he definitely wanted to remove the robe. Violence looked good on her.

Beau's cock twitched at the devilish, murderous excitement on her face.

He slung his arm around her shoulders and tugged her towards him. Pressing a kiss to her temple, he whispered, "That's my girl."

Clara beamed, then turned to the other male. "Go home, Finch. I'll see you tomorrow."

Finch nodded, and after a wave goodbye, he wandered off. Once he rounded a corner, Clara stood on tiptoes to whisper in Beau's ear.

"I won't lie, I'm a little turned on right now."

Beau spun quickly to face her, the movement causing her to stumble. Then he braced both hands on her waist and pressed his forehead to hers. His lips grazed over hers and he groaned. "Then for the love of gods, woman, lose the fucking robe."

Clara chuckled. It was such a sweet sound, and far too pure for the violence she was capable of, yet it fit her perfectly. "I thought you didn't believe in the gods."

Beau kissed her softly at first, then pressed harder against her lips. Like she was everything he needed to survive.

"I don't," he said, mouth still tight to hers. "But I believe in you. Let me worship you like one anyway."

CHAPTER THIRTY-TWO
BEAU

Clara grabbed the sides of Beau's face and crashed her lips to his. The taste of her was intoxicating. The world around him felt as though it stopped spinning and the only thing keeping him upright was her.

He ran his hands greedily down her sides, along her thighs, and cupped her ass. Lifting her up, he pressed her body as close to his as possible without him being physically inside of her. He moaned into her mouth, and she melted into him, which only deepened his need for her.

Without breaking their connection, he moved eagerly towards the house, not caring who might be in the common space. He strode down the hall to her room, as he knew the route without having to think or see, though he vaguely heard a female's gasp followed by tutting. Felicity would surely scold them later, but for now, he was too wrapped up in Clara to care.

She ran her fingers through his hair, desperately clinging to the fistfuls at his nape, the sensation sending shivers down his spine.

Clara gasped as Beau dropped her to the bed, and she propped herself up on her elbows, laid out before him like the goddess she was.

Her bathrobe had fallen open and her full breasts were on display, her nipples peaked and her skin subtly flushed. Clara's luscious ruby curls were draped over her fair skin, but her most enticing curves were wrapped in gold.

Fuck, she was stunning.

Beau greedily drank in the sight of her before he stalked to the door and flicked the lock. Clara giggled from the bed, rolling the sound into a deep moan.

Beau bit back a moan of his own, especially once he turned to see she now sat with her legs spread and her palms fondling her breasts. Her robe lay loose and discarded around her thighs. Fuck, if she wasn't the most divine creature he'd ever laid eyes upon.

His breath rasped out of him as he leant over Clara, her beautiful green eyes trailing his body. Beau took her wrists with one hand, raising them above her head, as he used his other hand to push her backwards into the mattress. The movement drew another gasp from her. Beau's cock twitched, rock hard and begging to be let free of the confines of his pants and sheathed to the hilt inside her.

As he forced her hands further into the mattress, Clara arched her back and pressed her naked body into his. He felt entirely too clothed.

Beau groaned as he inhaled the arousing scent of her, then from her jaw, down her neck and collarbone, Beau trailed firm kisses along her skin. Down her chest, to between the breasts he now cupped, having raked his hands down her body like the obsessed male he was. He pressed his fingers into her skin as he continued to drag them down her sides, along her hips, and down her thighs. Until Beau reached her knees, where he hooked his arms around her legs. When he looked up, he found her eyes already locked on him. Beau pulled Clara towards him, and the squeal she gave in response was glorious.

As quickly as he'd ever managed, Beau unbuttoned and removed his pants, his aching cock springing free, and it enticed another low approving moan from Clara. Beau threw his head back and closed his eyes, for a second cursing the torturous woman. It was difficult enough not to slam into her and fuck her, let alone when she made noises like that at the sight of his cock. *Fuck.*

He looked down at her, finding her still watching him, her gaze darting from his eyes to his dripping cockhead. Desire settled around her in a haze, filling those pretty eyes with lust. Beau smirked as he wrapped a hand around his erection, slowly stroking himself, while not breaking their stare. Closing the small gap between them, Beau dragged his aching cock along her opening until he was covered with her wetness.

Clara moaned, her delicate lashes fluttering, but she still maintained eye contact.

"Such a good girl," Beau crooned. "Remembering and obeying." Beau's smirk grew, as did the needy gasps escaping Clara's parted lips.

Her eyebrows drew together in a silent plea that Beau was all too willing to oblige.

Gently at first, Beau nudged his tip into her glistening cunt.

Then he fed her a little more.

Again and again.

She snaked her hand down her body, stopping her fingers between her legs, just above her perfect pussy. The heel of her palm floated over her clit, while her soft fingers stretched out and rubbed along his shaft as he thrust into her. Little by little, her whimpers grew, her legs wrapped around the backs of his thighs, and she wrapped her free hand around his forearm, her nails digging into his skin.

"Please," she whimpered.

The sound of her pleas, and the sight of her face twisted by pleasure and need, almost undid him. Beau groaned and leant over her, pressing one of his hands to her throat, his thumb stroking her chin and tugging at her bottom lip.

"Do you like it when I call you a good girl, Clara?" he growled out, his lips brushing her ear as he finally buried himself fully inside her. "Or—" Another deep, hard thrust. "Would you prefer—" And another. "I call you the perfect little slut that you are?"

Clara moaned so wantonly, so seductively, that Beau had to pause so he wouldn't blow his load then and there.

This stars-damned woman, this divine woman who rivalled the fucking gods. She ruined him, yet she was the only thing which kept him whole. She was the reason his heart beat, and most certainly the reason his cock hardened. He was already getting close to spilling inside of her tight, warm cunt. *Fuck.*

Beau growled in her ear, "My perfect, filthy whore."

"Yes, sir," she whined. "*Yes . . .*"

"*Fuck.*"

He pulled out with another growl, but before Clara could protest, Beau had flipped her onto her front, her round ass up and her pretty little face pressed into the sheets. He groaned, a husky sound which led Clara to arch her back further and shuffle towards him. Beau slapped her ass, one hand on each cheek, and the sound echoed slightly in the otherwise quiet room. He grabbed her plump globes, spreading her and marvelling at the sight.

Dropping to one knee beside the bed, Beau yanked her hips towards him and pressed his face to her slick pussy. Starting with his tongue flat over her swollen clit, he dragged it along and between her lips before dipping his tongue inside her.

Fuck, she tasted incredible. Sweet and addictive. Like pure bliss.

As he lapped and licked and devoured her, Beau fisted his cock slowly. He would please her, and only when she was entirely satisfied would he find his own release. Until then, he edged himself, rumbling out groans of satisfaction against her cunt. Every time he did so, Clara moaned a little louder, rolled her hips over his face, and tugged at the sheets more aggressively.

With another slap, Beau pulled away and asked, "May I?" as he traced his finger along her asshole.

"Please . . ." she repeated with a sultry moan, pushing her ass closer to him.

Beau chuckled, deep and low, before he spread Clara's cheeks wide and spat. With his middle finger, he traced circles around her now wet hole, then he pumped his finger in her ass, keeping in time with his tongue, which darted in and out of her cunt. Then he increased to two, then added one to her pussy as well. Beau flicked his tongue over her clit, curling his fingers inside her.

Clara moaned and whimpered, her hands raking the mattress. Beau's cock twitched and pulsed, stimulated simply from the sounds she made, and from her taste. Her whimpers turned to pleas and curses, her toes curling by his sides.

"You're going to make me come," she whispered, barely able to get the words out. Beau growled against her clit, maintaining his pace with his fingers. Clara drew in a ragged breath, then screamed Beau's name as she came on his face.

If his other hand was still wrapped around his bulging cock, he'd have exploded as well. The sound of his name, leaving her lips in a scream amongst sobs and curses, was a symphony Beau would never tire of hearing.

Only when her hand reached around to physically tap out did Beau pull away.

Fuck, he was so close.

He slapped her ass again, and grabbed a fistful of her flesh, leaving her fair skin bright red. She mewled under his hand, then arched and spun, and slunk off the bed.

With Clara on her knees before him, Beau knew it would only be a matter of seconds before he exploded. Clara smirked, her face flushed and glistening, her eyes filled with pleasure and contentment. She reached up, taking his throbbing cock in one hand and cupping his balls with the other.

"Fuck, Clara."

Beau's head fell back, his body sizzling with ecstasy. He held onto his release for as long as he could, wanting to savour the feel of her soft, warm hand pumping his cock. Though he never wanted to leave this torment-filled bliss of being so close to the edge it was painful.

"Come for me, Beau," she finally purred. Beau swore again. "Come all over me, please."

Fuck, the sound of her begging was all he could take. Beau grunted and opened his eyes to find Clara staring up at him.

"My face, my tits—"

"*Fuck*, Clara!"

Beau growled as his release barrelled through him, and he indeed exploded all over Clara. She opened her mouth like the good little slut she was, pressing her breasts upwards. He ground out another curse, revelling in the sight of her kneeling before him, painted in ropes of his cum.

She was an absolute fucking vision, and one Beau never wanted to forget.

CHAPTER THIRTY-THREE
ISOBEL

Somehow, the halls felt colder once Clara had left. More sterile and uninviting. She'd hardly even spent time at the palace, yet Isobel couldn't help but feel like something was missing now that she'd gone.

Isobel stopped outside the grand double doors which led to Elisabeth's bedroom suite. She took a deep, steadying breath, entirely uninterested in being spoken down to today, then knocked.

Elisabeth called out for her to enter, and Isobel swung the door inwards. She dipped her head in acknowledgement as she entered, but Elisabeth did not greet her in return. Her eyes stayed glued to the map of Elanist, which was spread over a small table in the centre of the room, its corners hanging off the sides.

"I'm afraid I have no update on the wolves, ma'am." Isobel averted her gaze, knowing the lack of progress would displease Elisabeth. "No one has been available to scout the secondary location in—"

With a hasty wave of her hand, Elisabeth cut her off.

"That can wait. Era and Tindal are missing."

Isobel's face scrunched as she tried to recall the last time she'd seen the two witches. Both were as gentle as an autumnal morning breeze, kind as the first splatter of rain after a week's worth of humid weather.

"Since when?" Isobel moved towards Elisabeth, peering around her hunched form to view the aged map.

"Two days ago," Elisabeth said with a sigh. "They went into Soil two mornings past on a shopping trip and no one has heard from them since."

"Where were they last seen?"

"Here. Only the two of them ventured out using the pendants." Elisabeth let out another frustrated sigh, perhaps now laced with a hint of fear.

"Has anyone questioned the Soil locals?"

Elisabeth only shook her head.

"What do you need from me?" Isobel asked solemnly.

"Go to the Earth Court and interrogate every fae you come across. Tindal is hard to miss and Era, bless her heart, frightens most folk. I want them found and brought home."

The urgency in Elisabeth's voice gave away just how much she cared for the witches. It was sometimes hard to remember that beneath her cruel tone and dismissive glances, Elisabeth's heart was soft at its core. That she *felt* something.

She'd been caring for the witches since long before Isobel arrived at the palace, the halls bustling with the short, manic creatures. Their smiles were contagious, only ever spreading warmth, peace, and encouragement.

From what Isobel knew, they'd originally come to Elisabeth searching for asylum. Some threat from their world was enough that they crossed the portal into Helenica, into the Spirit Court, which was already misted and concealed. Elisabeth offered them sanctuary and jobs, though Isobel still wasn't entirely sure what their work entailed.

Aside from the pendants for travel and a positive attitude, she didn't know exactly what they brought to the table. But what she knew was Elisabeth was frazzled. And *that* in itself was frightening.

"When do I leave?"

"Now."

The soil court was ripe with the smell of the outdoors, of harvest. With spring well underway, blooms of fragrance wafted from the damp grass, as freshly opened flowers stretched as far as Isobel could see, and the trees now appeared full of life and leaves. Colour burst all around her.

Isobel had only visited the home of the Earth fae once before, so when she arrived this time, she landed in the same open field. As she made her way to the town centre, she noted the lack of cobblestone roads or harsh pavements, and instead, lush green grass and soft dirt spread beneath her boots. The folk she passed waved and smiled. None wore shoes, even the vendors with food carts, the grocers with storefronts, and those herding and carting animals by wagons. She couldn't help the grin that spread across her face as Isobel remembered Clara's distaste for footwear.

Within a few seconds of entering the first grocer, Isobel was approached by a burly man with a wiry beard and moustache, eyebrows like caterpillars, and the widest smile a stranger had ever offered her. He clasped his hands before his round belly and asked if she needed help.

She explained she was looking for lost friends and gave a description of Tindal and Era. The man's smile faltered as he shook his head, telling her he'd not seen anyone who fit their descriptions.

The second vendor was the same, as were the third and fourth and fifth. Finally, at the sixth vendor, a short, skinny boy who carried crates of fruit and vegetables, recognised them.

"They were nice enough, but I'm afraid I couldn't look away from the one with the creepy eyes." He shuddered. "I wanted to, but I couldn't."

He explained they had left the store empty-handed and almost seemed to float towards the stall across the street, which was filled with herbs and dried flowers. Isobel thanked him and followed their path.

The woman she spoke to next was about as hopelessly romantic as they came, and she felt bad for trying to steer the conversation straight.

"Oh yes, I remember them," she said, nodding vehemently. "The only other patrons I had that morning were an elderly couple, still as wrapped up in each other as the moment they met. He held her hand, and with his other, he steered her around the vase collection, stroking her back the whole time." The woman clutched at her chest, a faraway look in her eyes. "She stared at him with so much love and adoration, oh it was so sweet!"

"Did the females purchase anything from you?" Isobel asked, gently redirecting the conversation.

"No," she said, with a confused pout. "As I was ringing up the couple— Oh! you should've seen the elegant bouquet they bought!"

"The women, please." Isobel offered a pleading smile.

"Of course. They asked for an ingredient I hadn't yet restocked, so I went into the storeroom downstairs to retrieve it. When I came back up, they had disappeared." The woman shrugged.

"What was the ingredient?" Maybe the answer would provide some insight. Hopefully.

"Sunflower seeds."

It was possibly the furthest thing from *insightful.* Sunflower seeds were one of the most frequently purchased ingredients by witches. They used it in everything from tea to snacks, fragrances, and healing tonics. Every time one of them went to the markets, they'd return with a minimum of one sack half Isobel's size, if not more.

"Have you seen them since?"

The woman shook her head, then apologised. Isobel politely excused herself and left the woman's shop. A small goat bleated in greeting as it raced past Isobel, and she chuckled softly. Her laughter quickly faded as both neighbouring stores denied having seen Era or Tindal.

After hours of scouring the town hub, the surrounding streets, and clusters of homes, Isobel still had no information to show for her efforts. It was as if they'd truly vanished. She'd asked dozens of patrons—whoever would stop to speak with her instead of apologising for being busy and continuing on their way.

Have you seen these females?

Last seen with satchel bags, wearing boots and corsets. This one wore pants, while the other wore frilled skirts and a piece of fabric hardly enough to classify as a shirt.

She recounted what Elisabeth had told her they'd been last seen wearing. How their hair was done. The milky, depthless eyes Era stared into souls with. Tindal's beacon of hair, and the distinctive clinking and clattering jewellery. Which one was taller, who would've been more likely to speak, how they carried themselves and spread light with every step. She asked about suspicious activity in the village, if anyone had noticed anything out of the ordinary around the time they'd been in town.

Where had they intended to go?

By the time the sun glared violently into her back, and her stomach ached with emptiness, Isobel conceded that the answers she sought would not be found here. Uninterested in going back to Elisabeth with no actual findings, she considered the possibility of another court having her wiccan friends. Of perhaps another fae who might be able to help.

After taking a calming breath to ease the suddenly rapid beat of her heart in her throat, Isobel placed her thumb on her pendant and transported herself to Clara's front door.

CHAPTER THIRTY-FOUR
CLARA

Clara lay on her back and twirled the crimson scale between her fingers, stared absentmindedly at the ceiling. Beau slept beside her, his back and wings pressed against her.

He'd given her the scale last night, along with the story of how he'd acquired it. Truthfully, he seemed as confused as she was.

Keep it close. Pass it on when the time comes. You'll know what to do, when to do it.

Such vague instructions.

Ryland's words echoed in her mind. Of how the daemdrana were in search of the one to free them of their curse. A female royal, not of the fire court but wandering through. Clara inwardly groaned at the possibility that it was her. She wasn't so foolish as to ignore the signs, but could not help hoping they were ambiguous enough to be misconstrued.

Clara sighed and returned the scale to her bedside table. The movement caused Beau to stir, though not wake entirely. He rolled onto his back, and the covers now only draped over half of him. He truly was beautiful.

Hair mussed and fallen over his eyebrows, his thick lashes pressed to his cheeks, and warm skin contrasted against the dusky pink sheets and ivory comforter. His body was toned and chiselled and dotted with various scars. Clara raked her eyes downwards to his half-hard cock.

For a moment, she considered waking him, before deciding that shaking him awake only to suck him off was far less enticing. Instead, she crawled between his legs and took his growing erection in her hand. Clara was a little surprised at how quickly he became fully erect while sleeping. Spitting on her other hand, she wrapped it around him as well before slowly working them up and down his cock. The faster she stroked him, the more rasped his breaths became, and excitement built low in her belly.

Beau moaned softly, and his eyebrows drew together slightly.

Clara hardly even cared if he was waking, taking pleasure from the act of jerking him while asleep.

She lowered her mouth and slowly but firmly licked her way from his base to the tip. Even now, she kept her eyes on him, just as he liked, as he demanded of her every time. She watched as his eyelids fluttered and his mouth dropped open. He was now breathing heavily, and rumbling moans left him as she took him in her mouth. Clara swirled and flicked her tongue, pressing it against his shaft as she bobbed.

Pulling back, she wrapped both her hands around his bulging cock and spun them as she stroked him. Clara then licked his balls, sucking one into her mouth.

It was then Beau woke.

"Fuck," he drawled, voice deep and husky.

Flutters erupted in her core, and Clara moaned at the sound.

He dragged his hands through his hair, and his head tilted back.

"Stars, I love you," he groaned out, reaching a hand down to stroke her hair. "Wake me like this every morning, I beg you."

Clara let out a low, sultry chuckle as she moved back to work his cock. She licked it again, and with her mouth pressed to his shaft, murmured, "It's nice to hear you beg for a change, sir."

"Don't get used to it," Beau said as he gripped her hair, pulling her into position and pushing her head down. He pushed her further and further down until all she could do was keep her mouth open and take him.

Just as he thrust up into her mouth, a soft knock came at the door. Beau snarled quietly, and Clara couldn't help but smirk as she pulled off him.

"Clara," her mother called from the hallway. "You have a visitor."

"I'll be out in a minute," she called back, her eyes locked on Beau's.

Her mother promptly responded. "No, dear, I think it best you be out now."

"Apologies, sir." Clara stood, throwing on a pair of trousers and a loose linen shirt. "Duty calls."

Beau was up and pressed against her body with preternatural speed. One hand was splayed at her lower back, and the other wrapped around her neck, his thumb gently stroking her jaw.

"I ought to take you against that door you're so eager to walk through. Calling me sir as you plan to leave is devious." His eyes flared with heat and need.

"Perhaps," she whispered, and she kissed him softly, then spoke with her lips still pressed to his. "You ought to punish me for it later."

Then she slunk from his grip and sauntered out the door. His growl echoed in her mind, though Beau did not follow her.

Elisabeth stood in the doorway to the hall, not quite contained within the open living space she normally kept to. Her eyes jumped around the room, but otherwise she showed no signs of being on edge. A niggling feeling suggested otherwise, though, and the soles of Clara's feet tingled.

"What's wrong?" she asked, not bothering with pleasantries.

"My apologies for the interruption." Elisabeth's tone suggested that she knew damn well what she'd interrupted. "We're having a slight situation at the palace, and it's made me realise you need to be completely prepared for what is coming. I cannot teach you much, but I will pass on every morsel of knowledge I have and enlist anyone I can to help you further. Times are dangerous and despite what you may think of me, sister, I care for you deeply. I will not allow you to stray further into harm's way through complacency or a lack of preparedness.

"Ryland will be along shortly. He will attempt to manipulate your mind in his full capacity, and I will teach you how to block him. The mind is simultaneously your greatest strength and weakness. It is also, from what I have gathered, the power you cannot control. Candor magic is an entity of its own, but it can be harnessed. Now, please get dressed, so wc may begin."

Elisabeth shooed Clara with both hands casually, like she hadn't just rapidly spewed the most heartfelt words since they reconnected.

Genuine fear laced every word from Elisabeth's mouth, and Clara found it disconcerting. She'd viewed Elisabeth as a hard, well-crafted stone. Strong, impassable, unswaying, and final. The energy surrounding her today was frantic and nervous, entirely uncharacteristic. So Clara didn't spit the harsh retort she would have previously, nor snip back or grumble. Instead, she nodded and walked back to her now empty bedroom to redress.

Heat radiated off Clara's back as she sat hunched in the sand. Elisabeth had asked which she preferred, sand or soil, and when Clara had answered, Elisabeth had clapped twice and left the house, after offering Clara's mother a brief nod and wave. Ryland had joined them only a few paces from the house, where he'd whispered something to Elisabeth. Whatever he'd said cast a grim shadow in her eyes and told Clara not to ask any questions, though he'd offered Clara a smile. She'd returned the gesture and followed silently, not taking note of where they were headed until they'd reached Ira Bay.

She'd been told to sit and meditate cross-legged on the sand with her hands splayed into the grains and her eyes comfortably closed. Elisabeth had explained how she'd learnt to harness her powers, to feel the future and speak into another's mind. How she imagined her mind tucked inside a small box and then placed inside a larger one. Then into a larger one, again and again, until the box filled with smaller boxes was locked behind a thick, solid iron wall.

"I've been doing it for decades," she'd said, waving her hand. "And now the boxes are always stacked away. You need to learn how to stack them first, rather than to correct momentary lapses or learn to reinstate your technique."

Clara had huffed at that. Of course, it couldn't be simple. Encouraging her deep, slow breaths, Elisabeth had sat before Clara and assured her she'd be successful. As soon as they found the technique which suited her.

Hours later, Clara could confidently say she'd tried all she could think of. The sun glared behind her and sweat pooled on her skin, dampening her hair and clothes.

She'd tried closing the doors in her mind, visualising a handle rotating and a lock clicking into place. Elisabeth had said the more vivid her block was, the more likely it would work. Then she'd tried building walls, brick by brick, then stone by stone, envisioning each addition in as much detail as she could.

Neither attempt had been successful, and Ryland had made his presence in her mind abundantly clear. He'd pulled at an arbitrary memory and repeated it back to her. Both times she'd clenched her fists, then grumbled about trying again.

At one point, she'd even imagined placing her mind in the oven at Nerrida's bakery. As if she placed it on a lined tray, then slid it inside and closed the door with a thud. That, too, had been unsuccessful, though she'd not expected otherwise.

Ryland had a good chuckle at her expense.

After multiple attempts, she'd only managed to push him back, not keep him out entirely. Her growls of frustration grew, as did her impatience and attitude.

"If you're not comfortable with me doing it, someone you can trust with your life, work harder." Ryland spoke matter-of-factly. He'd hardly broken a sweat; meanwhile, Clara's forehead and spine were drenched. "I'm not digging around in there, Clara. I'm simply entering. Your enemies will rummage and ransack, using whatever they find against you. What happens when they find *someone* they can use against you inside your mind?"

Flares of hot anger surged through her body, lighting her fingertips on fire and aggravating her throbbing head. At the thought of Beau being used against her, or in general, her mind turned as white as her rage, ivory as freshly pressed linen or rain-free clouds on a bright morning. At Isobel, and the few memories they'd shared, and the thoughts Clara had that never seemed to leave the confines of her mind. At the memories of Neven and her family.

The white fire burned sharp, clear, and strong.

Ryland flinched as though he'd been physically pushed, then a smile burst across his face.

For a moment, as Ryland commended her, Clara was proud too. She felt less so after another hour dragged by and her efforts hadn't been replicated. Her headache was now so bad all Clara could hear was the ringing in her ears, and a stabbing pain lanced down the sides of her face. It surged down her neck and spine violently. Nausea swirled in her gut while dizziness coated her vision.

"This is exactly when it is most important to keep going," Elisabeth insisted after Clara stood and declared their session done for the day. Her words sounded muffled and slurred, not as close as they should be, though Elisabeth stood directly in front of her. "Your mind is the most important tool you have, and you must keep it safe. You must hone it as sharp as any blade."

Black-and-white spots splattered the corners of Clara's vision. She threw a hand out to steady herself as her legs suddenly turned to jelly. Elisabeth caught her hand but continued in her attempt to convince Clara to stay.

"Mother forbid, if anything were to happen . . ." Elisabeth's voice trailed off, replaced by an ear-piercing scream.

Clara's body felt so light she couldn't feel it anymore, and before her stood a boy no older than three. His sobs racked his shoulders, his small body shaking and heaving with every gasped breath. His cheeks were streaked with tears, the lines of ash labelling him as a bereaved son now smudged.

Clara blinked, and instead of the small boy stood a young girl seemingly the same age, bearing the ashen marks of a bereaved daughter. She, too, sobbed painfully. Clara's heart cracked as her vision churned and changed between the children.

The scream grew louder and louder until Clara opened her eyes to realise that she'd been the one screaming. She blinked rapidly, trying to dispel her disorientation as she now lay against Elisabeth's knees, a wet cloth pressed to her forehead as gentle fingers wiped at her cheeks.

Tears had spilled from her eyes, as had blood from her nose. The bitter taste coated her tongue and Clara winced. Static tingles ricocheted along her arm as she reached for the bottle Ryland offered her.

"This will not be the end of our training, Clara," Elisabeth whispered as she stroked the damp hair away from Clara's face, then rubbed a surprisingly comforting hand along her spine. "But you're right, we're done for today."

Elisabeth let loose a deep, shuddering breath as Clara closed her eyes and tried to steady her breathing. Her sister helped her stand, then held both her hands as her gaze bored into Clara. Her expression suggested she wanted to say something but didn't know how.

"Thank you," Clara whispered, "for helping."

"I would like to be more help than hindrance, if you'll let me." The hope in Elisabeth's eyes was bright and bold. It tugged at an emotion Clara couldn't name. All she knew was that she felt lighter when she nodded her head, walking back to the house arm in arm with her sister.

CHAPTER THIRTY-FIVE
CLARA

The walk back home was made in comfortable silence. Elisabeth held on to Clara's arm, gently running her thumb back and forth. It was surprisingly pleasant . . . and welcome.

Ryland opened the door for them, then promptly said goodbye and left, explaining he had other commitments to see to. Clara smiled and bid him farewell before she entered the house.

Once they passed the threshold into the living room, Clara's heart skipped a beat excitedly, while the energy around Elisabeth grew cold. Isobel sat at the dining table, mid conversation with Clara's mother, though when she saw them, she stopped.

One side of her lips quirked up when her gaze fell on Clara, then a wince flew over her face when she noticed Elisabeth.

“Which of your orders led you here, Jeffreys?” Elisabeth asked, her hand moving from Clara’s arm, and she clasped it tightly in the other at her abdomen.

“Unfortunately, there were no leads in Soil. No actual information besides confirmation of Era and Tindal’s visit. I had hoped to—” Isobel’s mouth clamped shut as Elisabeth held up her hand.

“What could you possibly gain from visiting Clara?” None of the female from earlier was present. Her face was as hard as stone, and her tone was sharp, with no room for amicable words or understanding.

Clara balled her hands into fists and did her best to rein in her temper. “I’d like to help. And I would be appreciative, Elisabeth, if you refrained from speaking to Isobel in such a manner in the future. I’ve had a pleasant enough time with you today, despite my shortcomings. So please don’t ruin the start of a good relationship.”

Ire bubbled in her chest, and the bite of her words was thinly veiled. Though she’d enjoyed the sliver of Elisabeth she’d seen today, it meant nothing if she was going to treat Isobel like shit. Clara wouldn’t stand for it.

Elisabeth spun to face Clara. Disbelief and disgust filled her narrowed eyes.

Clara wanted to at least be civil with her sister, if not more than that. But the feeling she experienced at the sight of Isobel, then at hearing Elisabeth treat her in such a way—no, it simply would not stand. When it came to Isobel or Elisabeth, there was no choice to be made.

Elisabeth’s eyes widened a fraction, then her expression fell. “Alright,” she said, and turned back to Isobel. “My apologies, Jeffreys.”

Isobel's eyes widened, but she stayed silent, simply nodding as she looked away.

"Isobel," Clara corrected Elisabeth.

"Don't push it," Elisabeth fired back.

"Part of our troubles are caused by you not allowing me the space to decide who I spend my time with, not acknowledging I have a brain and a heart—and the capability to choose for myself." Clara spoke gently, placing a hand on her sister's biceps. "Thank you for today, Elisabeth. Tomorrow I will be physically training, and the following day I have work in the morning. Perhaps we could reconvene after work, and we shall see how well my fatigued mind fares."

Elisabeth sighed, much softer this time, and her face relaxed as she nodded. Clara saw her out and eagerly raced back towards the dining room, where Isobel waited.

Her hair had been pulled back and tied at the top, though it was too short for all of it to reach the binding. Sections of pink framed her neck, some tucked behind her ears, showing off a myriad of tattoos and body jewellery which hung from her ears.

Isobel smiled so brightly that Clara's insides warmed. She wanted to reach out and take her hand, but settled for placing her fingers just shy of Isobel's. Partly in fear of Isobel not wanting to hold her hand, and partly out of concern that Beau might wander in and see them. It didn't feel fair he should find out about Isobel that way.

"Thank you for that," Isobel said, a grimace scrunching her face. "She doesn't like me very much."

Clara rolled her eyes. "I think she likes her idea of me more than the *actual me*, so perhaps we're not all that different."

Isobel chuckled, a pure, musical sound, and immediately the weight of the day eased off Clara's shoulders.

"I think you deserve more credit than that."

“Why are you in her doghouse?” Clara pulled her feet up to rest on the edge of her chair, squirming until she found the right position. Clara could almost see the slew of wrong choices flashing in Isobel’s mind as she weighed each option, pondering what she wanted to say.

“I went behind her back—and orders—to see you at the ball in Tirenas. The festival, feast day, whatever they call it.” She spoke quickly, though not nervously.

“Why?” Clara asked.

“Because I felt drawn to you. I needed to meet you or at the very least see you in the flesh. I was in Tirenas anyway—”

“No,” Clara interrupted, with a slightly coy smile. “I mean, why did she say no?”

“Your sister knows about my past and likes to use it against me.” Isobel paused. “No, that isn’t true. She doesn’t like to use it against me, per se, but she will when it suits her. She told me to stay away from you because I’m a recovering drug addict. I’ve been sober for four years and seventy-nine days now, but who’s counting?” A quick smile flashed across Isobel’s face, though in truth, it looked more like a wince. “Anyway, I think she’s worried you’ll end up an addict, too, if you spend too much time around me. I’m also a raging lesbian, so there’s that.” Isobel shrugged while hope bloomed in Clara’s chest.

“Didn’t you say you’re in recovery and sober?”

“Yes.”

Clara rolled her eyes incredulously. “Then she clearly does not know how addictions or recovery or sobriety works. She is blissfully and dangerously ignorant.”

“Does it bother you?” Isobel’s blue-and-gold eyes flew to Clara’s, her striking stare piercing through every layer, almost searching for deceit.

"That my sister is kind of awful?" Clara scoffed, then remembered that wasn't entirely true. "At least in this respect."

"No. That I'm in recovery."

"Not in the slightest. What's in the past is in the past." Clara placed her hand on Isobel's after all, and her skin warmed on contact, her heart following suit as Isobel turned her hand over to interlock their fingers. "I won't dismiss your experiences by telling you they don't matter, but believe me when I say they do not affect the present, nor do I expect they will have much sway on the future. However, I will be bothered if you decide to listen to Elisabeth and follow her 'stay away from Clara' rule. Honestly, it hurt to watch you walk away after we danced, and I don't think I ever want to feel that way again."

Hope and desire glittered in Isobel's stare, in the almost smile on her face, and in her sharp, shuddering intake of breath.

"You say that as if we're to ignore the fact you're in love with a male." Isobel turned away, looking down at her free hand as she tapped the pads of her fingers to her thumb in her lap. "And that I am repulsed by their kind."

Clara shrugged as she squeezed Isobel's hand. "That I may be, but it doesn't mean I'm not interested in you. I like who I like, love who deserves it, and don't particularly care to label myself further."

"Well, I hope you deem me deserving."

"It's looking good so far."

Isobel spent an hour at the kitchen table with Clara. They sat and spoke and laughed. It was as if they'd never been apart. Though they had only met recently, it felt like they'd known each other forever. With each new piece of information Clara learnt, the tug in her chest grew stronger. The energy surrounding them pulsed with excitement and contentment.

Fascinated by her tattoos, Clara asked Isobel for the story behind each one. She got the dagger after she won a fight, claiming eternal victory. There were florals and insects, her sisters' names and symbols to represent her family. Then little pieces, which didn't really mean anything aside from the fact she wanted them forever etched on her skin. Clara wanted to ask about the thick black lines along her forearm, the almost lettering she didn't understand. Nervous bubbles erupted low in her gut whenever she opened her mouth, so Clara avoided the question.

Isobel stood and asked for the privy, and Clara pointed towards the hall. A lazy smile spread across her face as she watched the beauty walk away.

Not long after, Beau sauntered down the hallway. Clara stood to greet him, her face beaming as dark lust swirled in his eyes and danced along his smirk. He immediately moved to her and dragged his hands greedily down her sides before wrapping around her.

"Where have you been all day?" Clara asked, raising an eyebrow.

"I've had to spend the day distracting myself, so I was not walking around the house hard and horny." He growled the words so close to her ear, his breath sent shivers across her skin. His teeth grazed her earlobe as his hands pressed her into his body.

Clara chuckled, then whispered back, "I'm afraid you'll have to distract yourself a little longer. Isobel's here."

Beau swore, digging his fingers into her flesh as he pulled away. As his body left hers, Isobel rounded the corner, offering a sheepish greeting. Beau nodded in acknowledgement but otherwise stayed quiet. Irritation covered his face, and the prick didn't even try to hide it.

"Be nice," she scolded him in a hushed tone as her elbow collided with his side. He grunted, then offered a meagre smile, stalking to sit in the middle of the settee.

Clara sighed, reaching her hand out to Isobel, then moved to join him. She sat on the floor, leaning against his shins with her elbow propped on his knees, while Isobel took the seat to his left.

They sat in an awkward silence until Beau let out a resigned breath and asked Isobel how her day had been, and what had brought her to town.

Water blasted from the kitchen faucet and splattered in the sink. Both sets of eyes dropped to hers, and Clara's face scrunched in embarrassment. She stood to turn the tap off, while Beau and Isobel shared a look, then continued to chat.

Before long, they spoke as if they were old acquaintances. Not yet friends, but friendly amid the mild discomfort. Clara's cheeks ached at how much she smiled, her heart swelling and leaking warmth throughout her chest.

Perhaps Beau would fit exactly where he was, and maybe she didn't have to choose between them or give one up for the other. It was a conversation for another day, but hope grew with every shared word and the comfort which grew between the trio.

A week later, Clara was getting antsy. Her fingernails were raw from all the picking and her feet ached from the near constant pacing.

She'd worked at the bakery twice and practiced her spirit magic with Elisabeth three times. Each session left her more exhausted than the last, but she was making progress. She'd blocked Ryland for almost their entire last meeting, thankfully, with no more visions that left her bloody and unconscious. Elisabeth told her eventually she'd be able to entice a vision, calling out into the universe for one. It was not something she had the capacity to even attempt yet, but perhaps something to look forward to later.

Isobel had enlisted Poppy and Samara to help in the search for the lost witches, while also using her time to physically train with Clara and Beau. They took turns to spar. Though she felt a little guilty for diverting Isobel's attention away from something so serious, Clara couldn't help but be pleased anytime Isobel was with her.

There was still no sign of the Tirenas army, or the late king's twin daughters. Clara did not know why they were waiting, as Eveline did not seem like the patient type and Beau had told them what the twins were like.

Eveline was the natural leader of the two. Outspoken and fierce. She was a force to be reckoned with, though he couldn't say she'd ever displayed her magic. It left a sour taste in the air and a nervous energy surrounding them.

Solaris was kind and gentle. Far more reserved and opposed to violence. If they had any hope of talking their way out of this battle, she'd be the sister to sway.

The twins were close, and Beau had said there was an inseparable bond between them, more so than normal. Another heavy, nerve-filled feeling doused them.

Another training session had finished, and Clara had only a handful of bruises this time. The trio walked from the bay coated in sweat, Isobel bearing a scraped knee and Beau a split lip. He'd been paired with Oren, and that male refused to go easy. He unleashed all his power and muscle, which was for the best. But now Beau winced every time he touched his lip, or whenever Clara planted a gentle kiss.

Clara's feelings of pride at her progress had quickly dissipated when Finch mentioned upping the number of sessions.

"*We don't know when they'll come, but they* are *coming, and you need to be prepared.*"

Everyone was always telling her to be prepared, and the word itself now infuriated her. Clara dragged her feet and scowled as they walked towards town.

"What are they even waiting for?" she hissed, throwing her hands up in frustration.

As if in answer, the ground shook and screams echoed from the town centre. Clara froze, her eyes wide as she looked between Beau and Isobel. The former already had twin blades in his hands, the latter had her thumb poised over her pendant and free hand reaching towards Clara.

"You had to jinx it, didn't you, sweetheart?" Beau drawled, an empty smirk on his lips.

Isobel bristled beside her but said nothing.

Clara narrowed her eyes at Beau, then jogged towards the sound of chaos.

CHAPTER THIRTY-SIX

ISOBEL

Clara ran forward without a moment's hesitation. This beautifully careless woman erred on the side of recklessness. Isobel looked to Beau, who sighed, almost in resignation. He knew who Clara was, what fuelled her and filled her heart.

They set off after her, maintaining speed with each other. When they reached the town square, the smell of smoke hit Isobel first, then the flickering orange flames and billowing black clouds escaping a half-crumbled building. She couldn't tell what it once was, only that it had been populated. Water fae stumbled from the collapsed building, some coughing and others crying.

A male slouched on the cobblestone road, a female leaning over him, assessing his injuries. Her eyes held a hazy wrath as they flicked from the male to her surroundings.

"*This is his fault*," she hissed, over and over while she attempted to staunch the bleeding from his leg. A bone protruded from below his knee, but other than being littered with scrapes and soot, the rest of him appeared banged up but stable.

The female did not divulge who *he* was; instead, she crouched and placed her hands on either side of the open break and healed the man. It was truly remarkable how his skin slowly stitched itself back together and the bone receded into his leg as if the injury hadn't happened. Isobel wasn't ungrateful for the magic she possessed, but she had always been envious of the healers.

Stepping back from the couple, she observed and assessed her surroundings. By the second, more and more townsfolk adopted the same expression, shrouded in a cloud of haze, and began walking around almost in a daze. Varying degrees of anger filled them all, from balled fists and narrowed eyes to stomping feet and shouting. Their eyes took on a milky sheen, but Isobel wasn't sure if it was simply the polluted air affecting her own eyesight.

Beau had disappeared, but Clara remained in her line of vision. She stood before the burning building, her hands in front of her and face set in determination. Slowly, the flames receded until only puffs of smoke remained. Clara was putting the fires out.

In other locations, smaller fires flared.

Isobel stepped up, and drawing on her love for the woman already doing her part, she mimicked Clara's efforts and settled the flames. Reaching into the well of anger she kept as far from her heart as possible, Isobel waved an arm in one long stroke, guiding the smoke away. The wind picked up, tickling along her spine as it whispered violently in her ears of all the malice it wanted to inflict. She remained focused and pushed it away, leaving a mostly clear blue sky in the wake of charcoal clouds.

Beau jogged towards Isobel as she was catching her breath and insisted that she follow him into the building.

"I don't know what to make of it," he said, ushering her through the rubble into what used to be a narrow corridor. He pointed to a crater in the floor, surrounded by singed carpet, and at the walls on either side which were almost entirely destroyed. "It looks suspiciously like an explosive."

"The remnants of one at least," Isobel muttered, as she crouched down to inspect it further.

Beau stood stoically behind her, watching her closely as she hovered her hand above the shards before she picked one up. It was still hot to the touch, but not unbearable for someone with fire magic.

The smell of something familiar hit her first, then the colour, one she used frequently and replaced more often than any of her other paints. Isobel hummed, deep in thought. She couldn't tell why the smell was familiar, but perhaps the smoke had affected her senses, or perhaps it was only the colour she recognised.

Isobel dropped the shard and stood, glancing at Beau, who was clearly working through theories in his mind, though he voiced none.

The shouting from outside grew louder, as did the sound of glass breaking and the distinct twang of swords clashing against stone. Beau and Isobel bolted to the door, then to Clara, who was still working to put out the flames of fires which continued to flare up out of nowhere. More were ablaze now than when Isobel walked inside mere minutes ago.

Townsfolk continued to shout incoherently, words forming in their minds but not relaying from their tongues. Their anger, however, was prevalent and explicit. In her periphery, Isobel watched an axe fly and collide with a stone statue. Another male donned a large broadsword and smacked it against the smooth cobblestones as he stalked aimlessly.

Isobel turned to Clara, who turned to watch it unfold, then slid her gaze to Isobel's. Her expression asked a silent question, unmistakably confused.

What the fuck?

Isobel had no idea what was going on. Their trio formed a huddle.

"We need to sort this mess out before we deal with any of them," Clara said, jerking her chin towards the male with the sword. "No one here is going to think rationally while they're surrounded by flames. They're water fae."

Isobel and Beau nodded in sync, then Clara turned to where a café now burned. It'd been fine moments ago. Cool, dry, unmarred by the destruction. Where the fuck was this chaos coming from?

Not anyone here, surely. Clara had admitted as much. They were water fae, incapable of wielding flame.

Which meant an external force was at play.

She shook her head, committed to considering that thought later, then glanced up just in time to watch three arrows soaring towards her at light speed. Immediately her body jarred to the right, a powerful jab to her left side forcing her away. She stumbled and fell to the ground, pain radiating from her hands to her shoulders at the violent impact.

Immediately, a thud sounded from beside her as Beau's body hit the ground in an awkward heap. An arrow protruded from his ribs, the dip at his collarbone, and his temple.

A choked sob escaped her throat as Isobel rushed to him, inspecting his injuries. A steady flow of blood pooled at each site, less so from his head than the others. With only two hands available, she placed one over his ribs and the other on his collar to staunch the bleeding. Though her hands quickly became sticky, the bleeding did not slow.

"Why would you do that, you reckless male?" she screeched at him, tears welling. "Please don't die, oh Mother, *please* do not die." Her words flew from her mouth, and whether it was from understanding or incapability, Beau let her ramble. "She loves you, you absolute fool. If you die— *Fuck*. What were you thinking?! This will break her— I—"

Beau placed a weak hand on hers, silencing her poorly veiled fears. Her words no longer flew from her mouth, but still Beau said nothing. The colour leached from his face, replaced by a layer of sweat atop his forehead. His breaths drew closer, rapid and short. Isobel cursed again as her tears spilled. She pressed harder on his wounds, racked her brain for something to help. Her own breathing quickened as panic set in. Whispered curses and pleas flew from her lips to any divinity listening.

As Beau's eyelids drooped, Isobel screamed, "Clara!"

The most wonderful thing to ever happen to Isobel bounded into view and slid to her knees beside Isobel. It would be over now. Clara would see the love of her life pierced and dying before her because of Isobel, and she would rightfully want nothing further to do with her.

She placed a gentle hand on Isobel's as Beau's hand slid to the ground. Then she stroked a rogue lock of hair from Beau's brow. She gave him a smile that somehow looked apologetic and appreciative all at once.

"Oh dear," Clara murmured, then clicked her tongue. Beau's chuckle was feeble.

"*Oh dear*? Sweetheart, I've been shot. That requires a little more than an '*oh dear*'." His chest rose in bursts, not fluidly as it should have. Fear danced along Isobel's spine.

"Woe is you, right?" Clara joked. How could she be joking right now? Isobel wanted to shake Clara until she saw the severity of the situation.

"I'm so sorry," Isobel cried, the words spilling from her mouth. "I didn't see— I wasn't—"

"It's alright," Clara said softly, her beautiful green eyes earnest.

"When I said you'd be the death of me, Clara," Beau muttered, his words slurred, "I didn't intend for it to be so stars-damned literal. Fuck."

"Yes, well," she replied, the smile still gracing her face. "Technically, this one was Isobel's fault."

"I'm so sorry," Isobel repeated over and over, her voice quiet and small. Her hands shook despite how firmly she pressed them against Beau. "How can I help? How can I fix this?" She sniffed and pleaded silently to all the gods, to the Mother herself, that this was fixable at all.

"Oh, honey, please don't cry." Clara used her free hand to wipe a tear from Isobel's cheek. "He's okay."

"Umm . . ." Beau groaned. "He's dying, actually."

"Shut up," Clara muttered with a roll of her eyes. Then added more softly, "We'll wait for you."

Beau sighed, then groaned again, his breathing now more laboured than she'd ever seen on a living being.

Isobel choked out a sob, then turned to Clara. Isobel's eyes ached as they widened. "How are you so calm?"

"Beau is a Phoenix," Clara replied. "It takes some getting used to, and I worry every day whether he'll see the next sunrise without dying first, or whether he'll see tomorrow at all. The last time it happened, we'd argued just prior, and the fear on his face was obvious. He's not admitted as much, but I'm certain it was the fear that I'd walk away. That when he woke, I wouldn't be there.

"This time, he seems far more relaxed. I like to think me being calm is helping. He'll be reborn in a matter of hours, and I'll sit here until he's done. Then he'll need some assistance until he regains his motor function."

Clara sighed, a subtle exhale. She looked down at Beau's too still, too grey face with nothing but love in her captivating jade eyes. Her calm serenity seemed in such contrast to her personality up to this moment. Here she looked death in the eyes and sat still.

"That would've been good to know ahead of time," Isobel grumbled and took a deep breath. She pulled her hands from Beau, still covered in his blood, but now far less traumatised. Stretching her fingers, she saw they continued to shake.

"You're telling me," Clara huffed, with a sympathetic smile.

"What do we do about them?" she asked, jerking her chin towards the chaos still unravelling around them. The water fae now walked around in a confused daze, different to the cloud of anger they were entrapped in before. Some of them scanned the town and the destruction warily. Eyes darted between familiar faces, then to the trio who sat in a semi-circle of death, despair, and devotion.

Clara watched the townsfolk as they cleared away debris and pieced together what had taken place. She paused, then finally answered.

"I think some questions are in order, at the very least. I want to know who fired these arrows and why. And whether the individual deserves to keep their head. But for now, we wait." Her nonchalant movement was a deep contrast to the violence-laced words which had just spilled from her tongue.

“Can I wait with you?” Isobel asked quietly.

“Of course, I’d be honoured.” Clara paused, then sighed before she spoke again. “You know, I slapped him after the first time. It was rather cathartic, if I’m honest.”

A genuine smile tugged at the side of Isobel’s mouth, though it fell flat before it could spread far. “I thought he was dying—because of me, no less.”

“I know.” Clara spoke quickly, almost as if trying not to spook her. “And technically, he is dying, or dead right now, I’d say. But he won’t stay that way.” Clara squeezed Isobel’s hand, sending flutters—albeit weak ones—to her core and zaps of warmth up her arm.

“He shoved me out of the way. I wouldn’t have come back. I would’ve been dead.”

“He has a good heart under his acquired exterior.” Clara smiled genuinely at Isobel, then gazed down at Beau with the adoration Isobel was embarrassed to acknowledge made her envious. Now was not the time to be selfish, but she couldn’t help but wish Clara looked at her like that.

Isobel glanced at Beau as well. “I didn’t think he even liked me.”

“I cannot speak for him, but I know how much you mean to me, and he, too, is aware of that. So whether he saved you for you, or for me, or for his own slowly growing conscience, I do not know. But no matter why, I will be eternally grateful.”

CHAPTER THIRTY-SEVEN
CLARA

As soon as the pile of ashes drifted away and Beau's form took shape, Isobel let out a slow breath. She was likely relieved, and Clara couldn't blame her. Once he woke and sat up, Isobel slapped him, shoving her pointed finger into his chest, and called him a slew of names.

Toad was her second favourite.

Bag of dicks decorated with feathers was at the top of the list.

Clara was still chuckling.

Isobel had shouted for a long while, for herself and for Clara, which caused her heart to beat harder in her chest.

Beau did not appreciate her remark about it being a habit, or that he liked to keep secrets from pretty women who have to watch him die. Clara's chest flooded with pride and appreciation.

Still, Isobel helped him to stand and asked if he was okay, then thanked him. Quiet, but genuine. She then wandered off to question the surrounding fae. After almost half an hour of increasingly frustrated expressions and audible grumbles that could be heard from across the street, she returned.

"They all said the same thing," she huffed. "The past two hours have been a strange blur. The only thing they know for sure is that their bodies and minds were filled with rage and the Phoenix was at fault. He detonated the explosive, and they required retribution. I did not realise they meant you." She glanced at Beau as that last sentence left her lips. "The explosive itself, or what was left of it, looked or *felt* familiar. Maybe it was the smell, I'm not sure. I couldn't even tell where I'd come across it before or why it was familiar, just that it was."

"Could this have something to do with the witches?" Clara asked, brainstorming aloud. Truthfully, she did not know where these emotions and thoughts had come from.

"I think it might, but I think it may also be bigger than that."

"Why me?" Beau snapped.

"I don't know." Isobel shrugged. "But it was an intentionally targeted attack. Likely by someone who can manipulate the mind."

"Like one of Urian's twins?"

"Perhaps. What are their powers?" Isobel asked.

"Eveline's never displayed hers, that I noticed." Beau's voice held a hint of frustration. "Solaris has the ability to read minds and to sever and alter the physical brain. I'm not sure whether she can manipulate thoughts or actions."

“I need to find those witches, as surely they’re the key to this,” Isobel whispered, almost to herself.

“What were they shopping for the day they went missing?” Clara asked.

“Sunflower seeds, about a dozen different berries, cloves, firelily buds, charcoal, and a blue crystal I can never remember the name of.”

“Firelily buds react to certain types of crystals on impact.” Realisation, or perhaps hope, flashed in his golden eyes. “Some even explode, and depending on the quantity, could lead to this kind of destruction.”

“How do you even know that?”

“His mother was a professor, and she liked to practise her lectures aloud,” Clara answered without thinking.

Beau’s face lit up that Clara remembered the minor detail he mentioned in passing, and a similar memory danced across her mind of the time he did the same. She smiled softly at him, and he stepped closer to her, brushing his hand along hers before twining their fingers.

Isobel stared at their hands for a long moment, but said nothing.

The next morning, a loud rap from outside tore Clara from unbuttoning Beau’s pants. He’d fallen asleep as soon as he’d lain on the mattress, with no time to undress. Clara hadn’t woken him with her hand or mouth this morning, and instead Beau had woken her by planting hardening kisses along every inch of her body. She’d intended to remove his trousers and take his bulging erection in her mouth, something he was eagerly awaiting when the noise echoed through the house.

Beau narrowed his eyes as she stood. “Don’t you dare.”

Clara chuckled and threw a shirt on before she blew him a kiss and wandered from the room.

Jacob had left for school, and her mother had already gone to work. Evian hadn't been home consistently in some time, always choosing to be with Seren, so Clara didn't bother to take note of whether his door was open or whether he stood somewhere in the house.

Outside, Isobel stood poised to smack the wooden door again as Clara swung it inwards. Dark circles bloomed under her eyes, which looked far more grey than blue next to the undoubted signs of insomnia. Her hair was a mess, as if she'd tossed and turned for hours before giving up. She still wore the same clothes as yesterday, only now they were rumpled.

"I've been thinking," she said, not bothering with a greeting. Clara stifled her chuckle and ushered the chaotic beauty into her house. "The witches were taken in Soil. Then an attack was launched in Wave. Whoever took them did so to use them, I'm sure of it. The ultimate target is someone in Elanist. I don't think it's got anything to do with the twins. If they were going to do something, they'd do it themselves. Eveline's a queen, for heaven's sake. She needs no reason. Neither her nor her army were seen, no word from her at all. Next, the attack was on Beau—he was the target. Why? It has to do with you, Clara. I think it was meant to affect you. But I don't know why, or the end goal. What I know for certain is it's got something to do with you."

She finally took in a deep breath, and her shoulders relaxed as she exhaled.

"How do we find out?" Clara asked, as she collected a glass of water and handed it to Isobel.

"I don't have the foggiest idea." Isobel shrugged and shook her head before she took the glass, thanked Clara, and drained it.

"Perhaps some sleep will help?" Beau suggested from the hallway. He leant against the wall, his voice gruff but genuine. "You can take Clara's bed."

Clara raised a brow but didn't argue.

"I couldn't." Isobel shook her head again, looking away.

"We insist." Beau walked towards her, then with strong, warm hands Clara knew too well, he guided Isobel to the bedroom.

Isobel was asleep as soon as her head hit the pillow. Clara brought the blanket up to her shoulders and brushed a stray lock of vibrant pink hair from her face. Her hand lingered for a moment before Beau snatched her wrist and dragged her from the room.

She took in a sharp breath as he pressed her to the wall outside her bedroom door, closing it far more gently than he handled her. His thumb pressed just below her jaw as his hand wrapped around her neck.

"Your mother is at work, and your brother at school," Beau growled in her ear as he pushed his body against hers. "Evian is with Seren and Isobel is asleep. There will be no more interruptions, Clara, or so help me, I'll fuck you in front of them."

Heat coiled and seared her core.

"Beau!" Her tone remained hushed as she scolded him, though it was a weak protest, and the cocky bastard knew it.

"No. I do not care who walks through that door. You. Are. Mine. Now let me brand it on the back of your throat and deep, deep inside that perfect little cunt."

"Beau . . ." she repeated, the word more a moan than anything else. A breathy plea, one he answered immediately.

"Fuck yes, sweetheart. That's exactly what I want to hear."

He then dragged her into the bathing room, the floor still covered in puddles from Jacob's morning routine. Beau yanked open thc top drawer of the vanity and threw everything from the counter into it.

Clara watched him in the mirror, his face burning with desire, his eyes vibrant and fixed on her. Then her eyes flicked to herself. Hair unbrushed and wild around her face, a contrast that highlighted her eyes. Ample body and unblemished skin, delicate freckles, and a symmetrical bone structure. Clara had always liked what she saw when she stared at herself in the mirror, but she had never felt as beautiful as when Beau looked at her like he wanted to devour her.

Like he did now.

Perhaps when Isobel looked at her as if she was everything that brought the woman peace.

Now was no time for peace, though. Right now, Clara wanted the carnal hunger and depravity with which Beau willingly showered her.

He groaned as he lifted her shirt, praising her lack of undergarments as he threw the clothing to the floor. He removed his own clothes just as quickly, also tossing them aside. His hands dug into her skin and clawed down her sides until he grabbed her hips, then tugged her ass back into him.

Clara felt his already hard cock against her and let out a low purr.

Beau's grip deepened for a moment, then one hand released her, only to move up her spine. It wrapped around the back of her neck, and he used it to push her forward until her breasts pressed to the cool stone countertop, though he kept her eyes tilted towards him. Her quick gasp at the chill had Beau chuckling, deep and lazy and far too seductive.

He pulled away with hesitation and a rough groan to close the door. Behind it hung two robes, and Beau smirked as he tugged the tie from Clara's robe and stalked back.

"You don't object?" he asked coyly.

"And if I do?" Clara countered, splaying her hands on the counter.

"Then I would simply have to imagine having you tied up and at my mercy." Beau shrugged.

"I don't think you'll need your imagination today. Though that is good to know, for any potential future objections."

"I will never force you into anything, Clara," Beau said, his eyes locked with hers. He pulled a hand behind her back and then the other. "I will only ever do what you allow, regardless of what I want. I won't lie, though. The thought of you doing something purely to please me . . ." He shook his head, his amber eyes flaring with heady passion. Beau tugged her bound wrists until Clara's back arched and she could see even more of him in the mirror. Clara moaned, and he smiled, a truly devilish expression. "Fuck, sweetheart, I could just explode at the thought."

Clara pushed back into him as much as her body would allow. "Please," she breathed. "Have your way with me, sir. At least a little."

Beau wound his other hand through her hair and jerked her head back so she now faced the mirror, then snaked that hand around to squeeze her jaw, her cheeks, almost painfully holding her face in position.

"Watch," he growled. "I want you to see what you do to me. I want you to watch me fuck you. And I want to watch you watching yourself. You're a fucking goddess."

Then, without warning, he slammed his cock in to the fucking hilt. Clara shrieked and splayed her fingers, then dug them into her palms when she was unable to grab hold of anything else.

Beau's face contorted into a beautiful mix of relief, pleasure, and desperation. Hunger and passion were displayed in every violent thrust. His head tipped slightly, and he groaned a curse as he gripped both her bindings and face tighter. Stars, she hoped they'd bruise.

So she could walk around for hours—if not days—after with the marks of him still decorating her skin. He'd wanted to brand her, after all.

She tried to be quiet, knowing Isobel was asleep down the hall, but she couldn't. Each thrust sent a burst of fire along every nerve and shockwaves through her bones. She wanted, *needed* this pain surging through her body.

Heat quickly pooled at her core, threatening to send her over the edge far sooner than she'd like. She didn't want to stop, ever, wanting Beau to fill and satisfy her again and again.

Beau pounded into her so deep she wondered if he might actually bruise her insides, marking her as he'd claimed. Clara moaned and cried out louder every time he pulled back, only to thrust back in harder still. Her body crashed into the vanity and the items in the drawers rattled, though she could hardly hear it over the symphony of Beau's moans and swearing.

She watched as his body connected with hers, as he filled her with all of him. The sight was so insanely, unexpectedly hedonistic. Clara knew mirrors would play a far more active role in their lives from now on.

Beau let go of her face, using his now free hand to reach around and cup her breast.

"Your body is so stars-damned perfect," he muttered. "Like it was fucking made for me."

"Maybe it was," she breathed. "Maybe I am."

"Yes," he groaned. "Yes, you fucking are."

Her eyes raked over his chiselled body, and where his golden feathers were illuminated by the sun. If he thought she was a goddess, he was easily her godly counterpart. His sweat-dampened chest almost glittered as light hit him through decoratively panelled glass. Perhaps he was more than a god, and instead a universe of stars. Her universe.

His pace picked up again, and Clara screamed. The sound exploded from her chest, from her now breathless lungs and a body which sizzled with pleasure.

Beau tore his hand from where he was fondling her and yanked open a drawer. He pulled a washcloth from it and shoved it into her open mouth.

"As much as I love to hear you scream," he said, a slight smirk dancing over his plump lips, "if Isobel wakes up and wanders in, she's going to get quite the show, because I'm not fucking stopping until you're unable to stand. And then I'm going to keep going. There will be . . ." He paused, his smirk now gone and his face filled with need and determination. "No. More. Interruptions."

Every word sent a tingle down her spine and her clit ached to be touched. But if Beau continued this way, she wouldn't need it to be—he was going to drive her to climax with his cock alone.

Though slightly muffled, Clara's moans were still loud. Beau's deep grunts remained right by her ear. She rolled her hips as he thrust, mewling as Beau swore and pounded faster. The sound of skin slapping against skin echoed in the tiled room.

"Fuck, Clara, yes." Beau bucked into her wildly, and she knew he was close. His next words confirmed as much, as he groaned, "You're going to make me come."

His announcement was all it took, and Clara fell into an oblivion of blinding lights and fireworks. Release barrelled through them simultaneously until all that was left was the sound of their heavy breathing.

CHAPTER THIRTY-EIGHT
CLARA

For three nights, Clara had been plagued with restless sleep and disturbing visions.

The first night was nauseating and disorienting, with violent jumps through various landscapes and the seasons all in disarray. One minute it felt like summer, the warm sand swallowing her bare feet—though the ocean rolled above her head, replacing the clear blue sky. Then she stood in a barren, drought-affected river surrounded by an autumn-coloured field drowning in rain as torrential thunderstorms clapped and boomed. It was as if the seasons had become warped, and the land was confused and dying as a result. Right before she woke, a woman appeared before her clad in ornate gold jewellery. It was woven through her pale-blonde hair, pierced through her sun-kissed skin, and dangled from her long, spindly fingers. She said nothing, simply stood with a merciless and unapologetic stare.

The next night a repetitious montage played of Tindal and Era, the witches Isobel was trying to locate. Clara had been trying to help, as had Beau. She couldn't be sure it was a vision; it could have been her subconscious mind. Not everything had a magical root, after all.

Now Clara woke from a vision of a woman with dark hair and milky eyes. She had no other distinctive features, not even coloured irises—only cloudy eyes and hair like tar. She stood in the middle of billowing smoke, then disappeared as the puffs turned to splashes, leaving in her wake a puddle of oil, slick and dirty.

With the sun barely peeking out above the horizon, Clara had to get up for work soon anyway, so she threw back the covers and dragged herself out of bed. Beau grumbled from his side, but otherwise stayed asleep.

The sharp breeze bit at the back of Clara's neck and at her fingertips as she walked. Even though it was growing warmer, the mornings were still crisp. A niggling feeling at the back of her mind suggested it was more than the weather biting at her, but she pushed the thought away. With hardly enough sleep to keep her headaches under control, she needn't aggravate them with another problem. It would arise when it saw fit, and she'd deal with it then.

Mikhail arrived at the bakery at the same time as Clara, bouncing through the door on her heels. His energy was always chipper and eager, and truthfully, his bubbly persona was infectious. She couldn't help but smile when he was there.

His eyes, though, they held something deeper.

"What is it, Mikhail?"

Mikhail avoided her gaze as he hung his own coat and scarf. His mouth twitched as he put off answering, then finally he looked at her. Confusion and concern circled in his eyes and darkened the shadows on his face.

"Something's coming," he whispered with a shudder. "The birds can feel it and they're on edge. The air is heavy because of it."

Clara could see the fear filling the poor male. Someone so normally upbeat was now racked with worry. She knew he was right, and she trusted his judgement for reasons she couldn't understand. Clara did not like to see him this way, but did not wish to feed into it, so she waved him off. "No need to worry yourself with some uncertain, unknown conflict, Mikhail. Best we just focus on the job and get through the day."

The flat look he gave her told Clara he knew as well as she did her words were weak. He nodded anyway and turned towards the kitchen.

As they got to work, Clara did not forget his warning, though she managed to push it to the farthest corner of her mind and focused on her job.

Clara pulled the comforter up around her shoulders, tucking her hands beneath her chin, and stared blankly at Beau. He looked back at her with contentment, and slowly fading patience. For the first time in as long as she could remember, her mind was quiet. Almost numb.

A frightening revelation, truly.

Eerily empty, with no rampant thoughts or confusing questions battling for the title of loudest. She blinked slowly, trying to conjure something, *anything*, but nothing came.

Beau huffed a sigh and shifted his weight before he spoke.

"Spit it out, sweetheart."

Slowly, her eyes pulled up to meet his. It almost felt as if she was moving in a daze.

Before she answered, Evian knocked on her bedroom door and called out, "Elisabeth is here to see you, Clara." His voice rasped with sleep, and perhaps an inch of annoyance. As far as Clara knew, Evian had not taken well to Elisabeth. He was civil enough, even respectful, but he didn't like the woman.

Clara acknowledged her brother as she stood, then quickly dressed and left the room, Beau following silently. She entered the sitting room to find Elisabeth pacing.

Isobel stood by the edge of the settee and her eyes raked over Clara before they bounced to Beau. The change in her expression was subtle, but Clara saw disappointment darken her sky-blue eyes. A sharp pang of guilt flared in Clara's chest.

"Had you already fallen asleep?" Elisabeth enquired, sounding genuinely concerned.

Clara shook her head.

"Good." Elisabeth nodded and took a breath. "I wanted to let you know I'm glad to have been somewhat present in your life. I have thought about you for many years, and it's been an honour to meet the woman you've become."

"Elisabeth." Clara's alarm rose. "This feels an awful lot like a goodbye. What's going on?"

Her sister only smiled. A soft, sincere, and possibly sad smile which looked far too delicate on Elisabeth's sharp features.

"Not a goodbye." She shook her head, then took a deep breath. "I cannot tell you exactly what is coming, but it's going to change everything. It feels like the final spin in an intricate dance that could end in applause or ruin.

"The last time I said goodbye to you, I promised I would do everything in my power to protect you and to love you from afar. I promised you would grow tall and strong and beautiful, no matter where you were or who you were with. You would have no recollection of that day, as you were only a babe. But now, I want to tell you something I know you will not forget."

Elisabeth took another deep, shaky breath. Closing the distance between them, she took Clara's hands in her own and gently squeezed.

"Whatever happens, whenever it happens, I am proud of you. As our parents would be. As your mother and brothers are. I am grateful to call you my sister. I feel privileged to have glimpsed the ruler you will become." A tear slid free, falling from Elisabeth's face and dropping on Clara's hand.

"And if you wish to continue your relationship with Isobel, I will suffer in silence while you do so." While sincerity swirled in her light-green eyes, Clara couldn't help rolling her own. How typically Elisabeth to burst an almost perfect moment of familial bonding.

"That isn't the polite and accepting statement you think it is," she muttered.

"All I meant to say was I will honour your choice, and your word. You do not have my permission, but I respect your decision. I love you, little sister."

Clara wanted to say it back. Her chest warmed at the confession, and at most of their conversation. But since she was incapable of telling a lie and unsure if she truly loved Elisabeth yet, Clara was unable to form the words. A stinging pinch in her chest suggested she might regret her lack of response.

All she could do was nod and offer a genuine smile; one which Elisabeth accepted wholeheartedly.

Clara fell asleep quickly that night, but it was not restful, full of intangible visions which slipped from her mind as easily as smoke.

Beau slept beside her, while Isobel lay on the other side of the wall, likely curled up on the settee. Elisabeth slept in her mother's bed, as she was at work and not expected home until the following night.

Clara's eyes twitched open. A deep-charcoal haze haunted her vision, a tormenting reminder of the dream she could not remember.

The clock in the hallway chimed four times, the sky beyond her window still dark purple. Sunrise had not yet begun, but Clara had a feeling her day had.

As if in answer to her thoughts, a crow cawed in the distance. Once, then again. This time joined by what sounded like an army of its brethren. Clara took a deep breath and tried to slow her quickening heart. She swallowed and splayed her fingers in an attempt not to pick at her nails.

Then she slunk from her bed, dressed in silence, and stalked from her bedroom.

The twins had arrived.

CHAPTER THIRTY-NINE
CLARA

Clara strode through empty streets, not knowing where she was headed. She simply followed the caw of crows and the feeling of doom tugging painfully in her gut.

Not three streets from her home, Elisabeth materialised and fell into step silently beside her.

"Do you think it's wise for you to join me?" Clara asked, her voice hushed despite the streets being deserted.

Elisabeth raised her eyebrows at Clara, then her lips twitched up in determined malice.

"Did you think it was wise for you to go alone?"

Clara had no sensible response. She knew it was not wise. This was possibly the first time she'd ever considered every angle and every outcome before she acted. Her decision weighed heavily on her, but keeping Beau and Isobel safe far outweighed the inevitable wrath she'd receive once they woke to find her gone.

She trusted her magic enough to know that the sense of dread which lay heavy inside her was not a warning of her own making. Like the warnings she'd been given by Mikhail and Elisabeth, and the prophecy that drove her biological mother to suicide, these portents were not to be ignored.

Someone would die tonight; before sunrise, a heart would no longer beat.

However, that heart did not sit in Clara's chest. Of that, she was certain.

So who *did* it belong to? Clara did not know. She could only pray to the stars they'd keep watch over Beau, Isobel, her family, and loved ones, so their hearts would continue to beat come sunrise.

Clara walked onwards, Elisabeth matching her steps for nearly an hour until they reached a smaller army than Clara had expected.

The border between the Courts of Flame and Water was comprised of mountains and imposing terrain, but about an hour's travel into Wave revealed open plains with little tree cover. There were wide enough clearings that the open carriage of the Queen of Tirenas looked comfortable in the expanse. Her sister sat beside her, though when Elisabeth and Clara stopped before them, they stood.

Serenity graced Solaris' delicate features, whereas Eveline looked nothing short of furious. Her sharp nose and cheekbones, framed by narrowed eyes and pursed lips, gave away her emotion. She was the queen, though Clara couldn't help but wonder whether Solaris would've been a better fit upon the throne.

Their army was made up of a few dozen winged soldiers. More females filled the ranks than Clara had remembered, but they all projected the same negative expression. Ready for bloodshed, but wishing to be in bed. And Clara couldn't blame them.

Eveline clicked her fingers, and four soldiers stomped forward.

Without thought, Clara threw up a wall of air, barely containing her smirk when they simultaneously stumbled.

Eveline's gaze somehow grew colder.

"Clara Afron," she snapped, her voice thunderous. "You committed a heinous act of treason while present on my continent. The blood of our former king stains your hands, and his death your soul. You have been issued death marks and will be detained to return to Tirenas to await your execution. As I do not know this female, I will extend the last kindness my folk will show to you. Was she involved?"

Hope sliced through Clara's chest at the thought Eveline might ignore Elisabeth. Surprise quickly followed, as she hadn't been sure Eveline was capable of the act.

"No," Clara answered firmly, taking a half-step forward. Elisabeth inhaled sharply, but thankfully, kept quiet.

Eveline nodded once, then ordered Elisabeth away with a single word and a flick of her wrist. To which Elisabeth scoffed, but did not move.

"If you are so eager to refuse the orders of a queen, I am more than happy to extend the death marks to you." Anger laced Eveline's words.

"Is this not beneath you, *queen*?" Clara sneered. "To get your own hands bloody for a common girl?"

"You are no common girl," she snarled back. Her already fair skin turned white around her knuckles, where they tightened on the carriage railing. "You are a con artist and a murderer, and you will be punished for your actions! Your crimes will have consequences. I will see to it myself. My father was an unforgiving king, and I am his daughter."

"I'm sure he'd be proud." Clara scoffed. "Looking up at you with a sinister smile while his eternal soul rots in the pits of the underworld. If his soul had been put to rest, that is, but I incinerated it along with his waste of a body. As his daughter, I'd be more than happy to extend you the same courtesy."

Solaris stood and placed a gentle hand on her sister's forearm.

"Perhaps we could put the blades and barbs aside for the moment and discuss a course of action in a civilised manner." Her voice was softer than Eveline's, the pitch higher and the words far more graceful as they fell off her tongue.

"Perhaps I will bury my blade in your chest, so Her Majesty may watch you bleed out while Clara boils your sister's blood as it flows within her. While we're making grand suggestions, hmm?" Elisabeth's words flowed slowly, every syllable a violent threat. A murderous calm laced her tone, but her body was stiff and poised to strike.

"Elisabeth, please," Clara said, trying to dissuade her from violence. It was a strange feeling, to be the one trying to avoid chaos and destruction. The need for it flowed freely through her veins, her energy naturally pulled towards that side.

Today, though, the prickling in her nape turned painful at the mention of violence. Death lurked closely, eagerly awaiting whoever she was here to claim.

"Now that was a tad much. Solaris is the kinder of the twins. If anything, her end should be swift." Clara shrugged a shoulder far more nonchalantly than she felt.

Eveline clicked her fingers and waved an aggressive hand towards Clara and Elisabeth.

"You, Clara Afron, are under arrest for the murder of King Urian by order of the Tirenas crown and sentenced to execution without trial on the third sunrise. You, petulant woman, I care not who you are. For your assistance in Miss Afron's resistance and your threats against the royal family, you are under arrest and sentenced to trial in three sunsets. I would hate for you to miss the death of your sister, after all." Eveline grinned mercilessly as more soldiers stormed towards them, but Clara's wall held strong.

"Remove the wall, Clara. It's over."

Elisabeth's mouth opened, her face contorted in rage, but no sound came out. Solaris' body went rigid, her eyes as milky and pale as the woman from Clara's vision.

"I would be very careful with how you choose to proceed," Eveline said, as she, too, straightened and folded her arms across her chest. "Solaris currently holds this rage-filled woman's mind between her two very sharp and manicured fingers."

Clara scoffed, interrupting the queen.

"It is no laughing matter, I assure you," Eveline continued, seemingly unphased. "She need not break a sweat to break you, nor your sister. There will be no more futile games and threats. Surrender, now, or your sister will die, even while her body remains breathing. It truly is awful." Her sinister smile spread, almost as if she hoped Clara would choose wrong. As if eager for a decision that landed Elisabeth in death's open arms.

Elisabeth raises her arms, ready to strike. Twin blades fill her fists and Solaris' murky eyes narrow as her head cocks to the side.

A soundless scream tears Elisabeth's mouth open as she flings her blades forwards.

Time slows.

Even as the blades whirl through the sky and hurtle towards the queen's sister, the world shifts.

Ryn stands in the distance, far to the left of them all. Waiting. Beside her stands the little boy weeping, then the little girl. The child changes from the boy to the girl and back again until the blades hit their target, then everyone disappears. Only Solaris remains, a blade protruding from her eye and her chest, and Elisabeth, whose body contorts violently before crashing to the dirt.

Blood spills.

Hearts stop.

Death awaits no longer, nor her reaper.

"Elisabeth, don't!" Clara screamed, now returned to the present with an enlightened mind and a painful heart. She spun to her sister, but a second too late.

Drawing on her power of air, Clara flung her magic forward, intending to disarm Elisabeth and block her weapons from hitting their target. Instead, she removed the protective barrier, allowing Elisabeth to throw her blades. She then immediately fell to the ground.

Instant death was a blessing compared to the pain and suffering she would've been dealt by Solaris. With her actions, Clara had handed her sister into death's depthless embrace herself.

She should've told Elisabeth she loved her. She should have thanked her or at least given her something of value before she pulled the air from her lungs. Clara was no stranger to murder, and truthfully, she wasn't entirely against it.

But this was different.

Accidental. Unintentional. A mistake.

Her breath caught painfully in her chest and burned her throat. Hot tears stung her eyes, and a choked sob fell from her lips.

Another choked sound rang in her ears, and Clara looked up at the queen's sister.

Solaris blinked slowly, twin blades piercing her body identical to Clara's vision. Then she, too, fell.

Eveline's scream tore through Clara, echoing off the mountains in the distance and frightening the scattered crows at her soldiers' feet. In a heartbeat, Eveline was out of her carriage and storming towards Clara. Energy swirled around her for the first time today.

Clara wondered what Eveline's power was.

Eveline's face contorted in rage, and suddenly she was the spitting image of her father.

Cruel, uncaring, unforgiving.

Ruthless and murderous.

Clara didn't truly believe Eveline to be evil, but she was the product of a corrupt, tyrannical monster. The monster who was at fault for all of this. Why should Clara bear the blame for Elisabeth's death, when Urian had orchestrated the whole thing?

Warmth radiated down her arms while phantom flames licked and danced between her fingers. Without Urian's selfish obsession, none of them would be gathered here now. Solaris would be alive, and Clara would be none the wiser about her long-lost sister. She'd be living in blissful ignorance, and everyone would be alive.

Eveline opened her mouth, but Clara spoke first.

"*Enough*!" she shouted and pointed a now shimmering finger at Eveline.

Hot air whipped around them, forming beads of sweat on the soldiers' foreheads and necks. Others grew flushed wherever uncovered skin was present. Eveline's hair flew wildly around her face.

"I will lose no one else to your fucknut of a father. He has done nothing but cause misery, and even from the grave, he is still succeeding." Clara couldn't stop her lip from pulling back or her teeth from baring. "I was beaten by his hand and at his word. Beau died, Neven died, and countless others have either been corrupted or died." She turned her hard stare back to Eveline. "Now months after the barbaric ass himself died, my sister and yours are dead too. It. Is. Enough."

"Last I checked, Beau Hawthorne was alive and well," Eveline sneered, though it was a weak argument.

"That is irrelevant. He died *in front of me* without me knowing he would be reborn, and I grieved his death as such.

So no one else. Not another soul." Clara shook her head vehemently before locking eyes with every soldier willing to meet her stare. When she looked back at Eveline, uncertainty flashed in the young queen's eyes. Only for a second, but it was there.

"You cannot have my life, and I will not take yours. Death does not remedy death, queen. Take your loss and grieve, and leave me to do the same."

Eveline nodded slowly, her arms falling lax by her sides. She stepped so close to Clara, the next words out of her mouth were only audible for the two of them.

"He beat you?" she asked, in barely even a whisper. The look in her eyes, however, spoke volumes.

It was Clara's turn to nod.

"Then I am sorry. For the actions by his hand and his order."

Clara knew her words were sincere.

Eveline moved back two paces before raising her voice so those around them could now hear. "If you step even a toe onto my lands, I will have you tried for your crimes and the likely result will be execution. For now, however, I will be leaving."

With a swish of her hand, Eveline's soldiers returned to formation and turned towards the mountains. She paused beside her carriage for a long moment, staring at Clara intensely before she spoke. "Make no mistake, this does not make us friends. We are simply grieving the same loss."

Clara nodded in acknowledgement, then called out as the carriage made to leave.

“Elisabeth’s funeral will be held in four evenings’ time.” Her voice broke slightly on the words. “I do not know the Tirenas traditions, but you are welcome to hold Solaris’ here.”

“Why would I do that?” Eveline snarled.

“I am trying to extend some courtesy, *Majesty*, but I can easily revoke it.” Clara crossed her arms, then sighed before she added, “As I said, I am not well versed in Tirenas’ customs, but in many continents, funerals are held at or near the place of death. It’s symbolic.”

“Well, I do not know what a funeral is, so perhaps it is best we do not linger with the corpses of severed souls.”

Clara dipped her chin, then lowered herself beside her sister. Eveline’s carriage rode off, her entourage of winged fae stomping in unison around her.

After an inexplicable amount of time, a hand reached out to touch Clara’s shoulder. She wiped the few tears from her chin and turned her head to see Eveline once again, standing before her, uncertain and uncomfortable.

“What exactly does one do at a funeral?”

CHAPTER FORTY
CLARA

Eveline had been surprisingly receptive to holding a funeral for Solaris. Clara had expected a snotty, obnoxious response, or remarks about how Solaris deserved something classier than someone with no shoes could provide. She'd done a poor job of hiding her surprise when Eveline repeated the statement her father made all those months ago, *"I do not waste my time mourning the dead."*

Funerals simply did not exist in Tirenas, at least for as long as Eveline had been alive, and possibly even longer.

Sadness swelled in Clara's throat for a small child who never got to mourn her mother, or other relatives. Funerals were invaluable for the grieving process, and Clara pitied those in Tirenas who never got to experience that. More so, she pained for those who knew but were never allowed to acknowledge their loss.

Clara did her best to explain to Eveline her customs, though the confusion that flushed Eveline's cheeks suggested Clara might've rambled. She told her of the four nights' wait, in acknowledgement of the four courts from which they did not hail. And how the fifth day represented the deceased's home court, and a final send-off was given in the most patriotic of ways. That traditionally, the body was left undisturbed where it fell, so the soul could be gathered.

The queen assigned a winged female to stand guard over the bodies, while Clara explained that someone would be called for Elisabeth's. Bodies did not share watchers, as each was entitled to their own.

With a wave of her arm, she split her army in two. Half were sent home, while the other half were ordered to stay with their monarch. Clara offered accommodation recommendations, to which Eveline thanked her numbly and wandered off.

Clara knelt before Elisabeth's body, pressing two fingers to her lips, and then extending them in a gentle kiss to Elisabeth's forehead.

"I'm sorry," she whispered. "You know I was growing to love you, too, I think. I despised your presence—stars, merely the mention of you—when I first arrived home." Clara sniffed and didn't bother to hide her grin. "But that hasn't been the case recently."

With a deep breath, Clara stood and wiped the dirt from her knees. As she was about to call for Samara, an unfamiliar female voice called out from behind her.

"Pardon the intrusion, Miss," she said in a voice which was high-pitched but hoarse, like she'd been screaming for a week.

Clara gasped and spun, finding a familiar-looking winged fae, her eyes darting between Clara, Solaris, and the mountains behind them.

Her piercing blue eyes were oddly familiar, but Clara couldn't pinpoint from where, while mousy brown curls cast strange shadows in the rising sun. Wings the same colour as her hair rustled slightly in the breeze at her back. "I didn't mean to startle you," she continued, stepping closer to Clara. "My name is Lena."

"Hello," Clara replied sceptically.

"I've waited for what feels like forever to meet you!" Lena exclaimed as her smile grew. "My parents were not pleased when I joined King Urian's army. They weren't pleased when my brother joined either, but I'm sure you know how that goes. Brothers and sisters are never held to the same expectations."

A phantom touch down her spine told Clara to be wary.

"But now the king is dead, and so much has changed! And because of you, my parents no longer have to fear for their children." Lena's smile dropped, and her eyes darkened. "Instead, now, they only need fear for their daughter. Thanks to you, my parents grieve for their son."

Lena's steps were slower now and more deliberate as she closed the distance between them. Clara considered running, but knew it would not help her since Lena could fly.

"Perhaps you might like to extend that courtesy to your own parents?" Lena snarled. "No? Well, never mind. I'm happy to extend the courtesy for you."

She darted for Clara and had her tightly encased in her wings and arms in seconds.

"Any last words?" she whispered, but did not wait before plunging a blade into Clara's abdomen.

Clara bit her tongue in an attempt not to scream as pain lanced through her body. She would not give this serpent the satisfaction of hearing her cry out.

As soon as Lena's hold on Clara relaxed, she stumbled and braced her hands on her knees for support. Tingling raced through Clara's limbs. She felt heavy and too light all at once.

Lena sneered behind her—or maybe she was in front. The low cackling laughter came from every angle.

"Oi!" Clara called out, and the distorted sound of boots crushing on rock and dirt stopped. With a sharp inhale, Clara pulled the blade from her abdomen and threw it, pleading with the wind and her power to help the weapon reach its next target.

A shrill sound came next, quickly followed by a grunt and a thud. Clara silently thanked her magic, then added out loud, "Fuck you, Lena."

Blood gushed down her front, warm and sticky, and her vision was dark and blurred. The energy she'd grown to love reversed around her, as her magic dulled. The wind turned still, no longer dancing along her skin as it had done moments ago. Her fingertips throbbed as the cold embraced them. The ground felt so far away, as if she were floating. Her heart and lungs became tight.

Clara had been so sure she wouldn't die today, though perhaps death felt greedy.

A bitter laugh fell from her lips at the thought of her brother, now with access to healing magic but nowhere in sight. Truthfully, it was Clara who was out of their sight, as no one knew that she'd left, or where she'd gone when the crows cawed this morning.

Now she knew she was dying, both by the way time slowed around her, and the lack of fear churning her insides. The somehow growing and lessening pain thrumming through her.

Clara stood and stumbled a few steps towards town, towards her home, before her body grew too heavy. Her knees gave out, and she collapsed, her palms stinging as they took the impact. More blood filled her mouth, far more than what could've come from her biting her tongue.

She tried to stand, but her knees turned to jelly. Then so did her elbows, her fingers. Blinking away her tears, Clara pushed herself with every ounce of grit she had to crawl. To at least drag herself part of the way home, closer to someone—*anyone*—else. But in that, too, she failed.

Realisation set in, as heavy as her useless muscles and slowly failing body.

Death might welcome her today, after all.

As the first tear fell, Clara wondered if this was how Beau felt. More tears spilled as she considered the fact that she would not resurrect like he had, and so she would never get to see him again. She didn't say goodbye, didn't even leave him a note. She didn't give him a kiss before she left. Then she thought of Isobel, who was also entirely unaware and had been left without a goodbye.

Over and over again, Clara begged the gods and goddesses, the stars and the universe—hell, she even prayed to the Mother she was sure had abandoned her—that Evian found her body. That it wasn't her mother who stumbled upon her when she undoubtedly went searching.

Clara rolled onto her back, as the sun began its ascent, and tried to maintain an even breath . . . tried to hold on.

Blinking became difficult, as did keeping her eyes open. She couldn't feel her feet, or her arms where they lay by her sides. Soon her entire legs were numb, and licking her dry lips became near impossible. Her breaths no longer felt full, and her head swam as the world tilted around her. Clara silently screamed for Evian, as tears spilled down the sides of her face.

It wouldn't be long now.

Death curled her greedy fingers around the corners of Clara's waning vision.

Not long at all.

CHAPTER FORTY-ONE
EVIAN

An aggressive rap on the window pulled Evian from a dreamless sleep. He startled awake and bolted upright, turning towards the sound.

A small bird stood on the windowsill outside, forcefully pecking at the glass. He dragged a hand down his face and rubbed his eyes before he noticed the male standing outside as well.

In the farthest corner of his mind, he heard Clara calling his name, her voice no more than a whisper. Almost like a memory his mind had tried to recreate. His stomach flipped and settled heavily.

The male had shoulders wide enough to almost reach the width of the window and hazel eyes filled with concern, and he hurriedly waved for Evian to join him outside. Fear hardened his face and twitched at his mouth.

"Shit," Evian mumbled.

Seren still slept, and though he hated to wake her, Evian had a feeling she should not stay here. Nerves bubbled from his gut to his throat as he gently shook her, placing his hand on her cheek and brushing his thumb along her cheekbone.

"I need you to go to my house," he whispered. "Wait for me there."

"What about Clara?" she asked, her voice low and husky with sleep.

Evian shook his head, his brows furrowed. "I don't think she'll be there." He then hastily dressed and jogged around the back to where the unfamiliar male stood.

"My name is Mikhail," he said quickly. "I don't have the time to explain all the details and answer all the questions you will no doubt have. I work with Clara, and she's in trouble."

"What kind of trouble?" Evian interrupted.

"The bad kind. Please, follow me!"

Evian didn't hesitate as the heavy feeling in his gut grew. They ran for the longest half hour of his life, then his breath caught painfully in his throat.

He skidded to a stop, dropping beside Clara, who lay limp in the dirt. He hardly registered the sting of rocks and stones as they scraped his knees.

Evian sucked in a breath filled with fear and the smell of blood and death.

He noted the female soldier closest to Clara, then Elisabeth, and Princess Solaris. All lay dead. It was only a second before he returned his focus to his sister.

His eyes darted over her. Clara's arm dangled lifelessly beside her as Evian pulled her onto his lap, brushing stray locks of her usually vibrant hair—now damp and dull with sweat—from her forehead. His hands shook, as did his breath.

She could hardly open her eyes, her beautiful green irises so different from his dark grey. Her eyes, which normally glittered in the sun and shone in the firelight, now looked hazy and glassed over.

"What the fuck happened here?" He shook his head in disbelief. "We only just got you back."

Clara groaned, then blood spluttered from her mouth as she coughed. It was a poor excuse for a cough, but as she wheezed and gurgled and somehow struggled even further for breath, Evian felt it wasn't the time to point it out. If he had even the slightest hope he could rage-bait her into action, he would have.

Her entire midsection was saturated with blood and it still flowed from somewhere he couldn't pinpoint. It covered her abdomen and puddled around her. Truly, it seemed like a miracle she'd lasted this long.

"No," he whispered. His throat burned and eyes stung as they filled with tears. "No, no, *no*."

With trembling fingers, he checked her pulse, finding it thready and weak, while the barest puff of air left her open mouth. He sent silent prayers, over and over, that the Mother kept filling Clara's lungs.

"Please, Clara . . . hold on."

Evian sniffed, took a second unsteady breath, then shook his head to clear it of his unwanted, grief-stricken thoughts. She wasn't dead yet, and he'd be damned if he let her slip into the afterlife. The Mother had guided him here and had somehow sent Mikhail to him so he might find Clara in time. He had to believe.

"What can I do?" Mikhail asked. The smallest spark of hope flared in his chest.

"What's the time?"

"The sun's barely risen, but I don't have a watch."

Thoughts raced through Evian's mind. "How quickly can you get her to my house?"

Mikhail gave a slight shrug. "A few minutes—maybe ten."

Evian nodded, then looked up at Mikhail. "Fly her home, but keep Jacob in his room. Tell Seren to prep her. I'll be right behind you." His words sounded foreign as they left his lips. Authoritative and calm, despite the terror in his chest.

Mikhail gently tugged Clara into his arms, and more blood spilled down her cheek with the movement. This time, when her eyes closed, they did not reopen.

"Go!" Evian shouted as he stood and set off as fast as he could. The sound of wings flapping above kept him focused on something other than the ringing in his ears or the heartbeat in his throat.

Evian ran faster than he ever thought he could, almost keeping up with Mikhail as he flew overhead.

Almost ahead of his chaotic, racing thoughts.

Clara was already laid out on the kitchen table when Evian burst into the house. Isobel stood at her feet, her eyes unmoving, a rage-filled stillness illuminating her cold eyes. Beau paced behind the table, demanding someone do something more than sterilise the still-bleeding wound.

Seren hurried around, her tears falling. Her lip quivered when she saw Evian. He rushed to the table, squeezed Seren's hand, then began working.

Hovering his open hands over Clara's abdomen, he closed his eyes and drew on his magic. Pulled from the depths of his well, he focused on breathing slow and steady while he harnessed the anger surging through him. He didn't know who had done this, but he had no doubt karma would prevail. If not karma, then Beau or Isobel.

Whoever did this would rot in the pits of the underworld for hurting his sister.

Until then, his rage fuelled him as it had done when he'd healed Seren. It was the only other time he'd healed anyone. Fear threatened to overwhelm him. Healing was never something he'd truly cared for until Seren was injured, and following that, he'd thought of it only a handful of times. He did not want to be a healer, no more than he wanted to continue working as a server in town. This wasn't something he *wanted* to pursue, but he thanked every blessed morsel of this universe that he was capable now—when Clara needed him. He did not know what he was doing, and he only hoped he was doing it right.

Evian imagined her blood cells multiplying, surging into her wound and clotting instead of spilling out. He imagined her skin repairing, like an invisible needle and thread.

His breath became ragged and sweat formed on his brow and chest. He opened his eyes to find that she still lay deathly pale and unmoving, and when he checked her pulse and breathing, they were barely present.

Evian took a deep breath and considered what he could be missing. His own energy was waning, but he wasn't done yet. Perhaps there was more than a fatal wound. Evian made a split-second decision to search for something else, rather than solely heal what he could see.

How he found it, he didn't know. Nor would he ever be able to explain how he instantly knew what it was upon seeing the toxin slithering through his mind. But there it was in Clara's blood, like an iridescent green eel in a sea of red.

Instead of contemplating that, Evian focused on killing the beast inside his sister. He threw every ounce of magic he had at the slippery piece of shit. Watched it dodge his strikes until one landed. And the next. Then another, and another, until finally it disintegrated and vanished in his mind's eye.

Evian's knees wobbled, and he planted a hand on the table to brace himself. Opening his eyes again to check Clara's wound, he saw Isobel at her feet, and Beau now still, his fear-filled eyes darting from Evian to Clara. Seren pulled a knife from the kitchen drawer and hurried back to Evian's side.

She sliced her palm, then took Evian's and did the same. When she took his hand, she closed her eyes and began chanting under her breath.

Air rushed into Evian's lungs, and his body felt stronger than ever. His magic was fuelled and swirling in and around Clara once more. After what felt like an eternity, Evian and Seren dropped in exhaustion.

Clara's skin was blushed with colour, though she was still pale. Her breathing was now even, and Evian let out a sigh of relief. She did not move or wake, but she was alive. So much more than before.

Evian knew death would not take her today.

"Why are you stopping?" Beau growled with an angry step forward.

"There is nothing left to do," Seren whispered, but she took a quick breath and continued before Beau misunderstood. "The toxin is gone, and her wounds are healed. But now her body and mind need to catch up. The only way to do that is to allow her time."

His mouth opened without words, then pursed closed. Eventually, his face softened, though it was still stricken with fear.

"Was the mutual self-harm a requirement for healing her or . . ." His voice trailed off, the quip not as barbed as normal.

"It was the Converge." Seren shrugged a shoulder, while pulling a cloth from the table beside Clara's head. She wiped at her palm. "A minor version, but the ceremony, nonetheless."

Beau's eyes widened. "I thought it was too dangerous to attempt. A boy died the last time it was performed. *Clara* almost died to stop King Urian from performing it on her. Many others have died because of it."

Seren nodded, then answered softly. "Yes, it can be incredibly dangerous and almost always fatal when a participant is unwilling or the recipient is taking power out of greed. But it can also be beautiful. I suspect what the king wanted was permanent, though it can also be a temporary sharing of magical stores. Today it saved her life."

Beau nodded, then reached over to touch Clara's face gently. He swept her hair behind her ear, then took a cloth and dabbed it along her damp forehead.

Isobel's voice rang out in the quiet room. "Must she stay on the table?"

Evian shook his head as he looked at Isobel. Her eyes had not left Clara. "No," he said softly. "Give her a few moments and then she can be moved."

Moisture beaded at his palm and dripped down his wrist as Evian scrubbed the blood from his hands.

"You should also know," Evian said to Isobel, "Elisabeth is dead." Isobel sucked in a sharp breath, but otherwise didn't react. "Princess Solaris as well, and a female I don't know. Perhaps you might like to call for Elisabeth's second-in-command to watch over her body until the funeral."

CHAPTER FORTY-TWO
ISOBEL

Anger roiled through Isobel as she stood by Clara's feet. Never had she seen her so still—like Isobel, her need to fidget was as essential as breathing.

A surprising amount of grief stabbed through her chest. While she didn't truly like Elisabeth, she couldn't deny the woman had changed her life, and entirely for the better. Isobel was alive and sober because of her intervention, and as much as Elisabeth would hate to acknowledge it, she'd met Clara thanks to her.

Isobel would miss the cranky female.

"Where did you find them?" she asked Evian, her voice calmer than she felt.

"About an hour shy of the Flame border," he replied. "Head north-east. You won't miss them."

Isobel nodded, then turned to Beau. He wiped at Clara's forehead so gently. Isobel wanted to rip his arm from its socket, but instead she demanded he inform her if there was any change to Clara's condition.

The male had the nerve to scoff. "And shall I send a messenger pigeon to stars know where you're gallivanting off to?"

Isobel reined in her harsh retort, reminding herself that he loved Clara as well. He was prickly at the best of times, but now he was as riddled with fear as her—well, almost.

"I don't care how you manage it, Hawthorne, but I am trusting her in your care. You will send word and do so promptly."

"I do not take orders from you, Isobel." His glare would've hurt if it held any power, but the only reason she tolerated him was because of Clara. He meant a great deal to her. The surrounding air swelled and shrunk, dancing with murderous ambition. She had no more patience for pleasantries.

"If you want something," Beau said, his tone laced with his usual smug charm, "ask me nicely."

"You arrogant prick," Isobel muttered, then sighed. "Please."

"Of course." His smirk made her want to kick his teeth in.

Her rage grew with every step she took away from Clara's body, still lying limp on a dining table. Today she would not attempt to bottle her anger, or her aggression. Today she would let her emotions run wild and free, taking her in whichever direction they pleased.

Isobel left without another word, without the kiss she so desperately wanted to plant on Clara's lips. She told herself next time she'd kiss Clara with all the love and devotion she felt. The tiny voice in the back of her mind—that somehow was always the loudest—reminded her it was unlikely to be the case.

Isobel found the bodies soon enough, along with the spot where Clara fell, then dragged herself and then stopped again. Where she almost died while Isobel lay sleeping.

Anger swirled inside Isobel and in the air circling around her. Anger at herself, but more so at the female who had blood staining her wings. Lacklustre eyes Isobel knew were once bold—and cold in the most colourful way. This was a Dowling, similar in appearance to the others.

Isobel had encountered the brother and father many moons ago, passing through Tirenas while looking for exotic drugs. They'd been handsy and entitled, and she hadn't learnt to defend herself yet. Thankfully, Samara had been nearby, and heard Isobel shout, rushing to her rescue in all her frilly glory. They had underestimated the demure female in the lacy dress, to their detriment. Afterwards, Isobel stayed with Samara and then Elisabeth took her in. Samara taught Isobel self-defence and Poppy taught her how to be happy again, without the use of illicit substances.

But now Elisabeth was dead, and so was the one who'd tried to eliminate Clara. Though surely she didn't have enough brain cells to enact her plan alone, not if she was part of that family.

Isobel called to Samara, who immediately sent Ryland. After providing him with a brief explanation of what had happened, Isobel was eager to leave.

"Who will tell Christopher?" she asked, a fresh wave of grief washing over her for the boy.

The sweet, fragile boy would grow up far quicker than he ought to without a mother or father. His relatives were all dead except for an aunt he had not met, and a grandfather very much alive but not seen in years, thanks to his obsessions and thinly veiled selfish desires.

Ryland shook his head, then knelt by Elisabeth's side. He lay his hand close to hers, though their skin did not touch. He couldn't, not without the risk of causing discomfort to her soul. Elanist traditions put so much emphasis on the serenity of the dead, yet hardly any consideration for those left behind.

"I suppose I will," Ryland whispered.

Ryland was the closest thing to a brother, an uncle, or even a father the boy had ever known. His biological father had died when Christopher was young, though it wasn't like Elisabeth had shared any details. So now the excruciating task of informing the child he was now an orphan fell to the male grieving his closest friend. Isobel placed her hand on Ryland's shoulder and squeezed. As badly as she felt for him, Isobel hadn't the room to console him further.

She had to get away.

From the puddles of death and the nightmare she would thank every star, moon, and sun in the universe she didn't have to live within.

Shifting her focus, she pictured the barracks in the Cerulean Kingdom as the next destination in her search for answers.

Isobel materialised outside the soldiers' mess hall. Cheers and chatter floated from the open doors, the sound setting her teeth on edge. She stormed inside and marched up to the first group of soldiers who were sitting on the benches, eating their meal.

"Do you know the Dowling girl?" she snapped.

"Lena?" One of them asked, her mouth half filled with bread.

"Sure." Isobel gestured for her to hurry up.

She nodded. "She was in Elanist with Her Majesty. Why?"

Isobel ignored her question and instead asked one of her own. "Where does she bunk?"

“Who wants to know?” A male, a few seats down, inflated his chest and attempted to look foreboding.

Isobel held back her laugh—all puffing up did was make him look a fool. With hardly a thought, the air in his lungs evaporated, and he was left gasping and grabbing at his throat.

“I don’t like to repeat myself,” she said sweetly, with a facetious smile.

“Second level of the second tower. Fourth dorm on the right,” the female rushed out.

Isobel nodded and left silently, only restoring the air to the spluttering soldier once she was out the door.

By the time she reached Dowling’s dorm, the energy surrounding her roiled. Static buzzed along her skin, adding a furious bounce to her step—an eagerness she welcomed.

Three female soldiers lounged in the dorm room. One on the bottom of one bunk, the second on the top of the other, and the third with her back pressed along the opposite wall. They all jumped as Isobel threw open the door, slamming it to the wall behind. Drawing on the depthless hole of her rage, where her air magic was found, Isobel wound air around the females until they stood with varying degrees of anger and confusion and fear on their faces.

Without a word, Isobel turned and left the room, pulling the soldiers with her. Their protests were quickly silenced as Isobel stifled their breaths, slowly, until they got the message. Then she refilled their lungs, as there was no need for them to pass out before the real fun began.

Soon the winding halls straightened, and Isobel came to an unoccupied training arena near the far corner of the grounds. As far as she knew, these arenas weren’t used anymore. It was perfect, empty and secluded.

Isobel would revel in their pleas and screams.

Dumping them at her feet in the sand, Isobel closed her eyes and listened for the battle cry of her magic. The song of violence and pain she tried so hard to drown out. She used her fear for what could've been to pull roots from the ground and tie her captives. Her love for Clara, and the sparse but genuine love she had for Elisabeth, sparked a flame, and her anger blew it wide open until a bright-orange ring of fire encircled them all.

Silently, Isobel searched the soldiers one by one and took the weapons they possessed. The first was unprotected, bearing no weaponry at all. She was thrown into the fire and held down by the roots Isobel raised from the ground.

The taller of the remaining soldiers, with wings as dark as night and a glare to rival the flames, had a short sword strapped to her hip. She attempted to fight Isobel off, even landing a meagre punch to Isobel's lip, but the sting only fuelled her. In one clean swipe, the female's arm fell from her body, and her scream was as sweet as the war song filling Isobel's mind.

She smiled down at the now babbling soldier and took her own dagger in hand. Isobel used it to cleave the soldier's remaining arm, but she didn't remove it entirely. She left it partially severed, blood dripping at Isobel's feet.

The last female cowered—as she should—crying so quietly, but still pathetically loud. Three daggers were sheathed in a harness across her chest. Isobel took them forcefully, though this female did not fight. Instead, she begged and pleaded and sobbed. Pity.

Isobel took one blade at a time. The first landed deep in the soldier's eye socket. Blood sprayed across Isobel's bared teeth, warmth coated her tongue, and her snarl turned to a genuine smirk. That was how to end the female's blubbering, and she hissed crude, vulgar words at Isobel. Quickly coming to the realisation this female was not worth a damn thing, Isobel cut out her tongue.

Then Isobel took the third dagger and rammed it into the soldier's chest. She felt the resistance of bone and the grating of steel but pushed further, until there was no more resistance, and no more snarling or cursing from the dying female.

Angry noises came from her left, where the female whose severed arm filled the arena with the smell of charred skin now slumped. Isobel hardly heard whatever nonsense slewed from her mouth. All she heard was her pain and suffering, and rightfully so.

Her wrath not yet satisfied, Isobel hacked at the dead and dying bodies. Ripped the remaining arm from the mess at her feet, then hair and fingers and skin from whoever sat before her. She tore them limb from limb, with only a blood-filled smile and a sense of peaceful pride at the horror she'd inflicted.

Whether they deserved it, Isobel didn't care. She destroyed them anyway.

CHAPTER FORTY-THREE
CLARA

Golden hair like sunshine floats in the dank, colourless room.

Underground. Water flowing down above. No other way in or out.

But they try, try until their petite bodies seize. Until the tinkering of metal and jewels burns their skin, and waves of dizziness and nausea surpass the danger of the water trapping them in their cave.

A cell. A tiny, cramped, and unfitting room.

Treated like vermin, they sit and wait. But there is no escape.

Their pendants removed and power stifled, the witches cry at the knowledge sunlight will never again kiss their closed eyelids, nor the afternoon breeze brush against their cheeks.

They are going to die here.

Because no one knows that the Lady of Summer is plotting her revenge, using whoever she can in her twisted plans.

Alone, she is nothing.

Alone, she will fall.

But not before she destroys the others.
Not before she ruins them all.

CHAPTER FORTY-FOUR

BEAU

For two days, Beau sat by Clara's bedside. While he wanted to lie with her, he didn't want to disturb her more. So he'd pulled his armchair close to the mattress and sat vigil—still and scared.

After the first twelve hours, his rage had simmered, fading until fear was the only thing left coating his tongue and burning his throat. All he'd been able to think about for those twelve hours was how reckless she'd been. How selfish and foolish and careless. For a while, he was too angry to even touch her.

Then the tiny little nuisance of a voice in his head asked him what he would've done, had their roles been reversed. Would he have woken her and dragged her out of bed and into danger?

No. So a part of him understood.

He replayed the moment Mikhail kicked open the front door, barging past Beau and Isobel and so carefully laying her near lifeless body on the dining table.

Her blood dripped to the floor and echoed in his already ringing ears. How furiously and uncharacteristically still Isobel had stood, like a statue of wrath, a stoic guardian to keep death at bay.

His heartbeat skipped and shattered every time the image replayed in his mind, and then he couldn't bear not to hold her hand. To not feel the reassurance of her pulse every few minutes, or stare at her chest to make sure it still rose.

Isobel returned later that night, covered in blood and reeking of smoke. She hadn't said a word, just opened Clara's bedroom door, stared for a moment, then left. A moment later, a tap turned on, and half an hour after that she returned to the bedroom clean. She stayed as still and silent as Beau, sitting beside the door with her knees to her chest and her head resting on her forearms.

Late on the second night, Evian brought them trays of meat and vegetables. He set them down and lingered in the quiet before he cleared his throat. "Seren believes the toxin was a paralytic. Used to slow her heart until it stopped beating and preventing her magic from healing her."

Beau nodded, but Isobel didn't move.

"If she's correct, be prepared for Clara to be ill when she wakes," Evian added. "A side effect of not clearing it entirety from her system. She cannot expel it while unconscious, but the moment she wakes, the effects will be unavoidable. If we missed any, of course."

As Beau turned back to Clara, he saw her head dip backwards and slightly press into the pillow. Her lips parted and eyebrows furrowed. Beau stood, and in the next heartbeat, Isobel was beside him.

Clara murmured something incoherent, then her eyes fluttered open. Air filled Beau's lungs, and he was finally able to breathe. Isobel let out a shaky sob, her hand flying to her mouth, and without thinking, Beau brushed his hand along her back in reassurance. Isobel narrowed her eyes at his gesture before her expression softened. She nodded slowly at him, as her eyes welled with more tears.

"The witches are in Morrin," Clara croaked, then attempted to clear her throat. Isobel huffed a laugh while Beau rolled his eyes. "I think."

"That is the least of our priorities right now," Isobel said softly.

It was gentler than Beau was capable of at this moment, since all the anger he'd felt yesterday came crashing back in a wave—now that he knew she was truly alive, and mostly okay.

"Would you care to explain what the fuck you were doing?" Beau growled, unable to control his rising temper.

Clara, likely already expecting his outburst, sighed and gave him a flat look. "Can I at least have a hug before you berate me?"

Beau wrapped her in his arms and held her close enough he could feel her hot breath on his collar, and her strong heartbeat against his chest. His hand stroked her hair while he planted a kiss on her crown. He inhaled deeply, so he might never forget her cinnamon scent.

Clara groaned under the strength of his grip, and her body stiffened.

"I don't care," Beau muttered into her hair. "The fact that you can groan means you're alive and I, for one, need the fucking reminder." Beau squeezed once more before he pulled away.

Clara's expression softened when she faced Isobel, and a small smile crept over her face. Isobel seemed to shrink back against the wall, so Clara held up a hand in offering, then patted the mattress beside her.

Isobel looked to Beau, almost as if seeking reassurance. When he did not give it to her, a pang of jealousy flared, but he did not deny her either.

Reluctantly, Isobel crawled onto the bed at Clara's side. Clara wrapped an arm around her shoulders and pulled her close, then entwined the fingers of her other hand in Beau's.

"Who did this?" Beau demanded, as he rubbed his thumb over Clara's silken skin.

"It doesn't matter," she replied with a sigh.

"Like hell it doesn't," Beau growled. "I'll kill them. Tell me who—"

"You can't." Isobel and Clara spoke in unison, cutting him off. Beau's chest flooded with heat, which then surged along his skin.

"The fuck I can't!" he shouted. "I swear to the fucking gods, Clara, if you do not tell me—"

Again, she cut him off with a glare to match his own. "They're already dead."

Relief doused his fiery rage, and Beau's shoulders relaxed a little.

"All of them," Isobel muttered.

Beau raised an eyebrow at her, but she shook her head. They would talk later.

"Don't you ever do that again," he whispered through gritted teeth. "Ever."

"I would not willingly put either of you in harm's way."

"No." Beau couldn't help the hollow laugh that escaped him, nor did he miss the aggravated expression on Isobel's face. "Instead, you were perfectly fine winding up in the middle of nowhere, half dead and with no one to account for your whereabouts! Do you understand how stupid that was? How selfish?"

"Do not yell at me." Clara's voice hardened. "I made a choice. One I can promise you, that if the need arises, I will make again." She sighed, then tore her icy glare from him to look down. "You can call me selfish and stupid and whatever else you damn well please, Beau, but you will be alive to do so. That's what I was trying to do, and all I cared about. I will not apologise for that."

"It was incredibly stupid, and even more selfish. Clara, I don't want your apologies. I want you alive and safe. How do you think we would have felt to find you dead in the dirt—tomorrow or the next day—when it was too late to do anything to reverse it?" Beau shook his head, still riled and angry, more so than he'd expected. However, as he listened to her gentle voice, it wavered.

"And how do you think I could live with myself if something happened to either of you?" Her voice cracked a little, as did Beau's heart hearing it. "If my heart beat but yours did not, I may as well carve it from my own chest. I went through that once already, and I am not prepared to do it again." Clara's grip on his hand tightened, and she stared so deep into his soul he struggled not to melt under her gaze. "Do you hear me? You. Died. Already."

Beau's heart shattered as her voice broke. He remembered her desolate wails in the Cerulean Castle. He'd hurt her then, and it was the last thing he wanted to do.

"If your heart stops beating, Clara, I could carve apart a thousand men and it still would not replace my own shattered and irreparable one. If your heart stops, my world ceases to exist. I am begging you, do not put me in that position again, where I am left to wonder if I will ever breathe again."

"Perhaps," Isobel piped up, "we ought to focus on the fact that you are alive, Clara. That we can wake another morning, graced by your loud and colourful presence."

Beau realised what she was doing, and he appreciated Isobel's interruption. The last thing Clara needed now was more guilt, and he'd said his piece.

He understood her choice more than he'd care to admit, and why she could never promise to act otherwise despite his begging. He offered Isobel an appreciative smile, before he brought Clara's knuckles to his mouth and kissed them.

She softened at his touch, her shoulders relaxing as her body leant more into Isobel's side. She even rested her head on Isobel's, and Beau had the sense he should give them a moment. He didn't understand the tug they had towards one another, and jealousy as green as Clara's eyes and as fiery as her hair roiled in his gut. Though his ego was as easily bruised as her skin, he knew without a doubt Clara loved him. Perhaps she simply had more love in her heart than he wanted her to give.

His hand immediately felt cold as Beau stood and tugged it from Clara's grasp. "I'll be right outside," he said as he kissed her forehead. Each step away felt heavier, but he trusted Isobel.

With Clara's life and wellbeing, at least.

CHAPTER FORTY-FIVE

CLARA

Despite Evian giving her medical clearance, Clara had been forced to rest in bed until Elisabeth's funeral. Her mother scolded her whenever she tried to leave her room, each time with tears soaking her face.

The morning of the funeral finally arrived, and with it, a flurry of conflicting emotions. Relief and a sense of freedom at being allowed from her room, then guilt stronger than her grief, capped off by nerves at meeting the Tirenas queen once again.

Ryland momentarily hesitated as Clara arrived at the funeral site, then stood from where he knelt beside Elisabeth's body. He paused before he sighed and enfolded Clara in a tight hug.

"I'm so sorry," he whispered.

"Me too," Clara replied, and held him back.

As he pulled away, Ryland searched her face. "Are you okay?"

She nodded, and his gaze settled on Beau or Isobel behind her. She couldn't see their response, but Ryland dipped his chin and let Clara go.

She spared Elisabeth's body a quick glance before she walked to the soldier keeping watch over Princess Solaris.

They gave each other a silent greeting, and Clara confirmed the queen was coming. The soldier nodded, raising a hand to gesture behind Clara, and she turned to find the queen walking over, a hard expression on her face.

"What does one do at a funeral?" Eveline asked, as she stopped in front of Clara. No greeting, no niceties, though Clara should've expected as much.

"Honour the dead and grieve," Clara replied, with a gentle shrug of one shoulder. "Remember and celebrate the life you shared with them." She paused, taking note of Eveline's drawn brows and pursed lips. "We have traditions, but you can make your own. Did you share anything special?"

"We're twins. We share everything," she snarled, baring her teeth.

"Watch your tone. I'm trying to be civil, but that can quickly change."

Clara was not interested in politics today, nor did she have time to coddle and simper before the queen. Today was for loss and love, and Clara would not play to Eveline's ego. They grieved the same loss, one of a sister. While Clara knew the impact that loss had was different, she was extending a courtesy that only reached so far.

Eveline sighed and looked away. "She plays—*played*—the violin, and I would sing. Ever since we were small." Her voice shrunk with each word.

"Anything a musician here would know?" Clara asked, her tone softer now.

"Perhaps," Eveline mumbled.

Clara turned to Beau and asked him if he remembered where Seren lived. She'd pointed it out weeks ago as they'd strolled through town. He nodded, so Clara asked him to fetch her brother and inform him his musical services were required.

Before Beau returned, Samara materialised beside Ryland. She placed a hand on his cheek, and her eyes locked on his. He nodded, took her hand, and kissed her palm before he disappeared.

Samara's sweet, lilting voice filled Clara's mind. *I hate that it is under such circumstances, but are you ready to meet your nephew?*

She gasped. Then a new set of nerves twinged her heart and singed her throat.

"Does he know?" Clara asked, and Samara shook her head.

Ryland is telling him now.

"Is he prepared to see his mother's body? Should he see it?" Clara's eyes flicked to where Elisabeth lay. She wasn't sure how she would cope if it was her mother lying there. Christopher was young, not even school age yet. Clara couldn't imagine how this might fuck with him, and her heart hurt for the boy.

It doesn't matter. He is of royal blood, and tradition demands he be present. Samara paused, her head tilted. *Besides, does he not deserve the chance to say goodbye, regardless of his age?*

Clara knew Samara was right. She didn't want to deny the boy a chance to grieve properly, or to say goodbye to his mother. Still, it seemed cruel for someone so young to witness death so closely.

When he materialised with Ryland, his eyes were red rimmed and his cheeks streaked with tears. Dark-brown hair, almost black, dropped to his eyebrows and framed his precious, round face. Small fingers wrapped around Ryland's hand, holding it in a vice grip, so his fair skin turned white. His green eyes—even brighter than

Clara's—jumped from soldier to soldier, from the queen to Clara, then finally to his mother. More tears spilled then, in unending waves. All Clara wanted to do was snatch him up and hold him tight, to shield him from all this pain.

"Hello, Christopher," Clara whispered as she dropped to a knee before him. He did not respond, only searched her face. What for, she didn't know. Though when she held out her hand, he grasped it, as if some part of him recognised and felt safe with her. Clara's heart squeezed with relief, then as she stood she made sure her hand did not leave his.

"Which service would you like to hold?" Ryland asked quietly. Clara hadn't even considered the possibilities. Elisabeth came from a family of Vequil Inalis, though she only held Candor magic. Should the Candor service be carried out, or a mixture of them all, like Clara had done for Neven? How was she supposed to pick?

She shook her head, unsure and uncomfortable with the pressure.

"Might I offer some advice?" Eveline asked gently. Clara gestured for her to continue. "Your sister is dead. In Tirenas, at least by my father's standard, we do not mourn those who are no longer here. The living are all that matter, and so it is the living who call the shots. Choose the ceremony you want." She paused, taking a shaky breath as she looked towards her sister, then waved her arm towards Elisabeth. "Because they no longer have a voice to tell you anything."

"Flame," Clara whispered.

It was the court she felt most comfortable in, the magic she'd had the longest and felt the strongest connection. Fire destroyed with such power and ferocity. Fire also healed, warmed, and comforted.

Ryland nodded, then spoke quietly with Isobel as Beau returned with Seren and her brother. He held his violin in hand, and made his way to the queen, bowing low before they, too, spoke. Clara felt

Seren's eyes bore into her, but she couldn't look at the wide-eyed female yet.

Later, but not yet.

In the Court of Flame, memorials were brief. A few words spoken of the dead as their body burned, but otherwise the only sounds were the cries of the loved ones left behind. So Clara indicated they were to hold off burning Elisabeth's body until Eveline's song had been played.

As Seren's brother played, goosebumps erupted over Clara's skin. Tears welled as the haunting notes echoed in the open space. She did not recognise the song, even as Eveline's angelic voice sang lyrics of love and friendship, growing old together, of lives entwined and shared. She couldn't help but spare a glance at Seren, who, thankfully, had looked away as she dabbed at her own eyes.

Eveline's voice wobbled as tears drenched her cheeks. Then, the queen dropped to her knees, her song as broken as her voice. For a moment, all she did was silently sob, her shoulders hunched and face held in her hands. Seren's brother played on.

Christopher's hand squeezed Clara's, and in the corner of her eye the vision of a little girl flashed. She blinked, and the girl vanished, replaced by Christopher. He led her forward, towards where Eveline knelt in the dirt, his watery eyes darting from Clara to the queen.

"Why does she cry?" he asked, his voice as small as he was.

"Someone very important to her died," Clara said, unsure if she should've chosen a better phrase but unwilling to sugarcoat the situation.

"Me too," he whispered, his tiny lip quivering, and he looked away.

"Go to Ryland," Clara said, and jerked her chin towards the male. "I think he could use a hug."

Christopher nodded, and once his hand left hers, Clara placed it on Eveline's shoulder.

Seren's voice rang out from behind her. She'd always had a beautiful voice, though she didn't sing often. Whenever she did, Clara shivered from the magical tone. Today was no exception.

Eveline continued to sob even once the song ended. The sound of her cries hacked at Clara's chest.

"Are you ready for the burning?" Isobel asked, now standing beside Clara. Eveline looked up at them but said nothing. Clara only nodded, then took her hand from Eveline's shoulder and knelt before Elisabeth's body.

"Christopher first," Clara whispered.

Isobel placed her hand on Elisabeth's chest and closed her eyes. Flames burst to life quickly, engulfing Elisabeth entirely and warming Clara's face. A few more tears spilled as she watched the sister she'd only begun to know burn.

Isobel stood, her hand covered in charcoal, and she gave Clara a sympathetic look before she walked to Christopher. She whispered something to him before he closed his eyes, and Isobel drew a single vertical line down his cheek with his mother's ashes. His little shoulders shook, his eyes squeezing shut as his cries tore through the air.

"Why?" Eveline asked, her voice raspy as she came to kneel by Clara.

"So part of the dead remains with the loved ones left behind. So they continue to know a piece of their deceased is always with them." Clara paused and took a deep breath while Eveline looked longingly at her sister's body. "Would you like to do the same with Solaris?"

Eveline took a shuddering breath, clamped her mouth shut, and nodded. Clara patted her knee a few times before Isobel came back and placed her clean hands in the still raging fire.

Two horizontal lines were drawn across Clara's nose. She felt them, rather than saw Isobel mark her, as her own eyes were closed. Isobel's palms rested on Clara's cheeks for a moment before she planted a gentle kiss on Clara's forehead and stood.

Clara stood as Eveline did, and they slowly walked the few steps to Solaris' body.

"Ready?" Clara asked, sniffing.

Eveline only nodded, and Clara set the princess' body alight. After a moment of letting her burn, Clara crouched and placed her hand on Solaris' chest. When she stood, Eveline's eyes were tightly closed, her own chest and shoulders bobbing.

Gently, Clara dragged her thumb across Eveline's nose.

"Let it seep in," she whispered. "Let it soak into your soul and know a part of her will always kiss your skin. Always bask in the sunlight and relish under the moon."

When the marks were drawn, Isobel suffocated the flames and let the wind sweep the ashes away, clearing the dirt from where the women's bodies had lain.

"This does not make us friends, Clara Afron." Eveline spoke steadily, even as she sniffed and wiped away a tear. Like a queen. "Though perhaps we could be allies."

Clara extended her hand, which Eveline took willingly.

"I'm sorry for your loss, Eveline."

The queen only nodded.

CHAPTER FORTY-SIX

CLARA

Once Eveline and her soldiers left, Ryland took Christopher back to the palace with Samara. He made a comment about their throne requiring someone to sit upon it, but Clara waved him away. She wasn't ready to think about that right now, and he was more than capable of managing the kingdom until she was ready.

For now, she was only prepared to face one thing and had no space to contemplate anything else.

Beau and Isobel put up quite the fuss when she asked them to return home without her, but conceded after she assured them she wasn't staying back long, and she wouldn't be alone.

Seren stood with her brother as he packed his violin away. Clara offered him a sad smile as he rose, which he returned before dipping his chin and leaving. Seren turned to walk with him, but Clara reached out and grabbed her wrist, stopping her. She spun, eyes wide and full of emotion. The bright blue swirled with uncertainty and hope.

She opened her mouth, but Clara raised a hand, stopping her before she could speak.

"I am angry," she said, then sucked in a breath. "Angry and hurt because of your actions." Seren's gaze dropped, but it rose again when Clara snaked her hand into Seren's instead of having it wrapped around her wrist. "But I don't want to lose you. Irijna and David have gone. Neven and Elisabeth are dead. I almost died, for heaven's sake." Clara shook her head. "I don't want to lose anyone else, and I miss you."

Tears spilled from Seren's eyes, and she squeezed Clara's hand tightly as she whispered, "I miss you, too, Clara."

"Do you know what my first thought was after finding out I had a sister?" Clara asked, and Seren shook her head. "I never wanted a sister because you were enough. And I understand why you told them, and I truly hope your father is well and healed."

"I'm so sorry," Seren cried. She covered her face with her free hand. "If I'd known what—"

"No, don't," Clara interrupted. "You couldn't have done anything differently, and I don't blame you. I'd like to move on, if you wou—"

This time Seren cut her off, barrelling into Clara's chest and hugging her tightly. It was a comfort she'd not realised how greatly she'd missed, and Clara wrapped her arms around Seren and squeezed her back.

She knew she could always count on Seren. True friendship didn't require them to be joined at the hip and finishing each other's sentences.

It was the freedom to live as she wished. To be herself, without judgement, knowing there was someone waiting for her.

Three days later, Felicity bustled around the kitchen as Clara returned home from work. Mikhail had insisted on walking her home, both this shift and her last, though she insisted she was fine. He did not take no for an answer, and so she had an escort. Truthfully, she appreciated his—and everyone else's—concern, even if it was a little overbearing.

"This came for you," her mother called, holding up an envelope.

"Have you been holding it since it arrived, mother?" Clara teased.

"No, you cheeky bugger." Her mother chuckled, the envelope still in hand. "It arrived only a few moments ago, and I hadn't put it down yet. There's no return address, so I'm not sure who sent it."

Clara shrugged and took the envelope, opening it hastily and ripping the paper, causing her mother to grimace.

Inside was a beautifully scrawled letter.

A whisper on the wind told me your engagement ball will be held next week. I thought it prudent to send well wishes for health, happiness, and safety. Perhaps also some wisdom for the bride-to-be.

I think a dance with an old friend under the dim lights would do you some good. Wear pearls, as lace is unseemly for a queen.

Maja

X

At first glance, it seemed innocuous enough. To anyone unable to read between the lines, it appeared a congratulatory regard, and a suggestion to meet with an old friend, but Clara knew better.

Maja's letter not only informed her of a danger lurking in the shadows but also that Ora would be able to shed some light.

It had been a long time since she'd seen the Oracle—her friend and old boss at the pleasure house, The Pearl 'n Lace. Perhaps a visit was due.

The next morning, three envelopes arrived, slid through the slit in the door before anyone woke.

First was a letter from Prince Jude, announcing a string of balls to be held in honour of their betrothal. A masquerade ball to celebrate their upcoming nuptials, another mask-free ball for Clara to be formally introduced to Morrin society, and finally a traditional private ceremony between the betrothed couple and their immediate families, followed by another elaborate party. Clara's head swam, thinking about them all.

The second envelope contained her invitation to those balls, and to Morrin in general. Signed and sealed with a kiss, if the nearly illegible handwriting of Prince Jude was to be believed. And in the third, an invitation to whomever Clara wished to bring. Her mother, brothers, Beau, Isobel, and Ryland were listed by name, followed by the phrase, *along with any and all folks her future majesty sees fit to attend.*

Clara rolled her eyes but couldn't help the smile which twitched at her lips.

As she wandered back to her room to inform Beau and Isobel they'd be travelling in a matter of days, she was met with wild hands and raised voices. They'd managed to share a room in peace until now, if Clara could ignore the annoyed glances and narrowed eyes they exchanged when they thought she wasn't watching. Or the way Beau took up more of the bed than normal, so Isobel would stay on her portable mattress instead of climbing in with them like Clara so desperately wanted.

"What about me?" Beau flung his arms and smacked his hand to his chest. "Did you consider I might've liked to join on that particular adventure? No, of course not."

Isobel shook her head and pinched the bridge of her nose.

"It's not about you, Bird Boy. Nothing I do is ever, *ever* going to have anything to do with you."

"It's blatant exclusion and a pointed shot at my masculinity is what it is. Did you know about this?" He whirled to Clara, who shot her hands up defensively.

"He's angry that I left him at home and did all the dirty work myself," Isobel said over Beau's shoulder. "You know, you could do with being knocked down a few pegs. Your arrogance is showing."

"Is this about you murdering Lena Dowling's friends?" Clara asked and smiled when Isobel nodded.

"You told her?" Beau snapped.

"Of course I did," Isobel fired back, a smug look plastered on her face. "I've no intention of keeping secrets from her."

Beau growled in frustration and turned his back to Isobel, then demanded, "What?"

Clara's eyebrows rose further. "I don't think so. Try that again."

"You're so like each other, and I can only deal with one of you at a time," Beau muttered loud enough they both heard him.

Isobel smirked, but Clara only waited.

Beau sighed again, then in a much calmer tone said, "I'm sorry. What is it?"

"Invitations from Morrin arrived. We leave in two days."

Bags packed and filling the hallway, Clara did a quick headcount. Her mother, Beau, and Isobel stood by the door. In contrast, Evian had no bags and was hardly even dressed for the occasion.

"You aren't ready?" Clara commented, though it came out like a question.

Evian shook his head with a smile. "I won't be attending." Before Clara could say anything in return, her widened eyes and gaping mouth surely already speaking volumes, Evian continued. "As much as I hate to miss your announcement ball, I have another queen to see."

"What do you want with her?" Clara hissed, causing her mother to scold her, though her tone was hushed. The Tirenas queen might've left on civil terms, but Clara had no doubts her priorities consisted of herself, and herself alone. Eveline could not be wholly trusted, and nerves trickled from Clara's nape to her heels.

"Something more than this court can offer me, Clara. I'm going to inquire about joining her ranks."

"You're going to *what*?" their mother shrieked as she flew past Clara to smack Evian's shoulder. Clara barely stifled her laugh. "Did you even think of running this by your mother, Evian? No, because my entire family is determined to age me unnecessarily and put me in an early grave."

"Mother, please." Evian clutched the frantic woman's hands and planted a kiss on her forehead. "I am merely inquiring, and nothing may come of it. Enjoy your trip to Morrin."

Then he pulled away and looked back at Clara. He chuckled at her hard stare and narrowed eyes, but she did not relent.

"You will do well to remember who you plan to pledge your fealty to." She pointed a finger at her brother's chest. "And who raised her."

“I will,” Evian replied, as he pulled Clara in for a long hug. “I just cannot ignore the feeling that everything I need is in Tirenas. I don’t know what I’m looking for, but that’s where I need to start.”

“Be careful,” she hissed against his chest.

“Always.”

“And for fuck’s sake, Evian. Don’t die.” When Clara pulled back to glare up at him, her harsh expression weakened.

“I wouldn’t dream of it, little sister.”

CHAPTER FORTY-SEVEN

CLARA

Music vibrated along the glass walls and across the polished floor. Cheery, uplifting music, which Clara easily got lost in, swaying amidst the dozens of Morrinian nobles and high-ranking fae all decorated in the colours of winter—silver, blue, and beige. Their faces were adorned with masks of all different shapes and sizes, some held with ribbon or string, others twisted off bone and spiked handles. Isobel and Beau stood close by her on either side, though the dancers often swirled between the trio.

Beau's mask covered the entirety of his face, dust coloured and translucent from the nose up. It covered his jaw with a mandible, solid and unmoving even when he spoke. The top of his mask imitated the rest of a skull, though his face was visible beneath—mostly the glow of his amber eyes, which contrasted with the colours whirling about the ballroom. So, too, did his magnificent wings.

Isobel's mask also replicated a face, though hers was simple and porcelain, shielding her eyes only. Toned lighter than her skin, it had a gloss finish that shone under the magical lights in the ballroom, accentuating the feminine cosmetics across her makeshift eyelids and brows. Hues of lilac glittered around her eyes, drawing out every fragment of gold in her beautiful irises. Clara counted herself very lucky to be present with them both by her side. To have them at all.

Clara's own mask was far simpler. A patchwork of lace covered only her eyes and cheekbones, and was tied with silk at the back of her head. Strings of clear and cloudy gemstones hung from the fraying edges and dripped down her face. The ultimate effect looked almost like tears.

They matched the beads connecting her criss-crossed bandeau and sheer, draping skirt. Whether this was appropriate for a royal ball, Clara didn't know, and frankly, did not care.

The bold red colour was true to her character and her magic, but was also a statement. Red was the colour of power, of bravery, pride, confidence, and strength. No one else was dressed in such a daring shade, and Clara had expected as much. She was not here as arm candy for a prince, nor a toy for a future king. She was not a subject or a servant.

Clara was a force entirely unto herself and she would not be dulled or changed to fit their mould.

Her dress was half see-through and the colour of chaos, and she fought to hide her smirk at every look of surprise thrown her way.

Polite and welcoming conversation battled with the sound of violins and wind instruments. A subtle drum kept time in the background. Clara took a sip from her goblet, and some of the incredibly bubbly liquid spilled over her lip and down her chin. Racing to catch it, to dab and dry her made-up face before anyone noticed, Clara hadn't seen the clearly intoxicated male move beside her.

"What else does that pretty little mouth do, sugar?" he purred, though his letters ran together, along with his lopsided grin and swaying frame.

Clara bit the inside of her lip so she did not laugh. He seemed friendly enough. No malicious energy followed him, nor did any jittery feeling rake down Clara's spine. Sober enough to trust her judgement, Clara decided the best course of action was to brush the encounter off as nothing more than an innocent attempt at flirting.

After all, with her mask and no formal introduction, this male did not know Clara's identity, or who she was to become. She smiled and shrugged a shoulder as she answered him. "Complain."

The male lost his composure for a second, unable to hide his shock. He blinked a few times, then jerked his chin towards Isobel, who had closed the small distance between them, Beau at her side.

"She bites," Clara said with a wink, as Isobel flashed her canines in the most harmless and pretty smile Clara had ever seen her give a male. The conversation at its end, Clara took Isobel's hand and walked away.

Behind her, she heard a thud, as if Beau had clapped the male on the shoulder or back.

"It's true." His words were followed by a chuckle, and then Beau was in step behind her. She felt his burning stare on her ass as she swung her hips and smirked.

Not fifteen minutes later, another drunk male with a sloppy excuse for a smirk and arrogance—and perhaps entitlement—filling his dark-brown eyes approached Clara. Isobel had offered to refill her goblet, but immediately Beau insisted on doing it himself. In the end, they'd both gone, with the promise of wine and other treats upon their return. Now she watched as they stood bickering at the refreshments table, and Clara swayed to the lilting music.

Her peace had been interrupted by a crass voice and a far more malicious attempt at flirting. His eyes raked over Clara in the most unsettling way, his lips wet from his continual licking of them. He leant in far too closely, and all Clara could smell as he opened his mouth was one of the alcohols being served.

"I would refrain from your actions, if I were you, sir." Clara tried to keep the annoyance from her voice but feared she had failed. Though truthfully, she wasn't all that heartbroken by it.

The male bared his teeth as he snarled down at her. "And why is that, honey?"

His use of a pet name had Clara fighting not to physically recoil. The sleaze coating this male was so thick, almost visible to the naked eye. It was in his energy, in his eyes, and dripping from the words on his tongue. In the sheen of sweat at his hairline, the moustache that did not quite meet his top lip, and the hair intentionally spiked in too much gel. It took everything in her not to shudder or turn up her nose.

"Well, first of all, I think you'll feel rather foolish in the days to come when you realise that you are fantasising about groping your queen and calling her *honey*. Not to mention," she continued, as she waved a hand to Beau and Isobel, who now faced her, sporting nearly identical incredulous and irritated expressions, "my very protective, quick-to-judge entourage cut off limbs first and ask questions later. And they do not truly care for answers."

"She doesn't look all that scary," the male scoffed and puffed out his chest.

"Oh, she'll be extremely disappointed to hear that."

Then Jude was at her side, linking his arm through hers as he took in the stranger, still standing too close for Clara's comfort.

His mask had been pulled up over his hairline, though it didn't look stupid at all, and it eased Clara to see the prince so relaxed in such a formal setting. She hadn't realised how much tension had built until her jaw softened and shoulders sagged.

"You aren't my queen anyway," the male sneered.

Before Clara could offer a retort, Jude spoke.

"Give it a few weeks," he said in such an upbeat tone it took Clara a moment to register his words. Luckily, Jude whisked her away from the now agitated and spluttering stranger, and she hoped never to interact with him again.

"*Weeks*?" Clara shrieked quietly, though evidently, not quietly enough.

"Hush," Jude said, and patted her hand resting on his elbow. "You'll frighten the children."

His head turned to the side slightly, and his eyes darted further back. Towards where Isobel and Beau followed them, only a few paces behind. Clara let out a resigned sigh and shook her head.

"Don't forget," Jude continued, "tomorrow we have the gifting ceremony. It's tradition for the bride- and groom-to-be to present their in-laws with gifts. I think originally it was payment for permission to wed, but it has morphed throughout the centuries into appreciation for their child's hand. *Child* meaning offspring. We have never married off literal children."

"Good to know," Clara muttered. "So I will offer the King and Queen of Morrin gifts for their son's hand, and you will offer my mother a gift in kind?"

"Yes, exactly."

"And you didn't think to mention this *before* I arrived? Were you hoping I would make a fool of myself?"

"No, shush." Jude shook his head. "I'm trying to help you. My mother does not like thoughtless gifts. She has all the gold and riches she could ever need, so vanity and materialistic gifts will get you nowhere. She requires a more sentimental approach, though do not be open about it. In her mind, and from her tongue, she insists sentimentality is a show of weakness. Though she will never admit it, and blatantly refuses to acknowledge it, thoughtfulness is her favourite guilty pleasure.

"My father is a simple man at heart. He cares for appearances and good craftmanship. I do not know how that information will help, but it's the best I can offer."

"The best you can offer?" Clara repeated, pulling Jude to a stop. "Jude, the *best you could offer* would've been to prepare me ahead of time and not spring this monumental news on me mere hours before I need these items."

Clara pinched the bridge of her nose and attempted the calming breaths she'd seen Isobel take so many times. She'd evidently not mastered the act. Fucking stars. She was going to embarrass herself in front of royalty, though at least not for the first time.

However, this was the first time she wanted to do it right. Wanted to do well, to be presentable and demure and successful. To be princess-like.

"I have faith in you, Clara." Jude gently pinched her cheek before he cupped it with his large, cool hand. "Use that big, wonderful mind of yours to come up with something."

Clara sighed. "And what will you be presenting to my mother?"

"I can't give everything away, now can I?" Jude winked at her as he chuckled.

"Asshole," Clara muttered.

He pecked her on the cheek, then joined the flurry of folk dancing and mingling in the ballroom.

Clara had been given her own suite while staying in Morrin, as had her family. Ryland—naturally—had been placed in the first suite in one of the many guest wings of the Iridescent Palace, then her mother, then Isobel, then Clara, and finally Beau, lined up orderly along an incredibly long wall. The foyer of the wing was a massive landing, connecting it to the grand staircase that led deeper into the palace, and it was adorned with paintings and small tables covered in unique pieces of art and history. Clara knew this, as Ryland had gushed about his favourite pieces before the ball last night.

This morning, Clara woke in Beau's arms, after having refused to sleep on her own since she'd so long shared his bed. He hadn't stirred, so she did not wake him. Instead, she crept from the bed, donning a simple, gauzy dress that draped elegantly over her shoulders and tiptoed from the room. She left a note scrawled on a pad and placed it by his head. Something told her picking flowers was not a reason he wanted to be dragged from bed.

Clara wandered into Isobel's room to ask if she'd fancy a trip into the hills. She was torn about waking Isobel—the female seemed so calm as she slept, and it felt wrong to disturb her. Guilt riddled her chest, but hope and excitement won out when her fair lashes fluttered open, and her lips burst into a sleepy smile.

Isobel didn't hesitate, bouncing from bed and dressing similarly to Clara, in a supplied article of clothing she assumed was customary in Morrin and was likely also offered to Clara's mother. The two strolled from the castle arm in arm, towards the knolls and the recently risen sun, not yet at its peak.

"Are you nervous?" Isobel asked tentatively. She stood with her back to Clara, but the wind travelling uphill sent the smell of summer berries to caress her senses.

Clara sighed and ran her fingers along the velvet petal of a half-bloomed ruby rose. "More than I expected to be."

"Why?" Isobel's tone was gentle and inquisitive, but her question was vague.

"The last time I saw Queen Sylvina, she threw me in the dungeon." Clara shrugged and spun to face Isobel.

"Why?" she repeated, letting out a breath filled with audible disbelief.

"I may have inadvertently threatened her kingdom." Clara couldn't help but wince at the memory. "Including Jude and their dog. Apparently, she has a temper."

Isobel inhaled sharply. "Oh, my . . ." she trailed off. "May I speak freely for a moment?"

"Please never ask such a silly question again. I do not wish for you to wonder; you may do as you please."

Isobel dipped her chin, though apologetically or in acknowledgement, Clara didn't know.

"I believe in you, Clara." She spoke softly, twirling a handful of daisies in her grasp. "And I believe you're here in Morrin for more than helping a male find balance or allowing his life to remain full of love. There's something bigger at work. You're going to change the world one day, and it starts right here. Do not underestimate yourself." She paused, then added even more quietly, "I sure don't."

Clara's jaw dropped slightly. She hadn't known what Isobel would say, hadn't even wanted to guess, but that certainly was not it. Warmth flooded her chest, as did a thousand butterflies.

"Thank you," she murmured. "That was very kind."

"Did it help to settle your nerves at all?"

"Not even a little," Clara said with a frustrated exhale. "I think you've made them worse."

Isobel giggled sweetly, like cold honey on a summer's day. Clara couldn't help but join her, and before she knew it, the two of them were lying in the long grass and laughing together.

By the time Clara returned, the palace was alive with activity. Staff carried vases so enormous their heads could not be seen—they surely couldn't see where they were going. Others followed with trays stocked with dinnerware and glasses. She and Isobel passed nearly two dozen fae decked in powder-blue uniforms and pristine white gloves, who scurried past, narrowly avoiding knocking into anyone.

Tonight, as she had for the masquerade ball, Clara was free to dress as she pleased. However, unlike last night, she and her entourage had been instructed to dress within the parameters of the evening's theme: *Moonlight Meets Dawn.*

Supposedly, it symbolised the joining of the two kingdoms, each powerful in their own right, but more so together. It also represented how this unity would bring strength and magic like none had ever known, and beauty beyond measure.

Clara couldn't help but roll her eyes. Though if she were being honest, the hues of blue and gold were breathtaking, and she was excited to dress up again.

Beau wasn't in his room, but on her pillow was the note she'd left him with his messy handwriting scratched beneath. It informed her he'd gone for a suit fitting, though she wondered briefly how a fitting might work for someone with wings, whether a Morrin tailor would know how to make the adjustments or could lace the fabric with the same magic his other clothes held.

Though she did not think on it long, as Isobel zipped into the room and stuffed Clara into a beautiful flowing skirt and loose, sheer bandeau, which was far too revealing for a meeting with the king and queen. Isobel clicked her tongue but eventually agreed. With a pair of scissors she pulled out of nowhere, Isobel ducked under the many layers of tulle and silk of Clara's skirt and cut the slip.

"The skirt will be more uncomfortable now," she mumbled as she twisted the sheet of fabric across Clara's shoulders and midsection. While part of her was disappointed by the modesty, it was much more fitting for royal company. "But it'll have to do, and you look beautiful."

Clara smiled, her whole body warm and tingly from Isobel's compliments. Her approval.

Shortly after, Isobel dressed in an elegant, backless white gown, delicate gold beading draping across her back. She was stunning, the finery fit for a goddess.

An artist arrived and forced Clara into an uncomfortable wooden chair, then applied a dozen powders and creams to her face. Clara marvelled at her reflection, admiring the glimmer on her lids and the red stain on her lips. She looked beautiful indeed.

Though her arms felt bare without her bangles and bracelets, the dress was statement enough. Ready as she would ever be, Clara linked arms with Isobel, and together they strode towards the awaiting king and queen.

CHAPTER FORTY-EIGHT

CLARA

"Before we begin the passing of gifts . . ." King Taron's voice boomed through the hall from where he sat atop the dais in a burgundy wood throne, upholstered in a deep silver. The queen sat to his left, her throne near identical, except for size. "I would like to confirm the name you wish to be presented by at this evening's ball. Clarenna Hayes, or Clara Afron?"

Clara felt a painful tugging in her heart as she held back the answer she wanted to give—Clara Afron. That was her name, who she was raised to be, and the family she knew and loved. However, now betrothed to a future king, and descended from royal lineage herself, she knew it was not the answer.

Her mother squeezed Clara's hand, and when Clara turned to her, she found warmth radiating from her face, alongside contentment, pride, and approval. Clara was her daughter and holding a different name or title would never change that fact.

"Clarenna Hayes." Clara bowed her head low.

"And in private?"

"Informally, Clara is fine, Majesty."

"Alright then." King Taron clapped his hands and gestured for Jude to step towards Clara's mother. "Clara, come forward. What have you chosen to gift my wife, your future mother-in-law, Queen Sylvina?"

Heavens knew why he felt the need to tack on every title the female possessed. Quite frankly, Clara was sure it was the queen's preference to see Clara squirm.

"May I speak freely a moment, Your Majesties?" Clara asked, before dipping into a curtsy in front of the dais.

"For a moment," Queen Sylvina purred.

"Due to a miscommunication, I was left unaware of your traditions until last night. I request your understanding and willingness to overlook my shortcomings. I can assure you, this will not occur in the future. Your son can attest to that fact."

Jude grinned and entirely ignored the fire in her eyes. "Indeed," he crooned. "Though I'm sure there are no shortcomings to overlook, wife."

"Wife-to-be," Queen Sylvina corrected, as she tapped her manicured nails on the arm of her throne. Clara took a deep breath before she announced her offering.

"To you, Queen Sylvina, I present a bouquet I handpicked myself. My mother has a fondness for florals and my home is always bright and smells divine because of the effort she maintains. The flowers alone are not much, merely something pretty to look at, but with care, consideration, and intent, they can mean so much more.

"Please accept this token of my gratitude for you allowing my presence in your home and your palace, knowing that my only intent is to bring a little colour and life with me while I am here. That, and a love for your son which no other can offer him."

Clara finally took a breath, her cheeks warm. Her hands lay lax at her sides, so she appeared calm, not giving away the nervous energy that caused her stomach to flip-flop and the soles of her feet to prickle so intensely she wished she could run or jump.

A smile—even dare Clara say, an approving twitch of her lips—crossed Queen Sylvina's face. With the slightest dip of her chin, she sat back in her seat and placed both hands in her lap. It took all of Clara not to slump and praise the skies that she hadn't failed, but she also wasn't done.

"For you, King Taron, I present a gold brooch I designed personally and crafted. For someone in your position, appearances matter. I have great magic at my disposal, and for you I have learnt to harness it into crafting something both useful and attractive.

"Please accept this as a token of me handing a part of myself to you, your kingdom, and your son. It is forged and melded by my gold and my fire. I am here to serve and protect your kingdom and family alike."

King Taron burst into a deep chuckle as a guard first inspected the brooch and then handed it over. It was oval shaped, with the Iridescent Kingdom's initials raised atop it and small gemstones scattered across the shield.

"I am eager to wear it, Princess." The king's smile did not waver as he inspected his gift and Queen Sylvina sent hers to be placed in water and taken to her private quarters.

"You did well," Jude said in a hushed tone.

"I did what I could with piss-poor warning and the information I was given."

"I mean it," he whispered, then repeated more intently, "You did well."

Clara thanked him quickly before he turned to her mother and presented the most beautifully sculpted glass figurine depicting a small female with wings that stretched from her shoulders and wrapped around her ankles. In her hands was a single flower that reflected all the light in the room into a different colour on each angle. Clara didn't recognise the flower but marvelled at the figure, regardless. It seemed Jude had also done rather well for himself. Although Clara expected nothing less from the cocky prince, especially considering his ample time to prepare.

"Felicity Afron, mother of my bride, I present you with a crystalline sculpture of the Angel. In our culture, she represents the afterlife, and the flower she holds symbolises eternal, unwavering love. It is my understanding you lost your husband some time ago, and I offer my sincerest condolences. We do not believe in an immediate afterlife, as many in Elanist do. Instead, we carry the belief that those who pass linger alongside us, until we are ready to join them.

"Please accept this gift as a token of not only my appreciation for the hand of the daughter you have raised so well, but also a reminder that your husband roams the land and skies as you do. A guardian angel, by your side and in your heart, and now wherever you place this figure."

Clara's mother barely held back her tears, her shaking hand held to her mouth. Jude handed the angel to her personally and offered her a hug, which Felicity welcomed eagerly. There might've been tears welling in Clara's own eyes, but she blinked them away rapidly.

The grand hall soon emptied, and Clara was eager to join Beau and Isobel in the ballroom across the corridor, but King Taron stopped her just shy of the door.

"May I have a word, Clara?" he asked.

Her breath caught in her throat, and all she could do was nod. .

"First, I commend you on your gift selection. I am impressed you forged this yourself, and at how you managed to turn something as simple as handpicked flowers into something meaningful. Sylvina is not impressed easily, but she definitely approved."

Clara's heart somersaulted in her chest, beating so rapidly she feared the king might hear it, but she remained silent.

"Second, I wanted to speak with you regarding my son, and in turn, my kingdom, as it will eventually fall to him, and subsequently you." The king paused, his head cocked ever so slightly. "What are your intentions, Clara Afron?"

His gaze bore into her, his eyes searching for something she did not know. She offered him a sweet, demure smile and answered honestly.

"To love and support your son, Your Highness. Nothing more, nothing less. I may be Queen of Morrin one day, but this will be my kingdom in name and marriage only. This?" Clara glanced around her, gesturing to the room in which they stood and the surrounding palace. "Everything you and your queen have built belongs to Jude when you decide the time is right. I have another throne to occupy—I do not intend to take his."

"And here I was, concerned my worries would not convey." King Taron chuckled.

"Ah, do not fret, Highness. I am well versed in reading between the lines."

The humour dropped from his face, now serious and far less readable. "And what do you learn of Jude when reading between the lines?"

"That an intelligent, arrogant, well-raised, and well-meaning king will soon reign over Morrin."

“Clara,” King Taron pressed. “I am referring to his bed partner.”

“With all due respect, Your Highness,” Clara said, trying to keep the annoyance from her tone. “I know what you refer to, and I am intentionally ignoring your question. Who your son takes to bed weighs as heavily on me as a summer breeze might touch my cheek. I couldn’t care less whom he spends his intimate time with, as long as they are good and kind to him and he extends me the same courtesy.” She nodded and intended to turn, but the king had not yet finished.

“Forgive me. I needed to be sure.” He sounded earnest enough. His gaze dropped for a second before he inhaled and continued. “His mother is set in the old ways. While in Morrin, hetero-normative relationships are the majority, those are not exclusive among my kind. I do not worry so much, but she dreams of grandchildren and—”

Clara cut him off—a bold move, but necessary. The conversation felt painful, and it took all her willpower not to snap at the male, king or not. Though she’d learnt her lesson, after the last time she’d stood before the Morrin royalty, to hold her tongue and calm herself.

“Please assure your wife she need not fear. We shall produce an heir, perhaps even a string of them. However, I will not stop him from being who he is and loving who he loves. Especially considering I do not wish to stop loving those of my own choosing. Now, please excuse me, Highness, I have much to do before the celebration this evening. I look forward to seeing you there.”

Clara dropped into a curtsy, her eyes on King Taron’s boots.

He spoke as she stood, his tone gentle and almost proud.

“Save me a dance, Miss Afron. If you’ll allow me the honour.”

Clara smiled genuinely as her heartbeat slowed to its normal pace, and she dipped her chin.

“The honour would be entirely mine.”

CHAPTER FORTY-EIGHT

CLARA

"Before we begin the passing of gifts . . ." King Taron's voice boomed through the hall from where he sat atop the dais in a burgundy wood throne, upholstered in a deep silver. The queen sat to his left, her throne near identical, except for size. "I would like to confirm the name you wish to be presented by at this evening's ball. Clarenna Hayes, or Clara Afron?"

Clara felt a painful tugging in her heart as she held back the answer she wanted to give—Clara Afron. That was her name, who she was raised to be, and the family she knew and loved. However, now betrothed to a future king, and descended from royal lineage herself, she knew it was not the answer.

Her mother squeezed Clara's hand, and when Clara turned to her, she found warmth radiating from her face, alongside contentment, pride, and approval. Clara was her daughter and holding a different name or title would never change that fact.

"Clarenna Hayes." Clara bowed her head low.

"And in private?"

"Informally, Clara is fine, Majesty."

"Alright then." King Taron clapped his hands and gestured for Jude to step towards Clara's mother. "Clara, come forward. What have you chosen to gift my wife, your future mother-in-law, Queen Sylvina?"

Heavens knew why he felt the need to tack on every title the female possessed. Quite frankly, Clara was sure it was the queen's preference to see Clara squirm.

"May I speak freely a moment, Your Majesties?" Clara asked, before dipping into a curtsy in front of the dais.

"For a moment," Queen Sylvina purred.

"Due to a miscommunication, I was left unaware of your traditions until last night. I request your understanding and willingness to overlook my shortcomings. I can assure you, this will not occur in the future. Your son can attest to that fact."

Jude grinned and entirely ignored the fire in her eyes. "Indeed," he crooned. "Though I'm sure there are no shortcomings to overlook, wife."

"Wife-to-be," Queen Sylvina corrected, as she tapped her manicured nails on the arm of her throne. Clara took a deep breath before she announced her offering.

"To you, Queen Sylvina, I present a bouquet I handpicked myself. My mother has a fondness for florals and my home is always bright and smells divine because of the effort she maintains. The flowers alone are not much, merely something pretty to look at, but with care, consideration, and intent, they can mean so much more.

"Please accept this token of my gratitude for you allowing my presence in your home and your palace, knowing that my only intent is to bring a little colour and life with me while I am here. That, and a love for your son which no other can offer him."

Clara finally took a breath, her cheeks warm. Her hands lay lax at her sides, so she appeared calm, not giving away the nervous energy that caused her stomach to flip-flop and the soles of her feet to prickle so intensely she wished she could run or jump.

A smile—even dare Clara say, an approving twitch of her lips—crossed Queen Sylvina's face. With the slightest dip of her chin, she sat back in her seat and placed both hands in her lap. It took all of Clara not to slump and praise the skies that she hadn't failed, but she also wasn't done.

"For you, King Taron, I present a gold brooch I designed personally and crafted. For someone in your position, appearances matter. I have great magic at my disposal, and for you I have learnt to harness it into crafting something both useful and attractive.

"Please accept this as a token of me handing a part of myself to you, your kingdom, and your son. It is forged and melded by my gold and my fire. I am here to serve and protect your kingdom and family alike."

King Taron burst into a deep chuckle as a guard first inspected the brooch and then handed it over. It was oval shaped, with the Iridescent Kingdom's initials raised atop it and small gemstones scattered across the shield.

"I am eager to wear it, Princess." The king's smile did not waver as he inspected his gift and Queen Sylvina sent hers to be placed in water and taken to her private quarters.

"You did well," Jude said in a hushed tone.

"I did what I could with piss-poor warning and the information I was given."

"I mean it," he whispered, then repeated more intently, "You did well."

Clara thanked him quickly before he turned to her mother and presented the most beautifully sculpted glass figurine depicting a small female with wings that stretched from her shoulders and wrapped around her ankles. In her hands was a single flower that reflected all the light in the room into a different colour on each angle. Clara didn't recognise the flower but marvelled at the figure, regardless. It seemed Jude had also done rather well for himself. Although Clara expected nothing less from the cocky prince, especially considering his ample time to prepare.

"Felicity Afron, mother of my bride, I present you with a crystalline sculpture of the Angel. In our culture, she represents the afterlife, and the flower she holds symbolises eternal, unwavering love. It is my understanding you lost your husband some time ago, and I offer my sincerest condolences. We do not believe in an immediate afterlife, as many in Elanist do. Instead, we carry the belief that those who pass linger alongside us, until we are ready to join them.

"Please accept this gift as a token of not only my appreciation for the hand of the daughter you have raised so well, but also a reminder that your husband roams the land and skies as you do. A guardian angel, by your side and in your heart, and now wherever you place this figure."

Clara's mother barely held back her tears, her shaking hand held to her mouth. Jude handed the angel to her personally and offered her a hug, which Felicity welcomed eagerly. There might've been tears welling in Clara's own eyes, but she blinked them away rapidly.

The grand hall soon emptied, and Clara was eager to join Beau and Isobel in the ballroom across the corridor, but King Taron stopped her just shy of the door.

"May I have a word, Clara?" he asked.

Her breath caught in her throat, and all she could do was nod.

"First, I commend you on your gift selection. I am impressed you forged this yourself, and at how you managed to turn something as simple as handpicked flowers into something meaningful. Sylvina is not impressed easily, but she definitely approved."

Clara's heart somersaulted in her chest, beating so rapidly she feared the king might hear it, but she remained silent.

"Second, I wanted to speak with you regarding my son, and in turn, my kingdom, as it will eventually fall to him, and subsequently you." The king paused, his head cocked ever so slightly. "What are your intentions, Clara Afron?"

His gaze bore into her, his eyes searching for something she did not know. She offered him a sweet, demure smile and answered honestly.

"To love and support your son, Your Highness. Nothing more, nothing less. I may be Queen of Morrin one day, but this will be my kingdom in name and marriage only. This?" Clara glanced around her, gesturing to the room in which they stood and the surrounding palace. "Everything you and your queen have built belongs to Jude when you decide the time is right. I have another throne to occupy—I do not intend to take his."

"And here I was, concerned my worries would not convey." King Taron chuckled.

"Ah, do not fret, Highness. I am well versed in reading between the lines."

The humour dropped from his face, now serious and far less readable. "And what do you learn of Jude when reading between the lines?"

"That an intelligent, arrogant, well-raised, and well-meaning king will soon reign over Morrin."

"Clara," King Taron pressed. "I am referring to his bed partner."

"With all due respect, Your Highness," Clara said, trying to keep the annoyance from her tone. "I know what you refer to, and I am intentionally ignoring your question. Who your son takes to bed weighs as heavily on me as a summer breeze might touch my cheek. I couldn't care less whom he spends his intimate time with, as long as they are good and kind to him and he extends me the same courtesy." She nodded and intended to turn, but the king had not yet finished.

"Forgive me. I needed to be sure." He sounded earnest enough. His gaze dropped for a second before he inhaled and continued. "His mother is set in the old ways. While in Morrin, hetero-normative relationships are the majority, those are not exclusive among my kind. I do not worry so much, but she dreams of grandchildren and—"

Clara cut him off—a bold move, but necessary. The conversation felt painful, and it took all her willpower not to snap at the male, king or not. Though she'd learnt her lesson, after the last time she'd stood before the Morrin royalty, to hold her tongue and calm herself.

"Please assure your wife she need not fear. We shall produce an heir, perhaps even a string of them. However, I will not stop him from being who he is and loving who he loves. Especially considering I do not wish to stop loving those of my own choosing. Now, please excuse me, Highness, I have much to do before the celebration this evening. I look forward to seeing you there."

Clara dropped into a curtsy, her eyes on King Taron's boots.

He spoke as she stood, his tone gentle and almost proud.

"Save me a dance, Miss Afron. If you'll allow me the honour."

Clara smiled genuinely as her heartbeat slowed to its normal pace, and she dipped her chin.

"The honour would be entirely mine."

CHAPTER FORTY-NINE

CLARA

Pale-blonde hair and sun-kissed skin, haloed by the raging sun. She stands with her toes buried in sand, as the foamy swell laps around her ankles. Trinkets and charms hang from golden jewellery around her wrists and neck. The wind gently sweeps her hair around her and creates a delicate jingling sound as her jewellery sways.

She turns, no longer facing out towards the ocean's horizon. Now she faces inland, her striking blue eyes swirling with power and anticipation.

"Summer is coming," she whispers, her voice ethereal and chilling.

Clara's vision ended as rapidly as it started, and then she was thrown back into the Iridescent Palace, hand extended to open the ballroom door.

"Are you alright?" Isobel asked quietly, her hand brushing against Clara's.

She nodded slowly, then pursed her lips at Beau, whose scowl clearly said he knew she wasn't. Fae could not tell lies, but the rules only extended to verbal communication, and Clara often used the loophole to her advantage.

They would not be announcing her until the king and queen were present, so Clara took a few moments and slowed her breathing. Nerves built in her chest and stabbed at the soles of her feet, both at the impending warning of summer and in anticipation of her formal introduction as the prince's bride.

Summer.

Of all fucking things, was she to fear the change in the weather?

Though Clara suspected it wasn't the season she ought to keep watch for; instead, perhaps the mysterious Lady of Summer she'd learnt of in her last vision. The female who had captured Tindal and Era, locked them somewhere on this continent, and suppressed their magic.

Before she could contemplate it all, a familiar head of wild brown hair atop a being with rich-coloured skin decorated with chalk walked past. The female waved when she noticed Clara, her fingers now as straight as Clara's own.

"I'm surprised to see you back here," Clara said with a genuine grin. A familiar face was a welcome sight, regardless of where they'd met.

"As am I, Princess." She bowed slightly before Clara waved her off.

"Oh, don't do that," she hissed lightly. "I don't think cellmates are required to bow for each other."

The female laughed loudly.

"Cellmates? You know one another?" Isobel asked, her brows furrowed.

The female nodded while Clara pinched a crystal flute from a passing server.

“My name is Diedre.” She offered her hand to Isobel, who shook it gently. “I was caught stealing after my camp’s stores were raided. We were too far from home to journey back and hadn’t accounted for the additional supplies. The princess was placed in my cell and showed me incredible kindness. Thanks to her, I was healed and released.”

“Which camp?” Isobel asked. It was a strange question, but Clara brushed the thought away as she took a sip of her drink. Tastes of sweet and citrusy fruit exploded on her tongue and sizzled all the way down her throat.

“You recognise my face paint?” Diedre asked with a curious expression. Isobel only nodded. “Claw. We live in one of the mountain passes between Amber and Bloom. You’ve heard of us?”

Isobel let out a long breath before she shook her head and smiled, almost in relief.

“I’ve been looking for you for quite some time,” she said. “My late employer was hoping for an audience with your head of camp. While I hate to turn this evening into a business meeting, is this something we might be able to coordinate?”

Diedre smiled softly. “Of course. You may wait some weeks, however. Our head of camp, Peter, is still in the mountains, and I won’t return for at least a fortnight. What is it regarding?”

“My employer, Elisabeth Hayes, has a son. He is still very young and his power has not yet manifested, but Elisabeth had fears for his wellbeing. Of what nature I do not know. She had hoped to discuss the possibility of your camp, or one of the wolf clans fostering him. Of course, you would be generously compensated.”

Diedre nodded and collected her own glass as the server circled again. Clara’s mind whirled at the mention of wolf clans, though her recent vision left a lingering ache at the base of her skull, and any more confusion and her head might explode. She did her best to ignore the swirling possibilities and let the other females speak.

"I will pass your request along, though I do not see an issue myself."

"Thank you," Isobel breathed.

Clara did not know what fears Elisabeth held for Christopher, nor what her plans had been for the boy. She would have to discuss these with Ryland.

Tonight was not for her to wonder and worry about her remaining kin. Especially as the king and queen now entered, and the room fell into silence.

As the evening continued, Clara tried to learn the names and history of those she met. One male, in a suit covered in feathers and accessories of brushed gold, mentioned the Summer Court had been hit the hardest by the plague on the lands. He even asked if Clara was here to help fix it.

Rumours and speculation milled throughout the room that she was going to save them. Once someone overheard the first male, whispers spread, and before she knew it, half a dozen others approached her. They asked Clara if she knew what was wrong, how to fix it, and how long it would take, or even simply offered their sincerest gratitude. It felt as though a sharp bubble had popped, deep inside her gut, and all manner of unpleasant creatures had crawled out.

An unnaturally humid breeze flittered through her hair and danced along her exposed skin.

Did Jude honestly expect she'd fix his land, knowing nothing about the problem, and without a conversation? Nary a mention of this so-called blight and then a betrothal announcement is made, and what, she becomes their unknowing saviour?

No.

At the very least, her husband-to-be owed her an explanation, or she might simply let his lands rot.

So with her hands prickling with the surge of magic and a warm breeze swirling along her spine, Clara left Isobel and Beau to mingle in her wake as she stalked the room in search of her groom.

"You lied to me," Clara whispered with a jab of her pointed finger into Jude's abdomen. He was lounging with his elbows on the bar, one ankle crossed over the other. The perfect image of relaxed and arrogant.

"I did no such thing—I am incapable." Jude lifted a brow. "I merely omitted all the reasons I would like us to be wed."

He held himself so casually, spoke as if mentioning ducks on the lake. It had Clara clenching her fists, so she didn't smack the blasé attitude from him. Her eyes twitched and narrowed.

"And do you care to share those reasons now, considering half your court has pleaded and thanked me already?"

Jude sighed and offered her his elbow, which Clara wrapped in her hand and dug her nails in tight. He led her into a quiet hall. "I do need a queen, for as progressive a land as we have become, two kings would not sit well with my kingdom and my parents might die of it themselves. I do not wish to put them in an early grave. I want you to be my queen for a myriad of reasons, most importantly your heart. Who you are makes for a fair and just ruler, as despite your tendency towards haste, you are intelligent and considerate, gentle, yet you are ruthless. Qualities that do not always go hand in hand, and yet you've mastered the line between them. You're not so hard to look at, either."

"Flattery will get you nowhere, Prince."

"But honesty might." Jude gave her an awkward smile. He sighed and kept explaining. "I also need you as my queen for the magic you possess. There has been a rot growing in my lands for some time. I know not where it started or how, nor why it is here, nor what I can do to get rid of it." Jude shook his head before he looked at Clara almost pleadingly. "What I know is a queen of the elements is the key to fixing it, to healing this plague. I need your help, and while I'm laying all my truths bare, I'll tell you I was worried if you saw me pleading and desperate, that you might have thought me lesser. That you might've considered me a weak ruler and not wanted to join with me. It was a fear for my lands and my people that I did not share everything with you earlier, and I'm sorry."

Clara nodded, her face relaxing, as a fraction of the tension and nausea rolling around inside her eased. "I accept your apology, Jude. Though I won't pretend to understand royal politics, or any politics really. I will not insult you by speaking ill of your attempts at joining our kingdoms. I will threaten you, however"—Clara jabbed his chest again—"with calling off the entire engagement if you ever lie to me, by omission or otherwise, again. Am I clear?"

"As a glass house." Jude smiled, and Clara nodded.

"So, a rot on your lands?" Clara looped her arm back through Jude's and they strolled down the hall. Neither was interested in rejoining the party just yet.

"Do you know the history of Helenica?" Jude asked.

"I know very little history at all."

Jude chuckled softly before he continued. "Our continents used to be much closer, initially only a few hours' boat ride or a bridge distance apart. The tides rose, and some parts submerged, causing the edges of territories to drift further apart. Originally, the entirety of Helenica was ruled by one king and his queen, with various lords and ladies having dominion over each of their jurisdictions. One royal family to rule the world was the simplest of systems, the best in many ways."

Ryland would get along well with the prince, Clara realised. The corner of her mouth twitched upwards, but she made sure not to give away her ease or enjoyment. He did not need anyone to inflate his ego.

Clara gestured with her hand to hurry along, and Jude chuckled.

"The point is, the Golden Kingdom was the original royal house, containing the original rulers. They were not as gifted, one might say, as their lineage grew to be, but their line sat atop the throne first. Two of my ancestors were given the Autumn and Summer Courts respectively, and the Spring and Winter courts were given to familial lines since deceased. Urian's ancestors had the Day Court and Luellena's the Night Court. Eventually, the lineages blended and morphed, resulting in what they are today. Disjointed and separate." He shook his head before he added more quietly, "I truly believe we can become what we once were, as a species, dwellers of this planet as a whole."

Clara scoffed. "Eveline might not be so eager to give up her crown."

"What makes you think she was eager to receive it in the first place? There are many crooked crowns in our world, Clara. Help me right them. Please."

Pleading was not what Clara had expected when she'd confronted the prince. Though she had to admit, his words made her feel powerful, and not in the magical sense.

"So what you're telling me is you want to take over the world?"

"With you by my side, my queen."

Jude winked and Clara rolled her eyes, though neither said anything more. After a few moments of pleasant silence, the tension now cleared, the couple re-entered the ballroom.

CHAPTER FIFTY

CLARA

Their bedroom was at the end of the hallway, but she needed to pass by two other rooms before she reached her goal. For a moment, Clara had the vaguest sense she was upside down, or facing the wrong way, and it tickled at the back of her mind where her visions lay dormant as if her subconscious was trying to remind her of one she'd since forgotten, but it seemed so impossible, she ignored it. The first door was closed, and no light crept from under it, but the second was ajar.

Knowing it would be rude, Clara tried not to look, but she couldn't help herself. The sounds were too enticing, so she peeked through the gap.

A male she recognised from earlier in the evening was kneeling on the bed, bent forward, and clutching the head board so tightly his knuckles had almost turned white. Jude was on his knees behind him, his face pressed between the male's ass cheeks. One of Jude's hands was wrapped around his thigh, the other reached between his legs and stroked his lover's cock.

They were a beautiful sight. The male took a rasping breath as Jude's hand moved faster along his impressive length. Up and down, circling with each stroke.

"Fuck!" The word was low and drawn out, the male's head arching back, causing his blonde hair to fall from his face.

Jude growled in response.

Clara squeezed her thighs together. She knew she should step back, or continue to her bedroom, but she couldn't look away. Couldn't make her feet move.

Jude rose to his knees, both hands caressing his lover's thighs and hips, and from here Clara could see his hard cock jutting forward. Clara's mind raced as she pictured Beau, his hands running down her body, his erection pressed to every sensitive part of her.

Jude stroked his own cock leisurely, before he eased it into the male's ass. The sounds of pleasure from them both brought a soft moan from her lips. She wanted to be between them, or on top of them, or under the male as he was under Jude. No, she wanted Beau to wrap his hand around her throat as he whispered dirty things in her ear, his other hand stroking between her legs, while she watched Jude and his partner.

Jude didn't stop as he turned his head to look at her as she peered through the doorway. His grin grew wider and his thrusts deeper, as if he dared her to step through.

Her feet shuffled forward, and her shoulder bumped into the frame. As if the move knocked her to her senses, Clara shook her head and looked away.

"I'm so sorry, I should go," she mumbled.

"You don't have to," Jude crooned. Clara could easily picture the arrogant smirk on his face, though she kept her gaze firmly fixed on the floor. She shook her head, but he continued. "You'll have to join us eventually, wife."

"Wife-to-be," she corrected with a languid chuckle.

"You do not wish to bed me?" he asked, his voice joined by the moan of the male beneath him. Evidently, Jude had not stopped thrusting, did not pause fucking simply to have a conversation with Clara. Arousal built, hot and heavy inside her.

"Not currently."

"Is it Hunter you do not wish to bed, then?"

Stars, this prince was cocky, though at least he'd reminded her of the male's name. Hunter was an oddly fitting name for this strong and masculine featured male, with a whimsical air. After seeing him naked, she surely would not forget his name anytime soon.

"I am happily spoken for, and partaking in sexual activities with another is something I should discuss with him first. I apologise again for interrupting, prince, and it was lovely to meet you, Hunter." Clara offered an awkward wave, then stumbled from the doorway with Jude's chuckles following her. She immediately smacked into a solid, broad chest.

"Did you get lost, sweetheart?" Beau's deep voice vibrated through her already heightened senses.

"I might have," she mumbled, meeting his burning amber eyes which swirled with a playful allure.

"How much did you drink once the king and queen left the celebration, to have ended up in the prince's private wing and walked in on him fucking?"

Clara rolled her eyes and ignored his question.

"Is sleeping with another something you'd like to do?" he asked quietly in her ear, leaning down so his beard brushed against her cheek. Then his lips grazed along her jaw, breath warm on her skin.

"What?" she gasped, her breath suddenly evading her. "No, not right now." One of Beau's brows shot up. Clara shook her head again, looking over her shoulder, towards the thudding sounds coming from the prince's room. "I'd like to discuss it. As if I am to inherit his mother's throne, I will be required to bear an heir to the kingdom. That is, unless you know of another way to make a babe, I will have to fuck him sooner or later." She turned to Beau and lowered her voice. "Though tonight, perhaps, we could stop talking about the prince and instead focus on how you are far too clothed for my liking."

A devastatingly handsome grin spread across Beau's face, and Clara's core tightened in response. Fuck, he could look at her like that forever. Maybe not forever, as she also liked how he stared at her, as if he could devour her and still want more. Usually with his cock deep inside of her, before he tried to push a little deeper. *That* was the look which sent her into a spiral of desire.

"And here I thought you enjoyed watching them. You're so flushed I can see it even under the dim flicker of the sconces."

He was so stars damned smug. Clara would be lying if she said she didn't enjoy it, she loved every second.

"Well," she purred. "I do love to watch, sir."

His eyes flared as hot as the lust burning through her. "I'll give you something pretty to look at," Beau growled, and Clara couldn't help the mewl which escaped her parted lips.

His firm grip wrapped around her wrists before he pulled her back into Jude's bedroom, where they found Hunter laid on his back, a cushion propped under his hips and his knees up by his chest. Jude cursed as he thrust wildly and Clara inhale.

"Is this a private show?" Beau asked, his voice deep and husky, causing her heart to race, and flushed skin to warm.

Jude's laugh was low and his grin devious. "Pull up a seat." He didn't look away from Hunter as he spoke, though Hunter turned his face towards Clara and waggled his brows.

Beau murmured his approval, then pulled a plush chair in front of Clara. She hadn't seen where it came from, but she hardly cared, too enamoured by the males groaning and swearing on the bed.

"Sit." Beau's voice was so powerful that Clara obeyed him instinctively, his smirk and approving growl sending shivers down her spine and flutters deep inside her.

He dropped to his knees before her and forced her legs apart. His movement wild, as if he couldn't wait to taste her, Beau hiked up her multilayered skirt. The raw timbre of his growl turned frustrated at how many layers there were, and before she knew it, Clara's skirt had been ripped clean up the middle.

There was no salvaging this outfit, but she couldn't find it in herself to care. Not as he roamed his large hands over her thighs, pressing and dragging his fingers along her delicate skin. Nor when he leant in so close to her desperate entrance, and inhaled her scent as though he needed the smell of her to survive. His warm breath teased at her sensitive flesh, and she dipped her head back as a moan escaped her.

Beau's fingers grabbed her jaw, squeezed, and pulled her head back upright.

"No," he ordered. "Watch."

A breathless nod was all she could manage, though his smirk told her it was enough. His rough hand released its grip on her chin and lowered to her thigh, pressed so firmly on where her leg met her pelvis. A sensitive spot he knew and abused all too well.

With another sharp inhale and Clara's hand flew to the back of Beau's head, her fingers carding his hair. She swore as his tongue pressed and swirled against her clit, enticing a vibrating groan from his mouth. Then his hands were on the move again, one tightened on her hip, the other dragged further down until his fingers traced her wet lower lips.

Clara rolled her hips over Beau's face, and he groaned, sending more torturous pleasure through her.

Jude kept ploughing into Hunter's ass; their joint grunts and moans and pants hurtled Clara closer and closer to the edge. Though she didn't want to come yet, she wanted to stay locked in this bliss.

Hunter's arms flew out to his sides as his body stiffened, his neck arched, and head pressed into the mattress. He roared as his release tore through him, and ropes of cum exploded over his abdomen. Clara's core tightened, as pressure and pleasure rapidly built.

As if he could sense it, Beau inserted two fingers, then three, curling them inside her. Clara's moans grew louder, her fist now tight in Beau's hair. Then he pulled back and removed his beautiful tongue from her swollen, achy clit. He chuckled sensually at her pout, and then lifted so his breath caressed her ear and his free hand cupped her neck.

"Are you close, sweetheart?" he teased.

"Fuck you," she whimpered as he pressed the palm of his other hand to her clit.

"Forgive me," he whispered, hoarse and heavy, before he bit at her earlobe. The sting sent bursts of pain through her in the most satisfying way. "For wanting to watch you while you come."

Clara was unable to say anything else as Beau licked and kissed her jaw, her chin, and all the way down her neck until she was a writhing mess. The sight of Jude grunting and thrusting faster and harder into Hunter as he found his release tipped Clara so close to the damned edge.

Beau palmed her clit hard—near painful—as he continued to curl his fingers inside her. Then his pace sped up a fraction, and she bucked and screamed.

"Fuck," Beau growled, as his hand on her neck pressed deeper, her head swirling with every suppressed inhale. Each of Beau's rough and ragged breaths spiralled her further and further into rapture.

"Stars," Beau groaned. "You're fucking perfect. Come for me."

So she did.

Beau's rasping voice and coaxing words and praise; Jude and Hunter sweating and covered in each other's cum; all of it threw her over the dizzying cliff towards ecstasy. Clara screamed as her climax speared through her.

All too soon, Beau's fingers left her and she sat slumped in her chair, breathing heavily and riding the waves of pleasure and oblivion. She watched as Beau brought his hand to his lips, sucking her wetness from his fingers, and inhaled the scent of her from his skin.

Clara reached out and grabbed his wrist, sucking his fingers to her open mouth. She licked the remnants of herself from him, and his shudder in response. It threatened to relight the fire inside her he'd just put out. He growled in pleasure before he grabbed her face and smashed his mouth to hers.

They had just pulled apart, chuckling breathlessly, when Jude called from the mattress. "We will definitely be doing that again."

CHAPTER FIFTY-ONE

BEAU

Though the boat ride home was uneventful, exhaustion flared throughout Beau's body. He carried Felicity's bags inside, leaving them at the doorway to her bedroom, then returned to the entryway for his and Clara's. She followed him to her room, even more slumped than Beau, her eyelids barely open.

Isobel hadn't returned with them, which left Beau feeling pleased but conflicted. She'd held Clara so tightly before transporting to the palace in Candor, muttering about needing to speak with Ryland.

"Lie down," he suggested, as he flopped onto his side of the mattress.

Clara smirked, but when her eyes darted to the bedside table, her expression dropped, and she sighed. "I might run a bath instead."

"Would you like some company?" Beau asked with a wink.

Her rosy lips quirked, but she shook her head. So instead of joining her, Beau lay back on the mattress and let his mind conjure all the tantalising images of her naked and soaped up in the tub.

Beau was awoken by the sound of the bedroom door opening and Isobel's voice hissing, "Not again! Where is Clara?"

Her small hands pressed to his biceps, her fingers digging in so deeply he feared the tiny woman might leave a bruise.

"She was in the bath," he rasped, not yet fully awake. Rubbing sleep from his eyes, Beau sat up as Isobel rushed from the room, only to return a moment later with a crumpled piece of paper in her tight grip, her eyes now wide and her expression stark.

"Wrong," she snapped as she threw the paper at him.

I promise I'm alright x

The words were scrawled in Clara's neat but rushed handwriting, and his heart thumped violently in his chest. At least she'd left *something* this time.

"What did she say *exactly*?" Isobel demanded.

Beau sighed. "That she was going to run a bath . . . Shit."

Isobel's arms flew up. "We need to go. She could be anywhere. Where would she— Why— Get up, come on!" Words spilled from her mouth at a speed Beau could barely decipher.

"Take a breath," he growled, then thought better of his tone. He followed his own advice as he stood. When he placed his hands on her shoulders, Isobel stilled, though her nerves were written all over her face. "Stop and think for a moment."

He almost laughed at the absurdity of *him* being the one to calm *her*. Normally, Isobel was frustratingly chipper and upbeat. Between the three of them, he'd been labelled the grouch, and if not for Clara's tendency—although it had waned of late—to fly into a rage so easily, he'd have been named the hothead too.

His thoughts drifted to another time that Clara had left, and he'd reacted hastily. Due to his inability to think rationally, many had died, and the last thing he wanted was a repeat.

"No," Isobel whispered. She shook her head, but her eyes stayed fixed on his. "Something is wrong. Something terrible is coming."

"Terrible things have happened already, Isobel. Two powerful royals are dead because of it. Clara almost died."

Isobel's eyes narrowed, and her brows drew together.

"It was a touch anticlimactic, though, don't you think? Take the deaths and near death out of it. Clara said they mostly spat insults at each other. War brings far more than derogatory conversation, Beau. And it certainly brings more than two deaths."

The uneasy feeling spiralled in Beau's gut, though acknowledging it would only fuel Isobel. She needed to be calm and rational, and Beau hadn't been level-headed long enough to take the lead.

"What are you saying?"

"That Eveline and Solaris weren't the siblings we ought to fear. I don't think so, at least." Isobel continued to shake her head, her eyes darting away. "I'm not sure. Something feels like it's coming, something bigger and much, much worse."

Speculation was not helpful, but at least that's all it was. Talk and theory, but nothing concrete.

"Okay, well, this isn't it, so let's focus."

“How do you know?” Her voice nearly broke it wavered so much. “She almost died last time. I can’t—”

Beau cut her off with a gentle shake. “Hey, listen. I know you don’t give a rat’s ass what comes out of my mouth. You care very little for me, and that’s fine. But when I said I wouldn’t let her heart stop while mine remains beating, I meant it. If you recall, that includes keeping you alive and well.” Beau gave her a light-hearted, pointed look. “I can promise you that much, at least. Now focus.”

Isobel took a deep breath and nodded.

For a moment, Beau considered her intense reaction. Suspicion floated at the thought this woman might have feelings beyond friendship for Clara. The notion settled painfully as he considered whether they were reciprocated or unrequited. He shook the thoughts away—now was not the time to rile himself up.

“Can that thing take us to her if we don’t know where she is?” Beau pointed to her transportation necklace.

“No, it can barely take me places I’ve not physically been to yet. It needs a clear direction and ‘*find Clara*’ is not enough. She could be anywhere.”

“Well, not anywhere. She must have travelled by foot, as she doesn’t have a horse, nor does she have wings or one of those.” Beau jerked his chin towards the pendant.

“If running off is going to be a habit, I’d like to make sure she stays without one of these,” Isobel muttered.

“If she wants one, she’ll get one. You ought to know that by now.” Beau’s chuckle was flat. “Regardless, she doesn’t yet, so she’s walking. She can’t have gone far. What’s the time?” Peering at the clock on Clara’s wall, he added, “It’s been an hour, at best.”

“Or she’s enlisted the help of someone with wings.”

Beau hadn't thought of that possibility, and guilt lanced through him as memories of Neven surfaced.

"I know where he lives. Come on." Isobel gestured for Beau to follow.

He raced after her, unable to control his bulged eyes or comically high eyebrows. "How the fuck do you know where he lives?"

Isobel shrugged, so nonchalant. "Because I engage in friendly, information gathering conversation."

"Like a spy," Beau scoffed.

"No, Beau," Isobel said as she sighed and shook her head. "Like a regular, civilised being. Now, hurry. He's only a few streets away."

Despite his insistence they stay calm, his worry rose. Isobel stayed a few steps ahead of him the entire time, near floating down paths and around turns. Relentlessly and almost rhythmically, she tapped the pads of her thumbs to her other fingers.

By the time they arrived at the simple house with its curtains drawn and lights off, Beau's pulse raced. He pounded on the front door so hard it rattled until a light flowed through one of the windows.

The male Clara worked with answered the door. Beau might have forgotten his name, but not his face. In a blink, Beau grabbed the collar of his shirt and bared his teeth, barely suppressing the growl at the base of his tightening throat. The male pulled his own lip back, but otherwise stayed calm. Far calmer than Beau felt.

"Where is she?!" Isobel demanded. Surprisingly, she did not pull Beau back or separate them at all.

"In Breath," the male answered. "She asked me to take her."

"Are you capable of specifics, or interested in a beating?" Beau growled, and the male narrowed his eyes.

"The Pearl 'n Lace pleasure house. I left her in Florence Hills, but she mentioned where she was headed." His eyes dropped to Beau's still-fisted hands around his shirt. "Now please unhand me."

"I know where that is," Isobel said quietly and placed a small hand on Beau's biceps.

He shoved the male backwards and slipped his hand into Isobel's as she placed her thumb over her pendant. Before he could blink, they were standing outside a nondescript building. His stomach rolled and flipped, bile threatened to climb his throat, but he managed to keep the nausea at bay.

No windows lined the front or side that he could see. A single door stood in the middle of the building, with a lamppost set directly before it, and a small sign hanging beneath the dull orange light.

Pearl 'n Lace.

Why, of all places, was this where Clara had snuck off to?

Isobel opened the door with a shaky hand, her other still gripping Beau's tightly. Inside, the building was darker than he'd expected. An unmanned front desk stood to his left, while three closed doors lined the right wall. A fourth hung ajar, soft light spilling from it onto a flight of stairs heading downwards.

Silently, the pair took the stairs towards the sound of low music, clinking glasses, and hooting laughter. Isobel's hand turned clammy in his.

Once they reached the first landing, dim lights barely illuminated the expansive room. It was far larger than he'd expected from the exterior. His eyes flicked between leather-lined settees and armchairs, rich wooden tables decorated with individual candles and oil lamps which were spread throughout the space, and a bar lining the far wall, where many beings and creatures stood and sat with either drink in hand or waiting to be served.

The wall closest to him was lined with booths, some open, and others with heavy drapes drawn designed to separate whoever was inside from the rest of the room. Finally, he spied a dark hallway Beau dreaded to think Clara had followed. As he attempted to peer down its length, Isobel's grip on his hand tightened further and her free hand slapped against his chest. He spun, then followed her line of vision.

Any nerves or fear evaporated when he saw her. Scantily clad and bright-red hair illuminated by candlelight, her curvy body enticed everyone who looked her way. Simultaneously, Beau's body filled with jealousy and rage, arousal and awe. She was captivatingly beautiful.

On the stage, with a raven-haired female he did not recognise, was Clara.

CHAPTER FIFTY-TWO

CLARA

The familiar scents of pine, ash, and sweat cradled Clara in a way she hadn't expected. It had been a long time since she'd stepped foot inside the Pearl 'n Lace. Gwen waved her through, her face lit with an excited grin, and Clara smiled back as she continued down the stairs.

She sauntered past the booths—covered in a truly impressive number of bodily fluids—and the smoke wafting from the den, the usual array of expressions on regulars and newcomers alike. Some of the folk she'd known years ago noticed her and smiled or waved, dipping their heads in acknowledgement.

Clara made her way to the end of the barely lit corridor, noting that most of the doors were closed along the way. She'd been grateful for the soundproofing back then, and certainly now, knowing damn well what was going on behind the closed doors. At the end of the hall, Ora's office door opened a second before Clara raised her hand to knock. She chuckled and entered, immediately snatched up by the slim arms, which were stronger than they looked.

"Oh, I've missed you, girl!" Ora squealed as she squeezed her tight.

"It has been some time, huh?" Clara said and embraced her friend.

"Some time indeed," Ora said as she nodded and pulled away, then inspected Clara intensely. "You've grown up. Gold suits you."

Instinctively, Clara lowered her gaze to her abdomen. Ora couldn't see all her markings—not with her eyes, at least. Clara was dressed in long pants and a loose shirt, so only those along her hairline and collarbone were visible. Yet Ora could see with more than her eyes. As an Oracle, the female could see a great deal, and that is why Clara had come to her in the first place. Maja had suggested it for a reason, as no doubt more turmoil was ahead.

"Thank you," she replied. "But I'm afraid I'm not here on a social call."

"Oh, I know." Ora nodded. "I have little information for you, but I'll give you what I know. For the standard price, of course."

"Of course," Clara repeated with a nod. An exchange of services was always how Ora operated with friends and family, something she'd explained to Clara very early on in their relationship.

Money was less of an issue than it had been when she'd first arrived at Ora's door, especially since her betrothal to the prince. Though when she'd first come searching for not only employment but information about her father and his death, Ora had offered her a job and a trade.

One night's work in exchange for Ora's abilities and information, then she could continue working as a regular employee if she chose.

Now, she waited while Ora explained her trade for the evening: one act for the information Ora could provide.

"Only one?" Clara asked, her brows furrowed.

"It really isn't much information," Ora replied and shrugged. "I'm nothing, if not fair."

"Alright." Clara sighed and nodded, then ran a hand through her unbound hair. "Dance first, payment later?"

Ora chuckled, then ducked into the wardrobe behind her desk.

"No, that's alright. I trust you." She came out with a bright-turquoise garment, glittering with sequins. "Dress. You're not getting on my stage wearing that." Ora folded her arms and gave Clara a disgusted look after handing over the costume.

Clara scoffed and feigned offence, but the mood quickly dropped when Ora told Clara of her visions.

"The Queen of Tirenas and her twin were not the sisters you should fear." Her voice echoed in the otherwise quiet room, sinking a thousand razor-sharp teeth into Clara's bare skin. "In fact, three sisters are coming. The war has not yet arrived, and it is certainly far from over. Have you heard of Death's Daughters?"

Clara shook her head as she stepped around the sectional.

"I know little of them, truth be told, as until now, they've been manipulating and moving the pieces of their puzzle into place. They operate in the shadows and have others carry out their work for them. Though now they grow tired of their hidden games and are preparing to strike. I do not know when they will come, or how they will enact their plans, only that they are undefeated and ruthless. Many will die and you need to prepare for loss."

A chill settled over Clara that had nothing to do with how little she now wore, nor the cool touch of sequins and satin on her skin. Her heart beat loudly in her chest, and she wondered if Ora could hear it.

"Is there no way to best them? Surely you haven't just told me I will lose and it will end there."

"There are no winners in war, Clara."

The last thing Clara wanted to do after hearing that she and her loved ones were essentially doomed was perform. But a deal was a deal, and Clara would honour her word.

Tyra sat at the piano as always, sending Clara a wink before she struck the first note. Clara took a deep breath and rolled her neck, then sauntered on stage. As she swung her hips, the tassels on her dress flew around her, catching the light, making her sparkle. Hoots and cheers sounded from the crowd, and Clara relished in it. In the words and sounds that fed the pridefulness inside her and left her feeling incredible. Powerful.

Clara spun, keeping her toes pointed, and ran her hands sensually along every inch of her skin. Her head tipped back as she allowed the music to flow through her. She'd always enjoyed dancing.

Ora twirled up to her while her back was to the crowd, her hands roaming through her hair.

"I thought this was a single performance," Clara whispered as Ora wrapped her arms around Clara's neck.

"Your escorts have arrived," she replied, close to Clara's ear.

Clara propped up on her tiptoes to peek over Ora's shoulder, and sure enough, there they were.

Beau and Isobel stood out in the crowd, near the entryway to the den. Isobel's eyes were wide as she clung to Beau. He stood still, and Clara could see the fire surging through his body, even from far away. She wasn't sure whether it was arousal or anger he stared at her with, but he did not look away.

"Oh . . . they are *not* happy with me," Clara muttered, though she continued to move to the building crescendo of the music.

"Can you blame them?" Ora whispered back, her hands caressing Clara's shoulders and arms as her lips trailed along Clara's bared neck. "They both want you for themselves, yet are keenly aware of each other and everyone else in this room wanting the same." She paused for a moment, though her body continued to sway and grind with Clara's. "Stay up here for another minute or so, then you can leave. A teaser from a crowd favourite is payment enough, and I have no interested in coming between tethers. I'll find you once you're done."

Ora pressed gentle, suggestive kisses to Clara's shoulder from behind.

"I'll tell you right now," Clara hissed. "Kissing me is a surefire way to land yourself smack bang in the middle of whatever bond I'm forming with them."

"Oh, sweetie, it's so much more than a bond." Ora gave her a pointed look as Clara turned so her back was again towards the crowd. "Dip."

She did. With Ora's hand on the small of her back and her own wrapped around Ora's forearm, Clara arched her back until her hair traced the floorboards at her feet.

"I haven't even kissed her yet."

"I don't think that matters." Ora cupped her face for a moment before she pulled a chair from behind the stage curtains. Then she blew a kiss to Clara as she seductively sauntered off, and the crowd roared.

Absently—and with a silent plea to her air magic for stability and balance—Clara twirled around the chair. She traced her hands along its back and down her body, pointed her toes and tossed her head back, arching before she dropped into the seat. She swivelled, now straddling her prop with her back to the crowd and her chin dipped to her shoulder.

Quickly signalling to whoever was on curtain duty tonight that her act was almost over, Clara threw her head back and pressed her breasts up towards the glow of the dangling bulb over the stage.

One final look towards the crowd, to the Phoenix and fae she was certainly about to have words with, and then the curtain closed. Clara took a deep breath, then stood and reluctantly wandered towards her undoubted scolding.

Beau opened his mouth, his words caught in his throat for a second too long as a familiar face approached with a feline grin. Koa's dainty fingers traced Clara's shoulder before they wrapped their powerful arms around Clara's midsection and lifted her off the ground. Clara immediately embraced her friend.

"Long time no see," they purred, voice deep and warm, like a thick blanket Clara was once all too eager to curl up in. "Shall we see if our room is available?" Their eyes danced with mischief and excitement, sharp features highlighted by the flickering flames.

Isobel pulled her top lip back in a snarl. Clara welcomed the flutters the aggressive possessiveness emanating from the female's small frame drew from her core. Beau's feathers bristled, and he brushed his biceps against Isobel's, but said nothing.

"I won't be entertaining any more tonight, Koa," Clara said gently, her voice firm.

"I suppose seeing you on stage will have to suffice for now." They winked and ran a finger along her cheek before sauntering off. As Koa disappeared towards the bar, their hips swished and the delicate chains and jewels hanging from their near-naked torso jingled.

Beau looked all too ready to grab Clara's elbow and haul her outside, but she beat him to it, spinning Isobel and him forcefully and pushing them down the hall towards Ora's office.

"What are you two doing here?" she asked, far more calmly than Beau answered.

"What the fuck did your friend mean by 'long time no see'?"

Clara shrugged. "I used to work here. Koa has been my biggest supporter since day one. Did you two follow me?" She pressed her hands to her hips and narrowed her eyes. Isobel looked away, but Beau held her stare.

"Why, of all places, were you working here?" he growled, and his voice almost dripped with disgust as he spoke of the pleasure house.

"First of all, don't take that tone," Clara spat. "It's good money, and the patrons are lovely. We practice respect in Elanist, as well as normalising the acceptance of all kinds of sex work. I had a lot of fun working here."

"And we had a lot of fun having you," Ora chimed in sweetly as she exited her office, gently closing the door behind her. Perfect fucking timing.

Beau's expression hardened, and Isobel's lips pursed. Oh, they weren't happy at all.

"Hi," Ora purred as she held out her hand for Beau to take, which he ignored. "I'm Ora." She extended her hand to Isobel next, but she, too, kept her hands by her sides. Ora seemed unphased as she pushed her hands into her pockets. "It's a pleasure."

"Aura, as in you see colours?" Isobel asked quietly.

"No, dear. Ora, as in Oracle. I see futures." She gave a dazzling smile, though it was not reciprocated. "I make a living offering to read one's future, in place of a favour or payment on request." She lifted her palms up and mimicked weighing something in her hands before she chuckled dryly and lowered them again.

"So, you're what, some kind of she-devil?" Beau snarled.

Clara pinched the bridge of her nose. He was always full of attitude and so brutish.

"We do not discriminate with gender labels here, Phoenix. Devil is perfectly fine." After a momentary pause and an uncomfortable silence, Ora turned to Clara. "You're free to go, sweet, but do come back soon. The crowd loves you."

Clara sighed and shook her head. "Thanks," she muttered. "Alright, let's go. You two can berate me on the long walk home."

"Come change first," Ora called as the trio made to leave. "You two are welcome to wait in the upstairs lobby."

"Like hell—" Beau started, but Isobel cut him off. The glare he shot her would've killed if looks were able.

"If you're not out in five minutes, Clara," Isobel warned. The dangerous tone of her voice sent more butterflies to the deepest part of her belly. "We'll drag you out ourselves."

While she was glad they were getting on, uniting against her was not what Clara had intended. However, she nodded and hurried into Ora's office once they ascended the stairs.

Ora quickly closed the door, threw Clara's clothes at her, and shoved her behind the sectional. Her voice was now hushed and hurried as she spoke. "There's more you should know."

CHAPTER FIFTY-THREE

BEAU

"Beauregard."

The voice filled Beau's mind and surrounded his body. It sounded like a single whisper, yet an echo of three simultaneously. Rough and haggard, but somehow alluring. The combination dizzied him.

"What an awful name," Beau mumbled, still half asleep.

His body felt as though it were floating, and as he opened his eyes, he noticed the bedroom had disappeared. This room had no walls, no doors, no windows, no furnishings, and no end.

It was an empty, depthless black hole.

A pit of nothing.

Nerves crept along his skin, which he could scarcely see, as though his vision was waning. It was disorienting, to say the least.

"It is your name, is it not?"

That voice again, grating along his spine.

A hazy cloud formed far in the distance. Faster than smoke should be able to, it drifted, then wafted away, revealing a female dressed in wet, black fabric—maybe a cloak, or perhaps an ill-fitting dress. She might've even worn a veil, or maybe her hair was slick and hung to cover her face. He couldn't tell, as she did not come any closer.

"Stars, no," Beau said vehemently, turning his nose up. "That's revolting. It sounds like a male who wears a cravat and tucks his pants into his boots with decorative buckles. No."

"You may not like it, but it was the name given to you at birth. So it is the name I shall address you by."

"That isn't very progressive of you," Beau muttered, then turned away from the female, but she reappeared in front of him, the same distance away as before.

"I do not have time for pleasantries and chitchat, boy," she hissed in a painful sound that threatened to burst Beau's eardrums. "I am here with a warning; one you must heed."

"I don't know who you are, let alone whether I trust some phantom being." Beau narrowed his eyes and bared his teeth, yet the female was unperturbed.

"The name gifted to me upon my creation is Lorelai, though folk know me by many titles. Do you know of Death's Daughters or The Fates, perhaps?"

"My knowledge is limited." Beau was hesitant to give this woman any information about himself.

"My sisters and I each hold a place in the trio and have done since we were brought into existence. Our magic is fed by the balance of the universe and good versus evil. We keep the magical beings in check, neutralising threats to the balance, and intervene when one side is poised to tip the other. We maintain control and maintain order.

"Morana, the Veil, the shadow mistress, is the eldest and the deadliest. She revels in her role, and is unforgiving, unyielding. Cassandra, the Blade, the soldier, is in the middle. Following Morana's footsteps with ease and determination, she does not falter and slings her sword with more precision than you could ever hope to dodge. Every strike is fatal. I am Lorelai, known as the Whisper, the serpent, and the spell slinger. Precise in my words, which are marked with death, I am the first and last line of defence. I am the connection and the severance between us. I am their equal, though we are not the same."

Beau was not interested in her self-proclaiming monologue. He breathed deeply, attempting to remain calm and not anger the deity before him. "This information is only creating more questions. What do you want?"

"Do not use such a tone with me!" she bellowed. The sound shook Beau all the way to his bones. He threw his hands over his ears, but it still ricocheted in his mind and rattled and boomed inside him. "I could end you right here and you'd be none the wiser! Though your bonded may not appreciate waking up next to a corpse."

"I apologise," he said quickly and threw his hands up in submission. "What is the warning you wish to give me?"

"It is a warning, in part, but also a request." Subconsciously, Beau nodded. "I have been a deity of death for longer than your civilisation has existed, but I am millennia old, and I grow tired. I do not wish to aid in destruction any longer, so my warning is this:

"Clarenna Hayes is not the one with a target on her back. You, Beauregard, are the one being hunted. You will be marked, and death will claim you, or my sisters will settle for her instead. They do not currently want her, though they, too, grow tired of waiting for you and our manipulations have been going awry. They will take her instead, if you are not careful."

Fear dragged its spindly fingers down Beau's throat and clutched at his heart.

"Hang on, what about the king? He was going to drain her magic, killing her."

"What of him?" Lorelai asked, though it didn't sound as though she cared. "He was unsuccessful, was he not?"

The nonchalance and blatant apathy in her tone set his teeth on edge. "You just said she isn't the target and that your job is to keep the world in balance. Good and evil maintaining their respective sides. She's good, he was evil, yet he would've killed her. Did you pull any strings to free her?"

"No," she said imperiously. "We are no puppet masters, Beauregard. We simply watch, wait, and move pieces along the board as we see fit to keep the world in neutral balance. Without balance, there is nothing but chaos, and no one benefits from that."

"So, you would've let it happen? The convergence?"

"Yes."

Beau couldn't help but let his jaw drop and eyes bulge. Words sputtered in his throat, but none left his lips.

"Though if it eases you, we knew her future did not include dying by his hand."

"You are not selling yourself well here," he huffed out and looked away.

"For a time, yes, he was destined to destroy her. In every scenario he successfully performed the ceremony, you attempted to assassinate him, he had you killed for your crimes, and the threat was neutralised."

"What threat?" He couldn't keep the urgency from his voice. "Why am I a target?"

"We can no longer sit idly by. We expected Clarenna would not forgive you for the death of her shifter friend and that she would murder the king immediately after your death. She was then expected to level the kingdom and flee, either killing you in the process, or simply never seeing you again. The arrow that struck your ribcage that day should have landed in the tetherbond's chest. It would've killed the bond and Clarenna would've blamed you, or she would've chosen the bond.

"When you are taken, she might arrive too late. When she marries the prince, she might dismiss you, for a queen may only have one consort—and again, she would've chosen the tetherbond. In every scenario, she was supposed to leave you, and yet she has not, and we are now doubtful this is going to change. It is as if some meddlesome, infuriating, invisible string has bound you to one another, and every time your futures fracture, they rejoin even stronger than before. By conscious choice or otherwise, Clarenna is unable to stay away, so now *you* are the problem."

With no idea how to react, or what to say, Beau stood with his mouth open like a damned fish, Lorelai's words circling his mind viciously. Dread settled heavily in his chest, then hollowed his stomach.

Lorelai did not stop. She continued talking, adding to the fear and doom already overwhelming Beau's senses.

"Clarenna is a descendant of the Golden Kingdom bloodline, along with that of the Vequil Inalis fae. You are a Phoenix, a descendant of the bloodline responsible for creating hers. She is easily swayed, but veers on the side of good, as you are aware. She has many beneficial moves left on her board, and we do not want her to die. You have fewer good moves expected to come, and frankly, the only one worth noting is that you sway her further towards the light than darkness. However, if you breed, the offspring produced will be too powerful. This is our entire purpose, to keep the world in check, and we must neutralise anything that threatens to overthrow that balance."

All Beau managed to spit out was a strangled, "Why?"

Again, that almost shrug. "It is how it has always been, and likely how it always will be."

"If I sway her towards more goodness, does that not grant me a little leeway here?" The hope and desperation in his tone was bordering on frantic.

"You are not the only one capable of keeping her from falling to the wrong side, Beauregard."

"So I'm a problem because if I impregnate her, our child will be more powerful than you?" His anger built and consequences be damned. "And what, you and your sisters don't want any competition? Is this all some power trip and tantrum? Why are you telling me this?"

"Because I do not wish to take her from you." Lorelai's tone turned tired. "I will help you defeat my sisters and I, but it will come at a cost. Maintaining balance requires give—and take."

"How much?" Beau asked immediately.

"It is no numerical value, nor a monetary amount. It is not a cost you can pay yourself, but one you will inflict upon her if you choose to go ahead."

"Just tell me what it is!" he demanded, balling his hands into fists by his sides.

"I will help you kill me," she repeated. "Effectively destroying any power my sisters have, freeing Clarenna and those she has left. I will cease to exist and perhaps finally know peace." She paused for a long moment. "You simply must die."

"I am a Phoenix," Beau scoffed. "*Simply dying* is par for the course."

"Not if your wings are no longer attached to your body. They are what provide you with your regenerative power, as you surely know. You must shed your feathers and die for good, or my sisters will pick up where we left off. If that happens, you will lose."

"So let me be sure I understand." Beau sighed and dragged his hand roughly over his face. "You're giving me this warning, providing me with help, and I assume knowledge on how to kill you and neutralise your sisters. Then it will be how long before your successors arrive? The world cannot go on without its wardens of balance, now can it?"

"Not long."

"Right, so I get *not long* before your replacements arrive to kill me. Or will you be the one to sever my ties to the living? A sister, perhaps?"

"Either or."

"Right."

"But I will make it painless, so you don't feel a thing. Remove the wings, quick and easy, then a last death with my magic coursing through your mind to make the process easier. I can do that for you."

"Okay. You'd give me information and assistance, and I'd give you my death. Someone gives me a pain-free, one-way ticket to the Underworld and Clara gets to suffer because I want to keep her alive? Because I promised to her I'd die a thousand deaths before she met hers?"

"I'd like to confirm this despair-filled direction your tone has taken, and that your line of questioning indicates you're agreeing to an alliance?" Lorelai interjected.

"How do I know this isn't a trick?" Beau narrowed his eyes, scepticism falling over him.

"You do not, but ponder for a moment: is her life worth risking if you do not trust my word?"

She was right. Beau had no argument against that.

"I will ally with you, Lorelai, in this strange little suicide pact. However, I want this kept between us. I doubt you double-crossing your siblings will come up over a family dinner, but let me be crystal clear." Beau took a step forward, and surprisingly, Lorelai didn't float further away. “Clara is not to know of this. You are not to visit her as you have done to me. If she finds out about this by your tongue, the deal is off, and we’ll find another way to neutralise the threat.”

Beau turned from her, racking his already racing mind for a way out of this strange, empty plane.

“And make no mistake,” he called over his shoulder. “By threat, I mean to you and your sisters. No creature cannot be felled, after all.”

“So you *do* know of us.” Her tone held an edge of surprise.

He hadn’t thought he *could* surprise a warden of life and death. A deity whose existence revolved around watching, waiting, observing folk and beings and creatures alike. Their purpose was to maintain the balance, just as she’d said. That purpose came with benefits, like formidable power and magic, but also foresight.

“I may have limited knowledge,” he said dryly. “But I still have some. Do we have a deal?”

“You have a deal, Beauregard. My life and yours for hers, though she is going to loathe you for it.”

“Fine,” Beau spat, the word tasting of char and cinder. “Since it means she’ll be alive. There is nothing I wouldn’t do to keep her alive. Not a single fucking thing.”

ACKNOWLEDGMENTS

I have a habit of rambling and I know that by this point in the book, you're all either glad to have reached the end, to be able to tick it off as completed on Goodreads or wherever you're logging your reads – or you're hoping these last few pages are actually more of the story, more answers and less cliffhanger ending…

However, there are some people I have to acknowledge. There are people I listed in Shades' acknowledgement section–my friends, family, my husband–who will always have a place in these sections of my work. I legitimately cannot do this without all of you.

This time, I want to focus a little more on the newest additions to my "I don't know where I'd be without you" team. My ARC readers and Street team for one–you guys keep me motivated and excited about this world I thought up one random (probably) Tuesday night, and you're always keeping me inspired to keep writing. The fact I have *fans* is insane and I am beyond thankful for you. Each and every one of you has put a smile on my face and shown me so much support, I can't begin to thank you properly.

Sienna, thank you for every midnight brainstorm session, every minute to monumental piece of advice. Every time I rambled about a specific word choice or spiralled over spelling. You have helped me in so many ways and quite possibly more than you could ever realise. I hope you know how much I appreciate you and love being able to call you a friend.

Anne and Dahné, you have both been incredible. Your support is so greatly appreciated and I can't wait to continue working with you both. Thank you.

And I would be remiss not to mention my fantastic editor, Cat Jay PA & Author Services, and proofreader, Messenger's Memos - Fiction Editing Service. Yet again, my work has been taken to another level and polished so beautifully, thanks to your hard work and attention to detail. I'm so grateful.

To my readers, the fact you picked this up at all fills my heart with so much warmth. From the bottom of my heart, thank you for joining this insane ride.

I cannot wait to share the final instalment of the Crooked Crowns trilogy with you all! Book 3 is underway and coming late 2025! Be sure to follow along on my socials for somewhat-sporadic updates.

www.ingramcontent.com/pod-product-compliance
Lightning Source LLC
Chambersburg PA
CBHW010358310726
48979CB00006B/1090
* 9 7 8 1 7 6 3 5 9 0 3 7 3 *